西方人文论丛

Collection of Western Humanities

Shakespearean
and Jonsonian Comedy

莎氏喜剧
和琼生喜剧

《威尼斯商人》与《狐狸》比较研究
A Comparative Study of
The Merchant of Venice and *Volpone*

廖运刚 ◎ 著

四川大学出版社
SICHUAN UNIVERSITY PRESS

图书在版编目（CIP）数据

莎氏喜剧和琼生喜剧：《威尼斯商人》与《狐狸》
比较研究：英文 / 廖运刚著. — 2版. — 成都：四川
大学出版社，2024.1
（西方人文论丛）
ISBN 978-7-5690-6634-0

Ⅰ. ①莎… Ⅱ. ①廖… Ⅲ. ①喜剧－比较文学－文学
研究－英国－中世纪－英文 Ⅳ. ① I561.073

中国国家版本馆 CIP 数据核字 (2024) 第 047424 号

书　　名：莎氏喜剧和琼生喜剧：《威尼斯商人》与《狐狸》比较研究
　　　　　Shashi Xiju he Qiongsheng Xiju:《Weinisi Shangren》yu《Huli》Bijiao Yanjiu
著　　者：廖运刚
丛 书 名：西方人文论丛

出 版 人：侯宏虹
总 策 划：张宏辉
丛书策划：侯宏虹　张宏辉　余　芳
选题策划：张　晶　余　芳
责任编辑：余　芳
责任校对：周　洁
装帧设计：墨创文化
责任印制：王　炜

出版发行：四川大学出版社有限责任公司
　　　　　地址：成都市一环路南一段 24 号（610065）
　　　　　电话：(028) 85408311（发行部）、85400276（总编室）
　　　　　电子邮箱：scupress@vip.163.com
　　　　　网址：https://press.scu.edu.cn
印前制作：四川胜翔数码印务设计有限公司
印刷装订：成都金阳印务有限责任公司

成品尺寸：148 mm×210 mm
印　　张：11
插　　页：2
字　　数：416 千字

版　　次：2019 年 9 月 第 1 版
　　　　　2024 年 4 月 第 2 版
印　　次：2024 年 4 月 第 1 次印刷
定　　价：68.00 元

扫码获取数字资源

四川大学出版社
微信公众号

Acknowledgements

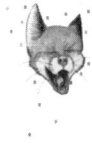

In his *Epigram* XIIII, "To William Camden," Ben Jonson writes of his Westminster School teacher William Camden: "Camden, most reuerend head, to whom I owe / All that I am in arts, all that I know, / (How nothing's that?) to whom my countrey owes / The great renowne, and name wherewith shee goes" (ll. 1 – 4. Herford & Simpson, Vol. VIII). Though I may never become a Ben Jonson, my gratitude to my mentors is comparable to his. When, fortunately, I was introduced to the study of Ben Jonson, I was "unlessoned, unschooled, unpracticed" (Shakespeare, *The Merchant of Venice*, III. ii. 159) in Elizabethan and Jacobean comedy. I had read about the playwright, but had not read any of his works. It was Professor Cheng Zhaoxiang, my supervisor, who has advised, directed and encouraged me in these years of pleasant studies of Ben Jonson and Shakespeare. Professor Cheng has enthusiastically responded to each and every of my requests, carefully listened to my reports, insightfully questioned my plans, patiently analyzed my explanations, and clearly pointed out my direction. I thank him for his guidance out of his profound and extensive knowledge of both English Renaissance literature and the latest research thereon; I thank him also for his hospitality, generosity and care.

During my study of Shakespeare and Jonson, Professor Thomas Rendall has always been my other Camden. He volunteered to be my guide, enlightening me about Shakespeare's and Jonson's works as I struggled to understand them. Over the past five years, he required that we read these plays one by one together, that I summarize and comment on, in particular, the Jonsonian plays we read scene by scene, and that we meet, first regularly, then upon my request, to discuss what I had read and written, even during his vacation time. Professor Rendall has provided me with the bibliography; for me he searched databases, photocopied essential chapters in books from North American libraries. He even asked his son, Bob Rendall, librarian of Columbia University, to bring an essential but heavy book about the Seven Deadly Sins from New York (I also take this opportunity to express heartfelt thanks to Mr. Bob Rendall for his help). I thank Professor Rendall for his erudition, guidance, generosity, patience and help.

This little book is based on my doctoral thesis. I'd like to take this opportunity to thank Professor Cheng Zhaoxiang and Professor Thomas Rendall again for their gracious kindness to grant me a preface.

I thank Professor Shen Hong for being my mentor for a year when he was professor of English with Peking University. It was he who introduced to me the importance of Jonson studies and its scarcity in China. Though my formal advisor for but a short time, Professor Shen comprehensively instructed me in European literature. Any progress I have achieved in understanding Jonson and Shakespeare, I owe to Professor Cheng Zhaoxiang, Professor Thomas Rendall and

Professor Shen Hong.

Many other professors in the English Department of Peking University have kindly helped me during my studies of Shakespeare and Jonson. I express my appreciation to all of them, in particular, Professor Liu Yiqing, Professor Gao Fengfeng, Professor Wang Jihui, Professor Hao Tianhu, and Professor Gu Zhengkun.

I would like to thank Professor David N. Tool for being my English language tutor, great friend, and helping colleague. I am for ever grateful to him for many of my references on Chaucer, the Seven Deadly Sins, *The Ben Jonson Journal*, and Shylock.

While a student in Peking University, I also taught at Beijing International Studies University (BISU). I thank all my leaders at BISU, especially Professor / Dean Zhang Xihua, my branch Chinese Communist Party (CCP) Secretary Cui Lili, Professor / Vice Dean Li Xiangming, Professor Cheng Jinneng, Professor Zhou Jianping, and Professor Xiu Yuezhen, and my former branch CCP Secretary Ren Chuanhui, for their kind support, consideration and generous arrangement of my teaching load. I also thank Ms. Yuan Lianrong, the former teaching secretary, for her considerate scheduling of my classes for the convenience of both my teaching and studies.

Many of my other friends or classmates have provided me necessary books. I thank especially Li Jun, Cheng Jiamin, Liu Wei, Cui Qingxin, Liu Guizhen, Hu Yonghua, Xu Ya, Feng Wei, Xu Jia, Xu Xiaodong, Hu Zhenming, Wang Jinghan, Wang Yuange, Zhu Ruiqing, Shi Xiaoying, Chen Liping, Zhang Xiaorong, Gao Xing and Ryan Ziegler for their generous and timely assistance.

Professor Sun Jianqiu, Professor Wu Fen, and Professor Sui Yun, all my teachers at University of International Business and Economics, have always been my guides and supporters. I gratefully acknowledge my indebtedness to them.

In this world of the Internet, it is easy to become indebted to international scholars. I asked for help from Professor Richard L. Harp of University of Nevada, Las Vegas and Professor Ian Donaldson of Australian National University. They both kindly and patiently answered my questions, and Professor Richard L. Harp even generously mailed a solid, heavy box of back issues of *The Ben Jonson Journal* to the U.S. home of Professor David N. Tool, who sent them on to me in Beijing, at his own cost.

Finally, I want to thank my family, especially my mother, who did not live to see the completion of my dissertation, my father, my parents-in-law, brothers-in-law, sister, brother, and most of all, my wife, Feng Haiyan and my son, Liao Zifan, for their unfailing love and support during my long years of study far from home. They have selflessly made it possible for me to concentrate on my studies. What I owe them is unrepayable even to the end of my life.

序　言

程朝翔

在早期现代喜剧中，莎士比亚的《威尼斯商人》和琼生的《狐狸》都是以威尼斯为背景。威尼斯是一个商业高度发达的城市，社会生活也呈现出典型的商业化社会的特点：一方面，经济利益至上，人欲横流，一些人唯利是图、贪婪成性；另一方面，为了避免大的冲突，为了社会的和谐发展，必须加强法制，弘扬主流的价值，并通过教化使法制观念和主流价值深入人心。这也正是《威尼斯商人》和《狐狸》这两部威尼斯喜剧的重要主题。贪婪和教化既是世俗的概念，又是宗教的概念；贪婪是世俗商人盈利的动力之一，是货币拜物教的体现，但也是基督教所谴责的七宗罪之一，需要世俗的或者宗教的教化来使之中和。因此，这两个概念具有超出自身的相当广泛的社会意义。

廖运刚的研究敏锐地抓住了这两个重要的主题，并且通过这两个重要主题，在风格似乎截然不同，甚至尖锐对立的两部喜剧中找到了最重要的共性，在莎士比亚和琼生之间架起了主题上的桥梁。这一研究能帮助我们深入了解这两部喜剧，反思贪婪与教化之间的辩证，反思这一辩证关系对于早期现代商业社会和法治社会发展的重要意义。

不过，在文学研究中，主题研究还是要落实到形式分析上。在运刚的研究中，对于文学形式的分析落实到了对于人物刻画的分析上，特别是对于气质（humour）和类型人物（stock character）的分析。所谓"气质"，其实指的是决定气质或者性情的体液——

西方从古代、中世纪到现代，都一直相信不同的体液导致了不同的性情或者性格。而所谓类型人物，指的是某一性格特征十分突出并相对固定化的人物，这是文学作品中相对脸谱化的人物，往往一出场就能被观众辨认出来。对气质和类型人物的深入分析，有助于了解剧中的人物性格，也有助于了解构成人物性格的戏剧形式以及戏剧形式之外的更广泛的社会背景。

对于气质和类型人物的分析，也指向了当代文学理论的一个重要方面，即精神分析学。弗里德里克·詹明信认为，弗洛伊德精神分析学将性格特征和神经病（neurosis）区别开来。有的人物具有十分独特的性格，"或烦躁不安，或焦躁易怒，或甜言蜜语，或低声下气"；但这都是性格，而不是病态。不过问题在于，这两者的界限何在？这一界限的意义何在？詹明信同时认为，弗洛伊德的精神分析学旨在发现病态并治疗病态，而拉康则认为精神病态无法治愈，我们只能接受生活在病态社区这一现实。就夏洛克和老狐狸福尔鹏尼而言，贪婪究竟只是他们的性格特征，还是已经成为他们的病症？这种贪婪究竟是可以治愈，还是根本就无法治愈？其病因何在？他们是否也只是病态社区的一个部分或者症候？细读两个文本，有助于找出这些问题的答案。

早期现代文本离我们已十分久远，阅读起来有一定困难，需要借助前人的研究。前人对于莎士比亚文本的研究较多，而对于琼生文本的研究相对较少。在研究过程中，运刚不仅尽量参考能找到的所有资料，而且还定期求教于在北大英文系任教的 Tom Rendall 先生，获益匪浅。有了扎实的文本细读的功夫，同时又大量参考前人的研究文献，保证了研究的质量和分量。

PREFACE

Tom Rendall

From Eliot's "Tradition and the Individual Talent" to
Kristeva's all literature is a "mosaic of quotations" we have
learned that it is impossible for any author to remain
uninfluenced by literary and cultural traditions. The time is
long past when scholars could argue a simple opposition
between Jonson's hidebound classicism and Shakespeare's
natural genius, or between Jonson's stern moralism and
Shakespeare's good-natured tolerance.

In this context, Liao Yungang's book asks the obvious
question "to what extent are the usual generalizations about
the differences between Jonsonian and Shakespearean
comedy valid?" Going beyond impressions and
generalizations, Liao's study approaches the problem through
close analysis of plays by each dramatist that share the theme
of avarice. *Volpone* and *The Merchant of Venice* provide a
test case for adding nuance to the traditional idea that
Jonson's plays are hamstrung by convention and didacticism
and that Shakespeare's "hold the mirror up to nature." The
well supported conclusion of this painstaking analysis is that
the traditional oppositions between Jonsonian and

Shakespearean presentation of character need to be either considerably more problematized or perhaps abandoned altogether. Jonson employs humours and stock characters, but his major characters are still complex and life-like, and although Shakespeare's characters may seem more naturally presented, his characterization still makes use of traditional humours and classical stock character techniques. In addition, Jonson is not alone in having moral aims that are expressed through explicitly didactic elements.

Dr. Liao's passion as a bibliophile is also well displayed in this study—not only in the voluminous bibliography but also in his incessant and detailed footnotes. This has produced a book which is almost Germanic in its willingness to pursue every detail, to go down every byway, providing the reader with not only copious background for the argument, but also interesting and useful supplementary documentation. In addition to a comparison of the two writers' dramatic methods, Liao provides independently valuable close readings of both plays, making many useful and illuminating points along the way.

In short, this book will be of interest not only to specialists in the dramatic texts of Jonson and Shakespeare, but also to all students of the popular and scholarly reception of the works of these great dramatists.

Notes on Sources

1. Unless otherwise noted, all Shakespeare quotations in this book are from *The Oxford Shakespeare: The Complete Works*. Eds. Stanley Wells, Gary Taylor, John Jowett and William Montgomery. Oxford: Oxford UP, 2004.

2. All Jonson quotations are from *Ben Jonson*. 11 vols. Eds. C. H. Herford, Percy Simpson, and Evelyn Simpson. Oxford: Oxford UP, 1925 – 1952.

3. All quotations from the Bible are from *The Geneva Bible*, *A Facsimile of the 1560 Edition*. Peabody: Hendrickson Bibles, 2007.

4. All quotations from Chaucer are from *The Riverside Chaucer*. 3rd ed. Gen. Ed. Larry D. Benson. 1987. Oxford: Oxford UP, 1988.

Contents

Introduction

Slightly more than fifty years ago, Jonas Barish remarked in his *Ben Jonson and the Language of Prose Comedy* (1960): "Shakespeare alone, in fact, who virtually invented linguistic satire on the English stage, wields it with a trenchancy and a sophistication equal to Jonson's" (284). In 2011, Laura Tosi in her article, "Shakespeare, Jonson and Venice: Crossing Boundaries in the City," wrote: "If we compare themes and characters in the three Venetian plays [*The Merchant of Venice* (hereafter *The Merchant*, or *MV*), *Othello*, and *Volpone*], the Shakespeare-Jonson polarity appears less defined and it becomes quite easy to pair and find correspondences between a Shakespeare play and *Volpone*" (147). These remarks are typical; they recapitulate two age-old facts in discussions of early modern English literature, especially drama: pair and polarity. Ever since the age of Jonson, Shakespeare and Jonson have been paired to compare with each other, for either convenience or effect of discussion. James Shapiro argues: "To present 'Jonson' was not possible without presenting 'Shakespeare,' and vice versa" (*Rival Playwrights* 148). This shows how often the two dramatists have been posited on opposite ends as if they have had to represent two contrastive dramatic worlds.

Even today, such binary oppositions are still prevalent.

Mick Jardine has summarized "a critical orthodoxy" of Jonson and Shakespeare (107):

- flat vs. round characters;
- satire vs. romance;
- rules vs. freedoms;
- comedy vs. tragedy;
- alienation vs. empathy;
- London vs. the universe;
- Classical vs. Romantic;
- constructionist vs. humanist;
- moralistic vs. non-judgmental;
- laws vs. nature;
- imitation vs. originality;
- Art vs. Nature.

(109-10)

While some of these "orthodox" oppositions that segregate Shakespeare and Jonson are ostensibly neutral about the characteristics of their dramatic art, like satire vs. romance, rules vs. freedoms, comedy vs. tragedy, Classical vs. Romantic, laws vs. nature, and Art vs. Nature, others are more or less straightforwardly judgmental, like flat vs. round characters, alienation vs. empathy, London vs. the universe, moralistic vs. non-judgmental, and imitation vs. originality. That these criticisms are "orthodox" means that they have been in critical practice for so long that they have become conventionality.

For certain, such a critically oppositional orthodoxy does not hold good universally. The above quote from Jonas Barish about Shakespeare's invention of linguistic satire is a case in point. Some may wonder at Barish's assertion that

Shakespeare's satire is as trenchant and sophisticated as Jonson's, if traditionally Jonson, instead of Shakespeare, is associated with satire. [1] The ascent of Shakespeare to the center of all English writers has kept him and Jonson apart, and the consequence is certainly not good for the appreciation of both playwrights. As Mick Jardine argues, putting Shakespeare at the center means the " danger " of "relegation" of other early modern dramatists, and "Jonson in particular " (105). After all, it was Jonson, not Shakespeare, who was considered the main figure of English drama in the seventeenth century and quite a large part of the eighteenth. Since the end of the nineteenth century, especially during the last one hundred years, Jonson has begun to regain some of the reputation he lost in the English romantic era. Now, although Shakespeare's central position has been "perpetuated," Jonson is acknowledged to be the greatest among Shakespeare's contemporaries. Jonson's works have at last been deservingly rediscovered and reappreciated.

Jonson's renascence naturally means renewed interest in his works, especially his best comedies. Rebecca Yearling claims that the scholars and critics of the eighteenth century who thought Jonson's works were for an age would be "amazed at the scale of the modern literary industry devoted to analyzing Ben Jonson and his writings, and at the

---

[1] I do not mean critics in history did not see or were unaware of Shakespeare's satire, which, in fact, they had identified. Charles Gildon (1665 – 1724) says that the design of *Measure for Measure* carries "an excellent Moral and a just Satire" (qtd. in Vickers, *Heritage* 2: 178). Lewis Theobald (1688 – 1744) considers Edgar's "whole Frenzy" in *King Lear* as "Satire levell'd at a modern Fact which made no little Noise at that Period of Time" (qtd. in Vickers, *Heritage* 2: 376). More recently (1943), Oscar James Campbell published his monograph *Shakespeare's Satire*.

popularity that many of the plays still enjoy on the stage"
(404). Indeed, studies and performances of Jonson's plays
increased continuously in the last century. According to
Robert Evans, scholarship on Jonson at the end of the
twentieth century "proliferated," and Jonson once again
seemed "truly central to discussions of his period" (188).
Evans also observes that while *Every Man in his Humour*,
Every Man out of his Humour, *Cynthia's Revels*, *Sejanus*,
The New Inn, and *The Devil Is an Ass* are still admired,
"Most modern attention focuses on *Volpone*, *Epicoene*, *The
Alchemist*, and *Bartholomew Fair*" (189).

Of Jonson's best comedies, the most popular and
influential is *Volpone*. According to Daniel S. Burt, *Volpone*
is rated twenty-third among the one hundred greatest plays of
all time (*Drama* 132). Stanley Wells, the great
Shakespearean scholar, asserts that "except for
Shakespeare's, no other comedies from the [early modern]
period have been so admired in later times" (*Shakespeare
and Co.* 147). Richard Dutton, the editor of *Volpone* for *The
Cambridge Edition of the Works of Ben Jonson*, shares
Wells's evaluation: "*Volpone* is the best known, most
performed and most studied of all of Jonson's plays, as it has
been for the last 100 years. . . . It is probably the best known
and most performed of all early modern plays, excepting
those of Shakespeare" (*Gunpowder Plot* 1; Introduction 17).
Murray Roston confirms Dutton's observation: "in the number
of professional performances during the twentieth century,
the play [*Volpone*] came second only to Shakespeare's most
popular comedies" (1).

Compared with Jonson's *Volpone*, Shakespeare's

Merchant of Venice is his most influential and most popular comedy.[1] Although one of the least popular Shakespearean plays in the seventeenth century, less popular than *Coriolanus* (Bentley 108, n. 2), *The Merchant of Venice* has in recent times been revived more often than any other Shakespearean comedy. M. M. Mahood, the editor of *The Merchant* for *The New Cambridge Shakespeare* series, points out that "*The Merchant of Venice* shares with *Hamlet* the distinction of having been more often performed than any other of Shakespeare's plays" (42). Charles Edelman notes that Shylock from *The Merchant* is so famous like Cervantes's Quixote and Dickens's Scrooge [from *A Christmas Carol*] that he has become "a common word, a distinction not even Hamlet can claim" (Introduction 1). As for critical studies, *The Merchant* is "notoriously an object of critical contention" (Danson 3). Lawrence Danson is certainly right in saying that "studies of Shylock are not the same thing as studies of Shakespeare's play" (2), but so far as I know, there has not been any other Shakespearean comic character that has attracted

---

[1] For the Jews, as Joel Berkowitz notes, "of all of Shakespeare's works, *The Merchant of Venice* holds the greatest interest" (172). In China, according to Alexander C. Y. Huang, *The Merchant* was "a site of fixation of the Chinese imagination," as it provides inspiration for "both the earliest documented cinematic and *huaju* ["post-1907 Western-influenced spoken drama theater, including obsolete subgenres"—Huang's definition, p. 7] Shakespeares" (8). The trial scene of *The Merchant* (IV. i) came to Chinese high school students as early as 1924 (Levith, *China* 90), and has been part of the "standard high-school curriculum since 1978" (Huang 257 n. 45; Levith, *China* 90). As Murray J. Levith observes, together with the tragedy *Hamlet*, *The Merchant* has been "enormously popular from the very beginning [in China]," and is "the most translated, produced, and written about of all of Shakespeare's works" (*China* 117). In Africa, *The Merchant* was the first Shakespearean comedy to be translated into Kiswahili—a language spoken extensively throughout East Africa (Banham, Mooneeram & Plastow 284).

as much attention as Shylock,[1] a sign of the influence and popularity of *The Merchant*.

The influence and popularity of *Volpone* and *The Merchant of*

---

[1]   Shylock's only close rival is Falstaff. To my knowledge, other than numerous operatic and dramatic adaptations, critical journal essays and even a biography, there have been five monographs on Falstaff: John Dover Wilson, *The Fortunes of Falstaff* (1943, rpt. 2004); Rupin W. Desai, *Falstaff: A Study of His Role in Shakespeare's History Plays* (1975); Charles Edward Phelps, *Falstaff and Equity: An Interpretation* (1901); James Orchard Halliwell, *On the Character of Sir John Falstaff* (1841); Maurice Morgann, *An Essay on the Dramatic Character of Sir John Falstaff* (1777). There is also a published dissertation: Jeffrey H. Aziz, *Of Grace and Gross Bodies: Falstaff, Oldcastle, and the Fires of Reform* (2007). Compared with studies on Shylock, almost all of these are rather old. There are many more books devoted to Shylock. In addition to Lawrence Danson's list [Toby Lelyveld's *Shylock on the Stage*, Jacob L. Cardozo's *The Contemporary Jew in Elizabethan Drama*, M. J. Landa's *The Jew in Drama*, Hermann Sinsheimer's *Shylock: The History of a Character*, Bernard Grebanier's *The Truth about Shylock*] (2, n. 4), there are four monographs: John Gross's *Shylock: A Legend and Its Legacy* (first ed. 1992), on the making of the character and his critical and stage history; Martin D. Yaffe's *Shylock and the Jewish Question* (1997), a book to correct misconception of Shakespeare's alleged anti-semitism by putting Shakespeare in his dramatic milieu with Marlowe, Bacon and in the context of Spinoza; Kenneth Gross's *Shylock Is Shakespeare* (2006), "an essay on Shylock's singularity" (K. Gross ix). There is also an edition by Harold Bloom: *Shylock* (1991), a collection of critical essays from the early nineteenth century to the end of 1980s, with a denouncing introduction by Bloom. There is a published dissertation: *Shylock and the Economics of Subversion in* The Merchant of Venice (2005) by Hesham Khadawardi, putting Shylock and the Shakespeare play into the context of the commercial conflicts of Renaissance England and today. Among other books that feature Shylock or the Jewish problem in *The Merchant* are: James Shapiro's *Shakespeare and the Jews*, about Jews on the minds of Shakespeare and his contemporaries; Janet Adelman's *Blood Relations*, on the relationship between the Christians and the Jews by examining *The Merchant* and its proximity with *Sir Thomas More* (1603 - 1604), a partly Shakespearean work, and Robert Wilson's *Three Ladies of London* (1584).

Venice have led to abundant critical studies on them.[1] However, it is curious that although general comparative discussions of Shakespeare and Jonson are easy to find,[2] specific studies comparing these two major English Renaissance comedies are scarce for no apparent reasons. To the best of my knowledge, David C. McPherson in his *Shakespeare, Jonson, and the Myth of Venice* explores, as the title indicates, the myth of Venice in Shakespeare's *Merchant*, *Othello* and Jonson's *Volpone* only because these three plays share an identical setting. In his barely two-and-a-half page conclusion, McPherson summarizes the "sharp contrast" between the two dramatists' use of Venice: Shakespeare uses it selectively so that the characters in his plays can move in and out of it, but Jonson confines his characters in Venice and causes Volpone especially to be "claustrophobic"

---

[1] For example, Matthew Steggle's edition of Volpone: *A Critical Guide* (2011); Richard Dutton's *Ben Jonson*, Volpone *and the Gunpowder Plot* (2008), on the dramatic circumstances in which Jonson created *Volpone*; Arnold P. Hinchliffe's Volpone: *Text and Performance* (1985); Katherine Eisaman Maus's "Idol and Gift in *Volpone*" (2005); C. N. Manlove's "The Double View in *Volpone*" (1979); William Empson's "Volpone" (1968 – 1969); Jonas A. Barish's "The Double Plot in 'Volpone'" (1953); Ralph Nash's "The Comic Intent of 'Volpone'" (1947) and other numerous journal articles on *Volpone*. Studies on *The Merchant of Venice*, besides the above mentioned *Blood Relations* by Janet Adelman, include Lawrence Danson's *The Harmonies of* The Merchant of Venice (1978), and two editions by Harold Bloom: *William Shakespeare's* The Merchant of Venice (2010) (from Bloom's Modern Critical Interpretations series), and *The Merchant of Venice* (2008) (from *Bloom's Shakespeare Through the Ages* series), and numerous other articles on *The Merchant*. Graham Holderness' *Shakespeare and Venice* discusses the dramatist's two Venetian plays, *The Merchant* and *Othello* in the context of Itanian Renaissance culture, including Shakespeare's Venice in fiction and on film.

[2] See, for example, James Shapiro, *Rival Playwrights*, esp. pp. 133-70; D. H. Craig, *Ben Jonson: The Critical Heritage*, and Brian Vickers, *William Shakespeare: The Critical Heritage*. Russ McDonald's *Shakespeare & Jonson, Jonson & Shakespeare* is an important comprehensive study of Shakespeare's and Jonson's plays, intending to bring down the traditional oppositions between the two playwrights, but it compares *Volpone* with Shakespeare's tragedies. There are also two good journal articles that compare Shakespeare's and Jonson's individual plays: Henk Gras, "*Twelfth Night*, *Every Man out of his Humour*, and the Middle Temple Revels of 1597 – 1598"; and Harry Levin, "Two Magian Comedies: *The Alchemist* and *The Tempest*." For more book and essay titles, see James Shapiro, *Rival Playwrights*, pp. 187-8, n. 14.

(117). McPherson believes that the similarities between these Shakespearian and Jonsonian plays lie in the motivative function of Venice in their characters; to give only two examples: Antonio is sad because of "the decline of Venice as a merchant power," and Volpone is passionate for theatricality because of "the extravagant theatricality prevalent both in ancient Rome and Renaissance Venice" (117-18). Another comparative study of Shakespeare's *Merchant* and Jonson's *Volpone* is also centered around their shared setting. Laura Tosi in her article "Shakespeare, Jonson and Venice: Crossing Boundaries in the City" discusses Venice's economic, social and political background in relation to the The *Merchant*, *Volpone* and *Othello* (143-65). Murray J. Levith's *Shakespeare's Italian Settings and Plays* contains a three-page comparison among *Volpone*, *The Merchant* and *Othello*, indicating that Jonson's Venice is more "detailed" and "specific" than Shakespeare's (16). Roberta Mullini in her essay "Streets, Squares and Courts: Venice as a Stage in Shakespeare and Ben Jonson" gives another study of the social, theatrical, political and legal background of Venice as the setting of especially *The Merchant of Venice* and *Volpone* in their historical context. In addition, Leo Salingar in his "The Idea of Venice in Shakespeare and Ben Jonson" surveys the two dramatists' reaction to English life and thought through examples from a number of plays including *The Merchant* and *Volpone* that use Venice as a metaphor. Beyond these examinations based on dramatic settings, I have not found any comparative studies between *Volpone* and *The Merchant*.①

① In China (including Taiwan province, Hong Kong and Macau Special Administrative Regions), studies on Jonson have been surprisingly scarce, and there have been even fewer studies of his individual works, not to say a comparative study between Ben Jonson and Shakespeare. Dr. Wang Yongmei's (王永梅) studies in Ben Jonson's masques are ground-breaking work in the area in China. In 2008, Dr. Guo Hui (郭晖), after graduating from Peking University earlier the same year, published her studies on Jonson's poetry, specifically his encomia. Jonson is briefly introduced in a couple of monographs on English literary history: in their *A History of English Renaissance Literature* (《英国文艺复兴时期文学史》, 1996), Profs. Wang Zuoliang (王佐良) and He Qixin (何其莘) gave Jonson and his works the most detailed introduction by Chinese scholars. There are other English or European literary histories written by Chinese scholars. Among the better known are Profs. Li Funing, and Liu Yiqing et al., ed., *A History of European Literature* (李赋宁、刘意青 等主编,《欧洲文学史》), and Hou Weirui, *A Comprehensive History of English Literature* (侯维瑞主编,《英国文学通史》). But these books have given Ben Jonson only passing introductions and comments. There is another monograph, *A History of English Drama*, by Prof. He Qixin, first edition 1999, and second edition, 2008 (何其莘,《英国戏剧史》, 1999 年第 1 版, 2008 年第 2 版). This monograph (2ⁿᵈ ed.) gave Ben Jonson and his works 25 pages, very detailed compared with other books, but in fact, the Ben Jonson section in this book is essentially identical to the Jonson discussion in the above book, *A History of English Renaissance Literature*, except for slight changes in sub-section and play titles, numeration, and typo corrections. Beyond these studies, there have been only eleven journal articles on Jonson and his works: Zheng Youzhi, "Ben Jonson: A Representative Playwright of the English Renaissance" (郑有志,《英国文艺复兴时期喜剧的代表作家——琼生》, 1993); Wang Pinpin, "Wine and Wreath: A Love Poem by Ben Jonson" (王品品,《美酒·花环——介绍本·琼生的一首爱情诗》, 1997); Lu Guirong, "*Volpone*: Ben Jonson's New Explorations of Comedy Creation" (卢桂荣,《狐狸 (*Volpone*)——本·琼生对喜剧创作新探索》, 2002); Lu Guirong, "An Analysis of *Volpone*'s Dramatic Setting" (卢桂荣,《〈狐狸〉 (*Volpone*) 的戏剧背景分析》, 2002); Lu Guirong, "Ben Jonson: His Life and Works" (卢桂荣,《本·琼生——其人其作》, 2002); Lu Guirong, "An Analysis of the Art of Deception in *Volpone*" (卢桂荣,《〈狐狸〉的欺骗艺术分析》, 2003); Yu Yongsheng, "The Perfect Combination of Dramatic Setting and Satiric Themes: An Analysis of *Volpone, or the Fox*'s Setting" (于永生,《戏剧背景与讽刺主题的完美统一——〈狐狸〉 (*Volpone, or the Fox*) 背景艺术分析》, 2003); Long Yue, "On the Harmonious Image and the Exquisite Rhythm of *To Celia*" (龙跃,《〈致西莉亚〉的意象与韵律之美》, 2005); Jiang Chunlan, "A Discussion of a Teaching Strategy of English Poetry Appreciation: Using Ben Jonson's 'It Is Not Growing like a Tree' as an Example" (姜春兰,《"英语诗歌鉴赏"教学策略探讨——以本·琼生的〈不像大树那样生长〉为例》, 2009); Wang Yongmei & Liu Lihui, "From Stage to Page: Ben Jonson and British Dramatic Canon Formation" (王永梅、刘立辉,《从舞台到页面:本·琼生与英国戏剧经典生成》, 2012); Wu Meiqun, "Tradition and Transcendence: A Study on Classicism of Ben Jonson's *The Forrest*" (吴美群,《传承与超越——试论本·琼生〈森林集〉中的古典主义》, 2016). Some of these eleven articals are general introductions to Jonson and his works. There have been four MA theses: Huang Xiuyuan, "The World of '*Volpone*'" (黄秀媛,《〈狐坡尼〉的世界》, 1980); Chen Shunlong, "Eating Strategy [sic.] in *Volpone*: Man as Animal" (陈顺龙,《狐伯尼剧中的饮食技巧:以兽喻人》, 1990); Zhong Peishan, "Foucaldian Discourse and Gender Politics in Ben Jonson's *Epicoene or The Silent Woman* and William Shakespeare's *The Taming of the Shrew*" (钟珮珊,《班·琼森的〈沉默女人〉与莎士比亚的〈驯悍记〉两剧中性别政治所呈现出的傅柯式论述之探讨》, 2001); Liu Chun (刘淳), "The Titanic Hero: The Tension between Life and Career in Ben Jonson's Poems of Occasion" (2005). There has been a research report done by Prof. Wang Yijun, who also directed the above Chen Shunlong's and Zhong Peishan's theses, on Jonson's inheritance of Lucianic tradition, entitled "Lucianic Tradition and Menippean Satire: in Ben Jonson and George Chapman" (王仪君,《陆西安传统和曼氏讽刺:论班·琼森及乔治·柴普曼》, 1994). The MA theses and research report have not been published.

It is my intention in this book to study these two comedies together. Since Shakespeare and Jonson are often mentioned together and compared in a general sense, why not a detailed comparison between *Volpone* and *The Merchant* in areas other than setting? Since we are used to categorizing plays into tragedy, comedy, tragi-comedy. . . and both *Volpone* and *The Merchant* are highly popular comedies by the two greatest early modern English dramatists, their comparison should result in a better understanding of both plays and their playwrights. They perhaps should be well compared even because of their shared genre and position in the history of English Renaissance drama. Moreover, in addition to the common setting and genre, *Volpone* and *The Merchant* share an important theme: avarice—the economic element that motivates and then eventually destroys some of their main characters.

Avarice has always been an important motif in English Renaissance literature, and one way of representing it is through the character of a usurer. According to Arthur Bivins Stonex, during the 90 years from 1553 to 1643, seventy-one plays were written which contain or seem to contain usurers (191). That is, on average, every year and a half one play containing a usurer was written. Some of these plays have become masterpieces of Elizabethan drama. Christopher Marlowe's *The Jew of Malta* (c. 1590), Thomas Middleton's *A Trick to Catch the Old One* (c. 1605), Thomas Heywood's *The English Traveler* (1633), and Francis Quarles's *The Virgin Widow* (1649) are a few examples. Jonson's *Volpone* does not contain a usurer, but it does portray an array of outrageously avaricious characters. Marlowe's *The Tragical History of Dr. Faustus* is an additional masterpiece that at least contains a clear reference to the theme of avarice (Scene V). A good understanding of the idea and motif of avarice is important to the appreciation of English Elizabethan literature, and especially to a comparative analysis of *Volpone* and *The Merchant of Venice*. However, this study does not focus on avarice. Instead, it uses avarice as a background because of this theme's dominant position in *Volpone* and *The Merchant*. The common important theme of avarice makes the two plays especially comparable; it makes the comparison between characters in the two plays illuminating and pertinent, since all of the characters to be discussed are either greedy or liberal. Since avarice was a repeated theme of secular and moral theater in the early modern period, consideration of this common theme is also important for the discussion of didacticism in the two plays.

The purpose of this study is to assess the validity of some of the binary oppositions traditionally seen between Shakespeare and Jonson. To realize this purpose, I have carefully selected two points for detailed examination: characterization and didacticism. Characterization is necessary because traditionally it is held as Shakespeare's main forte and as Jonson's main frailty. Aristotle says in his *Poetics* that "story [plot], then, is the first principle and like the soul of tragedy, and characters are second" (1450^a 39-40). Although Aristotle talks about the order of importance in tragedy, his remarks are often taken to refer to literature or narrative in general. My study will consider the extent to which traditional views of the opposing methods of Jonsonian and Shakespearean characterization are valid.

In my study of characterization in *Volpone* and *The Merchant*, especially of the actions and speeches of their major characters, I will also consider the usual assumption that Jonson's comedies are didactic while Shakespeare's are not. Many critics still hold that Shakespeare does not preach to his readers in his plays, while Jonson always does so. Jonson's plays are thought to be moralistic instruction and Shakespeare's non-judgmental entertainment. This study will challenge that view.

As Robert C. Evans points out, since the beginning of the twentieth century, with Jonson's "fortunes" having "rebounded" there began a "fairer, more methodical assessment of Jonson" (188). I hope that this study can be a fair and methodical reassessment of both *Volpone* and *The Merchant*.

I will begin my study with a brief survey of the traditional views about Shakespeare's and Jonson's comedies, selecting some of the topics that are most relevant to my comparison of *Volpone* and *The Merchant*, especially the most relevant binary oppositions. Then in Chapter 2, I will try to provide some important ideas about the concept of avarice as a background for the following discussions of characterization and didacticism. Chapter 3 addresses Jonson's and Shakespeare's didacticism as reflected in the two plays, to assess the oppositions listed in Chapter 1. Chapter 4 continues to respond to the traditional oppositions summarized in Chapter 1 by analyzing some important characters in *Volpone* and *The Merchant of Venice*, to again see if such binaries can hold validity. Then I conclude my book with a suggestion that although Jonson can be moralistic, and Shakespeare, non-judgmental, they are both didactic and entertaining, and both have created complex, vivid and well-rounded characters. Thus I hope my study will make a small contribution to the ongoing process of divesting ourselves of the usual stereotypes of Jonsonian and Shakespearian comedy.

1

Shakespearian and Jonsonian Comedy

I. A general view of Shakespearian and Jonsonian comedy

Despite their indefinite, protean forms,[①] comedies dominated the Elizabethan stage. Of English plays authored by the University Wits and produced during the Poetomachia, and in the Elizabethan and Jacobean playhouses and courts, comedies were the major form. According to M. C. Bradbrook, " comedies outnumber tragedies on the Elizabethan stage by nearly three to one" (*Growth* 3). William Shakespeare, according to Michael Dobson and Stanley Wells, perhaps the most generically balanced playwright of his entire age, wrote seventeen comedies, in contrast with eleven tragedies and ten histories (excluding

---

① See, for example, G. J. Mallinson, "Defining Comedy in the Seventeenth Century: Moral Sense and Theatrical Sensibility. "

the Shakespeare Apocrypha, xii). [1] Ben Jonson produced two tragedies and sixteen comedies, excluding masques. [2] Comedies in the Elizabethan age have been described in many ways: sweet and bitter comedies, romantic and satiric comedies, popular and intellectual comedies, and Shakespearean and Jonsonian comedies. Indeed, early modern English comedies are sometimes roughly divided into the Shakespearean and the Jonsonian, of which the first may be said to be characteristically Elizabethan, and the second Jacobean (Bradbrook, *Growth* 3).

Shakespeare's and Jonson's comedies have been given a general characterization: Shakespeare's comedies are romantic, spontaneous, popular, and funny; Jonson's, in contrast, realistic, contrived, satirical, and moralizing. Robert Ornstein puts the common opinion this way: "one romantic, positive and attractive; the other satiric, negative and (now and then) repelling" (43). Russ McDonald also summarizes some established distinctions between the two types of plays: "Shakespearian comedy is typically romantic, gentle, and reassuring, Jonsonian comedy critical, hortatory, and pessimistic" ("Visions" 132).

---

[1] The First Folio listed fourteen comedies, ten histories and eleven tragedies, excluding *Pericles*, which is categorized by Dobson & Wells as a comedy. This traditional categorization does not reflect some of the recent claims that other hands collaborated in plays attributed to Shakespear. Thomas Middleton, for instance, according to John Jowett, is now believed to have partly written *Timon of Athens*, *Macbeth* and *Measure for Measure* (17).

[2] Even *Sejanus His Fall*, Jonson's "most painstakingly classical play" (Dobson & Wells, "Jonson, Ben" 225), as well as his "first extant tragedy" (Drabble, "Jonson, Ben" 540), and in which Shakespeare was named among "the principal tragedians" (Dobson & Wells, "Shakespeare, William" 421), has "parallels" that are "obvious and important" with later comedies like *Volpone* (Knights 180). To borrow the words of J. A. Bryant, Jr., Shakespeare's and Jonson's comedies are two "fundamentally continuous" dramatic groups (155). Robert Ornstein refers to them as either "the twin pillars of Elizabethan comedy" or "its opposite poles" (43).

i. Shakespeare's sweet, romantic and popular comedies

Commenting on Shakespeare's comedies, M. C. Bradbrook says, his work "was nearly always described as ' sweet ' " (*Growth* 216, n. 5). The reputation of Shakespeare's comedies for sweetness was not first established by Jonson, but the use of the term in Jonson's encomium is the most famous. It was included in First Folio published in 1623. In this poetic preface, "To the Memory of My Beloved, The Author Mr. William Shakespeare: And What He Hath Left Us," Jonson celebrates Shakespeare's popularity:

> Sweet Swan of *Avon*! what a sight it were
> To see thee in our waters yet appeare,
> And make those flights upon the bankes of *Thames*,
> That so did take *Eliza*, and *our James*! [1]

(71-74)

In 1631, Milton in *L'Allegro* gave Shakespeare the superlative of the word:

> ... sweetest Shakespeare, Fancy's child,
> Warble his native wood-notes wild.

(133-34)

Indeed, according to Brian Vickers, the phrase " sweet Shakespeare" occurs "so often in the *Parnassus* plays, those trendy Cambridge satires, that one suspects a parody of stock

---

[1] Quoted from the First Folio (1623) facsimile, with u, v, j modernized. All other citations from this poem come from this edition. For a detailed argument about the tone of the poem, see Donaldson, *Magic Houses*, ch. 2, esp. pp. 7-21.

response" (*Heritage* 1: 2). Not only is *sweet* often used, but also its variations: " Honie-tong'd Shakespeare " (John Weever's address to the poet in 1595); "hony-flowing Vaine" (Richard Barnfield, 1598); "mellifluous" (Thomas Heywood, 1635); as well, there are in 1639, Thomas Bancroft's " Thy Muses sugred dainties " and George Lynn's " Smooth Shakespeare" in 1640 (qtd. in Vickers, *Heritage* 1: 2). [1]

What *sweet* means for Shakespeare and for others is different. For the poet himself, the word can refer to some pleasant smell (e. g. "When the sweet wind did gently kiss the trees," *Merchant*, V. i. 2), a pleasant sound (e. g. "Become the touches of sweet harmony," ibid. , V. i. 57); a vocative with the senses of " nice, beautiful, etc. " (e. g. "Sweet Portia, welcome," ibid. , III. ii. 222), and peaceful sleep (e. g. " How sweet the moonlight sleeps upon this bank," ibid. , V. i. 54). For Shakespeare's critics, however, when they say "sweet Shakespeare," they usually mean "the quality of eloquence" (Vickers, *Heritage* 1: 2). Whatever the meaning and situation, Shakespeare seems to have always been associated with the epithet *sweet*.

Today, Shakespeare's comedies are also *romantic* because they deal with sexual love and marriage. David Farley-Hills reasserts that "before 1600 Shakespeare's output

---

[1] Shakespeare himself uses *sweet* frequently. According to a corpus study by Beatrix Busse based on his dramatic works in the Riverside Edition, *sweet* is the second most frequently used word, next only to *good* (212-3). In his sonnets, in addition to his other poetry such as *A Lover's Complaint*, Shakespeare uses *sweet* frequently, too: "Thyself thy foe, to thy sweet self too cruel" (1, l. 8); "Mark how one string, sweet husband to another" (8, l. 9); "Since sweets and beauties do themselves forsake" (12, l. 11); "Thine own sweet argument, too excellent" (38, l. 3). Sometimes, *sweet* is used three times in a single sonnet (like 54). *Sweet* was also frequently found in late sixteenth century English correspondence (Busse 213).

had been devoted with remarkable consistency to romantic comedy and the long series of English history plays" (5), and *Twelfth Night* (1600-1) is "the last of Shakespeare's old-style romantic comedies" (54). Shakespeare's late plays, so called romances, invariably contain a love theme. Hazelton Spencer summarizes the relationship between Shakespeare's comedy and a romance in a direct and simple way: "to Shakespeare comedy was usually a vehicle for putting a romantic tale on the stage" (254).

But, *romantic* in Shakespeare criticism originally meant that Shakespeare's stories resemble those of romances, those tales of medieval chivalry and courtly love. Such a dramatic story can be found in *Much Ado about Nothing*, when Claudio says, "Lady, as you are mine, I am yours. I give away myself for you, and dote upon the exchange" (II. i. 282-84). When Charlotte Lennox, Mrs. Ramsay (1720 – 1804), poet, novelist and translator, comments about *The Two Gentlemen of Verona*, she says it carries "the romantic, the wonderful, and the wild to the most pleasing extravagance" (qtd. in Vickers, *Heritage* 3: 130). Because the medieval romances were often fanciful and dealt with sexual love, the British Romantics, who stressed inspiration and intuition, much admired and appreciated Shakespeare's comedies.

On the other hand, since Jonson's comedies, especially the best known ones, do not deal with sexual love or end in marriage, and since they mock at their characters' eccentricities or satirize their characters' vices, *romantic* is also used by critics to describe Shakespeare's comedies in order to conveniently distinguish them from Jonson's satirical comedies. In such a context, *romantic* means relationships between the sexes plus sometimes fantasy elements such as fairies and magic as Shakespeare's comic subject matter.

His sweetness, and the heroic, adventurous and mysterious plots of his plays demonstrate that Shakespeare was writing comedies in the popular tradition. According to A. L. Rowse, Shakespeare and every other Englishman of his time had grown up in the tradition of popular drama (116). Rowse also writes of Shakespeare as having "abandoned the learned models" and having gone back to "popular and unassuming traditions" (77) which he transformed. Anne Barton remarks that "the Elizabethan popular tradition achieved its finest realization in the comedies of Shakespeare" (*Dramatist* x). Barbara Everett remarks that even Shakespeare's mature comedies, like *The Merchant of Venice* and *Much Ado about Nothing*, were written for popular audiences (168).

Received opinion holds that compared with Jonson, Shakespeare followed the tradition that appealed to the common audience. His plays were less fettered by rhetoric, less academic, and more carefully suited to the taste of the popular audience. Jonson, in contrast, composed his plays with a stronger flavor of learning thanks to his educational background and social circle of learned friends and patrons.

ii. Jonson's cold, humorous, satirical, and learned comedies

Jonson immediately impresses readers or theater goers with his humour plays: *Every Man in his Humour* and *Every Man out of his Humour*. It was with these humour plays that Jonson's career as a dramatist began effectively. Humour in

Jonson means:

> A particular disposition, inclination, or liking, esp. one
> having no apparent ground or reason; mere fancy, whim,
> caprice, freak, vagary. (In this sense very frequent in late
> 16th and early 17th c., and ridiculed by Shakespeare and
> Ben Jonson.)
>
> (*OED* "humour")

In addition to the above mentioned two comedies, Jonson's other masterpieces *Cynthia's Revels*, *Poetaster*, *Volpone*, *The Alchemist* and *Epicoene* feature renaissance humours.

Indeed, Jonson is accredited the representative writer of humour comedies. M. C. Bradbrook, when calling *Every Man out of his Humour* a "new satiric comedy," assigns Jonson as "the only begetter" of this genre (*Growth* 144). According to James P. Bednarz, scholars once thought that Jonson had "revolutionized Elizabethan theater by inventing the comedy of humours" and that *Every Man in his Humour* was "the pivotal play" through which Jonson established a new comic paradigm (56). While Jonson's invention of humour comedies is well recognized, it is now generally accepted, according to W. David Kay, that *Every Man out of his Humour* "marks a watershed in Jonson's work" (231). Because Jonson's humour comedies mock their characters' eccentricities, they are certainly satirical comedies. The comedy of humours, as a distinctive feature of Jonson's dramatic work, is not challenged.

Jonson's comedies of humours are also known as comic satires,[1] "a new kind of drama that he conceived as an assault on existing theatrical conventions" (Bednarz 55). Jonson invented comical satire in 1599 with the performance of *Every Man out of his Humour* together with its forerunner, *Every Man in his Humour*, to ridicule of various humours such as venomous malcontent, cynicism, uxoriousness, fastidiousness, avarice and vainglory, irrational jealousy, and excessive concern. The comedies after *Every Man out of his Humour* are all comical satires.[2] Because Jonson's major dramatic works (excluding masques) are comic satires, many readers feel they are not as pleasant as Shakespeare's comedies. Some even find Jonson cold and repellent.

In his *The Companion to the Play-house* (1764), David Erskine Baker (1730 – 1767), grandson of Daniel Defoe, while joining many eighteenth century critics in praising Jonson's comedies, especially *Volpone*, *The Alchemist* and *The Silent Woman*, calling them the playwright's "Chef d'Oeuvres" and "perfections," regrets that there runs through all of Jonson's dramatic works "an unempassioned coldness in the language"

---

[1] A satire used to be thought of as related to satyr, a comic appendage to Greek tragic trilogies offered for competition, but the two terms have no connection with each other, despite their resemblances in spelling. A satyr is a humorous (funny) piece, a piece of comic relief, but a satire, originally from Latin, *satira*, from *lanx satura*, meaning "a full dish, a hotch-potch," is a poem or prose composition, in which prevailing vices or follies are held up to ridicule. For more, see *OED* entry "satire" or the entries "satire" and "satyr drama" in Drabble.

[2] According to Anne Barton, if Shakespeare, as the tradition has it, did recommend *Every Man in his Humour* to the Lord Chamberlain's Men against others' hesitation, then Shakespeare would with "characteristic openness of mind" have supported a kind of comedy "strikingly opposed to the mode he had explored himself in some six or seven Elizabethan plays". Barton also points out that in late 1590s London audiences were "not wholly unprepared for Jonson's new way in comedy" (*Dramatist* 44). This could mean either that the London audience had a wide range of taste or that a demand for a change in the manner of comedy was under way.

(qtd. in Craig 495). Besides " coldness," many other expressions that are associated with this feeling have been used to describe Jonson's comedies. David Erskine Baker uses "indifference" to describe the audience's response to the revivals of Jonson's comedies (ibid.).

Jonson's own intention was to always use comedies to make fun of human eccentricities or attack human follies in order to correct them and teach the audience. In *Every Man in his Humour* (1598), "a good example of Jonson's quickly maturing use of learning" (R. V. Young 46), Jonson mocks the "compulsive, mechanical" behaviors of the characters, especially Kitely and Bobadil. In *Every Man out of his Humour*, a detailed exposition of playwright's humour theory, Jonson ridicules the characters' obsessive peculiarities. With his more mature comedies, such as *Volpone* and *The Alchemist*, Jonson satirizes the destructive and yet hilarious greed of Volpone, Voltore, Corvino, Corbaccio, Mosca, Sir Epicure Mammon, Drugger, and many more. Through *Epicene, or, the Silent Woman*, the play Dryden praises as a "perfect play" (XV: 349), Jonson pokes fun at the pathological irritation of noise. Unlike Shakespeare whose aim as stated in *The Tempest* is to " entertain " (Epilogue, 1. 13), Jonson chooses to focus on human follies, reflect them in current life and warn people against them.

Jonson succeeds in making his audience laugh at human follies. Russ McDonald says "Jonson is nothing if not critical" (*Shakespeare & Jonson* 54). When comparing Jonson's and Shakespeare's comedies, Corbyn Morris says, "*Jonson* in his COMIC Scenes has expos'd and ridicul'd *Folly* and *Vice*; *Shakespeare* has usher'd in *Joy*, *Frolic* and *Happiness*. The

Alchemist, *Volpone* and *Silent Woman* of *Jonson* are most exquisite Satires" (qtd. in Vickers, *Heritage* 3: 127). Similarly, Samuel Rogers (1763 – 1855), Rector of Chellington, Bedfordshire, distinguishes between Jonson and Shakespeare as "appealing to the mind" and "the heart" respectively (qtd. in Vickers, *Heritage* 4: 3-4).

T. S. Eliot shares Rogers's view about Jonson. He goes on to link Jonson's comedies that "appeal to the mind" with the effort it requires the reader or audience to appreciate them. He says:

> When we say that Jonson requires study, we do not mean study of his classical scholarship or of seventeenth-century manners. We mean intelligent saturation in his work as a whole; we mean that in order to enjoy him at all, we must get to the centre of his work and his temperament, and that we must see him unbiased by time, as a contemporary.
>
> (67)

Eliot's claim can well be said to be a general opinion of Jonson as a playwright. Jonson the well-read satirist and intellectual demands a full occupation by his work, temperament and a fair treatment of him as a contemporary for proper understanding and appreciation.

To Dryden, the major critic of Shakespeare and Jonson in the seventeenth century, Jonson is respected as a teacher who is the English "Virgil," the "pattern of elaborate writing"; who has given the English "the most correct Playes," and has provided them with "as many and profitable Rules for perfecting the Stage as any wherewith the French can furnish us." Dryden's ultimate attitude towards

Shakespeare and Jonson is: "I admire him [Jonson], but I love Shakespeare" (XV: 354). If Shakespeare is Dryden's passion, then Jonson will be his reason.

Jonson's learning, or more specifically, education in the classics, was celebrated. He was fortunate to have had his friendly master William Camden (1551 – 1623), the "humanist scholar and educationalist" (McEvoy 3) and outstanding antiquarian and historian of the wonderful yet strict Westminster School, to whom he said he owed "All that I am in arts, all that I know" (8: Epig. xiiii, 1-2). Although his Westminster education was never completed, Jonson became a voracious reader well versed in classical writers, poets and philosophers alike. Murray Roston observes that through self-education Jonson became acknowledged as one of "the most learned men of his time" (15). [1] Julia Briggs calls Jonson's success of learning in Latin and Greek "an unusual accomplishment in a man who had not attended university" (196). His knowledge of Greek and Roman literature is evident throughout his works. During 1605 and 1606, Jonson toured with *Volpone* to Oxford and Cambridge Universities and was well recognized by the academic circles. Later, in 1619, Jonson, upon receiving from both universities a Master of Arts degree (Donaldson, *Life* 350), [2] became a celebrity and was followed by a group of admiring young writers known

---

[1] Murray Roston argues that Jonson had a strong "personal aspiration" for a formal academic training at Oxford or Cambridge, and when the "avenue" to it was closed to him, he was "embittered" but was determined to make amends by self-education (15). For details, see Roston, p. 15.

[2] Jonson's Oxford degree is controversial. Anne Barton (*Essays* 282; *Ben Jonson* 1) agrees with Herford and Simpson (1: 83) that it was an honorary M. A. Anne Barton, Herford and Simpson, and Ian Donaldson are acknowledged Jonson authorities. Sean McEvoy believes that Jonson was awarded an honorary "doctorate" (5). I thank Gao Xing (高幸) for assistance in this reference.

as the "Tribe of Ben." In 1616, Jonson collected some of his plays and published them in folio as *The Works of Benjamin Jonson*, which was taunted by Sir John Suckling (1609 – 1642), one of the Cavalier Poets, in his "A Session of the Poets": "For his were call'd Works, where others were but Plays" (1. 20). Despite mockery for presumption by some at the time, Jonson's learning and literary status similar to that of a classical writer were accepted by most of the contemporary readership. As D. H. Craig says,

> In the context of an English stage generally perceived as unworthy of serious attention, fed by makeshift, sensational, or merely trifling plays, the figure of the classic poet that Jonson constructed for himself could be seen as innovator and as reformer. His rigorously constructed plays, his well-differentiated characters, the dense and carefully weighed language he gave them, all supported the idea that his was a learned drama which would bring some standards at last to the theatre of his day.
>
> (4)

Jonson's works are learned and intellectual, but that does not mean that Jonson turns a deaf ear to the demands of the groundlings. As M. C. Bradbrook puts it, Jonson has "absorbed all that was best in the popular tradition," and the demands of popular audience have helped Elizabethan drama to "escape from the tyranny of rhetoric most completely" (*Growth* 42-43). In fact, for such great playwrights as Shakespeare and Jonson, it is hard to generalize their comedies in two or three words. This difficulty is to be discussed in more detail in Section IV of this chapter.

II. Shakespeare and Jonson in dramatic context

Shakespeare and Jonson are traditionally said to have followed two different dramatic traditions. According to M. C. Bradbrook, there are at least two traditions of the Elizabethan drama: the tradition of the revels and the learned tradition of rhetorical and satiric drama upon moral themes. Shakespeare represents the revel tradition, characterized by the "shapeless stories of the popular drama," and based often upon the "rambling medieval romantic tale." Jonson stands for the learned, satiric tradition, which stressed "order and formality." The great age of Elizabethan drama began thanks to the coalescence of these two sharply contrastive traditions (*Growth* 4).

i. Genius versus education

Many commentators consider Shakespeare's revel-tradition, popular comedy an achievement of his genius, opposed to Jonson's learned, intellectual and rules-bound comedy, his fruit of education. An eighteenth century critic, Samuel Rogers thus praises Shakespeare's genius and Jonson's learning, without failing to distinguish their strengths from their frailties:

> Great Shakespeare, with genius disdaining all rules,
> Above the cold phlegm or the fripp'ry of schools,
> Appeal'd to the heart for success of his plays,
> And trusted to nature alone for the bays.
> Despairing of glory but what rose from art,
> Old Jonson applied to the head, not the heart.

On the niceness of rules he founded his cause,

And ravish'd from regular method applause.

(qtd. in Vickers, *Heritage* 4: 3-4)

Roger's view is representative of many: Shakespeare has genius, appeals to nature, but cares not for rules; Jonson possesses learning, relies on rationality, and follows rules; and both have succeeded. Thomas Wilkes (d. 1786) praised Shakespeare's "force of heaven-born genius" as "the glories of their [Shakespeare's and Jonson's] age and nation"; Wilkes's encomium on Jonson's education is that Jonson possessed "the most consummate learning and art." Thanks to their respective merits, Shakespeare and Jonson "almost all at once raised the Stage to such dignity and perfection as has never since been out-done" (208). Charles Churchill (1731 - 1764), poet and parson, calling Shakespeare and Jonson the "two judges" of British poetry in his poem, *The Rosciad*, sings of the poetic power of Shakespeare's genius and Jonson's academic training:

> Things of the noblest kind his [Shakespeare's] genius
> drew,
> And look'd through Nature at a single view:
> A loose he gave to his unbounded soul,
> And taught new lands to rise, new seas to roll.
> . . . .
> Next JONSON sat, in antient learning train'd,
> His rigid judgment Fancy's flights restrain'd,
> Correctly prun'd each wild luxuriant thought,

Mark'd out her course, nor spar'd a glorious fault. ①

(265-68, 271-74)

In addition to numerous poetic commentaries on Shakespeare's genius and Jonson's learning, an anonymous essay was published in 1758 to give definite numerical values to their respective virtues as related to their forerunners and successors:

	GENIUS	JUDGMENT	LEARNING	VERSIFICATIONS
Chaucer	16	12	10	14
Spenser	18	12	14	18
Shakespeare	19	14	14	19
Jonson	16	18	17	8
Milton	18	16	17	18
Dryden	18	16	17	18

(qtd. in Vickers, *Heritage* 4: 326-27)

Based on his definitions of *genius* ("excellencies that no study or art can communicate: such as elevation, expression, description, wit, humour, passion") and *learning* ("not in an academical or scholastic sense, but that species of it which

---

① Among Churchill's admirers brought by the success of *The Rosciad*, a certain F-B-L published a poem, *The Rational Rosciad* (1767), to eulogize Shakespeare's genius and Jonson's art in emulation:

> JOHNSON to future times his fame may trust,
> Who is tho' seldom striking, always just.
> Tho' cool, correct, tho' modest, yet severe.
> Strong without passion, without dulness clear;
> Humorous with elegance, jocose with ease,
> Sublime to charm, satirical to please;
> SHAKESPEAR's strong genius ever unconfin'd,
> Darts on the soul, and captivates the mind;
> While JOHNSON, by more regular essays,
> Attacks the dangerous avenues of praise. (qtd. in Craig 505)

The praise of Jonson in this poem, according to D. H. Craig, is "measured," but only "a little beyond the conventional" (505).

can best qualify a poet to excel in the subject he attempts") (qtd. in Vickers, *Heritage* 4: 326-7), Shakespeare and Jonson score widely different numbers in the impression of the anonymous author. That is, Shakespeare has better genius, and Jonson, better learning (the highest possible score in each column is 20). An interesting point about this numerical contrast is that the commentator does not have a remarkably high opinion of any of the selected poets' learning, and Jonson, a little surprisingly, scores only 17, the highest, together with Milton. In any case, the anonymous evaluator gives Shakespeare's genius the highest points (19) among all the 29 poets in his list, including Alexander Pope (1688 – 1744) and James Thomson (1700 – 1748), who are in the original chart but not quoted here.

As is suggested in this numerical contrast, Jonson is also recognized as a literary genius. Not only is Jonson ranked at the same level of genius as Chaucer, but he's *Alchemist* is also commended by Sir Richard Steele (1672 – 1729): "This comedy is an example of Ben Jonson's extensive genius and penetration into the passions and follies of mankind" (qtd. in Craig 359). Shakespeare is certainly a dramatic genius, but Jonson is also one, although Shakespeare stands more remarkable in a comparison of this respect.

Since perhaps his life time, Shakespeare has been believed by many English Renaissance students to have a poor classical education compared with not only Jonson, but with many of his rivals such as Christopher Marlowe (1564 – 1593), Thomas Middleton (1570 – 1627) and George Chapman (1560 – 1634). He is claimed by Jonson to have "small Latine, and less Greeke" ("Memory" 31). Chapman, Marlowe,

Middleton went to either Oxford or Cambridge. Jonson did not make it to either university,[1] but he was lucky to have been educated by William Camden, who "wrote principally in Latin" (qtd. in Drabble, "Camden, William," 165).

However, opinions about Jonson's learning are not universally positive, nor are remarks on Shakespeare's want of classical education always negative. In reviewing the application of classical learning in Shakespearian tragedy, James Beattie asserts Jonson's "misfortune" was his learning: "not that he knew too much, but that he could not make a proper use of his knowledge; a misfortune which arose rather from a defect of genius or taste than from a superabundance of erudition" (488). Edward Young (1683 – 1765) regrets Jonson's encumbering learning while idolizing Shakespeare's genius in understanding nature and man:

> He [Jonson] was very learned, as Sampson was very strong, to his own hurt. Who knows if Shakespeare might not have thought less if he had read more? Who knows if he might not have laboured under the load of Jonson's learning, as Enceladus under Ætna? ... Perhaps he was as learned as his dramatic province required, for whatever other learning he wanted he was master of two books unknown to many of the profoundly read, tho' books which the last conflagration alone can destroy: the book of Nature, and that of Man.
>
> (81)

Despite Young's worship of Shakespeare's knowledge of Nature and Man, commentaries on Shakespeare's genius and

---

[1] David Erskine Baker claimed that Jonson went to St. John's College, Cambridge and Christ Church College, Oxford (264), but his opinion has been generally rejected.

naturalness are not unanimous, either. David Hume (1711 - 1776) somehow recognized Shakespeare's genius but regretted that he did not possess any other advantage:

> If Shakespeare be considered as a MAN, born in a rude age and educated in the lowest manner, without any instruction either from the world or from books, he may be regarded as a prodigy. If represented as a POET, capable of furnishing a proper entertainment to a refined or intelligent audience, we must abate somewhat of this eulogy. . . . A great and fertile genius he certainly possessed, and one enriched equally with a tragic and comic vein; but he ought to be cited as a proof how dangerous it is to rely on these advantages alone for the attaining an excellence in the finer arts.
>
> (127)

Hume effusively confirms Shakespeare's dramatic genius, but rather than seeing such genius as guaranteed resource, the Scottish philosopher cautions against it as a dangerous advantage to be solely relied on for excellence. For Hume, consequently, Shakespeare, despite his genius for both tragedy and comedy, had better resort to other advantages.

William Jackson (1730 - 1803), known as Jackson of Exeter, remarks that Shakespeare's verses are "very perfect" and the poet, "divine," but he criticizes Shakespeare's plays as often "generally so over-acted as to cease to be the ' mirror of nature,' " and holds that his characters are not "natural," either. He asserts, "Those who think that Shakespeare's personages are natural are deceived" (qtd. in Vickers, *Heritage* 6: 333).

Such are some of the representative criticisms of Shakespeare's genius and Jonson's classical education.

Genius is praised for its access to divine power, and education, its association with dramatic rules and art. However, Shakespeare sometimes is criticized for having relied only on his genius, and Jonson, good education but wanting in genius. The attributes of genius and education as distinctions between Shakespeare and Jonson, a part of a long-standing debate between the excellences of nature and art, has not always maintained unanimity.

ii. Nature versus art

Almost whenever Shakespeare and Jonson are considered together, the former is commended for his imitation of nature: the vividness of natural world and the human nature represented in his works. Jonson, on the other hand, is commended for his artistic techniques and moral principles. Russ McDonald summarizes many critics' views this way: "Shakespeare's 'country heart' kept him 'the genial natural,' and Jonson 'spat forth bilious satires' for his education and his 'sharp urban eyes' revealed him as 'the crabbed classicist'" (*Shakespeare & Jonson* 2). Jonson, "follwing an already threadbare convention of the time in contrasting Nature and Art" (Baldwin 5), praises his greatest rival in terms of both Nature and Art:

> Nature her selfe was proud of his designes,
> Andioy'd to we are the dressing of his lines!
> . . . .
> Yet must I not giue Nature all: Thy Art,
> My gentle *Shakespeare*, must enioy a part.
>
> ("Memory" 47-48, 55-56)

Four years earlier, in his conversations with William

Drummond in 1619, however, Jonson criticized Shakespeare because he "wanted Arte" (*Timber* 275).

Ever since these early remarks, a debate about Shakespeare's nature and art has been going on. Interestingly but not necessarily justly, Jonson is often mentioned in it as a contrast to Shakespeare.

As early as in 1631, while recommending their merry-making comedies, Milton asserted the dramatic difference between Jonson's learning and Shakespeare's naturalness:

> Then to the well-trod stage anon,
> If Jonsons learned Sock [comedy] be on,
> Or sweetest Shakespear, fancies [imagination] childe,
> Warble his native Wood-notes wilde.
>
> ("L'Allegro," 131-34)

Sir John Denham (1615 – 1669) dubbed John Fletcher, Shakespeare and Jonson "the Triumvirate of wit." In 1647, he commented on the difference between Jonson's artistic toil and Shakespeare's natural poetic inspiration:

> Yet what from JONSON'S oyle and sweat did flow,
> Or what more easie nature did bestow
> On SHAKESPEARE'S gentler Muse.
>
> (qtd. in Vickers, *Heritage* 1: 504)

Twenty years later, Denham modified his remarks slightly and began to hint at the superiority of nature over art:

> Old Mother Wit, and Nature gave
> Shakespeare and Fletcher all they have;
> In Spenser, and in Jonson, Art
> Of slower Nature got the start.
>
> (ibid. 11)

Richard Flecknoe (c. 1600 – c. 1678) directly contrasted Shakespeare and Jonson with nature and art: "Comparing him [Jonson] with Shakespear, you shall see the difference betwixt Nature and Art" (qtd. in Craig 234).

James Drake (1667 – 1707), a Tory pamphleteer and author of one play, claimed that Shakespeare "fell short of the Art of Jonson"; but "nature has richly provided him with the materials, tho his unkind Fortune denied him the Art of managing them to the best Advantage" (qtd. in Vickers, *Heritage* 2: 72).

Predictably, as an editor of Shakespeare's works, Nicolas Rowe preferred Shakespeare's natural talents to Jonson's artifice, "what Nature gave the latter [Shakespeare] was more than a Balance for what Books had given the former [Jonson]" (xiv).

Lewis Theobald (1688 – 1744), an influential Shakespearian scholar who wrote a preface to his edition of Shakespeare's works, compared the two playwrights in the usual vein: Shakespeare and Jonson are "the greatest Writers our Nation could ever boast of in the Drama," but Shakespeare "owed all to his prodigious natural Genius," and Jonson, "a great deal to his Art and Learning" (qtd. in Vickers, *Heritage* 2: 358).

Similarly, Paul Hiffernan (1719 – 1777), an Irish physician by training, in his published dramatic criticism (1754), claimed that "nature gave [Shakespeare] all the power she could: so art gave to Ben Jonson every resource" (qtd. Vickers, *Heritage* 4: 312). Corbyn Morris (d. 1779), a commissioner and author of a book about humours, compared in a context of their naturalness Jonson's works to exquisite cabinets and Shakespeare's, unfinished and irregular castles:

> Upon the whole, Jonson's Compositions are like finished Cabinets, where every Part is wrought up with the most excellent Skill and Exactness; Shakespeare's like magnificent Castles, not perfectly finished or regular, but adorn'd with such bold and magnificent Designs as at once delight and astonish you with their Beauty and Grandeur.
>
> (36)

Morris can be said to have specified Hiffernan's terms of "nature" and "art": Jonson's works are like finished cabinets, constructed with immaculate excellence, regularity, design and precision, whereas Shakespeare's, magnificent castles built with delightful and astonishing beauty and grandeur, but irregularity and roughness; Jonson stands for craftsmanship, and Shakespeare, with his "boldness," indicates his achievements of magnificence and splendor. Jonson's seriousness and diligence towards his plays as art is effectively summarized by J. B. Bamborough:

> He cared as much for his art as any other English writer, and more than all but a few, but there is nothing in him of the *petit maître*. Together with his fine sense of form and love of solid construction went a great vitality and creative vigor, and the two together give him his unique power. He belongs, as Milton does, to that class of serious and dedicated artists of whom Virgil (whom he admired so much) is the supreme example, and if he is not among the greatest, he is not unworthy of their company.
>
> (349)

The debate concerning Shakespeare's nature and Jonson's art is likely to go on. Critics, readers and audiences who prefer a natural imitation of reality may all find Shakespeare beautiful and pleasant, and when they examine Jonson's works, they will certainly be struck by his technique and artistry. Shakespeare's nature can be a result of his genius, but Jonson's art is definitely an achievement of his learning. Both approaches appear to have fulfilled the two dramatists' differing aims: Shakespeare's nature is entertaining, and Jonson's art, educational.

iii. Entertainment versus education

Audiences are important to playwrights. As Jane Milling points out, "one of the most significant factors in shaping a piece of theatre, both in the writing and performing, was the audience" (166). In the seventeenth century as today, audiences were essential to the success of a dramatist. As Dryden points out, first of all, writers belong to their times: to survive, after all, they "have to please their immediate audiences" (IV: 23). Both Shakespeare and Jonson must have been aware of this, but they displayed different attitudes to their audience.

According to M. C. Bradbrook, Shakespeare was grouped by John Webster (c. 1580 – c. 1625) with Thomas Dekker (c. 1570 – 1632) and Thomas Heywood (c. 1572 – c. 1650) for their "right happy and copious industry." She sharply notices the " absurdity the collocation may now appear," and especially what united them: popular theater. " All three practised a popular art," popular theater " without the professed loftiness of Chapman and Jonson" (*Growth* 137).

That Shakespeare was actively offering his London audience sweet, romantic and popular comedies is consistent with his theatrical philosophy. Shakespeare's intention to entertain the audience is well known, and he does not hide it. Although being an owner of the Lord Chamberlain's Men (later the King's Men) meant patronage from powerful people, even the King, as an actor and playwright in a highly competitive theatrical world, [1] Shakespeare was keenly aware of the necessity to sell theatrical performances to a large audience: [2]

> Gentle breath of yours my sails
> Must fill, or else my project fails,
> Which was to please.

> (*The Tempest*, Epilogue, 11-13)

The composition of *The Tempest* (1611) and other romances featuring noble heroes and heroines like *The Winter's Tale* (1609) and *Cymbeline* (1610) showed Shakespeare's nimble shift. These were for performances at the Blackfriars Theatre, which was patronized by more sophisticated upper class audiences. [3]

As M. C. Bradbrook has asserted, Shakespeare's comedies were "designed to appeal in the best ways to the widest possible audience" (*Growth* 5). Bradbrook claims that, for Shakespeare, it was "certainly the acting, not the plays, that built his fortune" (*Growth* 53). It is now accepted that plays were infrequently printed in Shakespeare's time.

---

[1] See, for instance, David Farley-Hills, p. 1.

[2] Although Shakespeare's tragedies, like *Macbeth* and *Hamlet*, were also written in the popular Elizabethan tradition, they are not discussed here because of the current topic of Shakespeare's and Jonson's comedies.

[3] The Blackfriars Theatre was taken over in 1608 by the King's Men as an alternative to the Globe. An indoor theater operated in candlelight. Its audiences were courtiers and wealthy Londoners.

According to Arthur Kinney, the reason for delayed or often abandoned publication of performed plays was not "the playing companies wishing to keep singular hold on their property," but rather, published plays "did not sell well in a market crowded with works of religious controversy, wondrous news, and household manuals" (ix). Luckily, Shakespeare "knew the exact quality of speech required to hold a large mixed audience" (Bradbrook, *Growth* 53), and that quality must be a mixture of both popular and some high-brow courtly elements, considering the "mixed audience" (ibid. 53), who were from "the lowest levels of society as well as the highest," and who "could be given to revelry but also riots" (Kinney ix). Naturally, the mixed quality of popular elements and high-brow poetry was embodied in both the writing and performance of Shakespeare's plays in order to please the largest possible audience. Gabriel Egan stresses Shakespeare's goal of business profit by pleasing the audience even more emphatically than Bradbrook and Kinney:

> We must think of Shakespeare, then, as primarily a man of business, specifically the theatre business. Whatever else he may have wanted to achieve in his work, he wanted, or rather he needed, his playing company to succeed in the competitive world of a vibrant entertainment industry. [1]

(12)

---

[1] The prevalence of imitation without the present sense of intellectual rights infringement helps to show how competitive the Elizabethan and Jacobean theater industry was. According to Roslyn Lander Knutson, " [Theater] Companies repeated the subjects and formulas that had been successful in their own offerings and in the repertories of their competitors. This principle accounts for the proliferation of offerings on a popular hero" (40).

Some scholars have speculated that Shakespeare's philosophy of the popular play may also have been a result of his failed attempt at courtly literature. To quote M. C. Bradbrook again, Shakespeare's ventures into courtly literature, *Venus and Adonis* and *The Rape of Lucrece*, "did not apparently reap the kind of reward that the older literary figure such as Spenser might have sought for" (*Growth* 53).① Despite their lack of profitability as court literature, however, the success of *Venus and Adonis* and *The Rape of Lucrece* as popular literature could have reinforced Shakespeare's intent to stay with the popular, for profit.② Books could be mass printed in Shakespeare's time, but because of wide-spread illiteracy and the higher prices of books compared with seeing a performance,③ writing plays could be more profitable than

---

① Despite favors from the royalty to his company and the legend that Queen Elizabeth ordered Shakespeare to write *The Merry Wives of Windsor*, Shakespeare was probably not so favored personally by either the Queen or James I as to yield significant patronage. As Anne Barton observes, "There is no evidence—and small likelihood—that Shakespeare ever enjoyed even that approximation to a personal relationship with King James that Jonson seems to have had." Although Shakespeare was made "a Groom of the Chamber in 1604," this honor implied "little more than the occasional need at court for extras to augment the native entourage during the visits of important foreign emissaries" ("London Scene" 125).

② Besides sometimes playing a leading or minor role, Shakespeare had other responsibilities in his company during his rise to prosperity. According to Ernst Honigmann, Shakespeare was, 1) "sharer, one of ten or so owners of the company's assets (play-books, play clothes, properties)"; 2) "house-holder," one of the owners or lease-holders of the Globe and Blackfriars theaters; and 3) dramatist (5). This also evidences Shakespeare's close economic ties with the revenues of his theater.

③ Shakespeare's books sold at high prices. For instance, *Venus and Adonis* was selling at 1 shilling, three times the average price of a book of its size, owing to a classification under erotica; and the *Sonnets* in 1609, 5 pennies. Notwithstanding, Shakespeare showed little concern for the publication of his works, because the theater was the "largest segment" of his income and publication for profit was not his "primary aim." Only *Venus and Adonis* seems to have been brought to a publisher by Shakespeare himself because it was written during the London plague year and the poet had to "boil his pot by his pen" (Murphy 16-17). In contrast, a ticket to a Globe performance could be as cheap as one penny.

printing books. This is why Shakespeare showed little interest in seeing his plays in print. Evidence of this is the First Folio, which was not published by the dramatist himself. Instead, his fellow actors, John Hemminge and Henry Condell collected, classified and published thirty-six of his plays in 1623, seven years after Shakespeare's death.

Different from Shakespeare, Jonson's aim and attitude seemed rarely to be pleasing a general audience. As J. B. Bamborough remarks, Jonson was a "proud and self-confident" man. "Circumstances might force him to take up playwriting, a despised occupation looked down on by the scholars and gentlemen among whom he felt his right place to be; very well, he would "make it his business to render it an accepted and valued profession" (337).

According to M. C. Bradbrook, "only in *Epicoene* did Jonson positively soothe the audience" because it was written for the private theaters, unlike its predecessor, *Volpone*, prepared for the King's Men (145). Jonson thought many popular elements of the contemporary stage vulgar.[1] D. H. Craig maintains that Jonson "takes pride in refusing to give the audience the vulgar entertainment it wants" (4). In this respect, Jonson did not care much about popular acclaim. His aim was to give his audiences something artistic, refined and instructive.

Jonson's disregard of the general audience could also stem partly from his relative failure to achieve success in the theater. Jonas Barish observes, "Jonson, despite a lifetime

[1] For Thomas Rymer, writing in 1692, Jonson writes irregularly like his contemporaries, with too much translation and too many interludes to please the crowd (Craig 11 & 326-27).

of writing for the stage, never arrived at a comfortable *modus vivendi* [peaceful coexistence] with his audiences" (133). In 1605, *Sejanus*, the first tragedy of which Jonson was proud and in which Shakespeare acted (Barton, *Dramatist* 92),[1] was hissed off the stage. The indignation from this failure is acutely recorded by the playwright himself in the quarto dedication to Aubigny, berating the audience by stating that the play "suffer'd no lesse violence from our people here, then the subject of it did from the rage of the people of Rome" (qtd. in Barton, *Dramatist* 94).[2] The failure of *Sejanus* was a watershed in Jonson's dramatic development.[3] After that, Jonson blamed the general audience's "poor discrimination" and believed that "its distaste for his offerings is itself a guarantee of quality" (Craig 4). In calling Shakespeare's *Pericles* a "mouldy tale," Jonson censured the audience for its "lack of appreciation" (qdt. in Hart 60). Jonson's conviction that the general audience lacked taste for plays of quality reinforced his intention to produce refined and cultured works, through which he meant to improve the audience aesthetically as well as morally.

Jonson's classical learning is well recognized. His

---

[1] McEvoy argues that *Sejanus* was not Jonson's first attempt at tragedy. Besides the lost *Richard Crookback* (1602), Jonson collaborated with Henry Chettle (c. 1560 – c. 1607), Thomas Dekker and John Marston (1576 – 1634) in *Robert II*. Merely Jonson's "additions" to *The Spanish Tragedy* (1592) of Thomas Kyd (1558 – 1594) survive in the only version of that play to have come down to us (32). Also, as Barton observes, "in 1598 Francis Meres was praising Jonson for tragedies, every one of which is lost" (*Essays* 286).

[2] Some audience members at the *Sejanus* performance did not think it a failure. One writer reported that he was one of those that hissed it off at first, "yet after sate it out, not only patiently, but with content, & admiration" (qtd. in Craig 11).

[3] In addition to *Sejanus*, at least two other Jonsonian plays, *Catiline* (1611) and *The New Inn* (1629) suffered similar mockery from the general audience. Sara Van Den Berg observes that Jonson felt "betrayed by the audience" because of such rejections (9).

erudition in the classics makes him ready and eager to apply the neoclassical rules, one of which was to educate the audience. He constantly teaches the audience about the educational function of a play "to profit" and "to tax the crimes"; he also teaches the audience not to take what is imitated in a play as truths, but truths "well feigned":

> The ends of all, who for the *Scene* doe write,
> > Are, or should be, to profit, and delight.
> And still 't hath beene the praise of all best times,
> > So persons were not touch'd, to taxe the crimes.
> Then, in this play, which we present to night,
> > And make the object of your eare, and sight,
> On forfeit of your selues, thinke nothing true:
> > Lest so you make the maker to iudge you.
> For he knowes, *Poet* neuer credit gain'd
> > By writing truths, but things (like truths) well fain'd.
>
> > > (Prologue (Another) to *Epicoene*, 1-10)

Harry Levin attests to Jonson's intention of using comedy to educate the audience. For Jonson, he says, comedy

> Is as a social corrective . . . The premise of Ben Jonson's "comical satire" was that the spectators, recognizing their faults and foibles, would improve their behavior. Caught up in a rearguard action against the uncompromising Puritans, Sidney and Jonson both conceived the drama as an object-lesson, a cautionary fable.
>
> > (*Playbills* 22)

Another important evidence of Jonson's aim to educate his audience is his control over the printing of his plays. As already mentioned, not only did he boldly and famously (infamously to some in his time) call his plays *Works*, a sign to position himself as an equal to classical poets, but he painstakingly monitored the publication of his plays, something in diametric opposition to Shakespeare who, as has been discussed earlier, cared almost nothing about publishing his plays for the education of future generations. Certainly, Jonson equalled his plays to his poetry. "Time and again he asserts the high place of poetry" (Bamborough 337). He must use his poetry to improve the world. And supervising the publication of his plays was important, especially for the appreciation of and education by his plays of future generations of readers and audiences.

Regardless of his dissatisfaction with the popular audience and despite his celebrated learning, Jonson set out to correct what he thought was wrong with the contemporary popular dramas and to provide intellectual plays to elevate the level of contemporary culture. "Jonson's critical strength lays in his formulated restrictions upon the license of popular art" (Bradbrook, *Growth* 103). In fact, according to D. H. Craig, Jonson's "achievement had been to establish an organized and official set of values among the privileged opinion-makers of English culture" (7). In addition to Jonson's success in winning academic audiences at Oxford and Cambridge, Jonson was able to attract the intellectual nobles at Court with his plays. According to Andrew Gurr, from 1603, Jonson "climbed socially by living with his noble patrons," and so "cultivated a circle of learned friends among the nobles and gentry" (6). Not surprisingly, as many intellectuals then depended on patronage, Jonson intended to please the aristocracy.

When he paid his celebrated visit to William Drummond at Hawthornden a few months after King James's enthronement, Jonson told the host "that he wished to please the King." This is one of the many demonstrations of Jonson's deference to authority (*Conversations* 135). Jonson's employment to write poetry for King James I, his gifts and regular royal pension, and his "verse manuscripts circulated among a select circle of gentlemen and ladies" (Riggs 3) all demonstrated his independence from the ordinary audience as well as a resulting dependence on the authorities. [1] This is also a difference between Shakespeare and Jonson: Shakespeare's dependence on the audience from groundlings to King James I for both economic and dramatic success, and Jonson's, on the nobility as patrons.

Therefore, scholars have traditionally seen the difference between the economic status of Shakespeare and Jonson, together with their distinct artistic concerns, as having significantly helped to shape their attitudes toward their audiences. Shakespeare's concern was first of all the profitable operation of his theater(s). Because the theater in Elizabethan England was a despised industry, Shakespeare in a sense had to please the theatergoers. To do this, he had to ensure both popular plays and entertaining acting to attract and keep the largest possible audience. He did not have much serious education in the classics, and was thus perhaps

---

[1] As Barton remarks, after *The Devil Is an Ass* (1616), Jonson "simply turned his back on the public theatres" and "could afford to," no longer "dependent as other playwrights were upon public means which public manners breeds [sic.]," at least for a while till the enthronement of King Charles I in 1625, partly because he was "secure in the favour of the king" (*Ben Jonson* 235; *Essays* 296).

not so aware as Jonson of the classical dramatic rules that were to dominate dramatic creation in roughly the next 150 years. On the other hand, Jonson turned to theater and playwriting not primarily to entertain the common audience, and he was first caught between entertaining the audience with popular plays and representing the classical rules of art. His classical knowledge and his failures in attempts at popular theater stamped the classical rules on his mind even deeper and hardened his opposition towards his audience, whom he considered uneducated; he meant to teach by bringing them intellectual plays and meticulously published books.

iv. Individual versus type in characterization

Despite the vicissitudes of character studies,[①] Shakespearian and Jonsonian characterization must be discussed in any comparative analysis of their comedies. Similar to the polarity seen by many critics of Shakespeare and Jonson in their dramatic intentions, these two playwrights' dramatic characters have also had disparate reviews. Kenneth Muir remarks that Shakespeare has become the most popular world dramatist because of his "unrivalled powers of characterization" ("Open Secret" 9). E. E. Stoll believes that " in character lies Shakespeare's supreme achievement" (89). Historically, M. C. Bradbrook asserts that it was Shakespeare's "characters which engage the audiences of his own day," and next only to the

---

① See, for example, Vickers, *Character Criticism*, pp. 11-21, and Yachnin and Slights, "Introduction," especially pp. 1-4.

"articulation of the fable," Shakespeare's "first great achievement," the "development of many-sided characters" was the playwright's second "great achievement" (*Growth* 81).

In contrast to the superiority of Shakespeare's characterization, traditional views are not highly favorable to Jonson's. When Jonson's characterization is discussed, there are usually disparaging remarks that his characters are insignificant and his art of characterization undistinguished. Augustus William Schlegel (1767 – 1845), the German Romantic and Shakespeare translator, while recognizing Jonson's "solidly and judiciously drawn characters" for the most part and appreciating his creation of Kitely in *Every Man in his Humour*, makes a harsh general criticism of the playwright for his "mechanical view of art." Calling Jonson's characters "caricatures" and mechanical imitation, Schlegel agrees with critics like Pope that Jonson's characters are "merely a personification of general ideas," in contrast to Shakespeare's "thoroughly delineated" ones with "a number of individual peculiarities," "their distinguishing property" and "a signification which is not applicable to them alone" (II: 135; 297-302). William Hazlitt shares Schlegel's opinion and becomes even harsher than his elder contemporary. While comparing Shakespeare's comic humour to a natural spring that "bubbles, sparkles, and finds its way in all directions," Hazlitt considers Jonson's comedy "far from being lively, audible, and full of vent: it is for the most part obtuse, obscure, forced, and tedious." Hazlitt continues to use the water metaphor to characterize Jonson's comedy of humours:

It [Jonson's comic humor] is, as it were, confined in *a leaden cistern*, where it stagnates and corrupts; or directed only through certain artificial pipes and conduits, to answer a given purpose.

(*Lectures* 73-74, italics mine)

To Hazlitt, Shakespeare's characterization of humours is lively and noisy, full of bubbles that go in all directions and break on the way; but Jonson's is stagnant and silent, without bubbles. When Jonson's humour does create bubbles, they have to go in certain fixed directions and break there. In a word, "Shakespeare's characters are men; Ben Jonson's are more like machines" (William Hazlitt, *Lectures* 73).

Hazlitt was not the first critic to use "machine" to describe Jonson's characters. Dryden had already said of Jonson: "Humour was his proper sphere; and in that he delighted most to represent mechanic people" (353). However, the difference is that Hazlitt's commentary is highly typical of the English Romantic Age, when Shakespeare was thought of as "everything," and Jonson, "different from his contemporaries," was "absent" in terms of influence and "marginalized" (Lockwood 1).

Such a polarity between opinions of Shakespeare's and Jonson's characterization has a long history. Charles Gildon (1665 – 1724), a playwright and anthologist, remarks that Jonson's as well as other comic writers' characters are types instead of individuals: "*Morose* is not a particular, but a general character, as I have observ'd; and the same may be said of almost all the characters of *Ben Johnson*." Meanwhile, Gildon shows preference for Shakespeare's

Falstaff as a combination from many follies like a bee's collection from different flowers: "Falstaff stands unimitated yet" (248). In an anonymous letter published in 1772, the author says while Jonson "pleased himself with personifying vices and passions," Shakespeare "drew characters, such as Nature presented to him, or such as she was capable of producing"; while Jonson "debased" the human species, Shakespeare "exalted" it (qtd. in Craig 530). George Colman (1732 - 1794), an English dramatist, echoes the view of Shakespeare's natural and Jonson's stereotyped characters:

> In this Character [Volpone], Nature is rather caricatured, which is the general, tho' only fault of this Author, in his Comic Writings. In this particular, without naming many others, *Jonson* is greatly inferior to *Shakespear*, the latter having excelled all the ancients and moderns, in the knowledge of human Nature, and, therefore, it is, that all his Characters are naturally drawn.
>
> (qtd. in Craig 522)

Even today, the traditional view that Shakespeare's characters are individuals while Jonson's are types is still held by some scholars. Harold Bloom asserts that "Jonson's characters, when successful, all are caricatures" (*Ben Jonson* 9), while Shakespeare's are "great originals," especially Rosalind and Falstaff (*Comedies* 1-2).

Such views on Shakespeare's and Jonson's characters are sometimes attributed to their differences in learning and life experience. Shakespeare, a country-born genius who loved nature and knew the details of trees, grasses and flowers in the Arden forest and on the Avon River banks, did not have the exact classical education of his younger rival. Shakespeare's relatively inconsiderable knowledge of the classics[1] might have resulted in his ignorance of classical or neoclassical models, or he might have chosen to disregard for them when it comes to creating dramatic characters. Consequently, in the seventeenth and eighteenth centuries, Shakespeare was criticized, even censured.

On September 29, 1662, after he saw a production of *A Midsummer Night's Dream*, Samuel Pepys wrote in that day's diary that that there was nothing pleasurable in the play, not even the currently celebrated characters Hermia, Oberon, Puck or Bottom. His only pleasure in it was seeing some "good dancing" and "handsome women." Pepys even decided that he would never see the play again (*Diary* 327). More surprising than this comment is that not even Falstaff could make Pepys laugh. Five years later, he saw a performance of *The Merry Wives of Windsor*, and wrote in his diary dated August 15, 1667, that the play "did not please me at all, in no part of it" (*Diary and Correspondence* 220). This time, even Falstaff, the hilariously bragging knight who had captivated so many, could not entertain Pepys.

In 1662, when a conflation of *Much Ado about Nothing*

---

[1] Apart from T. W. Baldwin's detailed exposition, Honigmann justifies the Jonsonian influential comment on Shakespeare's "Small Latin and Less Greek" by seeing it in the context of Jonson's own standards, but he has a little disagreement with it and claims that "Shakespeare probably read Latin as easily as most graduates 'with Honours in Latin' today." As to Shakespeare's Greek, he argues that the Stratfordian playwright "knew some Greek tragedies, either in the original or in Seneca's adaptations" (2-3). Andrew Murphy believes, Shakespeare is supposed to have worked as a proofreader at Henry Denham's in 1585, an experience that enabled him to proofread Holinshed's *Chronicles* and gain "a thorough knowledge of British history"; Andrew Murphy also supposes that Shakespeare's connection with Richard Field, a friend, another Stratfordian, and more important, a printer, allowed him to become familiar with North's translation of Plutarch's *Lives* (15). These suppositions are not certain, but they are believed by some scholars to be the sources of the knowledge that Shakespeare displays in his histories and Roman plays.

and *Measure for Measure* by Sir William D'Avenant (1606 - 1668) was performed, the audience found that all the comic characters in the latter play as well as Mariana in the former were omitted (Vickers, *Heritage* 1: 31). The same omission occurred again in Charles Gildon's 1700 adaptation of *Measure for Measure* (Vickers, *Heritage* 2: 97). In 1702, William Burnaby (c. 1672 - 1706), an author of a number of comedies of manners, alludes to Shakespeare's *A Midsummer Night's Dream* as an "unnatural farce" that looks like "sick Men's Dreams, compos'd of Parts that no Man can reduce to one Body" (235). The large scale adaptations of Shakespeare's plays in the second half of the seventeenth century and the first half of the eighteenth century also partly demonstrate the age's distaste for his characters. This distaste can be summarized by Dr. Johnson's remarks:

> In his comic scenes he is seldom very successful when he engages his characters in reciprocations of smartness and contest of sarcasm; their jests are commonly gross, and their pleasantry licentious; neither his gentlemen nor his ladies have much delicacy, nor are sufficiently distinguished from his clowns by any appearance of refined manners.

> (363)

However, despite the faults found by many playwrights and critics over the centuries, there has generally been strong commendation of Shakespeare's characters, especially since the Romantic period. Shakespeare is praised for his natural and varied characterization. John Dryden, despite his contradictory comments about Shakespeare and Jonson, asserts that "no man ever drew so many characters, or generally distinguished 'em better from one another" than Shakespeare, "excepting only *Jonson*," and "instances" Caliban to "show the copiousness of his [Shakespeare's] Invention" (qtd. in Vickers, *Heritage* 1: 223).① Dr. Johnson, to quote him again, writes that Shakespeare holds up to his readers "a faithful mirror of manners and of life," that his characters are not modified "by the customs of particular places, unpractised by the rest of the world; by the peculiarities of studies or professions," and that they are the "genuine progeny of common humanity, such as the world will always supply and observation will always find" (355).

During the Romantic Movement, panegyrics for Shakespeare's characterization consummated. Schlegel asserts that "never perhaps was there so comprehensive a talent for characterization as Shakespeare" (II: 134). William Hazilitt was straightforward about his dispute with Johnson's unfavorable comments on Shakespeare. Dismissing Johnson as an unqualified judge of poetry, let alone Shakespeare, Hazlitt refuted the doctor's opinion that Shakespeare's characters were species instead of individuals. Haliztt maintained that "every single character in Shakspeare is as much an individual as those in life itself; it is as impossible to find any two alike." It is "an injury" to call Shakespeare's characters "copies" of nature since they are as vivid as nature itself (*Characters* xi).

Hazlitt's eulogy of Shakespearean characters is just a specimen of the opinion of his age, when Shakespeare's

---

① Gerald Langbaine says he is not sure of Dryden's claim of Shakespeare's "creation" in Caliban: "As to the Foundation of this Comedy, I am ignorant whether it be the Author's own Contrivance, or a Novel built up into a Play" (464).

character portrayal was "the outstanding theme for praise and wonder," and "character study became the leading occupation" of literary criticism (Salingar 51). Hazlitt and his contemporaries seemed to have exhausted the vocabulary of Shakespearean encomia, and later critics could only but repeat what they said, the difference being only one of perspective. E. E. Stoll remarks that Shakespeare has a "greater power of individualization and differentiation" than Corneille or Racine or Ibsen; he is "less exact and careful in analyzing, ordering, organizing, but he has a more potent and magical touch" in words; all of Shakespeare's characters, "lord or lady, king or clown, prelate or layman . . . belongs unmistakably, though not always quite intelligibly, together, and to him or her alone." Shakespeare's characters "speak in propria persona" with "their own particular tongue, not the showman's" (112). To sum up, Shakespeare's characters are traditionally thought to be distinctively natural, lifelike and unique.

Concerning Jonson's dramatic characters, the comedy of humours comes to almost everyone's mind, which recalls the author's *Every Man in his Humour* and *Every Man out of his Humour*. In the middle of the eighteenth century, "Jonson's humour comedy was the official English comedy" (Craig 14). All Jonson's well-known characters are marked by their humours. Kitely stands out for jealousy, Bobadil, for braggartism and vanity, Morose, for eccentricity and for silence, Abel Drugger, for meanness, Sir Epirc Mammon, for avarice and extravagance, and Mosca, for slyness and avarice.

Despite the eccentric appearance of Jonson's dramatis personae, decorum is one of the most important points in the author's characterization, especially when compared with Shakespeare's. Developed from Horace's *Ars Poetica* (20 BC), decorum, or the propriety of the subject matter, character, action and language of a literary genre to match with each other, became increasingly influential during the Renaissance and neoclassical period. As has been discussed previously, Shakespeare, for several generations during his early reception, had been criticized for his violation of classical or neoclassical rules, including the decorum of characters. Jonson, a neoclassicist, in contrast, almost always created his characters according to the humours theory, a belief in a set, fixed and immoderate personality that required the conformity of a character's language to his action and story. This conformity is decorum. Some say that Jonson's characters were created based on his "loosely formulated (and inconsistent) theory of humours" (Anne Barton, *Dramatist* x). Peter Whalley remarked in his preface to his edition of *The Works of Jonson* (1756) that "a just decorum and preservation of character, with propriety of circumstance and of language, are his [Jonson's] striking excellencies, and eminently distinguish his correctness and art" (I: v), and "Propriety of sentiment, and decorum of character, are what we are principally to look for in the plays of Jonson" (II: 262).

Unnaturalness is also a conventional criticism of Jonson's characters in contrast with the naturalness of Shakespearian characters. This seems true when one considers the names of Jonsonian characters: Volpone, Mosca, Voltore, Corvino, Corbaccio, all of Italian origin and having meanings which represent the essential traits or humours: *fox*, *fly*, *vulture*, *carrion crow, raven.* The English names of Jonson's plays such as Cob, Kitely, Wellbred, Clement, Sir Politic Would-Be, Peregrine, Sir Epicure Mammon, Surly, Drugger, Morose, Ananius, Subtle, Dol Common, Face, Dame Pliant, Lovewit are immediately and inflexibly meaningful. Anne Barton has a good comment on this: "Most of Jonson's names like Politic Would-Be, Fastidious Brisk or Volpone [tended] to fix and define characters, depriving them of the freedom and flexibility that most of Shakespeare's people inherit with their more neutral names" (*Essays* 301). Because Jonson's characters reveal much of the roles they play, they do not seem to be natural.

Another aspect of unnaturalness in Jonson's characters that was traditionally asserted is their relation to specific persons of his time. B. Walwyn (b. 1750) suspected that such a Jonsonian character as Bobadill "may exist, and yet, it will rarely be found, but in *Every Man in his Humour*" (qtd. in Craig 552). However, most people felt that Jonson's characters were not fictional; instead, they were actual people with a different name. Alexander Pope was reported to claim that Morose was modeled on a real person of Jonson's time, and Sir William Davenant (1606 – 1668), Poet Laureate (1638 – 1668), Jonson's immediate successor of the then unofficial title, "knew the man" (Spence 9). Bennell Thorton (1724 – 1768), editor of *The Spring-Garden Journal*, agreed with Davenant, remarking that "had a modern Author drawn so unnatural a Part, that the Audience would have shewn very little Complaisance to his Humour, I will take upon me to say, this Character never existed but in Imagination" (15). It seems contradictory that critics in the seventeenth and eighteenth centuries thought that Jonson's characters were modeled both on real people and were imaginary, but the contradiction shows exactly the complexity or difficulty to judge his characters by some all-inclusive, general terms such as *unnatural*. If Jonson based his characters on his real contemporaries, then these characters would be historical, rather than universal, and Jonson was creating them of his time, for his time. Peter Whalley justified this by arguing that the decorum requirement of Jonson's plan "naturally led him to allude to particular persons and incidents of his own times" (qtd. in Craig 461). To Jonson's later critics, in changed times, consequently, Jonson's characters may not appear natural.

It is claimed that the verisimilitude of Jonson's characters is vastly different from the lifelikeness and naturalness of Shakespeare's. Shakespeare's characters are lifelike and natural because although the reader or audience know they are people in a play, they seem similar to people in their life, real neighborhood, not confined to a particular time, but " of all ages. " As Kenneth Muir remarks: " the characters [of Shakespeare] are *real*, not real people, but startlingly natural" ("Open Secret" 9). Stoll has a similar view: "they start up from the printed page before you" (89).

Traditionally, the difference inhuman reality between Shakespearean and Jonsonian characters was thought to be due to the authors' separate ways of characterization. Shakespeare's " essential" method, to quote Kenneth Muir, is dramatizing people with " ambiguities and ambivalences " ("Open Secret" 3). What is deficient in Jonson's characters is what Maurice Morgann means by the term " secret impressions" ("Open Secret" 3), or Schlegel, "nameless something" (293). Because Jonson's dramatic personae are based on humours or eccentricities, it is difficult to show them changing themselves or developing in insight. As Anne Barton comments: Jonson's "stereotyped humour characters . . . who are fundamentally incapable of growth or change, [are] measured against Shakespearean characters who learn from their experiences, becoming wiser and better in the course of five acts—or even, like Orlando's brother, overnight" (*Essays* 287). Moreover, Jonson, believing in the theory of the golden mean, strives to provide his audience with fun as well as instruction by satirizing his characters' excessive humours. A result of this is what Anne Barton observes of Jonson: "unlike Shakespeare, Jonson was a basically accumulative artist, who tended to reuse the same character types and situations in play after play . . . . *The Devil Is an Ass* . . . might almost be subtitled "The Further Adventures of Face and Subtle" (*Essays* 293). What she means is Jonson's repeated use of character types is a hindrance to create well-differentiated individual characters.

However, it must be remembered that both Shakespeare and Jonson created a whole array of characters, and it may not be wise to generalize what has been said of them too easily. Emma Smith suggests a way to study Shakespeare's characters: "looking at Shakespeare's characters as if they were, and with the expectation that they can be explained as, real people, may be more appropriate to some characters than others. It may also confine us unhelpfully or lead to questions the text is not supported to answer" (6). The same thing may be said of examining Jonson's characters. Jealous as Kitely and Corvino are, there are huge differences between them. Therefore, the safest way to obtain a reasonable and just interpretation of characters is through a close and thorough reading of a play *per se* in which these characters appear, with only cautious reference to previous generalizations about them.

III. Shakespeare and Jonson in historical context

Criticisms of Shakespeare's and Jonson's comedies can be roughly divided into three periods. The first is before the English Romantic movement, during which Jonson led in critical favor, and in which Shakespeare was appreciated, but also criticized and adapted. In the second period, between the English Romantic movement and the end of the 19th century, Shakespeare found surging and extensive critical acclaim, but Jonson with almost the same speed and extent sank to near oblivion. The third period, since the turn of the twentieth century, has witnessed a continued, secured Shakespearean supremacy and the rediscovery and re-appreciation of Jonson's comic art.

i. Before the English Romantic movement

As we have seen, before 1600 Shakespeare was well-known for his dramatic language, especially its *sweetness* or *gentleness*. When fellow dramatists, actors and theater-sharers referred to his plays, Shakespeare was praised for his industry, eloquence, pleasant personal qualities and legendary fluency. Francis Meres (1565 – 1647), a Cantabrigian and author of *Palladis Tamia: Wits Treasury* (1598), a commonplace book about Elizabethan poets, borrowed phrases from the *Officina* (1520) by J. Ravisius Textor to extol Shakespeare effusively and cloyingly: "so the sweete wittie soule of Ovid lives in mellifluous & hony-tongued Shakespeare... The Muses would speak with Shakespeares fine filed phrase, if they would speake English" (qtd. in Vickers, *Heritage* 1: 1-3). Shakespeare must have been popular with theatergoers considering the fortune made from the performances of his plays. To mark Shakespeare's death in 1616, there had been "only one elegy" by William Basse (Craig 6).

During the same period, Jonson was becoming known as a dramatist. According to D. H. Craig, he was selected by Francis Meres "among England's leading tragedians," although none of his tragedies from this period have survived. As for his comedies, Thomas Nashe gave *The Case Is Altered* a passing remark, calling it a "witty" play (2). The staging of *Every Man in his Humour* (1598) and *Every Man out of his Humour* (1599), however, launched Jonson onto a rising track, which was to have a clear pattern.

From 1600 to the beginning of the English Romantic movement, displaying respectively a rising and rising-and-declining route, criticisms on Shakespeare and Jonson carried on a prolonged controversy centered on the debate between nature and art.

Between 1600 and 1790s, Shakespearean criticism underwent a major, perhaps its only major, downturn, with the growing dominance of neoclassicism, starting from the English Restoration in 1660. Despite his failures in *Sejanus* and *Catiline*, Jonson's fame rose steadily with the success of *Every Man in his Humour* and *Every Man out of his Humour*.

In 1616, when he collected and published some of his plays as his *Works*, Jonson, despite disapproval even shock, was hailed as the first English dramatist to rival with the ancients. His plays were termed "innovative," "carefully finished"; when he died in 1637, he was celebrated "as the founder and chief representative of an English literary culture" (Craig 1), a "doughty champion of unpopular traditions the most incisive individual personality" (Herford & Simpson I: 118), "the most commanding personal force," "the rare, the incomparable, the unique, Ben Jonson." In terms of art, Jonson was both establishing his reputation as a classicist, an "adventurer" and an "opposition to contemporary popular culture" (Craig 4). Shakespeare remained Jonson's rival in this period. He continued to enjoy praises for his "gentleness," "sweetness," as well as receiving some idolatrous encomia as "inimitable," "divine" and "God-like" (Vickers, *Heritage* 1: 3).

The Restoration of Charles II further promoted Jonson to the pinnacle of English poetry and cemented his position there for roughly a century and half to come, while keeping Shakespeare's dramatic reputation relatively low. Despite the bawdy, cynical, witty, amoral and even violent[①] characteristics of comedies during the Restoration, Jonson's works continued to be enjoyed and highly appreciated for their art, justice, sound judgment, and observation of classical rules. A few of Jonson's plays were even "perfect" (William Carew Hazlitt 277). His authority was secure. In contrast, Shakespeare's plays were still performed, but with

---

① Brian Vickers notices that violence was "fashionable" on the Restoration stage (*Heritage* 1: 7).

massive adaptation. According to Brian Vickers, no work of a major artist was "altered in such a sweeping fashion" (*Heritage* 1: 5). In the adaptation of *Hamlet* by William D'Avenant (1606 – 1668),[1] over 300 alterations (although most small-scale) were made (Vickers, *Heritage* 1: 5-8). In remodeling Shakespeare's plays so much, adapters claimed they had "rendered him [Shakespeare] and the public some great service in rescuing a few worthwhile parts from an otherwise obsolete and useless work"; adapters worked with "remarkable freedom" in pruning Shakespeare's plots, characters and style of language (Vickers, *Heritage* 1: 5-8).

The reason for Jonson's continued strength and Shakespeare's extensive adaptation was fundamentally the change of taste that occurred with the revival of classicism. As Vickers points out, the return of the English king from France brought with him seventeenth-century French neoclassicism which stressed such elements as rules, decorum, propriety, and the unities in artistic creation. This new neoclassical attitude kept Shakespeare down for "several generations" (*Heritage* 1: 4). Jonson, as an early neo-classicist himself, was admired and even worshiped. The change of taste to neoclassicism was also a result of the downsized theaters and theatrical audiences. According to Vickers, in Shakespeare's London, five to ten theaters were open "at any one time"; a weekly audience was some 18,000 to 24,000, including courtiers and groundlings; but by

---

[1] D'Avenant was also the first poet laureate with the title, while Jonson, with a good sum of royal pension, is the first poet laureate *de facto*.

November 1660, only two companies were licensed.[1] In the Restoration, the remaining two companies had virtually become court theaters and their audience was a much more limited and select group: courtiers and noble family members (*Heritage* 1: 5).

The major views of Shakespeare and Jonson during this period were reflected in the controversy between nature and art. As has been discussed earlier, Shakespeare failed, or perhaps chose not, most of the time, to follow the (neo) classical rules—in all the senses from decorum to the three unities—but still was celebrated for his naturalness, ingenuity, and genius. What Dryden said of Shakespeare and Jonson can well summarize the views of the critics who did not recognize Jonson as superior to Shakespeare:

> Shakespeare was the Homer, or father of our dramatic poets; Jonson was the Virgil, the pattern of elaborate writing; I admire him, but I love Shakespeare. To conclude of him: as he has given us the most correct plays, so in the precepts which, he has laid down in his "Discoveries," we have as many and profitable rules for perfecting the stage, as any wherewith the French can furnish us.[2]

(354)

Another change that was to influence the Shakespeare-

---

[1] The two companies licensed by the crown were: the Duke's Men, managed by Sir William D'Avenant, and the King's Men, run by Thomas Killigrew (Vickers, *Heritage* 1: 5).

[2] Dryden was the most influential literary critic of late seventeenth century England, but his remarks on both Shakespeare and Jonson are distinctly ambivalent, as Hazelton Spencer writes, "Dryden's famous characterization of Shakespeare as the man 'who of all modern and perhaps ancient, poets had the largest and most comprehensive soul' is a striking and sonorous saying; but it means little, especially when compared with Dryden's other utterances. When he and his colleagues turn from phrase-making to detailed examination and criticism, there is much more of objection than of praise" (41).

Jonson criticism in their rivalry was taking place in the 1750s. According to Vickers, Shakespeare received gradual ascendancy in 1750s and 1760s (*Heritage* 3: 1).

It is necessary to bear in mind that during this period, despite the dominance of Jonson over Shakespeare, debates about their dramatic merits and defects were non-unanimous and continuous. Idolizing panegyrics of Shakespeare were mixed with the harshest criticism. " Effusive praise of Shakespeare during the eighteenth century went side by side with the most devastating criticism of him " (Vickers, *Heritage* 6: 7). As Vickers has it, in discussing Shakespeare's plots, characterization or language, Dryden either praised or blamed Shakespeare "according to the needs of the moment" (Vickers, *Heritage* 1: 15). Samuel Johnson, whose edition of Shakespeare "played a major role in establishing Shakespeare as the equal of any ' ancient, ' and the central figure in a canon of vernacular writing" (Mullan vii), said that Shakespeare "never wrote six lines together without fault" (qtd. in Vickers, *Heritage* 6: 7). Although Shakespeare was idolized under some of the Neoclassic dramatic categories for his " mastery over the passions, creating characters from nature, appropriateness of language," Vickers says that he had "violated too many of the other criteria of that system to escape without whipping" (Vickers, *Heritage* 6: 7).

But Shakespeare did rise, and his rise to the center of literary creation came at the expense of moving Jonson out of the central place. Bardolators used two effective ways. One was to rid Shakespeare of accusations of offences of rules and indecorum by promoting his excellence in characterization.

Leo Salingar rightfully notes that in the movement that established Shakespeare as the supreme dramatic poet in the course of the eighteenth and early nineteenth centuries, "progressively clearing him of reproach for offending against the neoclassical rules of construction, his gift of character portrayal was the outstanding theme for praise and wonder." Character study became the "leading occupation of criticism" (51). Jonson at the same time was driven from grace. According to D. H. Craig, "a good deal of propaganda" was generated in the course of the campaign against Jonson. "Genuine evidence, imaginary allusions, fictions admitted to or disguised" were all allocated to "establish the necessary myth of a gentle Shakespeare tormented by a malicious rival" (20). The efforts to displace Jonson were joined by changes in values. Earlier preferences for "satire over celebration" in comedy, for "correctness over inspiration," "art over nature," "learning over originality," "judgment over feeling," were simply "reversed," and together with them, Jonson's "supremacy" over Shakespeare (15). Therefore, critics now complained that far from striking chords with soundness and honesty, Jonson "fails to touch the heart," and this notion became "commonplace," and "more trenchant" as time went on (15). By and by, as the worship of Shakespeare gained more followers and intensity, the value of Jonson seemed to be "only as a sacrifice" on Shakespeare's altar (21).

Jonson's panegyric that Shakespeare was "not of an age, but for all time" was taken up by Shakespearian partisans in its reversed form to assess Jonson's own works, "declaring him no universal genius but of his time merely, interesting and important only to historians and scholars" (21). Critics started to believe that Jonson's plays were focused only on his contemporary London with its people, life and society. Unlike the works of Shakespeare that delineated the universal nature of characters, Jonson's were narrowly realistic and could only appeal to his Elizabethan, Jacobean or Caroline audiences. In general, as Shakespeare was found improper for Restoration audiences, Jonson at the end of the eighteenth century was increasingly blamed for pedantry, contrivance and unnaturalness.

ii. From the English Romantic movement through nineteenth century

In an age that preferred a dramatist who was not "shackled by prejudices, by arbitrary rules, and by the anxious observance of conveniences" (Schlegel 270), Shakespeare became the ideal. Schlegel praised Shakespeare for almost everything, from acting to theater management, from creative liberty to characterization (281-302). According to Brian Vickers, "an enormous consolidation of almost all the aspects" of Shakespeare's reception was seen in the last quarter of the eighteenth century. He was seen not only as "England's greatest writer" but as the "world's greatest," an altogether "exceptional human being" (*Heritage* 6: 1). When English actor Edmund Kean (1789 – 1833) was building up his great fame, Lois Potter informs us, " European anglophiles who had been struggling to read Shakespeare in the original were arriving in England to experience the great symbol of freedom at first hand" (190). The earlier faulty Shakespeare of the neoclassicists was now described by the Romantics as "the noblest genius," "the greatest master of nature," "the most perfect characterizer of men and manners," and "an immortal" (1-4). While an earlier generation had regarded Shakespeare as an equal of Homer, he was now worshipped as superior to even the Greek poet. Still, some critics were more prudent. They protested against the dangers of Shakespeare idolatry. In *The Critical Review*, Anthony Harrison's poem *The Infant Vision of Shakespeare: with an Apostrophe to the Immortal Bard* (1794), warned that

> Could Shakespeare see these praises of himself, he certainly would accuse the panegyrist of having overstept the modesty of nature. Neither Shakespeare, nor any other writer, can deserve to have it said of him that, without his writings, the world would be benighted and miserable . . . . Such hyperbole is worse than a want of poetry: it is a want of sense.
>
> (qtd. in Vickers, *Heritage* 6: 4)

Shakespeare's ascendancy during this time was accompanied by Ben Jonson's plunge. The Romanticists, as has been said, blamed Jonson for unnaturalness and moralizing. While Schlegel hailed Shakespeare, alongside his genius and naturalness, for the freedom and the spirit in the bard's creation, he accused Jonson of deficiency "in soul, in that nameless something which always continues to attract and enchant us" (293). Robert Evans summarizes the reception of Jonson among the Romantics: "By the early 1800s his influence languished: his works were sometimes read and respected, occasionally admired, but almost never staged and perhaps as rarely loved. The Romantics seldom valued this professedly classical author" (188). Although Jonson found a "devoted editor," William Gifford (1756 – 1826), whose defenses as reflected in his edition of the dramatist's works in 1816, though fierce, were usually "factual" (188), Gifford could not arouse much interest in Jonson to keep him on stage.

The rest of the nineteenth century saw a further ascent of Shakespeare's reputation and a continued descent of Jonson's. In his letter to J. H. Reynolds dated April 18th, 1817, John Keats wrote his friend that they would always "say a Word or two on some Passage in Shakespeare that may have come rather new," and that " must be continually happening," notwithstanding that they "read the same Play forty times" (17). In his letter, dated May 11, 1817, to another friend, B. R. Haydon, in talking about the presiding poetical genius, Keats asks: " Is it too daring to Fancy Shakespeare this Presider" (23). Keats could well be grouped as a bardolater with other English Romanticists like Hazlitt. In the same letter to Haydon, Keats says that he shall never read any other book except Shakespeare's because he is very near agreeing with Hazlitt that "Shakespeare is enough for us" (24). [①] Because of Shakespeare's strengthened dominance, contemporary dramatists were intimidated in their attempts to produce any great plays, tragedy or comedy. As Arthur DuBois asserts: " No great acting drama was written during the 19th century. Shakespeare was over-popular then. His popularity prevented the writing of great acting drama. Playwrights only imitated Shakespeare. Or else they wrote only potboilers, curtain-raisers or after-pieces

---

① The closing words of this letter read: " So now in the Name of Shakespeare, Raphael and all our Saints, I commend you to the care of heaven" (25). For Keats, Shakespeare was at least an archangel.

for Shakespeare" (163). ① England had to wait until *fin de siècle* for a resurgence of the theater when Oscar Wilde took the stage with his comedies.

As people were busy imitating Shakespeare, Jonson was left in a corner, almost forgotten. Craig has observed that in the nineteenth century reviewers mostly " contented themselves with assuring readers that there really was little reason to labour through Jonson's works, except to discover the occasional charming lyric" (1-2), and this age "brought only confirmation of the success of the campaign against Jonson" (21). According to Herford and the Simpsons, the most frequently performed Jonsonian play during the 1800s in Great Britain was *Every Man in his Humour*, which was revived seven times owing to special efforts by Charles Dickens, beginning on December 17, 1800, and ending, May 17, 1848. The first and only revival of *Epicoene* was on March 30, 1895. *The Alchemist* was revived on February 25, 1899, its only performance in the long nineteenth century. ② *The Sad Shepherd* was performed on July 23, 1898, and again, it was the only performance in the 1800s. Nearly all plays in the Jonsonian canon, tragic or comic, in terms of performance, were literally dropped out of the repertory in all venues, entertainment or academic, including especially surprisingly the big four: *Volpone*, *Epicoene*, *The Alchemist*, and

---

① Dubois even attributes the Romantic period's achievements in lyric poetry and the novel to the force of Shakespeare: "since Shakespeare's popularity was so great that they [writers] could not get audiences, they turned to lyric poetry or the novel" (163).

② Herford and the Simpsons discovered that Dickens attempted to revive *The Alchemist* in 1848, with himself as Mammon, but he got only as far as "two or three rehearsals. " An adapted version of the play into a low farce called *The Tobacconist* by Francis Gentleman ran from 1770-1815, but Herford and the Simpsons give it no more details (IX: 236-39).

Bartholomew Fair (IX: 163-258).

During the 1800s, a couple of Jonson's plays were translated into other European languages or performed outside Great Britain. *Volpone* was performed in both French translation and the English original in 1874 in Paris but both failed completely. Ludwig Tieck translated *Epicoene* in 1800, its only known translation in the nineteenth century. *Epicoene* had other translations, but they were all either in 1700s or 1900s (Herford & Simpsons ix: 163-258). Europeans and Americans might be enjoying Jonson's plays through reading, but their interest and influence were seriously limited. Although, according to Tom Lockwood, Jonson "maintained a presence in the late eighteenth and early nineteenth-century theatre far livelier and more various than has previously been recognized" (9) and was "available to writers of the Romantic age in more ways than we have previously been willing to grant" (11), in general, Jonson in the nineteenth century *was* far off the literary or dramatic center.

iii. Shakespeare and Jonson since the beginning of the twentieth century

Since 1900, Shakespeare's supremacy has continued, but Jonson has also been able to come out of Shakespeare's shadow. In the nineteenth century, when Shakespeare became synonymous with ideal plays, tragic, comic, or historical, a binary opposition was set up that put Shakespeare on one side, the bright one, and Jonson, on the other, the dark one. For a long time, Jonson's dramatic art was measured against that of Shakespeare. In 1919, T. S. Eliot tried to adjust the conventional biases. He did not agree that Jonson's genius was "unsuited to tragedy," calling this claim "too crude a statement to be accepted." He refuted the idea that Jonson's genius was for "satiric comedy because of the weight of pedantic learning," asserting that this claim "marks an obvious error in detail." He believes that "Jonson's drama is only incidentally satire, because it is only incidentally a criticism upon the actual world" (67-71). Eliot was an enthusiastic bardolater who said that a lifetime is "not too long" for the understanding of Shakespeare (viii), but his effort to remodel Jonson's image heralded the revival of interest in classic dramatic art of seventeenth century England, which made new appreciations of Jonson possible (Craig 23).

Increased performances of Jonson's plays were a sure sign of his revival. From 1902 to 1905, *The Case Is Altered*, *Every Man in his Humour*, *Eastward Ho*, *Epicoene*, and *The Alchemist* were seen on stage again, both in universities and professional theaters. The especially notable thing was the regular revival of the most important Jonsonian comedies, that is, *Volpone*, *Epicoene*, *The Alchemist* and *Bartholomew Fair* (Herford & Simpsons, ix: 163-258).

Maybe the best description of the changing relationship between Shakespeare's and Jonson's reputation is the following:

> By now [the end of nineteenth century], too, Shakespeare's clear triumph made further battles pointless. Thus began a fairer, more methodical assessment of Jonson. By the mid-twentieth century a renaissance was in full swing, helped by the superb Oxford edition (1925 – 1952). Finally, at century's end, Jonson

once again seemed truly central to discussions of his period. Scholarship proliferated ... If Jonson were living at this hour, even he might be pleased.

(Evans 188)

Robert Evans is just. Shakespeare in our time has decidedly won the battle against Jonson for dramatic supremacy although Jonson has begun again to recover lost ground on stage, as is echoed in Russ McDonald's observation: "the disposition of authors in the normal university English curriculum reflects that Shakespeare is much more important than Jonson: Shakespeare is given one independent course, ' contemporaries of Shakespeare ' another" (*Sceptical Visions* 131). Since "further battles" are pointless (Evans 188), it is time to strive for an unbiased and appropriate appreciation and assessment of Shakespeare and Jonson.

IV. The "rub" of generalization

It is not the intention of this book to set up Shakespeare and Jonson as binary oppositions for comparison and contrast. The aim of this exposition is to make a focused comparison of two comedies by the two dramatists, but alas, what Shakespeare and Jonson meant by comedy was so different, despite the name! David Galbraith has argued: "Comedy is notoriously resistant to theorization" (3), and this is certainly true of Shakespearian and Jonsonian comedy. Indeed, as discussed in the beginning of this chapter, even Shakespeare and Jonson themselves did not keep to a constant, fixed and stable definition of comedy. Stephen

Greenblatt has accurately remarked about the inconstancy of Shakespeare's plays in terms of genre:

> The fantastic diffusion and long life of Shakespeare's works depends on their extraordinary malleability, their protean capacity to elude definition and escape secure possession.

(1)

The "extraordinary malleability" of Shakespeare's comedies and their "protean capacity to elude definition and escape secure possession" explain the fact that the terms Shakespearian comedy and Jonsonian comedy themselves are not easily definable. As has been discussed in the beginning of this chapter, scholars have different ideas about the classification of Shakespeare's comedies. No one will believe that *The Taming of the Shrew*, *The Merchant of Venice*, *Every Man in his Humour* and *Volpone* share the same literary tone. As T. S. Eliot has pointed out, "it does not help us much to say that *The Merchant of Venice* and *The Alchemist* are comedies" (68); it is not fruitful to limit Shakespearian and Jonsonian comedies to certain characteristics or abstract features.

i. Shakespeare's Jonsonian comedy

Despite the celebrated sweet, forceful and popular qualities of Shakespearean comedies, his plays are not always so romantic and good natured as those terms may sound. Some of Shakespeare's comedies, like *A Midsummer Night's Dream*, *Twelfth Night* and *Much Ado about Nothing*, are sweet and romantic. Likewise, Jonson's comedies are known for their humours characterization and satiric tone, qualities characteristically different from Shakespeare's. Harry Levin has observed:

> Shakespeare and Jonson, in their respective venues, seem to confirm an inherent disparity between the romantic and the satirical modes of comedy. But romantic is never a satisfactory label, least of all for a dramatic vehicle.
>
> (167)

Not only is *romantic* a dissatisfactory label for many of Shakespeare's and Jonson's comedies, but some of Shakespeare's comedies, such as *Merry Wives of Windsor*, *Measure for Measure* and *The Merchant of Venice*, are certainly not romantic. They share something of the tone and qualities of a conventional Jonsonian comedy.

Throughout the seventeenth century when Jonson led in critical esteem, Shakespeare, according to M. C. Bradbrook, was admired for "such Jonsonian comedies" as *The Merry Wives of Windsor* (94). *The Merry Wives of Windsor*, observes Russ McDonald, a play that is "Shakespeare's brief detour from the path of romantic comedy," is "un-Shakespearean" because of its dark and scornful tone (*Shakespeare & Jonson* 54-5). In addition to superficially meaningful names (Falstaff, Shallow, Slender, Page, Nim, Pistol, Peter Simply, Mistress Quickly, etc.), the rare Latin lesson in the play's Act IV, Falstaff's attempt to seduce and fleece Mistress Ford and Mistress Page, the obsession with property, are all Jonsonian from the perspectives of comedy. More significant, as Dryden notes, this play is a "regular" comedy (qtd. in Vickers, *Heritage* 1: 219), that is, one that observes the three Aristotelian unities (time, place and action). Being Jonsonian, or following the neo-classical dramatic unities, is un-Shakespearian, but was at the same time the major reason for *The Tempest* and *The Merry Wives of Windsor* to become the "most often praised" of all Shakespeare comedies between the end of the seventeenth and the first quarter of the eighteenth centuries (Vickers, *Heritage* 2: 3).

Measure for Measure, probably written five years earlier than *The Merry Wives of Windsor*, is an outstandingly Jonsonian comedy. Anne Barton argues that "*Measure for Measure* is Shakespeare's most Jonsonian play.*" According to Barton, its Jonsonian elements include the play's "urban setting" —Vienna as a surrogate for London—its creation of a sense of "complex, ineradicable human evil beyond the capacity of its own comic conventions to control," and its ending which goes through all the usual Shakespearean motions in a Jonsonian way that "robs them of vitality and conviction" (*Essays* 292). Despite "Shakespeare's extension of the Jonsonian formula for realistic comicall satyre" in the play (Krieger 776), its satiric or ironic qualities are characteristic of Jonson. According to Murray Krieger, Shakespeare, when writing *Measure for Measure*, was introducing the "currently popular Jonsonian characteristics," trying to "graft the latter [Jonsonian] elements on to the fundamentally different [native Elizabethan] tradition of comedy to which he formerly was devoted." However, he "failed to blend the two" (782). In the play, Krieger points out, when the Duke's continuous and assuring presence, demanded by his function as intriguer, prevents the romantic element from involving too dangerous a situation, "we see here how a Jonsonian device helps maintain the play as comedy" (783).

In addition to elements of irony and satire, Shakespeare was also capable of creating humour characters. Dryden observes that Falstaff is "not properly one humour, but a Miscellany of Humours or Images" (XV: 356).

Shakespeare is less known for his humour characters than Jonson, but this does not mean Shakespeare did not employ them. Falstaff, Katherina, Benedick, and Antonio are all humour characters. One also should not forget that Shakespeare played the leading role in the debut performance of *Every Man in his Humour*, regardless of the legend that it was Shakespeare who supported the staging of the play. Certainly humour characters did not belong to Jonson exclusively.

Shakespeare did not immediately develop the romantic comedy in his career as a playwright. Under the influence of Italian Renaissance dramatic criticism that "demanded . . . learned Comedy (Commedia Erudita)," according to M. C. Bradbrook, he "briefly tried and rejected the learned formula of farcical imbroglio," and only gradually developed a "more complex plan" based on the medieval narrative tradition (*Growth* 77). Although Shakespeare had rejected "farcical imbroglio," the influence of learned comedy on him remained.

There are other Jonsonian qualities as well in Shakespeare's comedies. The close of its atrociously cruel and exquisitely funny sub-plot of the gulling of Malvolio in *Twelfth Night* is one of Shakespeare's most Jonsonian scenes. But the discussion above should suffice to show that Shakespeare's comedies often do have Jonsonian qualities.

ii. Jonson's Shakespearian comedy

Like Shakespeare, Jonson in his dramatic career could not have started from nowhere and did not stay with one style. Critics have classified Jonson's comedies as humorous or satiric to conveniently contrast to the romantic or popular comedies of Shakespeare. However, this contrast does not always apply.

Jonson can be romantic, too. Russ McDonald has given an example. He states that "for all its romantic conventions, its Elizabethan amplitude, its love story, and its harmonious ending, *The Case Is Altered* cannot be mistaken for a shakespearian comedy" (*Shakespeare & Jonson* 28). Percy Allen, an early twentieth century critic, also remarks:

> Jonson's first attempts at drama probably found him, temporarily, under Shakespeare's influence among the Romantics . . . Romanticism, however, could not hold Jonson for long. Eager acquisition and absorption of classical learning, working upon an intensely satiric and rationalistic temperament—together, no doubt, with a tinge of native jealousy—drew him swiftly, and permanently, away from Shakespeare and his fellow Romantics.
>
> (45)

Allen's claim about Jonson's "native jealousy" might be debatable, but his belief in Jonson's Shakespearian romanticism is historical and trustworthy. Eight years younger than Shakespeare, it was natural and reasonable that Jonson the newbie in the histrionic world should learn from the successful Shakespeare. *The Case Is Altered*'s romantic love story and its ending in marriage remind its audience of a Shakespearian comedy.

Jonson also bears traces of the native English tradition of popular comedy. Sean McEvoy has remarked, " Jonson's characteristic mode of theatrical representation also finds its roots in the humanist and popular drama of the sixteenth century" (13). Anne Barton points out that *The Case Is Altered* is likely to have been written "for Pembroke's Men and a popular audience" (*Dramatist* 31). Another Jonsonian play, *The New Inn* (1629), written more than 30 years after *The Case Is Altered*, also ends in the manner of a popular Shakespearian comedy in terms of courtship and marriage. This is Jonson's clear return from the classical and satirical tradition to the popular Shakespearian comic form.

Bartholomew Fair can be considered as Shakespearian, too. In this play, Jonson shows a tolerance and geniality that are not found in *Measure for Measure* or *Volpone*. No one in the end is punished. At the suggestion of Quarlous, all go to Justice Overdo's home to a feast and to hear the rest of Littlewit's play. These elements so resemble Shakespeare's plays that Anne Barton argues, " *Bartholomew Fair* turned out, in a sense, to be Jonson's *Measure for Measure*" (*Essays* 292).

There is still more to be said about the Shakespearian qualities in Jonson's comedies, but these illustrations are sufficient for the purpose of this chapter.

iii. Shakespeare's and Jonson's dark comedies

Both Shakespeare and Jonson wrote comedies that are neither romantic, sweet nor pleasant. Nicholas Rowe doubted

The Merchant of Venice was a comedy, considering it "design'd tragically by Shakespeare" (xix-xx). W. H. Auden suggests that this play should be classed among his "Unpleasant Plays" (221). V. Y. Kantak concedes that *Much Ado About Nothing* and *Twelfth Night* could be potentially Comedies of Manners, but he points out that "*The Merchant of Venice* can be read as a Tragedy of Shylock or as a plea for minority toleration" (11). *Volpone*, judging from its rather severe punishment of the greedy tricksters and gulls, does not go easily into the mind of a reader or viewer as a comedy. Robert Ornstein, in comparing Shakespeare's and Jonson's comedies, concludes that "Shakespearian comedy prevails over the wind and rain of Feste's song, even as it prevails over the tempests of the late romances, paradoxically, because it admits the possibility of tragic experience" (46). Shakespeare himself was well aware of the complexity of comedy, and in fact, of the difficulty of distinguishing genres in all plays in his time. Polonius thus praises the visiting players in *Hamlet*:

> The best actors in the world, either for tragedy, *comedy*, history, pastoral, pastoral-*comical*, historical-pastoral, tragical-historical, tragical-*comical*-historical-pastoral, scene individable or poem unlimited.
>
> (II. ii. 363-66, italics mine)

Polonius's division of plays displays Shakespeare's mockery of the attempts to classify dramatic forms or styles. As Kantak remarks, "Shakespeare seems to write his Comedy with little concern for conformity to the established genre. The tradition associated with the form gave but a general direction to his attitudes" (7).

Jonson, the first great English literary critic, describes his philosophy of the similarities between a tragedy and a comedy in his literary theoretical work, *Timber*: "The parts of comedy are the same with a tragedy, and the end is partly the same. For they both delight and teach . . . Nor is the moving of laughter always the end of comedy" (VIII: 2615- 19).

Shakespeare as represented by Kantak, and Jonson, by himself, are different in their theories of dramatic genre. The difference is verified by a look at their plays and their practice. Shakespeare only loosely associated himself with the terms of tragedy and comedy, and Jonson, from a functional point of view, stresses the similarities between tragedy and comedy.

However, no matter how different Shakespeare's and Jonson's comic theories and practices were, those theories and practices experienced a whole process of development. Being friends, Shakespeare and Jonson worked with, influenced and learned from each other. To them, the Globe was, as the geographical globe to us now is in the twenty-first century, a small world. It is only normal and understandable that they shared a number of similarities in their works.

At the end of such a long survey of traditional opinions on the differences between the comedies of Shakespeare and Jonson, a brief summary of the main points may be useful. As both contemporaries and rivals, Shakespeare and Jonson have quite often been studied side by side. It was once believed that Shakespeare was good at tragedies, and Jonson, comedies. However, this notion was soon amended. Shakespeare and Jonson are now both recognized as great comic playwrights, with remarkable differences between their comic styles.

Scholars have noted the importance of Shakespeare's inheritance of the English popular traditions. A great and humane genius, humanist and outstanding writer, actor and theater owner, Shakespeare was able to combine different traditions and sources to produce his unique, inimitable comedies. Traditionally the main features of Shakespeare's comedies have been claimed to be their sweetness, concern with male/female relationships, popular appeal and the purpose of entertainment. Compared with Jonson, Shakespeare's use of classical techniques and materials was limited. Shakespeare's lack of classical education was seen to be the cause of his violations of the dramatic rules laid down by Greek and Roman writers and renewed by the English and French neo-classicists.

Compared with Shakespeare, Jonson was regarded as more influenced by classical comic traditions. A well-read scholar of the classics, court poet and humanist, Jonson learned from the Greek and Roman dramatists while absorbing the English tradition of morality plays. He particularly drew much on contemporary London life. Traditionally Jonson's comedies have been considered learned, humorous, satirical and didactic. Dissatisfied with the current practices in playwriting, Jonson created humour comedies as a new genre based on his studies of classical literature and on his own literary theories. Being a drama theorist and critic himself, Jonson also produced comedies which deal with human follies aiming at warning against and correcting them. He was praised by both contemporary and future critics as a staunch observer of neo-classical dramatic rules.

Shakespeare's and Jonson's techniques of characterization have been thought markedly different. Shakespeare's characters have been considered unique, natural individuals that can be found in all ages and all places. They are always alive. Jonson's characters, in contrast, were considered not as unique individuals, but as types, for example, a bragging soldier or an old miser. They were alive in the dramatist's London, but not in other ages or other places. Shakespeare was praised for his naturalness and spontaneity; Jonson was blamed for his mechanicality and labored contrivance. Shakespeare was hailed for his nature; and Jonson, his art.

The past four hundred years have witnessed the vicissitudes of the reception of Shakespeare's and Jonson's comedies. From his death until almost the last quarter of the eighteenth century when neo-classical rules dominated the literary world, Shakespeare was largely criticized, extensively adapted and occasionally appreciated, while Jonson was avidly worshiped, carefully imitated and held up as the standard and culmination of dramatic comedy. The English Romantic movement radically changed this situation. With the new emphasis on " spontaneous overflow of powerful feelings " (Wordsworth 237), Shakespeare found great favor with the Romantics, who brought Shakespeare to continued ascendancy. The Romantics' elevation of Shakespeare resulted in ignorance and even rejection of Jonson, and an even lower place for him was still to come in the late nineteenth century, when most of his plays, especially his earlier, well-recognized, great Jacobean comedies, were disregarded. Since the beginning of the twentieth century, Shakespeare has continued to maintain his supremacy over Jonson, but Jonson's reputation has been able to turn a new leaf. With increasing revivals of his plays, Jonson has been rediscovered and re-appreciated. Putting the battle between Shakespeare and Jonson aside, readers, theatergoers and critics have all been able to find new ways to enjoy Jonson's plays.

Despite the differences between their comedies, Shakespeare and Jonson shared dramatic tones and techniques. Shakespeare wrote comedies with Jonson's characteristics; Jonson produced plays that sounded like Shakespeare's. Both Shakespeare and Jonson created plays that were not typical of either one. After all, comedy as a dramatic genre was not a definite thing to them. Neither of them could have, or perhaps, would have been constant in following the exact rules of comedy even if there had been such rules. However, as Nancy S. Leonard observes when studying *As You Like It*, *Volpone*, *Twelfth Night* and *The Alchemist*: " Neither Shakespeare nor Jonson is content merely to let a play be romantic or satiric by virtue of certain generic features " (47); " there are satirical elements in Shakespeare's comedies, and romantic elements in Jonson's, and the comic accomplishments of both dramatists are ' realized, rather than undermined, in their adaptations of the methods associated with the other ' " (69). Exactly, because Shakespeare and Jonson engaged in friendly competition against and learned from each other, both developed and progressed. As a result, future generations of readers and audiences have had the luck to relish their comic achievements.

The Theme of Avarice

There must be more money!

> D. H. Lawrence, "The Rocking-Horse Winner"

That disease
Of which all old men sicken, —avarice.

> Thomas Middleton, *The Roaring Girl*, Act i., Sc. 1. 134

I. Definition of avarice

Normally people do not make much distinction between *greed*, *avarice*, *covetousness*, and *cupidity* other than subtleties of connotation. *Greed*, according to the *Oxford English Dictionary* (*OED*), a backformed noun from *greedy*, which came into English from Old Saxon and Old High German, the earliest stage of the German language, was first used in *Beowulf*. Back then, *greedy* meant "an intense desire or inordinate appetite for food or drink," or simply "hungry," much like the meaning of *gluttonous* today. The earliest recorded use of *greedy* to mean " eager for gain, wealth" appeared in the year 1000. When "greed" first appeared in English in his *Anatomie of Humours* in 1609, Simon Grahame (1570 – 1614) gave it the meaning "inordinate or insatiate longing for especially wealth" and this meaning has stayed with us to the present.

Avarice, *covetousness* and *cupidity* all join the English language from Latin through (Old) French. Therefore, normally, *avarice*, *covetousness* and *cupidity* are stylistically more formal, learned and academic than *greed*. Otherwise, to most people, they all mean an excessive desire for wealth. In practice, they are used specifically to refer to a strong desire to acquire and possess material things, especially such forms of wealth as money and luxury goods that exceed one's proper needs. They may also be used to describe people who are miserly, that is, reluctant to give money where they should.

Carrying a stronger sense of inordinate desire than those four words, *rapacity* has its origin in "rape," from the Latin word *rapĕre*, "to take by force."

Webster's New Dictionary of Synonyms explains the niceties of *avarice*, *covetousness*, *cupidity*, *greed*, and *rapacity*. According to this dictionary, these words all mean intense desire for wealth and possessions. *Cupidity*, the most specific among the five words, stresses the intensity and compelling nature of the desire and often suggests covetousness. Compared with *cupidity*, *greed* denotes a weaker and more controllable but still inordinate desire; it connotes meanness and covetousness. Besides the meaning of "inordinate desire," *covetousness* also often alludes to the Ten Commandments of Moses and implies "longing for something that belongs rightfully to another." *Rapacity* implies both cupidity and the violence of seizing and snatching, like plunder, extortion and oppressive exaction. *Avarice*, although it involves the idea of cupidity, carries a strong suggestion of rapacity and stresses miserliness, implying both an unwillingness to let go whatever wealth one has acquired and an insatiable greed for more.

These differences of the words are contemporary, but they would also apply in the time of Shakespeare and Jonson. According to the *OED*, *cupidity* generally meant "ardent desire, inordinate longing or lust; covetousness." Specifically, it meant "inordinate desire to appropriate wealth or possessions; greed of gain." *Greed* meant inordinate or insatiate longing, esp. for wealth; avaricious or covetous desire. An example is from Simon Grahame's *Anatomie of Humours* (1609): "Whose avarice and gread of geare is such, that they care not whom with they joyne, so being they be ritch" (38b). *Covetousness* meant "a strong or inordinate desire (of)." *Rapacity* denoted "the quality or fact of being rapacious; the exercise of rapacious tendencies." *Avarice* signified "inordinate desire of acquiring and hoarding wealth; greediness of gain, cupidity." In this book, these five words, *avarice*, *covetousness*, *cupidity*, *greed* and *rapacity*[1] are considered nearly synonymous in Shakespeare's and Jonson's times.

Certainly there are other words that are closely related to these terms. Phyllis A. Tickle is right in saying that "greed has functioned under a multiplicity of aliases," ranging— beyond the five noted above—from "'acquisitiveness' itself to 'avidity,' and on to some of its more particularized metonyms like 'miserliness'" (15). But three of those five, *avarice*, *covetousness* and *greed*, with their derivatives, are the most frequently used in this book.

II. Praise and prosecution of avarice

i. Religious exhortation against avarice

Greed has traditionally been regarded by most people in

---

[1] There are other less commonly used synonyms in erudite English. *Philargyry*, now an obsolete term, was used earlier to mean "love of money; avarice, covetousness." Examples: 1) 1570 — 1576 Lambarde *Peramb. Kent* (1826) 249: The Popes laboured more and more with this incurable disease of Philargyrie. 2) 1631 R. H. *Arraignm. Whole Creature* xviii. 320: That Philargury or love of money which is called Covetousnesse. 3) 1652 Urquhart *Jewel* Wks. (1834) 212: In matter of philargyrie, or love of money. Another such synonym is *pleonexia*, meaning "covetousness, avarice, greed." Previous usages are: 1) 1858 Mayne *Expos. Lex.*, Pleonexia, term for greediness, grasping selfishness, overbearing temper or arrogance, regarded as mental disease. 2) 1892 *Daily News* 4 Nov. 5/3, Competitive, grasping fellows, cursed with the vice of pleonexia, of wanting more than their share. According to Richard Newhauser, "*Philargyria* is, of course, the more narrowly defined, depicting a literal love of money as the most material of worldly goods. *Pleonexia*, however, implies a broader sense of the vice (7). The "desire to have more" which can be identified in its etymology is somewhat open-ended, for while the majority of the word's uses is directed at the effort expended for material possessions alone, other occurrences place it in the context of fulfilling unclean desires of various kinds, including sensual ones" (*OED*, s. v. philargyry).

the West as one of the seven cardinal or deadly sins. ① Many cultures have philosophically and religiously denounced the practice of avarice, but for the purpose of this study, only a few examples in the Jewish, Christian, and Greco-Roman traditions are offered.

Arguably, the best known injunction against avarice to many people is the one② from the Decalogue:

> Thou shalt not couet thy neighbours house, nether shalt thou couet thy neighbours wife, nor his man seruant, nor his maid, nor his oxe, nor his asse, nether any thing that is thy neighbours.

> (Exodus XX. 17)

Here "couet" means an inordinate urge to possess something that is not rightfully one's own: a neighbor's house, wife and all the material things in the house, including livestock. According to Carol Meyers, "covet"

> does not refer to the simple and natural human desire that can be aroused by viewing an attractive object or person.

---

① According to Morton W. Bloomfield, a distinction between cardinal and deadly sins should be made: cardinal sins refer to the "most important sins," and deadly sins are the ones which "inevitably lead to damnation and the death of the soul." However, since the late Middle Ages, both individual theologians and laymen have often confused these two terms (43). Solomon Schimmel agrees with Bloomfield. He also asserts that the expression "seven deadly sins" is a "misnomer" whose "correct designation is the seven cardinal." But because of popular usage, he maintains the term of the seven deadly (22). Deuteronomy 7: 1-2, in which God casts out many nations, among which are seven stronger ones, for Israelites to conquer and destroy, may allude to the seven capital sins or deadly sins.

② Bible exegetic traditions have differed concerning the statement of Exodus 20: 17 as one or more than one Commandment, or Word, or Statement. Roman Catholics and Lutherans have tended to divide it into two Statements. Since the Jews call this verse one Statement, I am following them in talking about their tradition. Compare the Torah text of this Commandment: "You shall not covet your neighbor's house: you shall not covet your neighbor's wife, or his male or female slave, or his ox or his ass, or anything that is your neighbor's." While the text is identical, its chapter and verse number is 20: 14. See Barton & Muddiman, p. 81; Meyers, p. 163 for more.

Rather it denotes the intense desire that is generated by passion and thus is not easily controlled.

(178)

This commandment is repeated and extended to include spoils from defeated heathen nations in Deuteronomy:

> The grauen images of their gods shal ye burne with fire, *and* couet not the siluer and golde, *that is* on them, nor take it vnto thee, lest thou be snared therewith: for it is an abominacion *before* the Lord thy God.

(VII. 25)

This shows the Jewish God's detestation of people's inordinate desire for material things that do not rightfully belong to them, including even precious things that they should destroy. This commandment, together with others before it, has become law for the Jews.

Because this law, the warning against covetousness, is so important, God condemns avarice in many other places in the Old Testament. One story is told about Ahab, a great and victorious king of Samaria, in chapter XXI, I Kings. Ahab covets his neighbor's vineyard and is helped by his wife to murder the neighbor and seize the neighbor's land. Both Ahab and his wife are judged and punished by God. This story tells the reader that covetousness is not just a single sin or crime. It usually corrupts the human soul and leads on to other sins. That is how card Meyers explains the commandment against covetousness:

> To " covet " what is another's can have grave consequences for a community as well as an individual. This final precept is a perceptive psychological statement. If heeded, it can prevent the situations—adultery, theft,

and even murder and false testimony—that many of the other imperatives forbid.

(178)

The Old Testament exhortation to avoid covetousness is also expounded in the Christian Gospels. When He tells a rich man who wants to have eternal life to keep the commandments, Jesus says that he should go sell what he has, and "giue it to the poore," and he shall "haue treasure in heauen" instead of treasures in his house. Jesus warns his disciples that "it is easier for a camel to go through the eye of a nedle, then for a riche man to enter into the kingdome of God" (Matthew IX: 16-24; Mark X: 17-25, and Luke XVIII: 18-25). In fact, according to Jeff Cook, "Jesus spoke about greed more than any other sin" (89).

While coveting a neighbor's house and selling all one's (a rich man's) possessions are not the same thing, the essence of these Christian exhortations is not to desire unjust possessions. As Phyllis A. Tickle says, "greed, by any name, is the mother and matrix, root and consort of all the other sins" (15). The Christian teaching against avarice can be summed up in a well-known verse from St. Paul's first epistle to Timothy:

> For the desire of money is the roote of all euil, which while some lusted after, thei erred from the faith, & perced them selues through with many sorowes. ①

(VI: 10)

---

① Although "primarily a secular poet" (Miola 227), Jonson made frequent reference to the Bible. The version he used was the Latin Vulgate because this was the Bible found in his library. See, also, Herford & Simpson, Vol. I, p. 263. The King James Version was not published till 1611, so Jonson could not have known it when he was writing *Volpone* in 1606.

In the late Roman period, early Christian church fathers further elucidated the necessity to avoid greed. St. Augustine says that the true knowledge of things is "conceived either by desire or love" (34). Here for the English word *desire* he uses the Latin *cupiditas* (cupidity), and for love, *caritas* (charity). Worldly things like money, if desired excessively, mean an estrangement from love for God. Therefore, in terms of Christian theology, "cupidity" is anti-God and anti-charity. St. Thomas Aquinas warns that God "teaches that we should not demand our goods from motives of cupidity, and that we should be ready to give yet more if necessary" ("Treatise on Law," Question 108).

The "first great Christian poet in Latin" (Ruud 521), Aurelius Prudentius Clemens (348-413?) of Spain,[1] was one of the most influential writers for the next millennium. Prudentius's *Psychomachia* (ca. 405, *The Fight for Man's Soul* in English), "the first completely allegorical poem in Europe" and one of the "most influential poems of the Middle Ages" (Ruud 522), narrates a personified virtue-against-vice battle, in which avarice is depicted as follows:

'Tis said that Greed, her robe arranged to make a capacious fold in front, crooked her hand and seized on every thing of price that gluttonous Indulgence left behind, gaping with mouth wide open on the pretty baubles as she picked up the broken bits of gold that had fallen amid the

---

[1] Prudentius's birthplace is uncertain. H. J. Thomson decides on the Spanish (Roman then) Caesaraugusta or Saragossa (vii). Jay Ruud agrees with Thomson concerning Spain, but he claims that "Calahorra seems most likely," in addition to Tarragona and the common Saragossa (521). Both Thomson and Ruud assert that Prudentius was Spanish. Phyllis A. Tickle, however, claims that Prudentius was a "Briton" (24).

heaps of sand. Nor is she content to fill her roomy pockets, but delights to stuff her base gain in money-bags and cram swollen purses to bursting with her pelf, keeping them in hiding behind her left hand under cover of her robe on the left side, for her quick right hand is busy scraping up the plunder and plies nails hard as brass in gathering the booty. Care, Hunger, Fear, Anguish, Perjuries, Pallor, Corruption, Treachery, Falsehood, Sleeplessness, Meanness, diverse fiends, go in attendance on the monster; and all the while Crimes, the brood of their mother Greed's black milk, like ravening wolves go prowling and leaping over the field.

(454-69)

From this typical description of an avaricious person, Prudentius shows how Greed snatches the booty after violent battles between virtues and vices for the soul of man (here the defeat of Luxury by Sobriety). In addition to her pockets, she has turned every piece of her clothing into money-bags. She collects every piece of shiny bauble and broken bits of gold. Her money-bags are "roomy," but she is not satisfied as she stuffs them to the point of bursting. She is almost frenzied to scratch for gold with her right hand like a brass rake. What is even more frightening is that she is followed by a whole host of pains and vices: "care, pallor, hunger, fear, anguish, perjuries, corruption, treachery, falsehood, sleeplessness, meanness," and "diverse fiends" —all crimes associated with greed.

Apart from this vivid picture of greedy plunder, avarice is shown to produce a whole host of evils. She causes a soldier to kill fellow soldiers for the gems on their helmets, entices a son to rob his dead father's belt with shining studs, and stirs up civil wars. "The insatiable Love of Possession spares not his own dear ones, unnatural Hunger robs his own children . . . There is no more furious Vice in the world to envelop the life of the people of the world in such disaster, condemning them to hell-fire" (470-96).

What is also interesting in Prudentius's *Psychomachia* is Greed's disguise as Thrift when she is challenged by Reason. Because Greed understands that to her it is a large hoard of possessions that matters, not the way the hoard is achieved, "it matters not whether the prize of victory comes by arms or by guile," she transforms into a "noble bearing" (*Prudentius* 317) of Thrift that is called a Virtue and is able to deceive many people:

> In appearance, with austere mien and dress, she becomes the Virtue men call Thrifty, whose pleasure it is to live sparingly and save what she has; she looks as if she never snatched aught with greedy hands, and with her air of carefulness she has gained repute for the quality she counterfeits. With this virtue's likeness the false Bellona equips herself, so as to be thought not a greedy pest but a thrifty Virtue. With a delicate covering of motherly devotion she hides her snaky tresses so that the white mantle shall disguise the raging that lurks beneath and screen the fearful fury, and so display her plundering and thieving and greedy storing of her gains under the pleasing name of care for her children. With such semblances she befools men and cheats their too credulous hearts. They follow the deadly monster, believing hers to be a Virtue's work, and the wicked fiend takes them, easy, willing victims, and binds them with gripping shackles.

> (*Prudentius* 317-19)

Thus Greed has turned from a rapacious gold hoarder into a frugal parent, living sparingly and saving everything she can. Once a despicable greedy woman, she is now a virtuous member of a community. She claims to store up her wealth in the name of caring for her children. Such miserly claims have fooled people around her because they do not know what she really is (especially in a situation such as the current battle in the allegory is). Eventually, Good Works's arrival saves the situation. She defeats and kills Greed, and distributes Greed's hoards to the needy.

Besides such breath-taking allegorical narration, Prudentius also gives rational warning against avarice as the origin of other sins:

> The maw of greed swallows piles of money down its wide throat, since no limit of possession controls it and it only puts new desires on top of the riches it has amassed. For the hunger for gold only grows keener from the gold it has got. Hence comes a crop of sins and the sole root of evil, for the love of finery, that like a pander unlooses the restraints of modesty, strains all the gushing waters of streams and the buried ores, and misplaced zeal, probing the dirty earth, scrapes out what nature has hidden away in secret, in hope to find some little glistening stones in some of its diggings to reward its rummaging.
>
> (223)

Prudentius's admonition is reasonable because there is no end to the desire for more. As Jesus teaches his disciples not to worry about life, food and the future (e. g. Matthew VI: 19-34; Luke XII 16: 34), Prudentius writes:

> 'Tis the deepest rest to wish for nought beyond what

due need calls for, simple fare and one garment to cover and refresh our weak bodies in moderation, and when nature's measure is satisfied, draw us on no farther. When thou art going on a journey, carry no wallet, nor take thought, when thou goest, for another tunic to wear. And be not anxious about the morrow, lest thy belly lack food; bread for the day comes duly with the sun.

(Prudentius 321-23)

In short, Prudentius condemns avarice and exhorts us to be moderate with worldly riches, become generous and give what is beyond "nature's measure" to the poor.

ii. Secular eulogization of avarice

The human attitude towards avarice has had a mixed history. Not all people, current and ancient, have condemned avarice. In our days of financial accumulation, Bill Gates and Warren Buffet are adulated as icons for many people around the world. Gecko's "Greed is good" is a famous line from *Wall Street*, a 1987 Hollywood movie made when corporate greed began to be rampant and widely glorified in the United States. [1] "Many assume that the best motives for success are greed, competition, and hedonism" (Schimmel 182). A

---

[1] The movie *Wall Street* was directed by Oliver Stone, Twentieth Century Fox, 1987, screenplay by Stanley Weiser and Oliver Stone. Michael Douglas plays the role of Gordon Gecko, whose full speech on greed is: "Greed—for lack of a better word—is good. Greed is right. Greed works. Greed clarifies, cuts through, it captures the essence of the evolutionary spirit. Greed in all its forms: greed for life, for money, for love, knowledge, has marked the upward surge of mankind, and greed—you mark my words—will not only save Teldar Paper, but that other malfunctioning corporation called the USA. " See Matthew Robinson, and Daniel Murphy, p. ix for more. The movie had a sequel, *Wall Street: Money Never Sleeps*, in 2010, directed by Oliver Stone, written by Allan Loeb and Stephen Schiff, based on characters created by Stanley Weiser and Mr. Stone. Michael Douglas plays Gordon Gecko again.

classic example of this idea is from Max Weber (1864 – 1920). Although not without criticisms, Weber, in what is perhaps his best known book, *The Protestant Ethic and the Spirit of Capitalism* (1904 – 1905), argues that applying oneself to moneymaking is the greatest force that has made Western Europe a superpower. He lauds the Protestant ethic that would be considered avarice in many others' eyes:

> The summum bonum of this [Protestant] ethic, the earning of more and more money, combined with the strict avoidance of all spontaneous enjoyment of life, is above all completely devoid of any eudaemonistic, not to say hedonistic, admixture.
>
> (18)

Earlier than Weber, Adam Smith (1723 – 1790) in his celebrated *An Inquiry into the Nature and Causes of the Wealth of Nations* justifies avarice as a profit-motive, a mechanism that empowers the betterment of both the individual and the society at large:

> The natural effort of every individual to better his own condition, when suffered *to exert itself with freedom and security*, is so powerful a principle, that it is alone, and without any assistance, not only capable of *carrying on the society to wealth and prosperity*, but of surmounting a hundred impertinent obstructions with which the folly of human laws too often incumbers its operations.
>
> (540. Italics mine)

And

> He [every individual] generally, indeed, neither intends to promote the public interest, nor knows how much he is promoting it . . . he intends only *his own gain,*

and he is in this, as in many other cases, led by an invisible hand to promote an end which was no part of his intention.

(456. Italics mine)

Still earlier, Poggio Bracciolini (1380 – 1459), an Italian humanist of the early Renaissance, eulogizes avarice in his dialogue, *On Avarice*, in which he voices a "utilitarian, even modern, view" that "avarice is the compelling reason for business investment, the growth of cities, philanthropy, and wage-earning":

> It is obvious that avarice is not only natural, it is useful and necessary in human beings, for it teaches them to provide for themselves those things which are necessary for sustaining the frailty of human nature and for avoiding inconveniences.

(qtd. in Newhauser 17)

In Rome, Cicero condemns greed because no vice is "more offensive than avarice" (*De Officiis* II: xxii. 77). He goes on to say that when people commit wrong-doing to secure some personal end, "avarice is generally the controlling motive" (I: vii. 24), but he justifies the accumulation of wealth as long as it is not perversion or misuse of public right, which should be avoided: [1]

> Fine establishments and the comforts of life in elegance and abundance also afford pleasure, and the desire to secure it gives rise to the insatiable thirst for wealth. Still, I do not mean to find fault with the accumulation of property, provided it hurts nobody, but unjust acquisition

---

[1] See also Richard Newhauser (2000), p. 71, p. 176, n. 5, and Phyllis A. Tickle, p. 81, n. 49.

of it is always to be avoided.

(I: viii. 25)

iii. Secular criticism against avarice

In secular Greco-Roman literature, Midas, a king of
Macedonia (or Phrygia) who is not satisfied with his wealth,
is probably the best known incarnation of the sin of avarice.
When offered a wish (any one) by the god Dionysus, Midas
responds instantly that he wishes to turn everything he
touches into gold. Dionysus grants the wish, and Midas gains
his famous touch. Immediately, everything, including his
meat and fruit, and everyone, including his wife and
children, turns into beautiful, shining gold the moment he
touches them. Thrilled briefly and then frustrated horribly,
Midas has to beg Dionysus to take back the powerful touch
forever. The myth of King Midas illustrates the dangers of
greed. Midas's unreasoned and uncontrolled desire for gold
results in losses of family relationships, food, drink, and
almost his own life. As Solomon Schimmel says, Midas's
story shows that an "avaricious person is aroused by money
even as it is accumulated unused. That is what characterizes
the avaricious miser who will sacrifice almost anything in
order to fill his coffers and who hoards rather than uses his
wealth" (173).

Greek philosophers have thought profoundly about
greed. Aristotle exemplifies some of the most important
points. In his *Nicomachean Ethics*, the great teacher of King
Alexander argues that among the virtues that work towards
the ultimate goal of life, three are recognized as involving our

attitude to and practice of property: justice, liberty and magnificence. ① Justice, according to Aristotle, in relation to possessions, is:

> that in virtue of which the just man is said to be a doer, by choice, of that which is just, and one who will distribute either between himself and another or between two others not so as to give more of what is desirable to himself and less to the other (and conversely with what is harmful), but so as to give what is equal in accordance with proportion; and similarly in distributing between two other persons.
>
> $$(1134^{a}1\text{-}7)$$

In other words, the Aristotelian "justice" is taking or giving the right amount of property or wealth or possession, no more or no less than one's share.

Consistent with his idea of "justice" concerning wealth, Aristotle defines "liberality" as the mean of giving and taking of wealth. He argues that the liberal man has the best and right attitude and treatment of wealth, "riches, therefore, will be used best by the man who has the virtue concerned with wealth; and this is the liberal man" (*Ethics* $1120^{a}6\text{-}27$). Aristotle clarifies his definition of "liberality" by looking at

---

① According to Michael Pakaluk, although it "gets at the correct fundamental notion," "liberty" is "old-fashioned" in contemporary English. He uses in his discussion of Aristotle "generosity," the "least objectionable choice" of terms (173). However, David Ross, the *Nicomachean Ethics* translator being quoted here says, " 'liberality' reflects the connection of the Greek noun with *eleutheros*, free" (224, First Note to Book IV, Chapter I). At this point, Pakaluk is consistent with Ross. Pakaluk explains that the Greek word, *eleutheriotēs*, means " in a condition characteristic of a free citizen, as opposed to a slave"; it is "the virtue by which someone is not, as we would say, 'bound' or 'tied down' by concerns about his possessions; it is meant to be a posture by which someone 'rises above' his possessions, and, with a certain lack of concern, puts them to good use, in order to achieve admirable goals" (173).

two cases: giving and taking. In each case, the action can be mean only when the amount and timing of giving and taking are mean; the object(s) he gives to and the source he takes from should be just right, too. "He will give to the right people, the right amounts, and at the right time, with all the other qualifications that accompany right giving" (ibid. 1120^a 25-26).

Aristotle criticizes both prodigality and meanness because of their departure from the mean; he especially warns against the evil of meanness. If a prodigal person takes the right amount from the right sources, he is then "much better" (ibid. 1120^a 28) than a mean man who falls short in giving, because a prodigal can easily be cured by old age and poverty and move towards the middle state, but the mean person "benefits no man, not even himself " (ibid. 1120^a 29). Those who go astray from the mean in giving and taking, especially the "miserly, close, stingy, the cheeseparer and everyone of the sort," and those who "ply sordid trades, pimps and all such people, and those who lend small sums and at high rates" (ibid. 1121^{b}26-30-20), are "both incurable and innate" because "most men are fonder of getting money than of giving " (ibid. 1121^b 13-16). Aristotle warns, "meanness is a greater evil than prodigality" and "men err more often in this direction [meanness] than in the way of prodigality" (ibid. 1122^a 16).

The Aristotelian idea of " magnificence," or "munificence" in this situation, is comparable to that of "liberality" except only in scale—the former is larger than the latter. That is, "magnificence" refers to the expenditure on great projects or a large scale. A "magnificent" man can still be "liberal" if he spends according to his wealth. A poor man who spends too much is a fool; a rich man who spends too little where he should spend much is niggardly; and a wealthy man who spends too much where he should spend little is tastelessly showy. In each case, the man is not magnificent and has the character of vice (ibid. 1122[a] 18-1123[a] 33).

It can be seen that Aristotle's attitude towards wealth or money is the virtue of mean in amount, timing, and object. An excess is wastefulness, and a deficiency, avarice. Also, according to Aristotle, a just man takes and gives exactly according to his share, but " the unjust man is grasping [greedy]" (ibid. 1129[b]), and "when a man acts graspingly he often exhibits . . . certainly wickedness of some kind and injustice" (ibid. 1130[a] 20). He explains that "graspingness" is a "particular injustice" which is "concerned with honour or money or safety—or that which includes all these, if we had a single name for it—and its motive is the pleasure that arises from gain [taking more than one's rightful share]" (ibid. 1130[b] 1-3). Therefore, avarice is dangerous because a man will naturally satisfy his pleasure, and one pleasure for a greedy person is the motive to gain continually more wealth or money.

Aristotle's ideas of the golden mean and liberality are inherited and expounded vividly by Dante Alighieri (1265 – 1321) in his *Divine Comedy* (1307 – 1321). Dante vehemently condemns avarice's insatiability and evil. One interpretation of the enigmatic she-wolf of *Inferno* is that she represents avarice:

And she has a nature so evil and cruel that her

Greedy desire is never satisfied, and after feeding she
Is hungrier than before.

(1. 97-99)

Dante puts the avaricious along with the prodigal, unrecognizable as individuals and so undeserving a name, in the filthy fourth circle:

Bad giving and bad keeping has deprived them of
The lovely world and set them to his scuffling:
Whatever it is, I prettify no words for it.

(*Inferno* 7. 58-60)

Because of their greed ("bad keeping" and "closed fists") or prodigality ("Spending with no measure governed their spending" [*Inferno* 7. 41-42] and "bad giving"), the avaricious and the prodigal are exactly, in Aristotelian terms, neither moderate nor liberal. As a result, Virgil, Dante's guide, even disdains to find any superficially beautiful words ("prettify no words") for them.

Dante also shows well the connection between avarice and anger or violence. He condemns both in his masterpiece, too:

Oh blind cupidity and mad rage, that so spur us
In this short life, and then in the eternal one cook us
So evilly!

(*Inferno* 12. 49 – 51)

In addition to an everlasting hunger for more and injustice (in Aristotle's sense), avarice causes the greedy person to move away from God. Dante keeps this Augustinian idea in mind when he castigates avarice by showing the repentance of a soul in his *Purgatorio*:

Until that point I was a wretched soul

Separated from God, entirely greedy; now, as you
See, I am punished for it here.

What avarice does is shown here in the
Penance of the inverted souls, and the mountain
Has no pain more bitter.

Since our eyes, fixed on earthly things, were
Not raised up, so here justice has sunk them to the
    earth.
Since avarice extinguished our love for every

Good, so that our power to act was lost, so justice
Keeps us fixed here,
Bound and captive in feet and hands.

(Purgatorio 19. 112-24)

In this form of penance, the avaricious souls are shown to be going through bottomless pain. Since their eyes were always "fixed on earthly things," not raised to heaven, they are sunk to and fixed face down on the earth (19. 113-20). Such cleansing of sinners's avarice combined with studying examples of liberality are the only ways to correct their vice and prepare them for heaven. When Dante and Virgil continue walking on the fifth terrace, they hear the souls's calling out of such names as Mary, Saint Nicolas and Fabricius. Mary, Joseph's wife in the Gospels, readily accepted indigence and was chosen to be the Mother of Jesus; Saint Nicolas generously gave dowries to rescue three young girls from becoming forced prostitutes by their poor father; and Fabricius, the Roman consul, preferred honorable poverty to tainted material wealth. Dante gives such examples of generosity to harshly condemn avarice and clearly advocates Aristotelian liberality.

Censure for greed also abounds in English literature. Geoffrey Chaucer, Dante's English student in a sense,[1] in his *Canterbury Tales* criticizes avarice by satirizing both the pardoner and three revelers in the tale he tells. In *The Pardoner's Prologue*, the Pardoner brazenly talks about his own venality to his fellow pilgrims. He says that whenever he preaches in his church, he always quotes St. Paul's words to Timothy, " Radix malorum est cupiditas" ("The root of all evils is cupidity," 4), using a few words such as these in Latin to spice his preaching so that he can " stir hem to devocioun" (18). He deceives his believers into offering him " pence or elles grotes" (48) with some rags and animal bones that he claims to be relics of a saint and with what he claims to be "an holy Jewes sheep" (23).[2] He assures his believers that as long as they offer money to him, their sins, be them dreadful or adulterous, will be absolved by his " authoritee" (59). " He makes plain not only that he is greedy, but that his greed is vicious, sinful, a willful violation of holy things"

---

[1] For example, Albert Russell Ascoli states, "Poets throughout Italy and all over Europe—for example, Boccaccio, Chaucer, and Christine de Pizan—were treating Dante as a poetic model, an *auctor* comparable to ancients such as Virgil and Ovid" (4).

[2] In the Middle Ages, avarice of the clergy was a frequent target of satire, and " relics" was a euphemistic term for bribes of gold and silver to the clergymen. Commenting on one of the earliest surviving Latin satires, *Tractatus Garciae* [*Little Tract of Garcia*], written in 1099 or shortly afterwards, Laura Kendrick says, " The inflated account of the archbishop's ' epic ' quest for office, in which bribes of gold and silver are euphemistically called relics of the martyred saints Rufinus (ruddy gold) and Albinus (white silver), announces what will turn out to be the main theme of Latin satire for the entire Middle Ages: the greed or avarice of the clergy, and especially of those at the head of the Catholic Church. The pope and his curia, those who are expected to set a virtuous example, but, instead, through simony (bribe-taking), corrupt the entire body of Christian society" (54).

(Wetherbee 69). Indeed, he is ready to reveal that profit is the sole purpose of his hypocritical preaching:

> Of avarice and of swich cursednesse
> Is al my prechyng, for to make hem free
> To yeven hir pens, and namely unto me.
> For myn entente is nat but for to wynne,
> And nothyng for correccioun of synne.
> I rekke nevere, whan that they been beryed,
> Though that hir soules goon a-blakeberyed!
>
> (400-06)

As hypocritical and avaricious as the Pardoner are the three "riotoures" (revelers) in *The Pardoner's Tale*. After drinking, gambling, having fun at a tavern and then hearing of Death, a clandestine thief who has slain one of their friends, these revelers claim that since they are "one" and call each other "brother," they should act together to avenge their friend on Death:

> Herkneth, felawes—we thre been al ones;
> Let ech of us holde up his hand til oother,
> And ech of us bicomen otheres brother:
> And we wol sleen this false traytour Deeth.
>
> (696-99)

However, when they find a large heap of gold rather than the "traytour Deeth," their warm words of fraternity and mutual protection immediately turn into a scheme to murder their "brothers" in order to take the gold to themselves. Thus, they draw lots to send one away in order to divide the triad up for easy action. Once they are divided into two groups, the youngest, going to town for bread and wine, and the other two, staying to keep watch over the gold, begin their plans. Daggers are greetings the remaining revelers will give to their friend upon his return:

> Looke whan that he is set, that right anoon
> Arys as though thou woldest with hym pleye;
> And I shal ryve hym thurgh the sydes tweye,
> Whil that thou stroglest with hym as in game;
> And with thy daggere looke thou do the same.
> And thanne shal al this gold departed be,
> My deere freend, betwixen me and thee.

(826-32)

The youngest reveler on his way to town decides to use poison on his "brothers." After falsely telling a chemist about his intention to kill rats and a polecat, he succeeds in buying some deadly poison. Now,

> This cursed man hath in his hond yhent
> This poysoun in a box, and sith he ran
> Into the nexte strete unto a man
> And borwed [of] hym large botelles thre.
> And in the two his poyson poured he;
> The thridde he kepte clene for his drynke.

(868-73)

The killings occur as both parties have planned. When the youngest reveler returns, the other two rise and stab him to death; then these murderers sit down to drink and celebrate their success and are poisoned. All three covetous revelers receive the punishment they deserve.

In addition to vices such as gambling, lust, gluttony and blasphemy, Chaucer ruthlessly yet with grim humour attacks the sin of avarice, both of the Pardoner and the three revelers. As Winthrop Wetherbee points out, the Pardoner "shows us professional greed in its lowest form, reinforced by a ruthless exploitation of the authority of the Church and accompanied by vivid suggestions of personal corruption" (33).

Edmund Spenser, with whom Ben Jonson shares "convictions about the moral responsibilities and high calling of poets" (Barton, "Jonson, Ben" 1081), is another English poet to lash at avarice. In his *Fairie Queene*, Spenser exposes Avarice in a parade of the seven deadly sins:

> And greedy Avarice by him did ride,
> Uppon a Camell loaden all with gold;
> Two iron coffers hong on either side,
> With precious metall full, as they might hold,
> And in his lap an heap of coine he told;
> For of his wicked pelfe his God he made,
> And unto hell him selfe for money sold;
> Accursed usury was all his trade,
> And right and wrong ylike in equall ballaunce waide.
>
> His life was nigh unto deaths dore yplaste,
> And thred-bare cote, and cobled shoes hee ware,
> Ne scarse good morsell all his life did taste,
> But both from backe and belly still did spare,
> To fill his bags, and richesse to compare;
> Yet childe ne kinsman living had he none
> To leave them to; but thorough daily care
> To get, and nightly feare to lose his owne,
> He led a wretched life unto him selfe unknowne.
>
> Most wretched wight, whom nothing might suffise,
> Whose greedy lust did lacke in greatest store,

Whose need had end, but no end covetise,

Whose welth was want, whose plenty made him pore,

Who had enough, yett wished ever more,

A vile disease, and eke in foote and hand

A grievous gout tormented him full sore,

That well he could not touch, nor goe, nor stand:

Such one was Avarice, the forth of this faire band.

(Book I: iv. 27-29)

This Avarice figure riding a camel loaded with gold immediately reminds the reader of the biblical verses about the difficulty for a rich man to enter into heaven (Matthew XIX: 16-24; Mark X: 17-25, and Luke XVIII: 18-25). Spenser's Avarice is not ordinarily rich. His two big iron coffers are not only full of gold coins; he is also counting ("told") a heap of gold that his coffers cannot hold. Despite his vast hoard of gold, Avarice is neither satisfied nor faithful. He always wishes more; he makes gold his God, much like Israelites making a golden calf their God in the desert (Exodus XXXII: 1-8); he is accused of usury; in his balance, right and wrong are equally weighed. Despite his riches, he is old and diseased. His clothes and shoes are shabby; he starves himself in order to fill his money bags even though he has no children to bequeath his wealth to; he tries his best to earn as much as possible in the day and is worried at night about robberies of his gold; he has limited need for his wealth, but his covetousness for wealth is unlimited. Such is a typical Elizabethan miser, as Celeste Turner Wright has summarized: elderly, greedy, loathsome, coughing, huge-nosed, dropsical or gouty, starving at home but gluttonous at his guests' tables, shabby-clothed, attended by a famished servant, and hanged in the end (196-97).

Similar to the parade of Avarice in Spenser's *Faerie Queene*, a presentation of Covetousness as part of the procession of the Seven Deadly Sins is found in Christopher Marlowe's *Doctor Faustus*:

> I am *Covetousnesse*; begotten of an old Churle in a leather bag; and might I now obtaine my wish, this house, you and all, should turne to Gold, that I might locke you safe into my Chest; O my sweete Gold!
>
> (674-77)

Unlike Spenser's Avarice, an old man, Marlowe's Covetousness is a miser's child. Despite being a child, she sounding exactly like King Midas, is so avaricious that she wishes to turn everything into gold and lock it up safely in her chest.

Besides Covetousness in *Dr. Faustus*, Marlowe, born in the same year as shakespeare and eight years older than Ben Jonson, has created another greedy character, Barabas, or the Jew of Malta. In the opening scene of *The Jew of Malta*, Barabas is seen " in his counting-house, with heaps of gold before him" (I. i. , s. d.). This opening impresses on a reader / audience's mind immediately a calculating, acquisitive and money-seeking figure, as Barabas is no commonly greedy person. In the beginning of the play, he studies carefully the details of the columns of his accounts; he is even dissatisfied with his silver coins, which he considers " paltry" and " trash," although his coffers have been crammed full. He has been " tired all his life time wearing his fingers" to count his gold and silver coins. He now detests much sweating simply for gaining only a pound[1] (6-18).

> So that of thus much of that returne was made:
> And of the third part of the Persian ships,
> There was the centure summ'd and satisfied.
> As for those Samnites, and the men of Uzz,
> That bought my Spanish Oyles, and Wines of *Greece*,
> Here have I purst their paltry silverlings.
> Fye, what a trouble tis to count this trash.
>
> (I. i. 1-7)

He then begins to dream about winning gold by dealings with rich foreign merchants:

> Well fare the Arabians, who so richly pay
> The things they traffiquec for with wedge of gold,
> Whereof a man may easily in a day
> Tell that which may maintaine him all his life.
> The needy groome that never fingered groat,
> Would make a miracle of thus much coyne;
> But he whose steel-bard coffers are cramm'd full,
> And all his lifetime hath bin tired,
> Wearying his fingers ends with telling it,
> Would in his age be loath to labour so,
> And for a pound to sweat himselfe to death:
> Give me the Merchants of the Indian Mynes,
> That trade in mettall of the purest mould;
> The wealthy Moore, that in the Easterne rockes

---

[1] In Marlowe's time, one pound was a considerable amount of money. According to Park Honan, author of *Christopher Marlowe: Poet & Spy*, a grown-up assistant to Marlowe's father, a cobbler, received "up to £ 3 a year" (21). *Dr. Faustus*'s first performance on record, by the Lord Admiral's men at the Rose, on September 30, 1594, "earned a *handsome* revenue of £ 3. 4s. 0d. for Henslowe" (219. Italics mine).

Without controule can picke his riches up,
And in his house heape pearle like pibble-stones,
Receive them free, and sell them by the weight;
Bags of fiery *Opals*, *saphires*, *amatists*,
Jacints, hard *Topas*, grasse-greene *Emeraulds*,
Beauteous *Rubyes*, sparkling *Diamonds*,
And seildsene costly stones of so great price,
As one of them, indifferently rated,
And of a Carrect of this quantity,
May serve in perill of calamity
To ransome great Kings from captivity.
This is the ware wherein consists my wealth.

(I. i. 8-33)

Barabas fantasizes himself having pearls and other precious stones as many as pebble-stones. Because he has so much of them, he wants to sell them by weight, rather than by their number. A carat of his " opals, sapphires, amethysts" and rare "stones" "may serve in perill of calamity to ransom great Kings from captivity." He wants to give up his "vulgar trade" (I. i. 19-35) and take up some more profitable trade. A huge amassing of gold and precious stones are Barabas's aim.

Barabas's greed is further reinforced when he gives a Shylockian cry at his daughter's news of having retrieved his hidden gold:

Abigall.	Then father here receive thy happinesse.
Barabas.	Hast thou't?
Abigall.	Here, *Throwes downe bags*.
	Hast thou't?
	There's more, and more, and more.
Barabas.	Oh my girle,

My gold, my fortune, my felicity;

Strength to my soule, death to mine enemy:

. . .

Oh, girle, oh gold, oh beauty, oh my
blisse! *Hugs his bags.*

(II. i. 44-54)

Like Shylock whose money is the "prop" that "sustains
his house" (*Merchant* IV. i. 371-72), gold is Barabas's
"happinesse," "fortune," "felicity," "strength" to his soul,
"death" to his enemy, "beauty" and "blisse" (II. i. 48-50).
A special point to keep in mind here is the stage direction in
II. i. 54 that Barabas, instead of hugging his daughter
Abigall after she has found the hidden gold and "happinesse"
for him, prefers to hug the gold bags before her face. Despite
other differences between them, Barabas and Shylock's
avarice is the same.

Stevie Simkin correctly affirms that this soliloquy not only
establishes Barabas's "defining characteristic (his avarice),"
but also places "material wealth," or "human greed" firmly
at the "centre" of the drama (40). In depicting Barabas, a
Machiavellian villain,[1] Marlowe created a major Elizabethan
character of greed that was to influence a host of others,
albeit not necessarily avaricious ones: Aaron, Richard III,
Iago, Edmund and most of all, Shylock (Lynch vi).

---

[1] According to Stephen J. Lynch, "the name Machevil—suggesting a pun on 'make-evil' —was a
variant form of his name that circulated in Renaissance England, and that appears in the quarto
edition of the play" (3, n. 2).

III. Historical background of avarice

i. The rise of money

Towards the end of the Middle Ages, Europe was gradually turning from a feudal to a capitalist economy. Commerce, manufacturing, trade and finance greatly developed in the fourteenth and fifteenth centuries. Because gold and silver were in increasingly large demand, the more powerful economies, like those of Spain, Portugal and England, went around the world for them. Money was increasingly necessary as a means of exchange for the enhancement of trade. The result is known to all: gold and silver flowed in torrents from the New World into Europe to relieve the money shortage. [1] According to Michael Wood, Europe was so thirsty for gold and silver that "even if all the snow in the Andes turned to gold, still they [the Spanish conquistadors and exploiters led by Francisco Pizarro] would not be satisfied" (148). With this new love of money, even the age-old pride in hierarchy or social rank was affected, if not challenged.

The following description by Johan Huizinga summarizes the new situation:

In the later Middle Ages, the conditions of power had

---

[1] This problem was complicated by three aspects at least. One, mints were short of silver to produce fine coins; two, economic development needed an increasing amount of currency; and three, inflation was high. In England, the "cost of living increased by a factor of seven" from 1540s to 1640s, a "revolutionary inflation rate increase" in the price of bread by medieval standards. For more, see Ferguson, pp. 17-65.

been changed by the increased circulation of money, and an illimitable field opened to whosoever was desirous of satisfying his ambitions by heaping up wealth. To this epoch cupidity becomes the predominant sin. Riches have not acquired the spectral impalpability which capitalism, founded on credit, will give them later; what haunts the imagination is still the tangible yellow gold. The enjoyment of riches is direct and primitive; it is not yet weakened by the mechanism of an automatic and invisible accumulation by investment; the satisfaction of being rich is found either in luxury and dissipation, or in gross avarice. [1]

(19)

As it is part of the European Union today, England in the Renaissance paralleled the Continent in terms of economic growth. Despite such disturbances as the Wars of the Roses (1455 – 1487), the overall English economy developed rapidly in late Middle Ages and Early Modern period. The wool industry boomed; international trade surged; England's crushing defeat of the Spanish Armada in 1588 demonstrated its military and economic power. However, like the Continent, Renaissance England was severely short of money for increased commerce. According to John W. Draper, not only were the urban and rural aristocrats living on borrowed money, but also "miners, weavers, and other classes of artisans worked on small loans often at ruinous interest" (40-41).

ii. English literary context of avarice

In English literary history, the principal concerns of

---

[1] Huizinga singles out France and the Netherlands in his discussion, but the economic and financial conditions in England in the late Middle Ages were about the same as those in these two countries.

allegorical literature in the Middle Ages, such as those of morality plays, interludes and protestant drama, like Prudentius's *Psychomachia*, are the defeat of vices and triumph of virtues. John Watkins remarks that "The allegorical drama written in England during the fifteenth and sixteenth centuries is one of literary history's most static genres." Watkins calls these genres "static" because they always "tell similar stories of temptation, fall and regeneration" (767). Pamela King agrees with Watkins on the "static" nature of English medieval plays. She claims that "most surviving medieval plays in English are persuasive in purpose and devotional in content" (627). As popular entertainments of this period, morality plays "critique English society from a conservative perspective."[1] The principal vices of morality plays are "avarice, ambition, greed, extortion, and other sins" (Watkins 767). Expectedly, avarice is a major theme in English medieval allegorical literature.

Avarice is also a central concern in the literature of early modern England. According to Janel Mueller, the analyses of the English society in religious literature during this period are "remarkably consistent":

Despite the free and open circulation of God's Word,

---

[1] A full picture of medieval English literature, especially literature as related to entertainment, like drama, is yet to appear. According to Pamela King, "The full extent of the lost entertainment industry of medieval England is still emerging," and "No longer can we fall back on a secure, co-aeval body of 'mystery cycles' and 'morality plays.'" Popular as they were during the Middle Ages, there are, so far as we know, not many extant English morality plays. King believes there are only five, *The Castle of Perseverance*, *Mankind*, *Wisdom*, *Pride of Life* and *Everyman* (626), and Sarah Beckwith argues for a different list: *The Castle of Perseverance*, *Mankind*, *Wisdom*, *Everyman* and *Nature* (c. 1530) by Henry Medwall (89-90).

self-love and self-interest, expressed in rampant covetousness for money, goods and land, have deprived the people at large of hospitals and schools and have brought oppression, starvation and vagrancy upon the poor and humble.

(293)

Much of secular literature also shares deep worries about the sin of avarice. According to Christopher Warley, the "focus [of literature] on avarice is not unusual" in Tudor England. " Probably the most famous instance of such emphasis on greed is Hythloday's complaint in Book 2 of More's *Utopia* (1516)" (276). As Mueller summarizes, "covetousness is also the ubiquitous trope of Robert Crowley's *Philargyrie of Great Britain* (1551),[1] a satirical verse fable of a giant of immense strength and insatiable appetite for swallowing gold" (293). Nicholas Udall's (c. 1505 – 1556) *Respublica* (1553), which has been studied "largely as part of the prehistory of Shakespearean drama," features Avarice as the " clear leader of the other Vices, who act as self-interested courtier-counsellors to the widowed and somewhat feeble Respublica" (Warley 274-76). Apart from Marlowe's *Dr. Faustus* and *The Jew of Malta* as discussed above, many of the Elizabethan and Caroline plays depict important covetous characters, and the following are but a few well-studied examples: William Shakespeare's *The Merchant of Venice* (1596 – 1598) and *Timon of Athens* (1605 – 1608), Thomas Middleton's *A Trick to Catch the Old One* (c. 1605), Ben Jonson's major comedies, especially *Volpone* (1605) and

---

[1] See n. 1 on p. 86.

The Alchemist (1610), Philip Massinger's comedies *A New Way to Pay Old Debts* (c. 1625) and *The City Madam* (1632), Thomas Heywood's *The English Traveler* (1633), and Francis Quarles's *The Virgin Widow* (1649).

An important way to present the theme of avarice in early modern English literature is the dramatization of usury, the lending of money at interest. Whatever their actual practice in the business of money-lending, the English before and during the Elizabethan age did not have a positive attitude towards the usurer. Despite the pervasiveness of borrowing, Englishmen were clearly convinced that usury was condemned by both the Scriptures and Aristotle's *Politics* (I. iii. 23) as an unnatural way of gaining wealth. [1] Such an attitude is reflected in the large number of plays with usury as a theme. Arthur Bivins Stonex's reading of the Elizabethan and Jacobean plays reveals that the usurer in them is "rather surprisingly ubiquitous" (191), and during the 90 years from 1553 to 1643, seventy-one plays were written which contain or seem to contain usurers (190-91, including n. 3). Usury is closely linked with avarice. According to Lawrence Manley, prodigality is the gentleman's sin, and avarice, the merchant's. These two sins "linked to each other through financial practices to which preachers gave the blanket term 'usury.'" Manley further explains:

> Usury was traditionally associated with prodigal

---

[1] For example, usury is regarded as being as bad as taking bribes in the Old Testament: "he that giueth not his money vnto vsurie, nor taketh rewarde against the innocent (Psalms XV. 5). Usury is also treated as an abomination: "He that increaseth his riches by vsurie and interest, gathereth them for him that wilbe merciful vnto the poore [... shalbe an abominable]" (Proverbs XXVIII. 8-9).

borrowers and avaricious creditors who breached the intimate and informal terms of petty transactions; but by the later sixteenth century 'usury' denoted disturbing transformations in the social order—the changing relationships between land and money, between the aristocratic and business classes, and in the credit relationships of small producers to dealers, the developing relationship between wage earners and employers.

(406)

Despite the repeal of laws against usury under the reign of Elizabeth I, playwrights from the Middle Ages to the closure of theaters in 1642 condemned avarice. As Christopher Warley claims, "complaining about greed may be as old as humanity, but the intensity of the focus of Tudor writers on avarice as the key to social problems is conspicuous" (276). As the examples above show, the period Warley defines as "Tudor" can be extended to the reign of King Charles I.

Greed, together with its identical sisters, avarice, covetousness, cupidity, and rapaciousness, has been a focus of the attention of philosophers, theologians and narrative writers since the beginning of civilization. In the last few centuries, the birth and growth of commerce and capitalism have found some positive roles for greed and thus given it some credit in producing social and human achievement.

However, in most situations, religious, literary and historical, avarice has been condemned. Both the Jewish and Christian Bibles criticize avarice and teach their followers to shun it. Ancient philosophers, represented by Aristotle, carefully analyzed the right attitude towards money and suggested either the mean between stinginess and liberality as the standard when taking or giving one's share of wealth. An act beyond the mean, less or more, is condemned as injustice. Early Christian church fathers attacked avarice as one of the Seven Deadly Sins. In Medieval and Renaissance literature, avarice is personified in vivid stories as a character to be conquered or punished. And in history, avarice has been blamed as the excessive human desire for money that causes social problems.

In Shakespeare and Jonson's time, social concerns over avarice as represented by dramatists reached a new height. The definitions, religious, literary and historical backgrounds presented in this chapter will furnish a platform on which two of these dramatists' specific plays, *The Merchant of Venice* and *Volpone* can be discussed.

3

Jonson's and Shakespeare's Dramatic Didacticism

I. Introduction

The educational tradition of European literature dates as far back as the Greek era. Religious poetry such as the Septuagint and the Greek New Testament is certainly educational. Outside religious literature, in the secular domains, the Homeric epics are also meant to both inspire and instruct. Priam's ransom of Hector's body from Achilles is an affecting story of fatherly and brotherly love and filial piety. The ransom as arranged and aided by Zeus is meant to teach obedience to the highest authority and the need to offer godly mercy. Aristophanes makes a point through the character of Aeschylus that young people need poets as teachers (*Frogs* 11. 1249-50). Plato, one generation Aristophanes's junior, always holds that poetry should teach good morals. Because tragedy and comedy may mislead the guardians of the ideal state, Plato argues, both tragic and comic poets should be excluded from the republic (*Republic* 3. 394ᶜ). In Humphry House's view of Plato's ideas on poets in *The Republic*, "poets are to be allowed only if their work has a directly didactic aim linked to the purposes of moral education" (28). Later in *Laws*, Plato changes his opinion, granting poetry "an educative purpose in society" (Ferrari 107). Plato, in probably his last dialogue, recognizes that poets can "lead the younger men to take the proper enjoyment in worthy characters" (*Laws* 2. 670ᶜ 1-2). Aristotle, talking about the difference between speech and character in tragedy, remarks that "character is that which reveals moral purpose, showing what kind of things a man chooses or avoids" (*Poetics* 1450ᵇ 17). As for plot, the most important element in his idea of tragedy, Aristotle says that the best tragic plot is a complex one, one in which a man's "unmerited misfortune" arouses pity and fear in the audience (*Poetics* 1453ᵃ), and this "unmerited misfortune," as Isaiah Smithson points out, is Aristotle's "moral concern" (10). Also, Aristotle says in *Poetics* that "the incidents and the plot are the end of a tragedy; and the end is the chief thing of all" (1450ᵃ10-11). "End" in a moral sense was always Aristotle's advocacy for the value of art, as he asserts in *Nicomachean Ethics*, "Every art and every inquiry, and similarly every action and choice, is thought to aim at some good; and for this reason the good has rightly been declared to be that at which all things aim" (1094^{a}1-3). ①

During Roman Augustan times, when Latin literature flourished, both Greeks and Romans asserted that poetry must be didactic. Strabo (63 BC-23 AD), a Greek geographer, argued against the great Alexandrian scholar and scientist, Eratosthenes (c. 275-194 BC), who held that poetry should aim at entertainment. Strabo says, poetry as a sort of primary philosophy "introduces us to the art of life and instructs us, with pleasure to ourselves, in character, emotions, and actions;" and the reason the Greeks gave their children their first education through poetry is "not for the mere sake of entertainment," but "for the sake of moral discipline" (*Geography* 1. 2. 3). ②

Quintilian (c. 35-100) well recognizes literature's function of moral education. He exhorts children to be trained as orators to "begin [education] by reading Homer and Vergil" because they must learn "not merely what is eloquent; it is even more important that they should study what is morally excellent" (I. viii. 4).

It can be said that classical authors, be they poets or

---

① According to the great classicist D. W. Lucas, the Greeks had "no category of didactic poetry" ("Commentary on *Poetics*," 1. 1447^b 9). When he comments on the Aristotelian characters, Lucas says, "The activities of admirable people must reflect admirable standards of conduct. Whether we call this 'didactic' is a question of words" ("Commentary on *Poetics*," 2. 1448^a 2). *Cartharsis*, one of the essential concepts in *The Poetics*, is also closely related to morality. Daniel Javitch explains that if one wishes to "find moralistic function" in Aristotle's view of poetry, "*cartharsis* offered a good deal of scope, especially since Aristotle left it quite open to interpretation" (58).

② Strabo talks also about the difference between the education of children and adults, and the different mental development among adults. While assuring the education of children, illiterate, uneducated and "half-educated" men with "pleasing myths" and "fear-inspiring myths," Strabo suggests using philosophy for the well-educated "few." Strabo believes poetry to be "more useful to the people at large" in education than philosophy (1. 2. 8).

prose writers like Aristotle and Cicero, stress the function of morality in literature. As Daniel Javitch says, "Most ancient critics (Horace, among them) measured the effectiveness and value of a poetic work in terms of external standards of truthfulness and of morality," and "not by the degree to which it contributed to realizing what Aristotle took to be its particular form and function" (53). Indeed, the classical author to influence the English Renaissance most was not Aristotle, nor Cicero, although they were of course known and influential. For the several generations around the time of Shakespeare and Jonson, it was Horace whose teachings would be most important.

i. Horace's *Ars Poetica*

English Renaissance literary theory was dominated by classical criticism. As T. W. Baldwin points out, then "the classics were the standard of perfection" (6). Jonson encourages William Drummond to read Quintillian, Horace, Pliny, Tacitus, Juvenal, and Martial (III: 132). He also tells Drummond that "Quintilianes 6. 7. 8. bookes, were not only to be read but altogither digested. Juvenal, Perse, Horace, Martiall for delight & so was Pindar" (ibid. 136). In Jonson's library,[1] there were three volumes of Plato's books, one of Aristotle's, and books of the Greek and Roman dramatists, poets and philosophers. Although he was known to have had less education in the classics compared with Jonson,

---

[1] Jonson's library, or "libraries" in Anne Barton's words, famously caught fire in 1623 and "much was destroyed" (113). For more about the fire and destruction, see Barton, *Dramatist*, pp. 113, 219, 235; Donaldson, *Life*, pp. 367-70; McEvoy, p. 5, and certainly, Jonson's own poem, "An Execration upon Vulcan," collected in his *Underwood* 43.

Shakespeare, according to his excellent biographer, Park Honan, knew "more than most contemporary playwrights," "knew a good library before he wrote his *Henry VI* plays," and "could hardly have made deft use of historical sources without developing his reading habits after grammar school." Shakespeare had "a milieu not indifferent to learning and to history" as "one warm, favourable catalyst for an emergence of his talent" (68). Specifically, Shakespeare read Quintilian, enjoyed Arthur Golding's version of Ovid's *Metamorphoses*, and studied Cicero, Virgil and Horace in Upper School (Honan 52-56; Rowse 65). Both Jonson and Shakespeare were certainly familiar with the classics, either through directly reading Greek and Latin or through reading English translations.

But, among all the classical writers, Horace is the best known to both Jonson and Shakespeare in terms of poetics. Shakespeare, as Chiron says in *Titus Andronicus*, "knows it [a Horace verse] well (IV. ii. 22), although the Horace Shakespeare knew well is the Horace of *Odes*, not of the *Satires*" (Rowse 38). [1] According to Ann Moss, in sixteenth century Europe, including England, as far as poetics was concerned, "by far the most influential, as well as the most comprehensive, prototype was the *Ars Poetica* of Horace, in which the humanists had an authoritative text on poetic composition to set beside the old and the newly discovered rhetorical treatises of Cicero" (66). Moss observes that because

---

[1] See Perry D. Westbrook, pp. 392-8, for an analysis of Horace's influence on Shakespeare's *Antony and Cleopatra*, in which, Westbrook argues, the character of Cleopatra is almost certainly indebted to Horace's *Cleopatra Ode*.

of its popularity, ① the margins and appendices of the editions of *Ars Poetica* became "vehicles for transmitting the substance of quintessentially literary debates: on the related arts of discourse, rhetoric, and poetry; on the problematics of truth and fiction; on the ethical value of poetry, and, by implication, of all literature." She says that "the contributions of our commentators to these debates were rarely original, but it was they who set up the debates, and did so around the most widely read didactic work on literary composition" (76). ② Andrew Laird argues that "the importance Horace attaches to elegance, decorum, hard work, innovation, and the imitation of good models (in the *Satires* and in other epistles as well as in *Ars Poetica*) very much affected the way poetry came to be regarded and judged from the Renaissance onwards" (32). D. A. Russell asserts that as one of those "*aurei libelli* [golden booklets] treasured in medieval and Renaissance education as containing a particularly potent distillation of the wisdom of antiquity," *Ars Poetica* was for long "the most accessible source of the basic tenets of classical criticism: the doctrines of propriety and genre, and the underlying assumption that the poet, like the orator, sets himself a particular task of persuasion and is to be judged by his success in bringing it off" (339). As

---

① One important proof of the popularity of *Ars Poetica* is found in such phrases that have come into everyday English from the poem as "*in medias res*" and "Homer nodding." For more about common phrases coming from *Ars Poetica*, see D. A. Russell, p. 345.

② Cicero's *De oratore*, *Orator*, and *Brutus*, according to John O. Ward, can "lay a greater claim to being 'discoveries' of the fifteenth century (following the recovery of a complete manuscript of all three in the cathedral library of Lodi in 1421)." However, while Cicero was "not entirely unknown" to the Middle Ages, such Ciceronian treatises had "little impact upon the medieval rhetorical curriculum" (79).

Joseph Loewenstein says, it would be "difficult to over-estimate the influence" of *Ars Poetica* "on the literary culture of Renaissance England" (84). [1]

The unrivalled predominance of *Ars Poetica* in the Renaissance is a result of the importance of didacticism in literature. *Ars Poetica* remained "foundational" because its "didacticism fitted humanist pedagogical concern for a civic and moral rhetoric," because it was always or for many centuries "integral to the idea of tragedy" and because it was available (Reiss 237). According to George K. Hunter, literary criticism in the Renaissance was "tied to the humanist project of recuperating a classical literary and cultural order," and the principal interest of English literary criticism was in the "moral status of literature" (248). Consequently, when the already influential Horace met the English Renaissance need to morally educate with literature, *Ars Poetica*, an instructive epistle in the form of a poem, became a literary superhero.

Despite his "discursive and occasionally personal tone of an Epistle" and his lack of "completeness, precision, and logical order of a well-constructed treatise" (Fairclough 442), Horace repeatedly argues for a didactic purpose in poetry, especially dramatic poetry, because, according to Rushton

---

[1] The Horatian *Art of Poetry* was so popular and influential that even ideas in Aristotle's *Poetics*, incompatible with Horace's *Ars Poetica*, may have become commonplace and then been transferred to Horace by some intermediate sources. Or, in Ann Moss's words, Horace's text was opened up by its Renaissance commentaries to "absorb" Aristotle's ideas "much the same way as earlier commentaries had absorbed the medieval grammarians" (72). For more about the neglect, marginality and refraction of Aristotle's *Poetics* and the continuous popularity of *Ars Poetica* in antiquity through the Middle Ages to the mid-sixteenth century, see Javitch, pp. 53-57; Moss, pp. 71-76.

Fairclough, "fully one-third" of the whole poem is concerned with drama (442). It is Horace's didactic emphasis that we care about most for the subject in question in the present study.

Talking about good verse, Horace tells Telephus and Peleus, the Piso brothers, that it is "not enough" for a good poem to have just "beautie"; it must also have "a sweet delight / To worke the hearers minds, still, to their plight" (140-42). ① A poem is good not only because of its beautiful words, style, but also because of its moral to "worke" the hearers' minds, to engage, and affect them, and according to Fairclough's translation, even "lead the hearer's soul" (99).

When talking about plays as an art of imitation, Horace writes that sometimes even though a poem has no "grace, weight, art" and is not "in rimes," but "with specious places, and being humour'd right / More strongly takes the people with delight, / And better stayes them there" than a

---

① The citations of Horace's *Ars Poetica* in this book are from Jonson's translation, if not otherwise specified. Jonson's translation, according to Herford & the Simpson, was first published in 1640 in two versions. One was in his Duodecimo collection of his *Poems*, the other, a "carefully revised" one, in the Folio (VIII, 299). The citations are from the Folio revised version. Colin Burrow calls Jonson's translation of the Horatian poem "extremely literal" (3). Victoria Moul considers Jonson's translation of Horace "in varying ways and to varying degrees 'Jonsonian'" and "unfashionably 'close'" (8-9). Because this is a discussion of Horace's influence on Jonson, it is fitting to cite Jonson's translation of the Latin poet. However, I would like to provide another celebrated translation of *Ars Poetica* by Ross S. Kilpatrick, a twentieth-century classicist, in case a comparison is needed. Lines 140-42 in Jonson's translation, lines 99-100 in Horace's original (there is a big difference between the line numbers of Jonson's translation and Horace's original), are translated by Kilpatrick as "it is not enough that poetry be noble: it should impart delight, and transport the listener as it likes" (99). Other citations of *Ars Poetica* in the *notes* are also from Kilpatrick's translation if not otherwise stated.

matterless poem with only pleasant sounds (455-60). [1] Here "specious places" refer to beautiful passages, ones with instructive morals (Kilpatrick "splendid maxims"); "humour'd right," consistent with the ideas in Jonson's humour comedies, means correctly sketched characters. Therefore, a play with good moral teachings and decorous characters, although without good craftsmanship or powerful language, can give people more pleasure and hold them better than a play with only beautiful or mellifluous language.

When he writes about the function of the chorus in a play, Horace says that it "must favour good men" and be a "friend" to them; it must "both sway, and bend / The angry, and love those that feare to offend"; it must "praise the spare diet, wholesome justice, lawes, / Peace, and the open ports, that peace doth cause"; it must "hide faults, pray to the Gods, and wish aloud / Fortune would love the poore, and leave the proud" (280-6). [2] Let me cite Fairclough's rendition again to clarify Jonson's translation of these lines:

> It should side with the good and give friendly counsel; sway the angry and cherish the righteous. It should praise the fare of a modest board, praise wholesome justice, law, and peace with her open gates; should keep secrets, and pray and beseech the gods that fortune may return to the unhappy, and depart from the proud.
>
> (193-201)

---

[1] Kilpatrick: "From time to time a piece which has splendid maxims and a fine moral tone, even though lacking charm and without weight and craftsmanship, will give more pleasure and interest to people than verses devoid of substance, and musical triflesf" (309).

[2] Kilpatrick: "Let it favour the good, and give friendly advice; control the angry and support those afraid to hope. Let it praise the modest table, the benefits of justice and laws, let it conceal acts done, and pray to the gods that Fortune may return to the wretched and depart from the proud" (193).

Horace's words reflect a strong emphasis on teaching the audience through poetic justice: let the good stay good and be rewarded well, control anger, cherish the righteous, praise moderate diet, help the unfortunate and keep away from pride.

Then Horace summarizes his central ideas of good poetry:

> Poëts would either profit, or delight,
> Or mixing sweet, and fit, teach life the right. ①
>
> (477-78)

Poets should either instruct or delight, and it will be better if they give both pleasure and instruction.

Horace again and again stresses the moral aspect of poetry. He exhorts that good poetry needs not only to be beautiful and have the right diction and style. A poem must have the right moral to instruct the people; a play must have appropriate characters and correct ideas to lead the audience to moral behavior. Poetry must both delight and teach the hearers. As Leon Golden points out, "At the core of Horace's AP [*Ars Poetica*] is a profound respect for the importance and high purpose of poetry" (396). As George Kennedy says, Horace's "classic statement" that the poet "should both please and edify," developed out of Aristotle's "argument, ethos, and pathos," has been the "nucleus of what became the orthodox view of later times" (204). Kennedy is right. Horace taught the English Renaissance authors the importance of moral didacticism in dramatic poetry.

---

① Kilpatrick: "Poets wish either to benefit or delight, or else say things at once pleasant and suited to life" (333).

ii. Philip Sidney's *Defense of Poesy*

When Sir Philip Sidney died in 1586, Shakespeare was twenty-two years old and Jonson only fourteen. Sidney was not a personal friend of either Shakespeare or Jonson. However, Sidney, whose manuscripts were published posthumously and "dominated literary culture" in the 1590s (Gavin Alexander: xix), was a solid influence on both of them. [1] According to Kenneth Muir, Shakespeare derived his Gloucester subplot, "a perfect parallel to the Lear Story" (145) from Sidney's prose tale of the Paphlagonian King in the *Arcadia*. Park Honan remarks that Shakespeare's romances, something he used to cater for "upper sections of the play-going market" which his troupe needed to hold, have "affinities" with Sidney's *Arcadia* (365). A. L. Rowse points out that Shakespeare "clearly was reading Sidney and Spenser," although he was "no theorist" nor did he belong to their circle, the " conoscenti [connoisseurs] of Leicester House " (77). Also, Catherine Belsey observes that Shakespeare the dramatist draws on "strategies developed in Astrophil and Stella" to "construct the illusion of dialogue" (89). However, in aesthetic theory, Shakespeare, unlike

---

[1] According to Gavin Alexander, had Sidney not died prematurely, "his works might never have been printed" (xix). Sidney's works were circulated in manuscripts only among family members and close friends in his lifetime. For more about Sidney's publication, see Alexander, pp. xix-xxvii; Albert S. Cook, pp. xii-xv. However, the social connections of the Sidney family must have been extensive to let the message of *The Defence of Poesy* out. According to Albert S. Cook, "Sidney's *Defense* must have been extensively circulated in manuscript before its publication in 1595" because "extensive quotations from it are found" in George Puttenham's *Art of English Poesy* (1589), Sir John Harington's *Apology for Poetry* (prefixed to the first edition of his translation of Ariosto's *Orlando Furioso*, 1591), and Francis Meres's *Palladis Tamia* (1598) (xxxix).

Jonson, does not seem to have been much influenced by Sidney's *Defense of Poesy*,① although, according to Felix Schelling, the treatise "far outweighs all similar contemporary work [on poetic theory]" (223).

Sidney's impact on Jonson is wide and profound. Jonson personally interacted with the Sidney family. Gavin Alexander says that Jonson was "clearly on good terms with a number of Sidneys and Herberts" (143).② Anne Barton notes that Sidney "obviously obsessed" Jonson as "the realization of a personal ideal": the good poet and a conspicuously good man, whose life and art were in "harmonious accord," which Jonson "prized and found it so difficult in his own case to achieve" (*Dramatist* 4). To Jonson, Sidney was a poet at whose "great birth" "all the Muses met" (*The Forrest* II. 14). Jonson calls Sidney a "great master of wit, and language," in whom "all vigour of Invention, and strength of judgement met" (*Discoveries* ll. 908-9). Jonson sometimes also honors Sidney in his plays. He puts Sidney together with Plato and Heliodorus of Emesa (third century AD, author of the influential Greek romance *Aethiopica. The New Inne*, III. ii. 205-06). In Jonson's *Epicoene*, Dauphine defends poets by

---

① This treatise of Philip Sidney has had three titles. According to Gavin Alexander, *An Apology for Poetry* is the title of the unauthorized 1595 printing; *A Defence of Poetry*, a title invented in the Clarendon edition (1595); and *The Defence of Poesy*, the title with which Sidney's work appeared in its authorized 1595 printing and all subsequent reprintings (xiii).

② Mary Sidney, Sidney's sister, who "used her pen to celebrate the Dudley/Sidney alliance" and helped to promote the "glory" of the Sidney family (Hannay; x), married Henry Herbert, 2 nd Earl of Pembroke, in April 1577, but the connection between the Sidneys and the Herberts goes far beyond this marriage. See Brennan & Kinnamon, pp. xviii-xxiii, for more. In addition to having the Sidneys as patrons, Jonson was also tutor to William Sidney, Philip Sidney's brother, Robert's son. For details of Jonson as tutor to the Sidney family, see Rathmell, pp. 250-60. See also Gavin Alexander, pp. 143-47, 189-91, for Jonson's other interactions with the Sidney family, including with Robert Sidney.

telling Sir John Daw and Clerimont that "the noble Sidney liues by his [verse], and the noble family not asham'd" (II. iii. 117-18).

In terms of literary theory, Sidney's *Defence of Poesy* was "predictably appealing," and was one of the places where the minds of Sidney and Jonson "genuinely engaged" (Barton, *Dramatist* 5). [1]

Counterattacking *The School of Abuse* (1579), a "pleasant invective" on the surface but "venomous attack" in essence against poets, pipers, players, jesters as "caterpillars of the commonwealth" by Stephen Gosson (1554 – 1624), who dedicated it to Sidney without his permission (Leitch et al. 323), Sidney in his *Defence of Poesy* echoes Aristotle and Horace in their attitudes towards poets. Sidney claims that the goal of poetry, as "an art of imitation," that is, "a representing, counterfeiting, or figuring forth; to speak metaphorically," poetry's purpose is "to teach and delight" (9: 12-16). [2] Sidney divides poetry into "three general kinds" (9: 17): the religious (chiefly Hebrew and ethnic hymns and odes), the didactic or philosophical (moral, astronomical, historical, natural), and the creative, poetry by the "right poets," poetry in the strictest and truest

---

[1] Jonson and Sidney's poetic ideas often did not match. Anne Barton remarks that "most of Sidney's work" made Jonson "distinctly uneasy" (*Dramatist* 5). Jonson expresses his disappointment in his *Conversations* with Drummond that Sidney "did not keep a Decorūm jn making every one speak as well [beautifully] as himself" (3-5), and that Sidney makes every man "speak as well as themselves, forgetting decorūm" (611-12). In *Every Man out of his Humour*, Saviolina and Fungoso read *Arcadia* and find favorite phrases for their discourse. However, as half-wits, Saviolina and Fungoso's admiration of *Arcadia* is but making fun of Sidney's book, a mockery that "demeaned both them [Saviolina and Fungoso] and it [*Arcadia*]" (Barton, *Dramatist* 208).

[2] The first number in all citations from Sidney's *Defense* in this thesis refers to the page, and the second, the line or lines on the page.

sense (9: 17-10: 11). It is with the third of these that Sidney's *Defense of Poesy* is most concerned.

For Sidney, the "right poets" "most properly do imitate to teach and delight" (10: 20-21). To teach and delight are the purposes of creative poets. Sidney says,

> For these, indeed, do merely make to imitate, and imitate both to delight and teach, and delight to move men to take that goodness in hand, which without delight they would fly as from a stranger; and teach to make them know that goodness whereunto they are moved: —which being the noblest scope to which ever any learning was directed, yet want there not idle tongues as to bark at them.
>
> (10: 28-35)

Sidney stresses that mimetic as creative poetry is, its aims are "merely" to teach and to delight. Poetry needs to delight in order to "move men" to take goodness, and without delight, men would "fly" from poetry "as from a stranger." Poetry also must teach in order to make men understand what goodness they are moved unto. Therefore, both aims, to delight, and to teach, are necessary.

As for comedy, Sidney remarks that it is "an imitation of the common errors of our life," and it "representeth [those errors] in the most ridiculous and scornful sort that may be" so that it is "impossible" that "any beholder can be content to be such a one" (28: 1-5). Comedy handles "the filthiness of evil in our private and domestical matters" so that we get "an experience," "a great foil to perceive the beauty of virtue" (28: 7-11). Therefore, Sidney requests that "the right use of comedy will . . . by nobody be blamed" (28: 25-26). Sidney sees the use of laughter in comedy, but he stresses the difference between laughter and delight: "We laugh at deformed creatures, wherein certainly we cannot delight. We delight in good chances, we laugh at mischances" (51: 1-3). Therefore, he warns that "all the end of the comical part be not upon such scornful matters as stir laughter only." The end of poetry should stir laughter with "delightful teaching" (51: 21). Sidney constantly and consistently argues for teaching and delight as the goals of literature.

In summary, by fusing "Horatian and Aristotelian literary criticism" (Golden 395), and "adapting from classical and medieval models," Philip Sidney's *Defense of Poesy* "enjoys significance far beyond its occasion for its synthesis of the Renaissance understanding of classical literary theory" (Leitch et al. 323). As Vincent B. Leitch and others point out, Sidney's view of poetry as an art of mimesis is "based on a religious belief in providential design" which means that the universe is the product of divine wisdom (325); therefore, the poet is to imitate the universe to teach and delight the reader.

II. Jonson's didacticism

i. Jonson's theories on dramatic didacticism

Thanks perhaps to his learning in the classics and his debt to medieval and contemporary writers such as Chaucer, Dante and Sidney, Jonson was a literary moralist who strongly advocated and practiced the didactic function of poetry. Jonson told Drummond that " of all stiles he [Jonson] loved most to be named honest" (*Conversations*

631). Felix E. Schelling calls Jonson a "great moralist" in despising contemporary popular literature and advocating for the judicious (232). Herford and the Simpsons tell us that "Jonson, a lifelong student of Horace, Juvenal, and Martial, followed their tradition" (IX: 397). According to Katharine Eisaman Maus, Jonson has significantly inherited in poetics from such Roman moralists as Seneca, Cicero and Horace who most appreciate virtues of temperance, self-reliance, fortitude, and altruistic self-sacrifice (*Ben Jonson* 5). Jonson plainly exemplifies his didactic theories in his works.

1. Epistles, inductions and prologues

In contrast with Shakespeare who never includes an induction to his plays to pronounce dramatic theories, Jonson often uses epistles, inductions, prologues, and even epilogues to explicitly explain or stress his critical ideas. A reading of such Jonsonian passages reveals that Jonson's dramatic theories can be summed up by one word: classicism. In the context of Jonson, classicism, according to Victoria Moul, means "among other things, self-conscious imitation of the style and form of Greek and Roman writers, including Juvenal, Seneca, Tacitus, Martial and Cicero among the Romans, and Lucian, Homer and Pindar among the Greeks," and for Jonson, "imitation" carries "a moral as well as aesthetic force" (2, n.4). [1] This is easily understood in the light of the previous discussion of Jonson's indebtedness to the classical authors. Moul claims that Jonson's "classicism"

---

[1] However Jonson purports to imitate the ancients, he is no slave to the Greek or Roman authors, who, he tells us in his *Timber, or Discoveries*, despite their supreme importance conducive "to letters . . . to all the observations of the Ancients, wee [contemporary English writers] have our owne experience. " The ancients are "Guides, not Commanders" (129-39).

is a "critical commonplace" (ibid.).

Among all classical authors, Jonson's relationship with Horace is the most special and significant. Horace is Jonson's "chief literary model, the man whose memory he honoured and whose achievement he claimed to outdo" (Moul 2). Moul even remarks that "Jonson liked to think of himself as Horace" (2). When his *New Inn* received hostile critical reception, Jonson blamed the critics and called himself "thine owne *Horace*" in the "Ode to Himself" appended to the play (43). The Horatian dictum of profit and pleasure is central to Jonson's poetics.

As a meticulous author who went over every detail of the printing of his texts,[1] Jonson put his most favorite Latin quotation from Horace's *Ars Poetica* on both the Quarto and Folio title-pages of *Volpone*: "simul et iucunda et idonea dicere vitae [1. 334, Jonson's translation: Poets would either profit or delight, / Or mixing sweet and fit, teach life the right]" (Donaldson, *Ben Jonson* 617). The printing of his favorite maxim on the title pages of his plays epitomizes Jonson's steadfast belief in Horace's ideas. In the text of his plays as well, Jonson typically remembers to stress the profit and pleasure theory. He "characteristically" uses the "inductions" of his plays to lecture his audience on this subject (Herford & Simpsons, IX: 406). In the Grex (chorus) after the Second Sounding of *Every Man out of his Humour*, his second successful play to be performed and first to be printed, Jonson promises to "mixe with attentive

---

[1] For Jonson's scrutiny over the publication of his texts, see Herford & Simpson, vol. IX, pp. 13-86, especially pp. 45-52.

auditors in industrie" who will "joyne their profit with their pleasure" (200-22). In *Epicoene, or the Silent Woman*, one of his most successful plays, Jonson tells his audience that "the ends" of all playwrights "are, or should be, to profit, and delight" (2nd Prologue 1-2). In his *Bartholomew Fair*, Jonson, while echoing Philip Sidney's identification of the poet as a "maker," hopes in the Prologue to the King (who was present in the theater) that his play will give the audience "a fairing, true delight" (11-12). In this context, "a fairing, true delight" carries Jonson's usual moral and didactic tone, because, in his Epilogue to the same performance of *Bartholomew Fair*, Jonson says he wants to make sure that the King has seen a pleasant play. He asks the King to judge if he will "rage, or licence breake, / Or be prophane, or make prophane men speake" (7-8). Sometimes, when Jonson does not try to expound the Horatian theory in an "induction" or prologue, he stresses it, as in the passage just quoted, in an epilogue. When *The Staple of Newes* ends, Jonson immediately reminds the audience that they should have "seene the Makers double scope, / To *profit*, and *delight*" (Epilogue 1-2). Again and again, Jonson points out to his audience that dramatic poets must blend the double purpose of profit and delight in their plays. In other words, with Jonson, it is not enough for plays just to please the audience; good plays must at the same time teach the audience moral lessons.

Besides being a classicist, another important reason for Jonson to assert the didactic function of literature was his detestation of popular works. For Jonson, popular literature, especially popular drama, meant cheap pleasure obtained from such crude devices as loud noise, profanation and violence that cater to the low tastes of the audience. In the dedicatory Epistle to Oxford and Cambridge Universities prefaced to *Volpone*, "the most important document we possess of his [Jonson's] notions in criticism, and of his mind about his own art" (Herford & Simpson II: 49), Jonson complains that in his age "*Poetrie, and the Professors of it heare so ill* [foul language], *on all sides*" (10-12). One of the reasons is "*too-much licence of* Poetasters" has "*much deform'd their Mistris*" (14-15). Because of the "*manifold, and manifest ignorance*," and the "*petulancy*" of poetasters, the "*diuine*" skill of poetry has fallen "*under the least contempt*," and "*nothing*" of the "*dignitie of Poet*" but "*the abused name*" remains. "*In* dramatick, *or* (*as they terme it*) *stage-poetrie, nothing but ribaldry, profanation, blasphemy, all licence of offence to God, and man, is practis'd*" (15-38). In addition to using *Volpone* for the "instruction, and amendment" of audiences, Jonson reaffirms in the play's prefactory epistle that "*the principall end of poesie*" is "*to informe men, in the best reason of liuing*," and it is fitting that "*the office of a* comick-Poet, *to imitate iustice, and instruct to life, as well as puritie of language, or stirre vp gentle affections*" (103-23). With critically negative reference to his contemporaries including Shakespeare,[①] Jonson pledges he will "*raise the despis'd head of* poetrie *againe, and stripping her out of those rotten and base rags*" (129-30). Good dramatic poetry must be able to give pleasure and profit, or to entertain and teach, with proper moral example and language.

In this famous epistle prefaced to *Volpone*, Jonson also points out the qualities of a good poet. Dissatisfied with his contemporaries whose "manners" and "natures" are both "inuerted," Jonson says that an impartial and upright poet must first be a "good man," who is able to "informe youngmen to all good disciplines, inflame growne-men to all great vertues, keepe old-men in their best and supreme state, or as they decline to child-hood, recouer them to their first strength." Jonson believes that only from a "good man" can come forth "the interpreter, and arbiter of nature, a teacher of things diuine, no lesse then humane, a master in manners." Also, a "good man" who is "no subiect for pride, and ignorance" can alone or with a few "effect the businesse of man-kind" (20-34). A poet needs first to be a good man because he is to inform the youth of good disciplines, encourage adults to embrace great virtues and keep the old in their best state as a right interpreter and arbiter of nature

---

① As Anne Barton explains, during the 1590s, Jonson "developed a distinctive poetic and (more particularly) a distinctive comic mode by reacting against a generalized Elizabethan norm" and became in this respect "the exact opposite" of Shakespeare, who "forged his own style during the last decade of the sixteenth century by assimilating and then transcending the native tradition" (*Dramatist* 6). Jonson in *Every Man in his Humour* in the 1616 Folio edition, as suggested by G. A. Wilkes in his edition of Ben Jonson's plays, adds a Prologue and alludes to characters like Caliban as "monsters" (l. 30, note). *The Tempest* was first performed in 1611. James Shapiro seconds Wilkes' opinion (*Rival Playwrights* 153).

and a teacher of divine things. Clearly, Jonson's emphasis on the good poet being first a good man is completely in line with his constant affirmation on the educational purposes of poetry.

Jonson's insistence on the Horatian principle of poetry as providing both profit and pleasure is also harmonious with the English Renaissance ideas synthesized in Sidney's *Defence of Poesy*. This is also one of the reasons that Jonson was held as the preeminent English neo-classicist of his age. In fact, he was also considered such even among the English Romantics who, as shown in Chapter One, raised Shakespeare to the throne of literature and reduced Jonson to the lowest point ever. Even in the age of bardolatry, Jonson was able to find support. Coleridge identified Jonson's point of a good poet being a good man with Strabo's writing and commented that he agreed with Jonson that "there can be no great poet who is not a good man, though not, perhaps, a *goody* [*OED*: good in a weak or sentimental way] man." Coleridge says that the poet's heart must be "pure," and he must have "learned to look into his own heart, and sometimes to look *at* it; for how can he who is ignorant of his own heart know anything of, or be able to move, the heart of any one else?" (245)

Jonson not only stresses the morally instructive function of literature, but also discusses in detail the technicalities of dramatic poetry. As will be pointed out in Chapter Four, Jonson tries to give an accurate definition and application of the humour theory in his plays. As Percy Simpson asserts, Jonson "took care" to prefix "the seuerall Characters of euery Person" to the text of *Every Man out of his Humour* "to prevent any misunderstanding" (lv). In *Cynthia's Revels*, Jonson went further and included eight character sketches in the text and "thus forced his analysis on the playgoer" (Simpson lvi). And again, in the Prologue of *Every Man in his Humour*, after talking about the "deedes, and language" and "persons" for comedy, Jonson claims that comedy, showing "an Image of the times," should "sport with humane follies, not with crimes"; and by "follies" Jonson means "our popular errors" (21-26). Such matter for comedy is a direct response, as discussed earlier in this chapter, to Sidney's opinion in his *Defence of Poesy* that comedy is "an imitation of the common errors of our life" (28: 1-2). In Marvin Carlson's words, these ideas of Jonson are repetition "in much abridged form" of Sidney's "arguments for the unities" and echoes his "aim of comedy" (84).

In his later comedies, Jonson continues to hold to his principle of entertainment and instruction. In *The Staple of News*, Jonson asks the audience to distinguish between "Poetique elues" who "dable in the inke / And defile quills" and real "Poets" who can "thinke, / Conceiue, expresse, and steere the soules of men," and can "instruct your youth, / And keep your acme in the state of truth" (Prologue, 19-26). Still dissatisfied with this warning that good poets should teach moral lessons, Jonson returns to his advocacy at the close of the play. He explicitly intends to ensure that the audience sees his "*double scope*," which is "*to profit and delight*" (Epilogue 1-2). In *The New Inn*, the last play whose proofs were read by its author, and a play whose author "turned away from the popular morality tradition" (Barton, *Dramatist* 258), Jonson sets out to warn his audience in a polemical tone against their poor taste, as if he foresees the unpopularity of this play. He metaphorically tells the audience that if some meat is set to a "*wrong taste*" and so does not taste good, the meat is not to blame; instead, the mouth is "*displac'd*" and its "*sick palat*" should be removed. The reason for such a wrong taste is the audience have been feeding "*too much*" on "*sharpe, or sweet*" in a "*weake, sick, queasie age.*" Jonson requests the audience to "*vnderstand, /Concoct, digest*" his "*meat*," that is, his play (Prologue 7-23). *The New Inn* haplessly failed at first performance. Indignant, Jonson wrote "*The iust indignation the Author tooke at the vulgar censure of his Play, by some malicious spectators, begat this following Ode to himselfe.*" This diatribe was appended to the play at publication, blaming the audience as " having no taste" because their "appetites are dead" (42, 44). However, Jonson was not beaten. He encouraged himself later in the " Ode" to take "thine owne Horace," " strike that disdaine-full heate / Throughout, to their defeate " (43, 46-48). In Martin Wiggins's words, " Jonson was most comfortable with established and academically respected forms" (106). He always believed in his poetry and his poetic principle of profit and delight.

2. *Timber, or Discoveries*

As " the greatest English literary critic of his time " (Steward 175), and "the first English dramatist to produce a significant body of critical commentary" (Carlson 84), Jonson wrote his *Timber, or Discoveries* as a commonplace book on a wide range of topics from social manners, oratory, education of the young, writing skills, poetry, painting to the art of drama. This book is the "last major work of English Renaissance criticism" (Carlson 86). Jonson's ideas in this book are authoritative opinions, although, as Stephen Orgel has said, they are "rarely" Jonson's ("Jonson" 140).

Jonson's diverse ideas in *Timber* are universally didactic. He teaches about money and poverty, saying wisely that "money never made any man rich, but his mind" (1373). He warns the reader against avarice and the pursuing earthly things, questioning the need of "silver dishes, multitudes of Waiters, delicate Pages, perfum'd Napkins" (1380-91). He exhorts us to watch out for obsession with "too much desire and greedinesse" which can make the body "unfit, or unprofitable" (1470-71). When he gives instructions on training a good poet, one of the things he recommends is wide but selective reading. He suggests that the poet "must read many; but, ever the best, and choisest." By "the best" and "the choisest," Jonson means "those, that can teach him any thing, hee must ever account his masters, and reverence." Specifically, Horace and Aristotle "deserve to bee the first in estimation" because Aristotle, "hee that taught him [Horace]," is "the first accurate *Criticke*, and truest Judge; nay, the greatest *Philosopher*, the world ever had" (2507-13).

However, what concerns us most in *Timber* here are Jonson's remarks on poetry, especially drama. Jonson follows the classical writers and his predecessor Philip Sidney in defining poetry as an art of imitation, representing properly the life of man in nature. He says, poetry, like painting, is "busie about imitation" (1510); "A Poet is ... a Maker, or a fainer: His Art, an Art of imitation, or faining; expressing the life of man in fit measure, numbers, and harmony, according to Aristotle" (2347-50). More importantly, Jonson holds, as he always does, that a poet must be a moral teacher, not just someone who writes. He remarks, "hee is call'd a Poet, not hee which writeth in measure only; but that fayneth and formeth a fable, and writes things like the Truth" (2347-54). "Truth" in Jonson's usage is not a philosophical but a moral term. He blames the moral defects of Euripides's plays by comparing the tragedian to Aristophanes: "many things in Euripides hath Aristophanes wittily reprehended; not out of Art, but out of Truth. For, Euripides is sometimes peccant [guilty of moral fault], as he is most times perfect" (2574-76).

Jonson considers the poet closest to the orator because of their similar function in expressing "all his virtues" (2528-29). And the comic poet, especially, is the very closest among the poets to the orator because he "chiefly excels" in "moving the minds of men, and stirring of affections" (2531-34). After pointing out the similarities between the poet, especially the comic poet, and the orator based on their moral merit, Jonson stresses the Horatian literary principle he always advocates: "The parts of a Comedie are the same with a Tragedie, and the end is partly the same. For, they both delight, and teach" (2625-27).

For Jonson, "delight" means to entertain, to raise pleasure, but it does not solely mean to raise laughter. Again, Jonson echoes Sidney to differentiate delight and laughter in comedies. Sidney claims that it is "very wrong" for comedians to think "there is no delight without laughter" because though laughter may come "with delight" but "not of delight, as though delight should be the cause of laughter. " For Sidney, there is a kind of "contrariety" between laughter and delight: "Delight hath a joy in it either permanent or present; laughter hath only a scornful tickling" (23-34). Jonson also praises delight but despises laughter: "Nor, is the moving of laughter always the end of Comedy, that is rather a fowling for the peoples delight, or their fooling" (*Timber* 2629-31). To Jonson, laughter, as he cites Aristotle, means "to seeme ridiculous," which is "a part of dishonesty and foolish" (*Timber*, 2640-42). He believes that "true and naturall" jests "seldome raise laughter, with the beast, the multitude," who "love nothing, that is right, and proper" (2658-61). Clearly Jonson is too arrogant in associating the multitude with the beast. He is too readily critical of the commoners and as well as of the poets of his day; as Russ McDonald comments, Jonson "is nothing if not critical" (54). Jonson criticizes his audience and his contemporaries because he is dissatisfied with them for catering too much to lower tastes and for failing to practice the dual function of poetry: to entertain and to teach.

To be sure, Jonson is no empty literary theorizer who is only good at systemizing principles. As he comments on being a critic in *Timber*, "to judge of Poets is only the facultie of Poets; and not of all Poets, but the best" (2078-79), he is conscious that he takes labor "in teaching others," and he is also ready to bring his "Precepts into practise" (1755-57). Having surveyed Jonson's theatrical ideas on didacticism in literature, we can now discuss how he practiced what had preached.

ii. Jonson's portrayal of humour as didacticism

The "continuity" of Jonson's ideas of humour can be read from his own plays. In *Every Man in his Humour* (1598), Jonson defines humour this way:

> Cob. Humor? macke, I thinke it bee so indeed: what is this humor? it's some rare thing I warrant.
>
> Piso. Marrie, ile tell thee what it is (as tis generally receiued in these daies) it is a monster bred in a man by selfe loue, and affectation, and fed by folly. ①

(III. i. 154-58)

Here Jonson's definition of humour is compared to a monstrous vice bred in a man. He stresses its self-love, affectation and foolish qualities, all moral aspects of the term.

In *Every Man out of his Humour*, Jonson gives a more detailed definition of *humour* than the one in 1598:

> So in euery humane body,
> The choller, melancholy, flegme, and bloud,
> By reason that they flow continually

---

① In his *Omniana*, Coleridge says that Jonson's borrowing from Strabo that a good poet must first be a good man is a "just and noble sentiment" (304). Jonson made extensive revision to the 1601 Quarto of *Every Man in his Humour* for it to be included in the 1616 Folio. The following quotation, taken from the 1616 Folio to compare its corresponding lines in the Quarto version, as Dutton observes, for its "neatening, tightening, and contemporary flavour [e. g. "gallantrie," as recorded by the *OED*, was first used by Shakespeare in 1606 and so was a fairly new, maybe fashionable expression in 1616]" ("Significance" 248), remains essentially the same with the original in the meaning of the idea of *humour*. Cob. Humour? mack, I thinke it bee so, indeed: what is that humour? some rare thing, I warrant. Cas. Mary, Ile tell thee, Cob: It is a gentleman-like monster, bred, in the speciall gallantrie of our time, by affectation; and fed by folly. (III. iv. 18-22)

In some one part, and are not continent,

Receiue the name of humours. Now thus farre

It may, by *Metaphore*, apply it selfe

Vnto the generall disposition:

As when some one peculiar quality

Doth so possesse a man, that it doth draw

All his affects, his spirits, and his powers,

In their confluctions, all to runne one way,

This may be truly said to be a humour.

(Induction, 98-109)

An echo of the classical and medieval physiology and psychology of humour, this analysis of the term, as pointed out by James D. Redwine, Jr., constitutes its "basic definition, a sort of keystone which supports Jonson's theory of humour characterization" (318). Jonson clearly associates his theory with that of the bodily fluids, "choller, melancholy, flegme, and bloud," and their "not continent" or continual and unconstrained mixture, as previously discussed. Then Jonson goes beyond *humour*'s physiological property to its psychological features: metaphorical application of the term to "generall disposition" (Induction 108). As Redwine notes, "disposition" here means "the prevailing aspect of one's mind as shown in behavior and in relationships with others" (318). The Elizabethan idea of disposition in relation to humour can be further seen in the characteristic adverbs associated with humours in Jonson's *Cynthia's Revels* (1600), the successor to *Every Man out of his Humour*: "To phantastikely melancholy, too slowly phlegmaticke, too lightly sanguine, or too rashly cholericke" (II. iii. 126-27).

In this light, Jonson's definition is clear enough: in the

interaction ("confluction") of the four humours, if one becomes so much that it subverts the balance among the four, then the man's "affects," "spirits," and "powers," flowing together, "all to runne one way," constitute his dominant *humour* (*Every Man out*, Induction 108). This Jonsonian definition of the psychological humour is considered by Redwine as "succinct, and a more or less precise summary of the best that had been thought and said on the subject" (318). These two aspects of *humour*, physiological and psychological, are two essential ideas of the term for Jonson.

According to Redwine, one of the "two most popular explanations" of Jonson's humours has been that "they constitute a psychology" (326). On the psychological level, Jonson's *humour* is closely linked with *passions*. Jonson says when a man is possessed by a "peculiar quality," the "peculiar quality," that is, "a true humour," draws "all his affects" (*Every Man out*, Induction 105-09). Here, "affects," according to the Oxford English Dictionary, means *affections*. In *The Passions of the Minde in Generall*, a widely read Renaissance book that Jonson prefaced, its author, Thomas Wright, says: "Those actions then which are common with us, and beasts, we call Passions, and Affections, or perturbations of the mind" (7-8), and "Passions ingender Humours, and Humours breed Passions" (64). Redwine observes that conventionally, moral philosophers of the day would point out "the intimate relationship between the passions and the humours" (328). Lily Bess Campbell, scrutinizing moral philosophy in Shakespeare's day and anatomizing passions, points out that the melancholic and choleric humours "are also represented as passions" (77). Herford and the Simpsons speak of passion as one of the three humour "currents," and "the stock Elizabethan analysis of character was the simple and summary one of the dominant trait of master-passion" (I: 339). In other words, the expressions of *melancholy*, *choler* and *passions* were interchangeable for Elizabethans.

However, Jonson's *humour* means more than physiological fluids and psychological dispositions. It includes manners, too. In 1610, when he finished his *Alchemist*, Jonson equated humour with manners:

> Our *Scene* is *London*, 'cause we would make knowne,
> No countries mirth is better then our owne.
> No clime breeds better matter, for your whore,
> Bawd, squire, impostor, many persons more,
> Whose manners, now call'd humors, feed the stage:
> And which haue still beene subiect, for the rage
> Or spleene of *comick*-writers.
>
> (Prologue 5-11)

The author says that the "manners" of London's "whore, bawd, squire, impostor, many persons more" as represented on stage are *humours*. An equation between *humours* and manners may seem off the mark to current readers in light of the traditional meaning of *humour*, but, as Redwine perceptively argues, to Jonson's contemporaries, it would have been "precise and apt" (332). Jonson himself does not reach this equation by caprice. In his last comic satire, *The Magnetic Lady* (1632), Jonson reinforces this equation:

> The *Author*, beginning his studies of this kind, with *every man in his Humour*; and after, *every man out of his*

Humour; and since, continuing in all his Playes, especially those of the *Comick* thred, whereof the *New-Inne* was the last, some recent humours still, or manners of men, that went along with the times, finding himselfe now neare the close, or shutting up of his Circle, hath phant'sied to himselfe, in *Idaea*, this Magnetick Mistris.

(Induction 99-106)

Here Jonson reinforces his meaning of humours as manners, something, he asserts, he had continually dealt with since *Every Man in his Humour*, ending with "this *Magnetick Mistris*." As Redwine keenly observes, "not only does Jonson's criticism of comic characterization begin with his theory of humours; it ends there too" (334). Jonson's moral understanding of humours as manners are thorough and constant.

Jonson's character Crites in *Cynthia's Revels* speaks of *humour* in strong moral terms:

> O how despisde and base a thing is a man,
> If he not striue t'erect his groueling thoughts
> Aboue the straine of flesh! But how more cheape
> When, euen his best and vnderstanding part,
> (The crowne, and strength of all his faculties)
> Floates like a dead drown'd bodie, on the streame
> Of vulgar humour, mixt with commonst dregs?
> I suffer for their guilt now, and my soule
> (Like one that lookes on ill-affected eyes)
> Is hurt with mere intention on their follies.

(I. v. 33-42)

On the surface, we find such terms associated with *humour* as "despisde and base," "groueling thoughts," "vulgar," "commonst dregs," "guilt," "ill-affected," and "intention on their follies," to use Redwine's words, "unmistakably moral" (321). Read more closely, the phrase "t'erect his groueling thoughts aboue the straine of flesh" and the lines "my soule / Like one that lookes on ill-affected [that is, ill-humoured] eyes / Is hurt with mere intention of their follies" immediately remind the reader of the admonitions of moral philosophers, especially the Church Fathers, with some of whom Jonson must have been familiar. [1] Crites's disquisition sounds as if it is echoing St. Augustine's warning in *De Doctrina Christiana*:

> For since it will be the case after the resurrection that the body will live for ever in a state of utmost tranquility and total subservience to the spirit, it should be our concern in this life that the tendency of the flesh is reformed and not allowed to resist the spirit with its unruly impulses.
>
> (I. 52)

We should be concerned if our low thoughts of the flesh are changed towards a wrong direction because of the "unruly impulses," i. e., inordinate desires, or excessive humours. St. Augustine suggests that man should not let his excessive humours take precedence over his love for God.

In fact, excessive humours to an Elizabethan mind would result in excessive passions. As Lily B. Campbell tells us, "it is apparent that in the thinking of the Renaissance, humours might move passions, and passions might cause the distemperature of the humours" (77). Robert Burton, four or

---

[1] For a more detailed analysis, see Redwine, pp. 321-23.

five years Jonson's junior, in the name of Democritus Junior[1] in his *Anatomy of Melancholy*, writes that the body's workings on the mind by its "bad humours" will trouble "the spirits," send "gross fumes" into the brain, and consequently disturb "the soul, and all the faculties of it, with fear, sorrow, & c." On the other hand, the co-workings of the mind's "passions and perturbations" will produce "miraculous alterations, as melancholy, despair, cruel diseases" (Part I, Sect. II, Memb. III, Subs. I). According to Burton, passions are commonly reduced into two groups: "irascible" and "concupiscible," which include "Love, Joy, Desire, Hatred, Sorrow, Feare: The rest, as Anger, Envy, Emulation, Pride, Jealousie, Anxiety, Mercy, Shame, Discontent, Despaire, Ambition, Avarice, & c." (Part I, Sect. II, Memb. III, Subs. III). Thomas Wright sums up the effects of inordinate passions:

1) Blindness of understanding,
2) Perversion of the will,
3) Alteration of humours, and
4) Maladies and diseases together with troublesomeness or disquietness of the soul.

(48, qtd. in Lily Campbell 78)

Wright's summary is a clear reflection of the Elizabethan understanding of passions as a destructive force to both the physical health and wellbeing of the soul. Lily B. Campbell points out that the "fundamental moral concern of the period" was with "the passions and the reason" (68). Such

---

[1] Burton's selection of the name Democritus was suitable to the tone of his work. Democritus, the laughing philosopher, was the first to *anatomize* the particles that constitute all matter. And *his Anatomy*, a medical treatise on the surface, is a satire in effect.

connotations of passions are no doubt moral. The implications of *passions* are even more apparent in writings of moral philosophy than in superficially medical works. Bishop Edward Reynolds (1599 – 1676) thus writes of the difference between the passions of sinful men and those of Christ:

> The *Passions* of sinfull men are many times like the tossings of the Sea, which bringeth up *mire and durt*; but the *Passions* of *Christ* were like the shaking of pure Water in a cleane Vessell, which though it be thereby *troubled*, yet is it not *fouled* at all.
>
> (40)

How Crites's comparison of humours to "commonst dregs" (Jonson, *Cynthia's Revels* I. v. 39) sound like Bishop Reynolds's description of sinful men's passions! Gail Kern Paster has perfectly paraphrased Reynolds's description: "Dirt and mire are like sin, but dirt and mire are also like the liquid humours coursing through human flesh." She says that the humours are "imbued with moral density and spiritual import" and the passions act within the body as "the forces of wind and waves act in the natural world" (*Humoring* 6).

The word *manner* in another meaning in Jonson's theory of humour, was also a moral term. Besides his synonymous usages of *humours* and *manners* in his plays, Jonson also uses *manners* in a moral sense in his prose works. When talking about the best curricula for youth at the best timing, Jonson prudently argues:

> For besides, that the mind is rais'd with the height,
> and sublimity of such a verse, it takes spirit from the
> greatnesse of the matter, and is tincted with the best

things. Tragicke, and *Liricke* Poetry is good too: and *Comicke* with the best, if the manners of the Reader be once in safety.

(Timber 1810-15)

By taking special heed in suiting good study materials to the readiness of a youth's mind, Jonson points out that the instructor must first know the "safety" of the "manners of the Reader," that is, when the mind is "rais'd with the height" of the materials so that the youth "takes spirit from the greatnesse of the matter [of the things read]."

Jonson's use of *manner* in a moral sense is also found in his translation of Horace, the poet who appears in *Poetaster* as Jonson's representative, and whom Jonson uses "meticulously close to express his own authorial *freedom* and autonomy" (Moul 175). Horace in his *Ars Poetica* as translated by Jonson says,

> And I still bid the learned Maker looke
> On life, and manners, and make those his booke,
> Thence draw forth true expressions.

(453-55)

Horace urges the writer who has learned the art of imitation to look to life and moral characters and then draw living expressions from them.

Another important moral aspect of Jonson's humour theory is the Renaissance doctrine of *decorum*. As Herford and the Simpsons point out, among the Elizabethan dramatists and critics of the academic and courtly schools, to which Jonson belonged, *decorum* " in the treatment of character—involving a similar dominance [as of a master-passion] of a single trait—held rank, from the seventies onward, as literary orthodoxy" (I: 339). Decorum has always been a term of moral philosophy. Cyrus R Edmonds, when translating and commenting on Cicero's *Moral Duties*, remarks that *decorum*, together with truth, justice, and fortitude, is one of the four qualities of virtue (vi). In Cicero's poetic usage of the term, *decorum* is about morality in human character, the "gracefulness" poets observe when a person " speaks and acts in that manner which is most becoming his character. " Cicero alerts poets that they must "form their judgment of what is becoming in each individual according to his character" (xxviii. 49). When Jonson was writing, not only was Cicero still one of the Roman masters for him to imitate (Moul 2, n. 4), but also the idea of decorum, as noted by James D. Redwine, was held unanimously by Renaissance theorists to be "based in good part upon moral philosophy, and decorum is nowhere more important than in characterization " (333). According to Redwine, in Horace's "classical pronouncement on decorum" in *Ars Poetica*, Jonson finds his " defense of humours. " " Horace's decorum begins in the moral philosophy of Socrates and ends in the humour characterization of Jonson himself" (334). [1]

---

[1] Decorum as a term of moral philosophy finds also an inheritor of Socrates and Cicero in David Hume. In his *An Enquiry Concerning the Principles of Morals*, Hume writes: "DECENCY, or a proper regard to age, sex, character, and station in the world, may be ranked among the qualities, which are immediately agreeable to others, and which, by that means, acquire praise and approbation. An effeminate behaviour in a man, a rough manner in a woman; these are ugly, because unsuitable to each character, and different from the qualities which we expect in the sexes. It is as if a tragedy abounded in comic beauties, or a comedy in tragic. The disproportions hurt the eye, and convey a disagreeable sentiment to the spectators, the source of blame and disapprobation. This is that indecorum, which is explained so much at large by Cicero in his Offices. " (Sect. VIII. 12)

Concerning humour's several moral aspects, such as passions, manners and decorum, we may borrow again the words of Redwine to sum up Jonson's ideas of humour theory: "The real subject of Jonson's theory of humours is neither psychology nor aesthetics, but moral goodness (330). Here [moral goodness] is the proper context in which Jonson viewed his theory of humours. Socrates is at least as relevant to Jonson's theory of characterization as is Galen" (334).

Although Chapman started the vogue of the comedy of humours, Jonson is perhaps the most important practitioner of the genre. According to R. V. Holdsworth, *Every Man in his Humour* was, as Jonson himself became well aware, "a watershed in the development of English drama" (11). Chapman's *An Humorous Day's Mirth*, Shakespeare's *The Taming of the Shrew*, and Jonson's own *The Case Is Altered* all played with humours, but *Every Man in his Humour* was the first to make "personality, rather than narrative complications" the primary interest (Holdsworth 11). As for Chapman's earlier play with the idea of humour, they say: "Chapman anticipated Jonson in using the Humour motive in drama, but he did not anticipate the Jonsonian Humour play" (ibid.). In the words of Herford and the Simpsons, Jonson's innovation in *Every Man in his Humour*, more important than just representing character from a "new" perspective, was to make the exhibition of humours "the sole function of plot" (I: 343-45). Susan Bruce and Rebecca Steinberger consider Jonson "the first to significantly elaborate on these [humour] personalities or to use the natural tension and conflicts between them to motivate a dramatic plot" (116). William W. Demastes enthusiastically claims that Jonson was "of course,

the master of humours on the English Renaissance stage"
(57).

Jonson's career of developing the comedy of humours was
long and expanded. Starting from *Every Man in his Humours*
in 1598, it stretched to 1632 with his *Magnetic Lady, or
Humours Reconciled*, the author's last comedy of humours.
The drive headed by Jonson to produce comedy of humours
was to continue on and on till the beginning of the eighteenth
century in England, a clear sign of the significance and impact
of Jonson's didactic comedies based on humours.

iii. Jonsonian didacticism in *Volpone*

In *Volpone*, Jonson warns the audience against avarice
and hypocrisy through the humours of its characters. Jonson
uses Voltore, Corbaccio, Corvino, the Politic-Would-bes,
Mosca, Volpone and the Avocatori to carry out the action
either individually or collectively. Three of them—Corvino,
Mosca and Volpone—will be analyzed in detail in Chapter
Four. For the purpose of this chapter, it is sufficient to
recognize their chief vices at the moment. They are all
avaricious, calculating to compete with others and gull others'
wealth to themselves. Corvino and the other legacy hunters,
that is, Voltore, Corbaccio and Lady Would-be, offer things
they think important to flatter Volpone in hope of winning his
inheritance. They even collaborate to bear false witness at
court to exempt Volpone, Mosca and themselves from guilt.
Eventually, they find their briberies and perjuries fruitless.
Mosca pretends to work hard and tactfully for his master
Volpone to cozen the legacy hunters out of their wealth. But
after they are defeated, he suddenly and secretly turns

against Volpone, attempting to collect all the wealth Volpone has accumulated and his status into his own hands. Volpone first cooperates with Mosca by feigning death to deceive the legacy hunters. However, Volpone is overly confident in the loyalty of his parasite Mosca and almost loses all he has fleeced into the parasite's hands. In the end, in a passion of pride, Volpone decides to reveal himself and unveil everyone else, resulting in punishment of vices and reward of virtues. The stories of the legacy hunters, Mosca and Volpone are clearly entertaining and instructive, or, to borrow Jonson's terms, delightful and profitable.

However, Jonson's *Volpone* is much more than a collection of stories to achieve poetic justice. As a dedicated expounder of the Horatian and Sidneian principle of profit and delight, Jonson explicitly asserts the principle in this comedy.

As an important theme in *Volpone*, avarice is criticized in the characters' speeches as well through their action. In the beginning, the single and childless Volpone satirizes his "clients," that is, the legacy hunters, "women, men, of euery sexe, and age," who bring him "presents" from "plate, coyne" to "iewels" and "expect / Each greedy minute," and hope that he should die so that they can reap returns "ten-fold." However, because he sees clearly their "couetous" tricks, Volpone finds it easy to "play with their hopes" and eventually treats them like unlucky chop-cherry players that find "the cherry against their lips" but can never bite it (I. i. 73-90).

Among all the legacy hunters, Voltore the lawyer is perhaps the most educated and crafty. Mosca says that

Voltore has a "gift" that will never let him "want, while there are men, / And malice, to breed causes [legal cases]" (V. iii. 89-91). However, wily as Voltore is, he is mocked by Mosca for his sole aim to make money regardless of moral integrity. Mosca on behalf of Volpone tells Voltore that lawyers are "admir'd" because they could speak "to euery cause, and things mere contraries" according to the law, that they, "with most quick agilitie, could "turne, / And re-turne; make knots, and vndoe them; / Giue forked counsel" [ambiguous advice] so as to "take prouoking gold / On either hand, and put it vp." Lawyers not only receive money from opposing parties, but also lie. However, as Mosca sarcastically remarks, they "would not wag, nor scarce / Lie still, without a fee; when euery word / Your worship but lets fall, is a cecchine [a gold coin]" (I. iii. 52-66). Such lawyers as Voltore will legally argue any case so long as they can receive money.

Another explicit teaching against avarice in the comedy is Volpone's satirization of greed in old age as represented by Corbaccio, another legacy hunter, a decrepit, deaf dupe with a sinister heart. Corbaccio first intends to poison Volpone with "an opiate" that he claims to be from his "owne Doctor" (I. iv. 13), but is frustrated by the more wily Mosca. Then he is tricked into disinheriting his son and making Volpone his heir in the hope of winning Volpone to do the same to him, naming him heir. The reason for Corbaccio to run such a high risk is his fancy that he certainly shall out-live Volpone, a fancy that makes him "yong againe, a score of yeeres" (I. iv. 55), and therefore, he thinks he certainly is to inherit Volpone's estate. Seeing Corbaccio's wretched acts,

Volpone cannot help sighing, "What a rare punishment / Is auarice, to it selfe?" (I. iv. 142-43). Volpone understands that it is natural that old age is attended on by "so many cares," "maladies" and "feares"; it is a fact of life that in old age, people's "limbs faint," "senses dull," "seeing, hearing, going / All dead before them," and "their very teeth . . . fayling them." However, Corbaccio refuses to understand his own situation. Because of a hope to get Volpone's wealth, Corbaccio "flatters his age" and wants to "haue his youth restor'd." Such a hope grows so delusive in Corbaccio that he begins to believe that "fate / Would be as easily cheated on" until, in the end, "all turnes aire!" (I. iv. 144-59)

Such a delusion formed from covetousness in Corbaccio is also ridiculed by Mosca when the legacy hunters are so obsessed with their hopes to inherit Volpone's estate that they can even collaborate in perfect harmony to work for the same goal despite the rivalry among them. The parasite remarks,

> Each of 'hem
> Is so possest, and stuft with his owne hopes,
> That any thing, vnto the contrary,
> Neuer so true, or neuer so apparent,
> Neuer so palpable, they will resist it—
>
> (V. ii. 23-27)

"Possest" (possessed by the devil) is a key word here. Each of the legacy hunters possesses a hope for Volpone's estate, and they are also possessed by their desire so that they are deluded. They know they are rivals against each other, but each is confident that he or she has the only chance because he or she is selected by Volpone and Mosca.

Their hope and confidence in this delusion of possession are so strong that they become blind, a delusion that is "neuer" so "true," "apparent," or "palpable." Therefore, when they are possessed by their covetousness, they will resist anything that may come in its way.

Ironically, although Volpone and Mosca have both explicitly commented upon the degenerative, even destructive power of avarice, and have laughed at the legacy hunters possessed by covetousness, they, together with the objects of their mockery, are defeated by the same vice: the desire to keep wealth to themselves. They are compelled to lead their life until there is no way out unless a judge is to appear and teach them a lesson: "Mischiefes feed / Like beasts, till they be fat, and then they bleed" (V. xii. 149-151). Their desires to gain others' wealth or estate "feed" and grow like beasts. When they are fat enough, they become the target of hunters or butchers, and that is their time to bleed and die.

Volpone not only satirizes avarice, but also criticizes hypocrisy. Park Honan asserts that Jonson, after his "comical satires," was "using the freedom of a boys' coterie theatre to expose social hypocrisy" (278). We know that Corvino, Mosca and Volpone are fakes. Corvino maintains an army to watch over the activities of his wife in order to ensure that he will not be cuckolded, violently condemns and terrorizes her after seeing her drop a handkerchief from her window to buy medicine; but when he spots a possibility to "prostitute" his wife for Volpone's wealth, he, in person, forces his wife to go to Volpone's bed (III. vii. 75). Until the court scene in Act V, Scene ii, Mosca always tells Volpone and every legacy hunter that he is working only for him or her. In the end, he is unveiled to have been actually working only for himself. Together with Corvino and Mosca, Volpone is perhaps the most sincere, or rather, the least insincere. He frankly admits the ways he cozens the legacy hunters. He does not hide his desire for a voluptuous life. However, he feigns dying, especially at the vital moment of being a witness at court, to escape judgment. He satirizes the covetous Corbaccio, but is himself covetous of Corbaccio's and others' wealth. He tries to seduce Corvino's wife Celia by telling her that he is her "worthy louer" (III. vii. 187). These are three of his major hypocricies in *Volpone*.

The avaricious advocate Voltore is also a hypocrite. Besides Mosca's mockery at his reception of money from both the accuser and the defendant, or in Bonario's rightful disdain of his "mercenary tongue" whose "soule moues in his fee" (IV. v. 95-96), his dramatic acting before the court judges is a striking representation of his hypocrisy. Hoping to get Volpone's wealth, Voltore flatters him with a silver plate and hypocritical wishes. He organizes a system of perjuries to confuse the judges and almost succeeds in turning the innocent Bonario and Celia into the guilty parties. When he finds his hopes of inheritance thwarted, he instantly betrays himself and his gang of perjurers. However, when he is told again that he still has hopes to inherit Volpone's wealth, he betrays himself again, feigns possession by a "deuill . . . in a shape of a blew toad, with a battes wings" (V. xii. 28, 31), confuses the judges again, and almost succeeds in keeping his guilt covered up if Mosca does not appear to insist on Volpone's death and his inheritance of Volpone's estate. As he does in the court defense, Voltore is the leader of the hypocrites.

Different from the vocally prejudiced but dignified Duke in *The Merchant of Venice*, the magistrates in *Volpone*, the Avocatori, are also shown to be hypocritical. In the beginning, they appear to be just and circumspect, listening to and examining carefully all the parties. However, when they hear of Mosca's inheritance of Volpone's estate, two of them immediately change their attitude towards the parasite, even when Voltore is accusing Mosca of fraud. Particularly, after Mosca appears at court, still charged by Voltore, those two Avocatori start to treat him as a gentleman, ordering those in the court to " make him way" and give him " a stoole. " One of them immediately begins to admire Mosca, calling him " a proper man" and is ready to marry his daughter to him (V. xii. 49-62). When Volpone is turned away by Mosca and faces whipping, the Avocatore cannot hold his patience any longer and asks Mosca if he is married (V. xii. 83). Thanks to Volpone's self-exposure, Mosca is deservedly punished and the proposed marriage between Mosca and the judge's daughter is aborted. However, the judges' acts are enough to reveal their hypocrisy.

Still, more things can be said of the instructive purposes in *Volpone*. Volpone's decision to unveil himself and accept sentence and punishment may be considered a result of his pride. Such bad humours as Mosca's sloth and envy, and Volpone's lust and luxury can also be used to teach charitable and moral behavior. However, the above discussions suffice to show Jonson's advocacy and observation of the traditional poetic principle of profit and delight. Jonson successfully creates his story or "fable" to embody the principle (Prologue

28).

In this chapter, I have discussed the didactic intentions of Jonsonian comedy. Instruction is an important end of Jonson's comedy. Jonson's erudition in the classics made him a devout observer of such ancient masters as Aristotle and Horace. The influence of Philip Sidney and Jonson's social relationship with the Sidney family reinforced Jonson's conscious conviction of the moral purpose of literature. One reason Jonson despised some contemporary popular literature was its sole intention of entertainment. John Donne, in his Latin commendation of *Volpone* "fully registers and applauds the success of Jonson's stupendous ambition to surpass the supposed poverty of contemporary literature and restore the aesthetic glory and moral power of ancient dramatic poetry" (qtd. in Whitney 125). In addition to suggesting that viewing Volpone can "possibly increase one's chances for salvation," Donne essentially praises Jonson for " accomplishing the daring and towering goals he had set for himself" (ibid. 244).

Volpone is as much a comical entertainment as an educational play about morality. In fact, Jonson's greatest achievement in the play is his welding of moral instruction and hilarious entertainment. Russ McDonald has a good summary: "Jonson's [mature] plays [of which *Volpone* is a representative] are moral acts, but their profound morality is a function of the great risks the artist has allowed himself to take" (134). Commenting on Volpone's stepping forward at the end of the play as the chief of Jonson's works to "rightly" request the reward of applause for "having so splendidly entertained us with his immoral doings," Harriet Hawkins says that Jonson, "through his glittering grotesque sinners," has shown us "things like truth" about certain ways of the world, and thus "deserves thanks for a black and gold comedy" which is "so much more than a piece of moralistic propaganda implying an inevitable triumph of virtue over vice" (111-12). Donne is right. Jonson in *Volpone* has successfully brought his "Precepts [of profit and delight] into practise" (*Timber* 1755-57).

III. Shakespeare's didacticism

i. Shakespeare's dramatic theory

Shakespeare's most explicit statement of his literary theory is Hamlet's directions to the players in the context of using a play to try Claudius's guilt: actors should avoid "inexplicable dumb-shows and noise" when they speak the lines; they should "suit the action to the word, the word to the action;" they should control the movements of their hands; to sum up, they should be realistic and natural and not overdo anything; or, in other words, hold "the mirror up to nature; to show virtue her own feature, scorn her own image, and the very age and body of the time his form and pressure" (III. ii. 12- 24). While Hamlet's directions may be Shakespeare's voice and so are important to show his commentary about contemporary theater performances and remarks about good and effective acting, these directions are rather technical and scarcely have anything to do with moral education. Other than these lines, there is hardly anything explicit about literary or dramatic criticism or theory in

Shakespeare's writings.

However, Shakespeare's lack of explicit theoretical statement does not mean his want of dramatic theory. Shakespeare disperses his theory into his plays. While Philip Sidney claims that nature's world is "brazen," the poets only deliver a "golden" world (8: 3-4), Shakespeare holds up the mirror to nature to show "her own feature" and "her own image." Pauline Kiernan argues that Shakespeare does not attempt to represent "the original subject or original moment in history," nor does he seek to uncover a Sidneyan 'golden world' in which art attempts to "outdo nature in the timeless perfection of artifice," but is concerned with finding ways of "creating an art which can exist within the mutable, 'brazen world' of nature." Kiernan points out that Shakespeare's drama "privileges the living human body, the organic matter on which it is created"; the "living human body" that Shakespeare "reinstates" is "where art does not aspire to the absurdity of being 'livelier than life'" (11). Although Shakespeare "rarely commits himself to an established theoretical attitude," he "more often than not" reveals "an eclectic versatility in subscribing to whatever ideas best serve his immediate demands" (Kiernan 8-9). As this chapter now shows, Shakespeare not only has a dramatic theory, but also can be didactic.

In *Timon of Athens*, when Painter and Poet talk about a picture as "a pretty mocking of the life," Poet opines that "it tutors nature. Artificial strife / Lives in these touches livelier than life" (I. i. 35, 37-38). Again, in the voices of Painter and Poet, Shakespeare embeds his artistic and didactic theory, or rather, a contra-didactic criticism due to the passage's satirical tone. ① Whether or not Shakespeare wrote this part of the play in a state of "artistic crisis," John Jowett glosses "tutors nature" (1. 37) as "instructs nature as to how it should be," and goes on to assert that Shakespeare "conflates two claims for poetry in Philip Sidney's *Defence of Poesy*: that it makes 'things better than nature bringeth forth' and has the ability 'to teach and delight' " (1). While Poet's phrase " tutors nature " may jokingly echo the traditional, Sidneian and even Jonsonian principle "to teach and delight," the play is certainly didactic with regard to its lessons on materialism and true friendship. Certainly, Shakespeare is conscious of the importance of didacticism in literature, and has written much to teach wisdom concerning life.

ii. Shakespeare's didacticism in humour characters

One way for Shakespeare to teach is through humour characters. The lack of a definite date for *The Merchant of Venice* makes it difficult for us to trace its relation with Chapman's *Comedy of Humors* (1597) or *The Blind Beggars of Alexandria* (1596) in terms of the humours comedy vogue. ② *The Merchant* was probably not seen as a comedy of humours by the Elizabethan audience, at least not a popular

---

① According to John Jowett, new evidence has proven that *Timon of Athens* was collaboratively written by Shakespeare and Thomas Middleton, but Act I, Scene i is suggested to be by Shakespeare (1-2).

② John Russell Brown suggests the date of *The Merchant of Venice* between July 30, 1596 and July 22, 1598 (Introduction, xxvii); Burton Raffel agrees with Brown on 1596 – 1598 (xvii); Jay L. Halio, 1596 – 1597 (27-29); Harold Bloom agrees with Halio (*Merchant* 172); Charles Edelman suggests 1596 by listing the play's performance(s) in 1596 (*Merchant* xvi), although he may also agree with Bloom on 1596 – 1597 (Edelman, *Merchant* 2); and M. M. Mahood, 1597 (2).

one, considering its short stage life in Shakespeare's era. [1] However, even if *The Merchant* was composed before the performance and success of *The Blind Beggar of Alexandria* and *The Comedy of Humours*, [2] this should not keep us from analyzing Shakespeare's application of the idea of humours to see his creation of humour characters in *The Merchant*. After all, as Lily B. Campbell has remarked, "Shakespeare, much more than has generally been thought, was a man familiar with the learning of his day, a student of philosophy, and a purposive artist" (vii).

Humours was one of the hottest topics among the Elizabethans. According to John W. Draper, between 1532 and 1601, at least twenty-eight books on humours were published. During the period from 1586 to 1613 when Shakespeare was probably in London busy with a life in and out of theaters, at least twenty-seven books on humours were published or reprinted (120-22). Considering the capital's

---

[1] Although editors of *The Merchant* all suggest its performances at its composition time (Edelman, 1596 (*Merchant* xvi) ; Mahood, 1597 – 1598 (42) ; Halio, 1596 – 1597 (59) ; John Russell Brown gives no specific date except the one in 1605, on which all agree (Introduction xxxii)) , the play was then not seen on the English stage until 1701 (Edelman, *Merchant* xvi ; Halio 61) or 1741 (Brown, Introduction xxxii ; Mahood 43).

[2] Wiggins believes *The Merchant* came out in 1596 (92). However, Wiggins suggests Shakespeare was already vaguely representing humours before Chapman. "The attentive eye," Wiggins argues, " may detect traces of *The Two Gentlemen of Verona* [1590-1591] and *Love's Labours Lost* [1594-1595] [in *The Comedy of Humours*]" (64).

small population of 200,000 in 1603,[1] these numbers of publications were large. The frequent reprints of publications showed the popularity of such books.[2] The popularity of books on humours in the English Renaissance was also a result of the wide circulation of books on popular philosophy, especially moral philosophy. According to Lily B. Campbell, a survey of publications in England before 1605 " shows a massive array of works in many editions dealing with moral philosophy" (47). Because of the close internal relations between humours and moral philosophy, a big moral philosophy readership would make humours an everyday topic, about which Shakespeare must have known. As Draper points out, to believe that Shakespeare is behind his time in his use of humour in its Elizabethan sense "is merely to insist that he was not an Elizabethan, that he did not write in Elizabethan English with Elizabethan concepts, and that he

---

[1] Despite repeated political disorders and plague outbreaks, population in London grew quickly in late sixteenth and early seventeenth centuries. According to Douglas Bruster, London had 180,000 people in 1576, when Shakespeare was twelve years old, and 350,000 in 1642 (19). Lawrence Manley holds that London's population in 1600 was 250,000, and that it was the second largest metropolis in Europe by the later seventeenth century (399). Certainly estimations of London's population vary. Even in the same book, *The Cambridge History of Early Modern English Literature*, another author argues that "in 1600, London held 200,000 souls, and was growing by about 8,000 a year (half the annual population increase for England and Wales)" (Butler 569). It seems more scholars would agree on the number of 200,000. James Shapiro says, "in 1600, in an England of four million, London and its immediate environs held a population of roughly two hundred thousand" (*A Year* 9). The most authoritative statistics probably comes from Roger Finlay, the outstanding librarian demographer, who informs us that the population of London in 1600 was 200,000 "approximately" (7).

[2] According to John W. Draper, P. Barrough's *Method of Phisicke* was reprinted in 1590, 1596, 1601, 1610, 1617, 1624, 1634, and 1639 after its first publication in 1583; T. Cogan's *Hauen of Health* was published in 1584, and then reprinted in 1588, 1589, 1596, 1605, 1612, and 1636 (*Humors* 120-21). It should be kept in mind that health then meant mostly the balance of the four humours. For more examples of such frequent reprints of humour books and handbooks, see Draper, *Humors*, pp. 120-22.

was so incompetent a playwright that he made his text mislead his audience" (11).

Despite Shakespeare's almost certain knowledge of humours theory, we do not have any definition of it from him. Certainly Shakespeare seemed to have not theorized a definition of humour, whether inside or outside a play. He never wrote a prologue to a play in the Jonsonian way to introduce his ideas. [①] Compared with Jonson, Shakespeare does not seem to have applied many moral connotations to the word *humour*. In fact, despite the similarities of physiological and psychological meanings in Shakespeare's and Jonson's use of humour, Shakespeare "rarely invokes the humors in Jonsonian fashion" (Paster, *Humoring* 24).

Of Shakespeare's comic characters, or characters in his comedies, Corporal Nim is probably the one that impresses the audience most with humour. In *The Merry Wives of Windsor* (1597 – 1598), Nim repeatedly uses the word *humour*:

> Nim. He was gotten in drink. His mind is not heroic. Is not the humour conceited?
> Sir John. I am glad I am so acquit of this tinderbox; his thefts were too open. His filching was like an unskillful singer; he kept not time.

---

① Indeed, based on the Riverside edition, of all Shakespeare's plays, he had prefixed only two inductions (one to *The Taming of the Shrew*; the other, *the Second Part of King Henry IV*) and five prologues (to *Troilus and Cressida*, *Henry V*, *Henry VIII*, *Romeo and Juliet*, and *The Two Noble Kinsmen* respectively). All these seven brief inductions and prologues are used to introduce the play's plot. Jonson, in contrast, had typically included an induction or a prologue, and quite often, both an induction and a prologue to his plays. Sometimes, he also wrote an expanded "To the Reader" or "Dedication" in the front of his plays. Jonson's inductions, prologues, and dedications often introduce the play's plot, but also his theory concerning plays in general, or the play proper.

Nim. The good humour is to steal at a minute's rest.

(I. iii. 20-25)

Nim. The anchor is deep. Will that humour pass?

Sir John. Now, the report goes she has all the rule of her husband's purse; he hath a legion of angels.

Pistol. As many devils entertain, and 'To her, Boy!' say I.

Nim. The humour rises; it is good. Humour me the angels.

(I. iii. 46-50)

Nim's persistent use of the word *humour* may easily impress the audience that the Corporal is an Elizabethan *humoral* character. He can be regarded in this way if one takes into account his almost programmed articulation of the expression *humour(s)*, or *humorous*. However, a *humorous character* should not be considered to be so simple as merely a character with a particular habit of language.

The reason for Nim's pervasive use of the word *humour* is not certain. According to John Dover Wilson's supposition, Nim is "a character of travesty," whose glaring speech of humour "lacks sap for us in our ignorance of the occasion," and Nim's use of humour would be more "juicy for us if we but knew just what, or whom, it is travestying" (Introduction xxxi). Wilson suggests that Shakespeare was ridiculing Jonson as a result of the Poetomachia. Thus the passage targets Jonson's analyses of humour characters in successive plays, his physical swellings of the head, his experience as a soldier and more importantly, his starring as *Hieronimo*, Marshal of Spain in Kyd's *Spanish Tragedie* (Introduction xxxi-xxxii). [1] Whatever the reason for his obsessive use of the word *humour*, Nim is not sufficiently serious for the word to mean much, as Anne Barton has said, "Nim has latched onto the word humour as though it were a diamond discovered among the pebbles on a beach and uses it to cope with all contingencies, with the result that it rapidly ceases to have any meaning whatever" (*Merry Wives* 288). Gail Kern Paster agrees with Barton on Nim's meaningless dependence on the word humour: "For Nim, the possibility of verbal recourse to 'humor' —as a placeholding word that makes up for his lack of ideas and vocabulary—makes his world full of self-evidence." ("Bodies, Fluids" 50)

The next Shakespearean comic character a reader will associate with humour can be Sir John Falstaff. As the No. 1 famous character in the entire seventeenth century from all Shakespearean and Jonsonian comedies (Bentley 120), Falstaff seems to deserve a natural association with humour. Besides all his wit and conviviality, Falstaff is known to be a braggart, a fat vainglorious knight, and a butt for Prince Hal. Here are the prince's remarks about Falstaff:

> Why dost thou converse with that trunk of humours, that bolting-hutch of beastliness, that swollen parcel of dropsies, that huge bombard of sack, that stuffed cloak-bag of guts, that roasted Manning tree ox with the pudding in his belly, that reverend Vice, that grey Iniquity, that

---

[1] For a detailed and persuasive discussion of his analysis of Shakespeare's travestying Jonson with the use of the word *humour*, see Wilson, Introduction, pp. xxxi-ii. While many scholars decide that the date of *The Merry Wives* was 1597 – 1598, thus setting the play one or two years before the outbreak of the Poets' War, many others, including Wilson, argue that the play was written after Henry IV, Parts I and II, but before Henry V, in 1599. This is also why Wilson warns that Nim's travestying Jonson in *The Merry Wives* should be taken for "a guess and no more" (xxxi).

father Ruffian, that Vanity in Years?

(I Henry IV, II. v. 454-59)

Prince Hal is right to call Falstaff a "trunk of humours," and a "swollen parcel of dropsies" because Falstaff is not a man dominated by a single humour. He is a combination of different humours: overconfidence, lecherousness, lust and obscenity in *The Merry Wives of Windsor*; vainglory, merriment, boasting, gluttony, covetousness, drunkenness, debauchery, cowardice and phlegm in *Henry IV, Part I*. Perhaps because Falstaff is such a huge "trunk of humours," critics often do not talk of him as a humour character.

Although he did not give a clear definition of humour and might not have verbally stressed the moral side of the knight's humours, Shakespeare definitely has demonstrated his moral concerns through his portrayal of this corpulent and corrupt character. Bernard Spivack has argued:

> The shadow of a serious moral judgment hovers about him [Falstaff], disturbing us as it disturbed Maurice Morgann; and when it finally closes in on him, Falstaff succumbs to the moral severity which is always present in the traditional stage image of the morality vices, no matter how comic their performance.

(459)

Despite such moral concerns about Falstaff, the knight has impressed many as a lovable merry-maker instead of a deplorable and choleric devil. For a real Shakespearean comic devil who reflects a running of more than one humour, we have to turn to Shylock, another character as famous as Falstaff to us moderns, and yet perhaps, a much more complex one than all other comic characters in Shakespeare's plays.

iii. Shakespearian didacticism in his plays

It is easy to remember explicitly didactic passages from Shakespeare's plays. When Laertes in *Hamlet* is ready to board his ship for France, Polonius famously gives his son a "few precepts" such as "give thy thoughts no tongue" and "to thine own self be true" (I. iii. 58, 59, 78). Polonius's "precepts," though meant to be comic prate, are certainly didactic. If one takes Polonius to be a fool and thinks that Shakespeare means his speech to be a joke, then he will definitely find other characters seriously moralizing. Prospero in *The Tempest* fears that his daughter Miranda may lose her virginity prematurely. In an aside, Prospero decides that he must make "this swift business [of falling in love between Ferdinand and Miranda]" "uneasy," "lest too light winning / Make the prize light" (I. ii. 453-55). As David Bevington points out, Prospero's decision "reinforces the play's insistent teaching that sexual fulfillment should not precede marriage" (206).

Indeed, seen from the perspectives of major motifs, most of Shakespeare's mature tragedies, which were staged before Jonson's *Volpone*, are didactic if not explicitly, at least by implication: *Hamlet* warns against jealousy and an-eye-for-an-eye revenge; *King Lear*, pride and wrath; and *Othello*, jealousy. As another important part of Shakespeare's dramatic art, his comedies are also partly didactic, if not so thoroughly as the tragedies. In *As You Like It*, Shakespeare's "sweetest-tempered play" (Bloom, *Invention* 205), there are lessons about life to be learned from Adam, Jacques de Boys and Orlando's old servant. In the eyes of Orlando, Adam resembles "the constant service [faithful servant] of the antique world, / When service sweat for duty not for meed [undeserved reward]" (II. iii. 58-59). Orlando admires Adam because he is not like many servants at the time when "none will sweat but for promotion." For those servants, even if they can get "promotion," the "promotion" will "choke their service up." However, Orlando's Adam is not that kind of servant; "it is not so with thee [Adam]" (II. iii. 60-63). Orlando's appreciation of Adam is a lesson on how to be a good servant, or generally, a good worker, teacher, student, etc. Responding to Orlando's appreciative words, Adam agrees with his master that many people seek "their fortunes" when they are young, but it is far too late for him now at the age of "almost fourscore." Adam believes that "Fortune cannot recompense me better / Than to die well and not my master's debtor" (II. iii. 72-77). Adam's refusal to worship fortune and his dedication to loyal service or a work ethic can also be a lesson in accordance with Orlando's words. Moreover, Adam's words offer a lesson on how to live a responsible and peaceful life, not as a "debtor" to his master. In the context of Christianity, as we discussed in Chapter Two, worshipping God instead of fortune, or money, is to love God. One who spends a life loving God, who is the final master, will not be a debtor at the end of his life. Andy Mousley remarks that Adam represents "one kind of literary humanist lesson in how to live" (141). Although the dialogue between Orlando and Adam is not explicitly didactic, it is clearly teaching an accessible message.

In *The Merchant of Venice*, my focus of study, there are also plenty of didactic passages. In addition to the implicit criticism of prodigality, money worshipping and hypocrisy embodied in the characters of Bassanio, Portia and Shylock, which will be discussed in detail in Chapter Four, there is more explicit teaching in the play that necessitates a relevant examination here.

iv. Shakespeare's didacticism concerning mercy in *The Merchant of Venice*

As some of the best known dramatic lines in all Shakespeare's works, Portia's speech is a straightforward didactic lecture on the virtue of mercy. For the convenience of analysis, it is worth quoting in full:

> The quality of mercy is not strained,
> It droppeth as the gentle rain from heaven
> Upon the place beneath. It is twice blest:
> It blesseth him that gives, and him that takes.
> 'Tis mightiest in the mightiest, it becomes
> The thronèd monarch better than his crown.
> His sceptre shows the force of temporal power,
> The attribute to awe and majesty,
> Wherein doth sit the dread and fear of kings;
> But mercy is above this sceptred sway.
> It is enthronèd in the hearts of kings,
> It is an attribute to God himself,
> And earthly power doth then show likest God's
> When mercy seasons justice. Therefore, Jew,
> Though justice be thy plea, consider this:
> That in the course of justice, none of us
> Should see salvation. We do pray for mercy,
> And that same prayer doth teach us all to render
> The deeds of mercy.

(IV. i. 181-99)

Nineteen lines! This is quite an oration in which Portia means to teach Shylock as well as the play's audience a lesson of heavenly love. She says that mercy, like the rain, drops freely to the earth. It is "twice blest" as it blesses both the taker and the giver. Although appropriate to a king, mercy is even more powerful than monarchs. Mercy is an "attribute to God himself." Therefore, Shylock should renounce his claim on punishment, embrace mercy and forgive Antonio because "no one" should see "salvation" in the course of strict "justice."

Some critics consider Portia's speech a lecture from the perspective of New Testament laws of mercy against the Old Testament or Jewish law of justice,[①] which is narrowly conceived by Shylock as "revenge" (III. i. 63). However, the idea of "revenge" in Shylock's intention, or under the cover of "justice" from his mouth (IV. i. 200), cannot find support in the Jewish or Christian Bible. Jay Halio has precisely pointed out that neither Shylock's religion nor Christianity "condones or sanctions vengeance. Quite the contrary: both systems of religious belief stand adamantly opposed to it, condemning it as a corruption of the human spirit" (46). Halio also adds that "in the sixteenth century, both church and secular authorities vigorously opposed blood vengeance" (46, n. 1). In this light, Portia, dressed as Balthasar, a Doctor of Laws, assumes the role not only of a Christian preaching forgiveness, but of a secular authority, sermonizing Shylock to abandon violence.

Expectedly, Shylock does not accept this lesson from

---

① See, e. g. , Coghill, pp. 256 – 88.

Portia and is eventually punished by justice "more than thou [Shylock] desir'st" (IV. i. 313). Indeed, Portia is not the first to teach Shylock to be merciful. In the beginning of the trial scene, Act IV, Scene i, Antonio implies that the Duke has already tried to teach Shylock to show pity, taking pains to moderate "his rigorous course" (7). However, Shylock is "uncapable of pity, void and empty / From any dram of mercy" (4-5). Then when Shylock is brought into the court, the Duke patiently and politely exhorts Shylock to forgive Antonio. The Duke tells Shylock that he should show "mercy and remorse more strange / Than is thy strange apparent cruelty," that he should not only "loose the forfeiture," but also "forgive a moiety of the principal" out of "human gentleness and love" (19-25). Trying to persuade Shylock, the Duke uses two techniques. One, the Duke tries to mediate the situation, saying that Shylock is only pretending to be cruel, and eventually at the court, he is going to give everyone a pleasant surprise to show mercy and pity. Two, he tries to arouse Shylock's "human gentleness and love" so as to soften his demand, by referring him to biblical teachings such as God showing "mercie vnto thousandes" who love Him and keep his commandments (Exodus XX. 6; Deuteronomy. V. 10), one of which is not to kill other people (Exodus XX. 13). For the Christian audience of Shakespeare's original productions, the Duke's words must also have reminded them of Paul's First Epistle to the Corinthians: [love] disdaineth not: it seketh not her owne . . . thinketh no euil" (XIII. 5). Shylock answers the Duke's teaching politely, but, instead of following it, stands firm to claim his penalty, which he thinks is "due and forfeit" (IV. i. 36).

Then Bassanio follows the Duke and tries to convince Shylock to change his mind, telling him that all men do not "kill the things they do not love," and "every offence is not a hate at first" (65, 67). Regrettably, Bassanio's rough words with accusation are easily rejected by Shylock. Bassanio's words may have even hardened Shylock because now even twice as much money cannot excite Shylock's greed so as to prefer money to his bond (IV. i. 84-87).

Now the Duke interrupts to ask Shylock how he shall "hope for mercy, rendering none" (87). To this charge, Shylock seems able to fight back more easily than before. He believes that he is "doing no wrong," and therefore he shall dread no judgment (88-89). Then he satirizes Christians' hypocrisy of keeping and maltreating slaves. So far, Shylock has been lectured well but is still not accepting the teaching. As will be discussed in Chapter Four, he will only learn his hard lesson when he is punished according to the justice based on the strict letter of the law. Jay Halio remarks of Shylock's punishment: " by rejecting Portia's several invitations to show compassion, Shylock fails to rise above the lowest level of humanity and convert incipient tragedy into the ' merry sport' he claimed it was when he first proposed the bond (I. iii. 134-48)" (51). Shylock's failure is also a lesson from which the audience is to learn.

v. Shakespeare's teaching concerning superficiality in *The Merchant of Venice*

Besides preaching in favor of mercy and against greed, Shakespeare obviously also teaches about telling appearance from reality in *The Merchant*. Most of this didactic comment

of the play is found in the scenes in which the suitors choose
their caskets. Of the three caskets, gold, silver, and lead,
only one contains success—Portia's picture. Choosing the
other two involves a serious risk: an oath never to marry a
"lady" (II. i. 41) or a "maid" (II. ix. 13) in this life.

The first suitor to decide on a choice is the Prince of
Morocco. He ponders at each casket: gold with an inscription
of "who chooseth me shall gain what many men desire,"
silver, "who chooseth me shall get as much as he deserves,"
and lead, "who chooseth me must give and hazard all he
hath" (II. vii. 5, 7, 9). Surveying the inscription on the lead
casket, Morocco despises it as threatening, claiming that it
is not worthwhile to "hazard for lead" because "men that
hazard all" are for a "hope of fair advantages," and "a golden
mind stoops not to shows of dross." For the silver casket,
Morocco believes that he deserves Portia in every respect:
"fortunes," "graces," "qualities of breeding," and even
"love;" as for the gold one, the African prince well recognizes
its inscription because "all the world desires her." Examining
the caskets back and forth, Morocco makes his decision on
the gold casket because "never so rich a gem / Was set in
worse than gold." He dismisses the lead one as a
"damnation" to think that Portia's picture can be put in such
a humble and ugly casket, which is associated with death; he
also abandons the silver one, calling it "a sinful thought" that
Portia can be "immured" in something "ten times
undervalued" to gold (14-60). Expectedly, Morocco chooses
the casket according to the value of the container. The result,
unfortunately, is disappointing, maybe disastrous, if a prince
is literally forbidden to marry. So Morocco fails, reads the

explicit moral contained in the casket's message, and receives along with the audience of the play a lesson from his choice that "all that glisters is not gold." Many a man sells his life just to see a person or thing's "outside." The Prince should have been "as wise as bold, / Young in limbs, in judgement old" (65-71). Therefore, everyone should be careful of the difference between appearance and interior matter. [1]

The next bold suitor to make a choice is the Prince of Arragon. Like Morocco, he thinks lead is too "base" for him to give or hazard anything, and so easily passes it by. The inscription of "what many men desire" on the gold chest sounds to him like something that would attract "the fool multitude that choose by show." Arragon seems to have an insight to distinguish essence from appearance. He says that he will not be like those "fool multitude" who are "not learning more than the fond eye doth teach," whose eye "pries not to th' interior"; therefore, he "will not choose what many men desire" because he will not "jump with common spirits" and rank himself "with the barbarous multitudes." Arragon readily agrees with the inscription on the silver casket: "let none presume / To wear an undeservèd dignity." He remarks that if everyone wore his honor according to his "merit" without corruption, many people's honorable hats would be taken off; many commanders, commanded; and the positions of "low peasantry" and "the

---

[1] Some may argue that Morocco is not all wrong in his reasoning. He thinks the picture of such a lady as Portia whom many men desire should be well kept. In the present case, it is appropriate to keep it in the gold chest instead of lead, just like the English gold coin, on which an angel is stamped (56-57). Still, this would be a lesson on the propriety to suit one's appearance to his interior.

true seed of honour" might be exchanged. For these reasons, Arragon chooses the silver casket but fails just like Morocco has. The explicitly didactic lesson from the scroll he gets out of the "blinking idiot's head" is: some people kiss shadows to get joy, and therefore, such joy can only be like a shadow. Such people are like court officials who pretend to be old and experienced with silver ornaments (Halio, note to II. ix. 68). These people are foolish and a choice made by the outward attraction only is just like a selection by such people (II. ix. 24-68).

We will discuss the speech and choice of Bassanio, the third suitor to choose his fortune in Chapter Four. However, he makes the right choice, and his assertion that "The world is still deceived with ornament" is instructive (III. ii. 73-74). It teaches people not to be deceived by ornament. In this way, one will be able to get the fortune Bassaino receives. As the scroll in the lead chest informs him: "You that choose not by the view / Chance as fair, and choose as true" (131-32). Therefore, choice made not only by the outward appearance will be rewarded. According to John Russell Brown, "this theme [of appearance and reality] was often in Shakespeare's mind about the time that he wrote *The Merchant*" (lii.). Indeed, if we consider *King Lear*, in which Goneril and Regan appear to be kind and loving by their sweet words, but turn out to be cruel and treacherous children, and even disloyal spouses, we can say that Shakespeare perhaps was thinking about this theme longer than the period mentioned by Brown. In any case, the speeches made by Morocco, Arragon and Bassanio make up a good lesson on the need to judge by looking sufficiently at both the exterior and the interior of an issue. [1]

From the discussion of Jonson and Shakespeare's didacticism in this chapter, we can see that Jonson is an adamant advocator and practioner, while Shakespeare is less frequent and usually was implicit in teachings.

Jonson always cares about a didactic purpose in his plays. As a careful student of Horace, Jonson is articulate about the dual purposes of profit and pleasure of poetry, which are in good harmony with the ideas of English Renaissance writers headed by Sir Philip Sidney. Jonson prefaces most of his plays, comedies or tragedies, with either an induction or a prologue or both, and ends them quite often with an epilogue, affirming and explaining his intention or idea of writing or producing that play, and sometimes checking with the audience in the epilogue if his purpose has been achieved. In his *Timber, or Discoveries*, itself a didactic work, Jonson continues to expound his theories of profit and pleasure, as well as many other such ideas as those on the creation of the comedy and tragedy.

Jonson practices what he preaches concerning the principle of profit and pleasure. Most of his plays serve to instruct as well as to entertain the audience. In *Volpone*, specifically, he synthesizes several stories of legacy hunting, which are in turn the cause of other episodes, to lecture the audience against avarice and extravagance of people of different ages and professions. By sporting with their follies,

---

[1] John Russell Brown enumerates many other lines to show the repetition of the theme of appearance and reality in *The Merchant*, including the one in the comic ring scene; see p. lii for details.

also their crimes, Jonson hopes to teach the audience to live moderate and virtuous lives. The overall tone of *Volpone* is didactic, but there are only two or three speeches of direct didacticism. Jonson's didacticism in *Volpone* is achieved mainly through its action.

Unlike Jonson, Shakespeare does not seem to care much about the didactic purpose of his plays. He rarely affirms anything theoretical in his inductions or prologues, which are also rare. However, similar to Jonson, Shakespeare can be didactic. Some of his comedies, romances and most of his mature tragedies are meant to teach the audience life lessons.

The Merchant of Venice is a typical Shakespearean comedy in that it has no induction, prologue or epilogue, nor does it advocate any dramatic theory. This comedy, however, is highly didactic. Through its action, it teaches such important lessons as mercy and the deceptiveness of appearance. More significantly and in contrast with *Volpone*, *The Merchant of Venice* contains several long and straightforward didactic speeches. Portia's sermon about mercy is well known; the speeches of Morroco, Arragon and Bassanio are also familiar to the audience. Also, in *The Merchant*, many other characters, Shylock, the Duke, and others can also be regarded outright didactic.

Therefore, the traditional views discussed in Chapter One about Shakespeare's emphasis on entertainment and Jonson's contrasting emphasis on education in their plays is not borne out in *The Merchant of Venice* or *Volpone*. The two plays are both entertaining and educational. While it is hard to tell which is more entertaining, *The Merchant*, or *Volpone*, it is clear that *The Merchant* is certainly more didactic in its speeches than *Volpone*. The important point is that both are great comedies.

4

Characterization in *Volpone* and
The Merchant of Venice

PISTOL With wit or steel?

NIM   With both the humours, I.

I will discuss the humour of this love to Page.

(*The Merry Wives of Windsor* I. iii. 72-73)

As has been discussed in Chapter One, Shakespeare and
Jonson have provoked critics' contrastive opinions about their
characters: Shakespeare's are natural individuals from real
life; and Jonson's, mechanic types based on humours. Such
oppositional opinions are exclusive. It means that
Shakespeare did not create characters based on humours,
and Jonson did not shape realistic ones. Since the
overwhelmingly prevalent opinion of Shakespeare's characters
in the twenty-first century is still not much changed,[1] I shall

---

[1]   For example, Michael Bristol claims in his article (2009): "His [Shakespeare's] characters are
like us . . . They are people who live in a world we can understand" (38). M. H. Abrams and
Geoffrey Galt Harpham claim Sir Epicure Mammon (from *The Alchemist*), a "*humours character*"
whose name "says it all," is "in contrast to the roundness of character in Shakespeare's
multifaceted Falstaff" (43).

begin this chapter's discussion with views on Jonson's characterization.

The criticism that Jonson's characters are humoral types touches on two closely related subjects: humours and types. Let us now take a good look at them.

I. Humours and character types

i. Definition of humour

A study of Jonson's use of humour is as fundamental in analyzing his characterization as it was to discuss his didacticism in the previous chapter. James D. Redwine preceptively asserts that "it is with his humours that an analysis of Jonson's theory of characterization must begin (316), because "all of Jonson's plays, especially the comical satires and the comedies, have been 'humour plays'" (330). In Redwine's words, there has been "a continuity of characterization if not of form in all of Jonson's plays" (330).

Humour, as Herford and the Simpsons precisely point out, in our literary usage here as "a frequent synonym for the dominating trait of character," was "not of literary origin at all" (I: 340). [1] A survey of dictionary entries demonstrates

---

[1] English writers have long written about humour and health or represented characters by conveying their dominant humours. Chaucer in his description of the "Doctour of Phisyk" in the General Prologue of *The Canterbury Tales* shows the poet's command of the traditional knowledge of the theory of humours: "He knew the cause of everich maladye / Were it of hoot, or coold or moyste or drye / And where it engendred and of what humour. / He was a verray parfit praktisour" (419-22). Chaucer also briefly portrays two distinct humour characters in the General Prologue. He describes the Franklin in these words: "of his complexcion he was sangwyn" (333). Different from the Franklin's optimism, Chaucer's Reeve is irascible: "The Reue was a sclendre colerik man" (587).

the conventional association of humour with bodily fluids. *Humour*'s first two definitions out of the six in Onion's *Shakespeare Glossary* are "moisture" and "bodily fluids" ("humour"). Of *humour*'s three definitions in *Johnson's Dictionary*, the first is moisture. In the *Oxford English Dictionary* (*OED*), the first three of the nine definitions of *humour* are fluids. Definitions of humour as "whim" or "mental disposition" following those of moisture or fluids in Onion's *Shakespeare Glossary*, *Johnson's Dictionary* and the *OED* confirm the Elizabethan's inherited conviction that a person's character was closely connected with his *humours*, that is, his bodily fluids. The Elizabethans receiving knowledge from popular books of medical science (a combination of physiology, psychology, alchemy and astrology) thought that a humour was constantly moving in their bodies, both independently and together with others. *Humour* became an English word as a medical expression (Burnley 237). According to Ian Johnston, Galen's medical and philosophical treatises "remained an integral part of the medical curriculum into the second millennium" (10). In both classical (Aristotle and Galen, for example) and medieval (e. g. Avicenna and Bartholomeus Anglicus) physiological writings, *humour* referred to the four major fluids of the human body—choler (bile or yellow bile), melancholy (black bile), phlegm, and blood. The proportion or balance of these humours determined a person's physical health as well as his or her psychological disposition, or temperament. Thus, the movement of the humours resulted in different temperaments: a balance of all the humours caused a perfect temperament and health, a kind of golden and rare Aristotelian mean, but an imbalance, both in quantity and quality, which was most often the case, brought about a peculiar disposition. [1] To be exact, as Linda Ehrsam Voigts has summarized from James Yonge's English translation in 1422 of the "widely read pseudo-Aristotelian *Secreta secretorum* (*Secret of Secrets*), a manual on statecraft that deals extensively with the human body": [2]

> A person has a melancholy complexion when dominated by black bile, cold and dry like the earth; a choleric complexion when dominated by yellow bile, hot and dry like fire; a sanguine complexion when dominated by blood, hot and moist like the air; and a phlegmatic complexion when dominated by phlegm, cold and moist like water.
>
> (42)

By the later sixteenth century, according to Herford and the Simpsons, humour had come to "denote whatever element of character, through unequal mixture of the fluids, was dominated by the rest" (I: 340).

---

① According to Harry Levin, Juan Huarte, an "ingenious" Spanish physician, even published a treatise in 1575, *Examen de ingenios para les ciencias*, "suggesting that all infants be examined at birth and assigned to their subsequent careers in accordance with their temperamental predispositions." Although this "deterministic program" came under the "strictures of the Inquisition for its implicit challenge to the freedom of the will," the book was translated and circulated in England, where it was "undoubtedly read" by Ben Jonson (182).

② Herford and the Simpsons have a different view. They hold that Sir Thomas Elyot, a pupil of Thomas Linacre, whose Latin translation of Galen's book, *Of Temperaments*, was published at Cambridge in 1521, "did most to popularize the idea [of the connection between humours, health and temperaments]." They reveal that Sir Thomas Elyot's book, *Castel of Helth* was published by Berthelet in 1539 and, up to 1618, "fifteen editions" (IX: 391) were recorded.

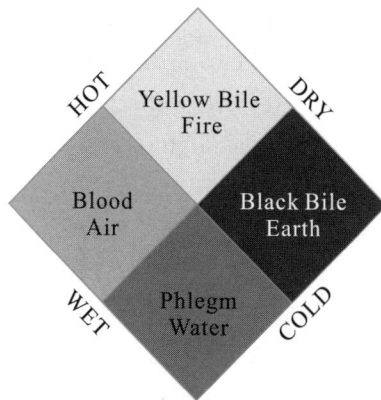

Fig. 4 - 1   The four major humours and their relationship to the elements and qualities, reproduced from Brian M. Fagan (63)

However, as Herford and the Simpsons point out, the term humour "rarely preserved the neutral usage of science" (I: 340). Humour, as a "ready formula for human infirmities . . . acquired a predominantly satiric usage, a suggestion of something odd or overbalanced, which coloured the entire Elizabethan usage of the term" (I: 340-41). Harry Levin suggests that "more casually, humor could be conceived as a person's state of mind at the moment: a mood, a caprice, a whim, an inclination to be indulged—or humored" (182). Levin's opinion can be found in previous scholars. The Furnesses's *New Variorum Merchant of Venice* lists Sir Walter Scott's definition of humour as "irresistible propensity of the mind, a peculiar quality," and Halliwell-Phillipps's as "an indescribable exaggeration of its meaning as applied to whim, caprice, or any propensity, any peculiar quality or turn of mind" (n. to IV. i. 47). However, David H. Bishop, in analyzing humour in *The Merchant of Venice*, proposes that "caprice" or "whim" is the "secondary" meaning of *humour*, and should be distinguished from its primary sense of physiological fluids " indicating a fixation in character " (175). ① Moreover, as Herford and the Simpsons point out, "the medieval love of classifying and cataloguing human infirmities," which culminated in *The Ship of Fools* (1494) by Sebastian Brandt (1457 – 1521), "persisted far into the Elizabethan period, and still survived at its close, under the new terminology of 'humours'" (I: 341).

It is difficult, as M. A. Harris argues, to "fix the source and trace the growth" of the use of humour as a person's eccentricity because of "lack of material bearing directly upon the history of humours" and "the necessity for a wide view of the times" (44). In any case, as Percy Simpson observes, English literature in the late sixteenth and seventeenth centuries is "full of metaphors and allusions" derived from the physical idea of humour (xxxvii). John Addington Symonds (1840 – 1893), writing of Ben Jonson's time, also says: "At this date humour was on everybody's lips to denote whim, oddity, conceited turn of thought, or special partiality in any person," and it became "a mere slang term for any eccentricity" (qtd. in Harris 44).

Nevertheless, Harris powerfully suggests the Greek models of character sketches, especially those of Aristotle

---

① John Dryden compares *humour* in early modern English comedy with *humeur* in seventeenth century French comedy, especially Molière's, which is not extensively used in drama and is "ill imitations of the ridiculum, or that which stirred up laughter in the old comedy" (356-57). Through his comparison, Dryden unites humour as a peculiar personal propensity with humour that arouses laughter: "by humour is meant some extravagant habit, passion, or affection, particular (as I said before) to some one person, by the oddness of which, he is immediately distinguished from the rest of men; which being lively and naturally represented, most frequently begets that malicious pleasure in the audience which is testified by laughter" (357). Dryden is among the earliest English writers to associate *humour* with (arousing) laughter, but this was well after Jonson's day.

and Theophrastus, as the origin of both the English Character writing and the popular idea of humour. According to Harris, the rise, growth, prosperity and waning of English, French and German Character writing and humour presentation coincide not only with the rise and fall of Greek and Latin studies in the Renaissance in those cultures but also with each other. In England, the heyday of Character writing was also the peak time of humour portraiture. Harry Levin confirms that it is "a predominant humour or ruling passion, a master faculty or *idée fixe*" that "animates the stock figures of the comic stage" (182). Herford and the Simpsons do not agree with Harris's suggestion that the Elizabethan popular idea of humour as caprice or whim and English Character writings share an origin. They say both the stock Elizabethan character analysis and the literary fashion of the typical character-sketch in the latter half of Elizabeth's reign were "quite independent of the 'humor' fashion" (I: 339). However, they point out that the literary currents of character analysis and character sketches in the late sixteenth and early seventeenth centuries England, together with "the Renascence doctrine of decorum in the treatment of character—involving a similar dominance of a single trait," called in the "piquant and flexible catchword [of humour] to their support, modifying its content but also themselves taking its colour" (I: 339). The presentation of humour as a simplified personal disposition, Elizabethan stock character analysis and English Character sketches joined with one another in a confluence of dramatic tradition.

ii. Character types

Aristotle, so far as we know, was the first writer known to have sketched characters. In his *Nichomachean Ethics*, Aristotle describes the characters of the liberal and the prodigal (1119^b21-1122^a18). Northrop Frye believes that Aristotle separates four archetypes of comic characters: the alazon (impostor, boaster, a hypocrite, etc.), the eiron (hero or heroine), the bomolochos (buffoon), and the *agroikos* or churlish, literally "rustic" (272-76). However, Edward Chauncey Baldwin credits Theophrastus's *Characters* as the "origin" of the character sketch as a literary form (193). Theophrastus (c. 372 – 287 BC), a disciple of Plato, and friend of Aristotle, sketched thirty-one[1] characters, such as the dissembler, the adulator, the garrulous, the rustic, the plausible, the ruffian, the shameless, the parsimonious, the blunderer, the busy body, the stupid, the morose, the old trifler, the malignant, the penurious, the vain, the proud, and the suspicious. According to Herford and the Simpsons, Theophrastus's sketches "powerfully promoted" the English literary fashion of Character writing in the early 1590s (I: 340).

Indeed, Character writing in England began, according to M. A. Harris, as early as 1567, when Thomas Harmon published his twenty-four Characters (45). Harris also observes that such kind of writing was "remarkably frequent in the first thirty-five years of the seventeenth century, a period coinciding with the working years of Jonson's life."

---

[1] Edward Chauncey Baldwin says thirty-seven (193).

During this period, publications of character sketches included the twenty-eight (my own counting is twenty-seven) Characters (1608) by Joseph Hall (1574 - 1656), forty-nine by Nicholas Breton (1555 - 1626), the seventy-nine (1614) of Sir Thomas Overbury (1581 - 1613), seventy-six of John Earle's (1601 - 1665) *Micro-cosmography* (1628), and many more (Harris 45). John Earle, especially, appends to his *Micro-cosmography* an annotated chronology of publications of Character writing between 1567 and 1700. According to Earle's chronology of publications (excluding his own), one Character writing book was published in 1567; one in 1605; thirteen between 1614 and 1634; and forty-two from 1641 to 1700 (five of them are supposed to be printed before 1700; the remaining thirty-seven bear definite dates) (246-314). Some of these publications issued new editions, which are not counted in the numbers above. The popularity of this kind of composition continued through the seventeenth century in England, the last publication possibly being the eighty-four Characters of Samuel Butler in 1680 (Harris 45). Moreover, there were books in the last quarter of the sixteenth century England teaching actors to play stereotyped characters. According to Oscar J. Campbell, Leone di Sommi wrote a book between 1567 and 1590 to "instruct actors who expect to play the role of the lout" or country rustic (5). Apparently, literary character sketches and dramatic character types had been associated with each other before Shakespeare and Jonson had had their first play performed.

As a voracious reader, Jonson certainly knew Theophrastus's Characters well. According to Percy Simpson, Jonson had read the Characters of the Greek author, who is "too near to comedy for any direct contribution to have been ignored" (lvii). Edward K. Graham says that "Theophrastus is, of course, the source and model of the English character-writers" (299). Graham also points out that the very popular character-writers "may have got suggestions from Jonson," although "their form was from Theophrastus" (300). In practice, Jonson is not known to have joined with the English writers in publishing any independent volume of character sketches. However, he did, in his first published play, *Every Man out of his Humour*, prefix fifteen "brief concise" sketches of the characters in the play. It is time here to look at one example from this play (Herford & Simpson, I: 374):

> Asper his Character. He is of an ingenious and free
> spirit, eager and constant in reproof, without feare
> controuling the worlds abuses. One, whom no seruile hope
> of gaine, or frosty apprehension of danger, can make to be a
> Parasite, either to time, place, or opinion.
>
> ("Character of the Persons" 1-6)

In this brief description, Jonson creates a free-willed and fearless critic who yields to no "seruile hope of gain or frosty apprehension of danger." Asper, according to Herford and the Simpsons, is Jonson's "ideal poet" (I: 388). Although Asper is a "notable creation," more "human and sympathetic" than any other figure in *Every Man out of his Humour*, he in this sketch remains a simplified character of an eccentric: the free-spirited poet of "unalloyed passion" (Herford & Simpson I: 388). Without other details, Apser is seen to be one-sided.

It is possible because of Jonson's portraiture of humours in *Every Man in his Humour* and its sequel, *Every Man out of his Humour*, and his character sketches in the latter play that critics such as Charles Gildon, John Dryden, Augustus William Schlegel and William Hazilitt call Jonson's characters types. From his own brief description of Asper, Jonson's characters do look like types, or stock characters. Edward K. Graham admits that in *Every Man out of his Humour*, Jonson did "present certain types acting under the influence of a dominant characteristic" (299). Indeed, as Graham sees, anyone else can also realize that Jonson easily impresses his readers with creating character types rather than individuals because he gives his dramatis personae suggestive names: Knowell, Brainworm, Downright, Wellbred, Justice Clement, Carlo Buffone, Fastidius Brisk, Fallace, Sordido, etc. These people, as Graham says, are "to a great extent the people of the character-writers" (304).

However, Jonson's characters are not always like ones from character-writers, nor are they all types. Edward K. Graham agrees that Jonson "in his early plays presents character not at all" (304), but "with the great plays of Jonson's middle period comparison with the character-writers fails, and for a significant reason." He believes that in his middle comedies, Jonson's characters "underwent a change that is fundamental" (304-05). Tyrone Guthrie, the great actor and director, claims in his *Life in the Theatre* that "every seriously ambitious young actor should have played at least three of the important *young* classic roles at the right age— Hamlet, say, Romeo and Benedick; or Mosca in *Volpone*, Young Hardcastle in *She Stoops to Conquer*, and Valentine in *Love for Love*." Paralleling Mosca with Hamlet, Guthrie calls them "great parts in great plays" (178). If Jonson's characters are all types, Guthrie could not have had such a view. Given the predominant opinion that Shakespeare and Jonson are the greatest English Renaissance dramatic poets, it is now necessary for us to examine the true nature of some characters in the two plays.

II. The fortune hunters

i. Corvino

1. Corvino the legacy hunter

After discussion of humours and character types in the context of the popular Character writing in early modern England, we can now use this discussion as a background to look at some characters from *Volpone* and *The Merchant of Venice*. For convenience of comparison, we may categorize these characters up as the legacy hunters, the facilitators and the comic villains, each pair represented by Corvino and Bassanio, Mosca and Antonio, Volpone and Shylock, respectively. Let us begin with the least dominant pair: Corvino and Bassanio.

Corvino first impresses the readers as an avaricious legacy hunter. He has a strong passion for Volpone's estate, which he plans to win through good gifts. When he hears of Volpone's dying, he comes to visit Volpone with the most expensive gift of all: an orient "rich pearle" that "doubles the twelfe caract" (I. v. 13-14), defeating the other legacy hunters' silver plate and gold coins. Then when he tries to greet Volpone but does not find the "sick" man responding to him, Corvino acts again and offers a diamond. All Corvino wants to achieve with these precious gifts is a mentioning of his name as at least one of the heirs if not the sole one in Volpone's will.

Therefore, when he hears Volpone's parasite Mosca say "The weeping of an heire should still be laughter, / Vnder a visor" (I. v. 22-23), Corvino becomes exceedingly excited and instantly asks for confirmation: "Am I his heire?" (I. iv. 23) Corvino's apparent anxiety is exploited by the shrewd parasite who fabricates a confidential will unshowable until his master's death but assures Corvino of the greatest hope. Obsessed, Corvino is easily gulled, trusting the parasite and eagerly expecting to become Volpone's heir.

While he anticipates Volpone's death, Corvino is shown to face a major trial. He is told that instead of dying quickly, Volpone has recovered and is receiving young women as comfortresses,[1] including possibly a virgin—a physician's daughter, from competing legacy hunters. Frustrated as he is, Corvino decides to follow the suggestion from Mosca of offering his own wife by the following reasoning:

> If any man
> But I had had this lucke—The thing in't selfe,
> I know, is nothing—Wherefore should not I
> As well command my bloud, and my affections,
> As this dull Doctor? In the point of honour,
> The cases are all one, of wife, and daughter.
>
> (II. vi. 68-73)

Considering his effort for Volpone's legacy "lucke," Corvino now believes that "the thing" (his wife to sleep by

---

[1] 1 Kings 1: 1-4 tell about the old and weak King David's shivering from coldness and a lovely young virgin Abishag seeking out to take care of him, sleeping by him and keeping him warm.

Volpone) " in't selfe is nothing " because he trusts that
Volpone is decrepit and impotent. As for honor, it is only a
case of wife or daughter. Therefore, his only question is
whether it should be his wife; although to use one's wife as a
property for investment is unethical, or illegal to other people
even in Elizabethan England (we know Venice is London
under a thin veil) ,[1] Corvino decides to ignore the question of
ethics or law after this quick debate in his mind. Corvino
announces to Mosca;

> We will make all sure. The party, you wot of,
> Shall be mine owne wife, Mosca.

(II. vi. 80-81)

Thinking he can " make all sure" that he will win the
legacy competition by offering his wife, Corvino thus wills to
offer his wife.

Once decided, Corvino urges Mosca to go quickly back
home and prepare Volpone for his wife Celia's attendance
"lest they [other legacy hunters] should be before vs" (II.
vi. 91). When Mosca goes home, Corvino immediately cajoles
Celia to put on all her " best attire," and her " choicest
iewells" and go to Volpone's (II. vii. 14). Quickly both
Corvino and Celia arrive at Volpone's home only to surprise

---

[1] In Elizabethan England, although a woman was "under the governance of a man for most or all of
her life," and a married woman was "subject to her husband who had the final say," a husband
who "governed arbitrarily would sooner or later find his home in crisis," not only because the wife
could find "routes of recourse," but also because the Equity courts and church courts were open to
a woman should she need them (Forgeng 42). Nicholas Breton's advice to a husband might be a
hint of how a man should then treat his wife; "Cherish all good humors in her; let her lack no silk,
crewel, thread, nor flax, to work on at her pleasure, force her to nothing, rather prettily chide her
from her labor, but in any wise commend what she doeth" (Forgeng 42). For parallelisms between
Venice and England / London, see Brian Parker, pp. 20-21.

Mosca, who has told them not to come until he sends for
them:

> Mosca. Death on me! you are come too soone, what
> meant you?
> Did not I say, I would send?
> Corvino. Yes, but I feard
> You might forget it, and then they
> preuent us.
> Mosca. Preuent? did ere man haste so, for his hornes?

$$\text{(III. vii. 1-4)}$$

Corvino is blamed by Mosca for rashness to offer his wife for
legacy, hinting at cuckoldry, perhaps the one thing Corvino fears
as hell. However, he explains with a reason at which even
Mosca, the planner of the deception, is appalled. Corvino tells
Mosca that he has speedily come because he is afraid that Mosca
might forget to send for them so that other legacy hunters may
"preuent" him, or come before him, a reason invoking Mosca's
contempt in an aside that no man has ever hasted so much as
Corvino "for his hornes," or to be cuckolded.

As Joseph Hall writes, the covetous man is "a servant to
himself"; he "doth base homage to that which should be the
worst drudge; a lifeless piece of earth is his master, his god:
which he shrines in his coffer, and to which he sacrifices his
heart" (116), Corvino is such a covetous man. For a hope of
gaining Volpone's legacy, his gold, Corvino has sacrificed a
diamond and an orient pearl; now he is willing and ready to
sacrifice his wife, at whom he, in another situation, fears the
most even to have others cast a look. In this sense, Corvino
represents the obvious stock character of the covetous man.

Driven by his avarice, Corvino tricks his wife into arriving with him at Volpone's house. Corvino tells his wife the reasons why they have come. However, when she understands her husband's intention, Celia shows such perfect qualities of virtue and chastity that she refuses to obey his command. She begs Corvino to "affect not these strange trials" (III. vii. 24). Celia tells her husband that she would rather be locked up forever at home than sleep by Volpone. Telling his wife that he has "no such humor" (fear of her unfaithfulness) (III. vii. 28), Corvino assures her that he is "not horne-mad" (III. vii. 30), nor crazy with fear of being cuckolded. When Celia shows suspicion of some serious trial for her, Corvino tells her about his interests in the legacy competition again:

> Corvino. I' haue told you reasons;
> What the phisitians haue set downe; how much,
> It may concerne me; what my engagements are;
> My meanes; and the necessitie of those meanes,
> For my recouery: wherefore, if you bee
> Loyall, and mine, be wonne, respect my venture.
> Celia. Before your honour?
> Corvino. Honour? tut, a breath;
> There is no such thing, in nature: a meere terme
> Inuented to awe fooles. What is my gold
> The worse, for touching? clothes, for being look'd on?

(III. vii. 32-41)

For the first time in the play Corvino clearly and frankly tells Celia that he has intended her as a "venture": his interests in competing for legacy which is, in turn, important to the recovery of his other investments. Corvino wants his wife to obey him to show respect for his "venture." As for Celia's question about his "honour," Corvino sniffs at it. When honor is put together with business ventures, Corvino considers it just "a breath," "a mere terme invented to awe fooles." Corvino compares Celia to his gold, his money, which does not become "worse" or less by being touched or being looked on. On the contrary, it is "a pious worke, mere charity, for physick / And honest politie" that she shall go to Volpone (III. vii. 65-66). In addition, Corvino assures Celia that no other people will know that she is going to sleep by Volpone except for themselves and Mosca, and Mosca is not going to tell because his "lippes" are in Corvino's "pocket" (III. vii. 51). Neither of them will tell about it unless Celia herself shall "proclaime't" (III. vii. 52). In other words, the reputation of being a cuckold is of no importance to Corvino as long as only few people know about it and he can exchange it for enough monetary gains.

Theophrastus has written the character of the Self-seeking Affability, "a sort of behaviour which provides pleasure, but not with the best intentions" (51). According to Theophrastus, the character of the Self-seeking Affability, as the name indicates, will flatter someone excessively for self-interest. Corvino, now trying to coax his wife into sleeping by Volpone for his hope of legacy, clearly bears such a character.

However, seeing that his persuasion and coaxing cannot move Celia to Volpone's bed, Corvino furiously invokes a violent threat: to drag her home by the hair, call her a strumpet through the streets, rip up her mouth unto her ears, slit her nose like a raw red gurnard, bind her alive together with a killed slave, hang her up and etch words of a devised crime into her naked body (III. vii. 96-106). Corvino's threat bears such a harshness of behaviour that he is shown to be just like another character that Theophrastus describes: the Surly man (77).

To his frustration, both Corvino's plausible arguments and his violent threats fail him. He finally decides to follow Mosca's suggestion, leaving the scene but forcing Celia to stay alone with Volpone, who, after many failures of attempted seduction, almost succeeds in raping her. The long process of Corvino's offering his wife to sleep by Volpone eventually terminates with Celia's continued resistance and narrow, lucky escape. During the whole process, Corvino is shown to be maniacally obsessed with getting Volpone's legacy, flattering him with his diamond, pearl and finally his wife. As Michael Taylor notes, between sex and money, two of the "great themes" of literature dealing with the city, money— and the real estate that advertises its possession—is ultimately the more important" (vii), Corvino's avarice for Volpone's wealth eventually dominates all his motivation, which is displayed in his self-interested cajolement and enraged threatening of his wife.

2. Corvino the jealous husband

The Elizabethan husbands cared deeply about the faithfulness of their wives. As Jeffrey L. Forgeng points out, one of the most serious insults to a man then was "to imply unchastity on the part of his mother (whoreson) or wife (cuckold)" (50). We remember Othello's violence against Desdemona. We also remember well Benedick or Kitely's feared humiliation of being cuckolded. Corvino is not only avaricious, cajoling and surly; he is also a jealous husband, fearing extremely to be cuckolded. He is exactly like Kitely in this respect: a jealous merchant husband. Similar to Kitely who has his wife monitored when leaving home, Corvino puts his wife Celia under heavy surveillance when he goes out:

> There is a guard, of ten spies thick, vpon her;
> All his whole household: each of which is set
> Vpon his fellow, and haue all their charge,
> When he goes out, when he comes in, examin'd.
>
> (I. v. 123-26)

Not only is Celia closely watched by Corvino's "spies" at home, but also she is, according to Mosca, kept at home. She "never do's come abroad, neuer takes ayre / But at a windore" (I. v. 119-20).

It is the window where Celia takes fresh air that drastically worsens Corvino's treatment of her. Because of Corvino's close watch of Celia, Volpone has to disguise as a mountebank working under Celia's window to entice her out to satisfy his unstoppable desire to see her. When Celia finally appears at the window and is tricked into throwing down her handkerchief for his fake medicine, Volpone cannot help giving a prolonged speech about the medicine to keep Celia at the window. Expectedly, Corvino sees the scene and

becomes desperate and violent. [1] Beating away Volpone, his
followers and others, Corvino cries out to the mountebank:

> Spight o' the deuill, and my shame!
> . . .
> Signior Flaminio, will you downe, Sir? downe?
> What is my wife your Franciscina? Sir?
>
> (II. iii. 1, 3-4)

After bemoaning Volpone's seeing his wife as his
"shame," Corvino deplores the fox and his wife for putting on
a *commedia dell'arte* performance,[2] in which the
mountebank is Signior Flaminio, the young lover; Celia,
Franciscina, the saucy maidservant. Then he laments a
possible consequence to befall himself:

> Hart! ere to morrow, I shall be new christen'd,
> And cald the PANTALONE di besogniosi,
> About the towne.
>
> (II. iii. 7-9)

This is his real fear: becoming a Pantalone. A Pantalone,
according to Herford and the Simpsons, is a "stock Venetian
character" in the *commedia dell'arte* who was presented as

---

[1] Handkerchief-tossing "to an early modern audience was seen as flirtatious" (McEvoy 60),
although Celia, who cannot get out of the house to buy from the mountebank and therefore has to
use the handkerchief for wrapping money and medicine, may not mean as much as such. We
remember Desdemona's inadvertent dropping of her handkerchief. In fact, Jonson may have been
parodying Shakespeare in this handkerchief-dropping scene. Brian F. Tyson, studying the
numerous similarities between *Othello* and *Volpone*, points out the possibility of Jonson's
"conscious parody": "the handkerchief which fans the flame of Othello's anger, causing him to
accuse his wife of harlotry, is transmuted for comic effect in *Volpone* into the handkerchief thrown
by Celia to the disguised Fox, an act that incenses her husband, who instantly accuses her of
harlotry" (62). Howard Marchitell has also discussed the "parodic form" of the handkerchief
scene in *Volpone* in relation to that in *Othello* (287).

[2] For Jonson's knowledge of the Italian *Commedia dell'arte* and *Volpone*'s resemblances to it, see
Brian Parker, pp. 21-24.

"a lean old man, wore loose slippers, a black cap and gown, and a red dress. " He is often depicted as "a jealous dotard" or as a " cuckold," and " this is the point of Corvino's allusion" (IX: 709). Jonson's knowledge of the Pantalone is another strong proof of his familiarity with character writing, including that in Italian. [1]

Returning home after Volpone and all other people are beaten away, Corvino storms at Celia for having put "death of mine honour, with the cities foole" (II. v. 1). Accusing Celia of smiling graciously at the mountebank and the onlookers, Corvino calls Volpone a "iuggling, tooth-drawing, prating montebanke," and the onlookers, "noted lechers," "Satyres," and "hot spectators" (II. v. 2-9). Then he flays Celia in horribly abusive language filled with sexual innuendos:

> Well! you shall haue him, yes.
> He shall come home, and minister vnto you
> The fricace, for the moother. Or, let me see,
> I thinke, you'had rather mount? would you not mount?
> Why, if you'll mount, you may; yes truely, you may:
> And so, you may be seene, downe to th' foot.
> Get you a citterne, lady *vanitie*,
> And be a dealer, with the vertuous man;
> Make one: I'le but protest my selfe a cuckold,
> And saue your dowrie.
>
> (II. v. 15-24)

In this condemnation, Corvino compares Celia to a lascivious woman who may "mount" another man, to be seen

---

[1] Jonson's language skills in Italian are proved by Mark Bland, p. 379, n. 39, p. 389, and Herford & Simpson, I, p. 156, n. 92.

in public "downe to th' foot," a prostitute with a "citterne" (stringed musical instrument), a "lady vanitie" (i. e. seductress), and an adultress to make himself a cuckold and "saue her dowry."

Then Corvino tells Celia that he is a restrained German ("Dutchman"), not a sexually passionate "Italian." He threatens Celia that if she fails to understand this,

> Thou'ldst tremble, to imagine, that the murder
> Of father, mother, brother, all thy race,
> Should follow, as the subiect of my iustice!
>
> (II. v. 27-29)

In other words, if Celia dares to be unfaithful, Corvino will consider it so outrageous a crime that he is to seek justice by killing her entire family. At this point, Corvino draws out his sword and waves it at Celia as he continues to threaten her:

> What could'st thou propose
> Lesse to thy selfe, then, in this heat of wrath,
> And stung with my dishonour, I should strike
> This steele unto thee, with as many stabs,
> As thou wert gaz'd vpon with goatish eyes?
>
> (II. v. 30-34)

Corvino is telling Celia that as long as she dishonors him, even by being looked upon, he would be so wrathful as to stab her, as many times as she has been "gaz'd vpon."

After the death and sword-stabbing threat, Corvino decides to forbid his wife to appear at her window. Indeed, he is going to have it shut up for ever ("haue this bawdy light dam'd vp"), and before it is done, he is going to "chalke a line, some two, or three yards off" the window, and warns

Celia not to overstep the line, not even by "chance." Otherwise, "more hell, more horror, more wilde, remorcelesse rage" shall seize upon her than those that might seize a conjurer by his devils accidentally let out. Then he holds up a chastity belt ("locke") and tells Celia that he will hang it upon her. This is still not all yet. Corvino informs Celia that she shall spend the rest of her life "backe-wards," that is, in the back of the house, unable to see any outside views or breathe any fresh air through the window facing the public street (II. v. 50-61). [1]

Having planned these strict measures, Corvino is still not satisfied. He makes another threat of violence against Celia, warning her that if she does not let him prosper, he will make her "an anatomie," dissecting her by himself for both physiological and moral analyses, and "read a lecture" upon her "to the citie and in publique (II. v. 70-72). Howard Marchitell notes that "the threat posed by a 'dishonest' wife is a major theme in a diverse range of Renaissance texts . . . that often elicits a profound violence (not always only verbal) aimed at women" (288). Corvino's hysterical strictures of his wife's appearing at the window and tossing her handkerchief in public eyes, and his threat of using violence on her if she becomes unfaithful to him show that Corvino is desperate to protect his honor from being smeared. Corvino's definition of unfaithfulness, at least for Celia, is showing up in public, except for one or two rare appearances in Church. This is again seen in his command for Celia to hide away and not be

---

[1] Cynthia Lewis discusses women's moral agency at a window in early modern British drama. See "Actor," esp. pp. 479-82 in Section II, for a discussion of the theatricality of Celia at her window, an excellent analysis of Celia's gullibility and even foolishness.

seen when he hears a knock at his door:

> Away, and be not seene, paine of thy life;
> Not looke toward the windore.

(II. v. 67-68)

Corvino so cherishes his honor and is so afraid of being cuckolded that he now forbids his wife to show her face in public, not even from a window.[1] Richard Dutton, in discussing *Volpone*'s Venice, points out historically that although Venetian men "were inclined to kiss each other, they went to great lengths to prevent other men from kissing their wives," and it would be "typical behaviour" (also reflected in the dialogues between Sir Pol and Peregrine in Scenes II. iii. and II. v. of *Volpone*) for Corvino to treat his wife as he declares (*Gunpowder Plot* 96). Historically true as this is, Corvino's maniacal and violent abuses of his wife prove him to be a "pathologically jealous" husband (Maus, "Horns" 565).

What is worth noting is that although Jonson characterizes Corvino partly as a jealous husband, he probably did not have classical archetypes to refer to. Theophrastus did not include a sexually jealous character. Herodes (living probably before 240 BC), who did dramatize a jealous lady in one of his mimes, might have been known to Jonson but this has not, to my knowledge, been proven, not even by Herford and the Simpsons in their exhaustive collection of Jonson's classical sources. Joseph Hall in his *Characters of Virtues and Vices*, published two or three years

---

[1] For a psycho-analytic discussion of cuckoldry in Jonson and Thomas Middleton, see Gary Kuchar, pp. 1-30; See esp. an analysis of Corvino, pp. 3-12.

after the first performance of *Volpone*, included the character of the envious as its last item (124-25), but this character is about the general envy of a person's goodness or achievement, rather than a man's sexual jealousy concerning his wife or even a woman. Among his seventy-six characters, published twenty-two years after *Volpone*'s first performance, John Earle also included one as the last item: the character of the suspicious, jealous man. However, this character is much more about a suspicious character than a jealous man, and nothing about sexual jealousy is mentioned (208-10). [1] This lack of models is highly curious in the context of abundant dramatization of jealousy among husbands and wives in English Renaissance literature.

Sexual jealousy was a major theme in early modern English literature, not limited to literature of dealing with the city. Katharine Eisaman Maus notes that "anxiety about sexual betrayal pervades the drama of the English Renaissance": not only does "jealousy dominate the plots of many plays," but songs, jokes and saws about the cuckolded, the abandoned, the unreliability of wives and lovers "turn up in other plays on the slightest of pretexts" ("Horns" 561). Thomas Middleton's *A Mad World, My Masters*, John Ford's *'Tis Pity She's a Whore*, John Webster's *The White Devil*, George Chapman's *Bussy d'Ambois*, and Thomas Heywood's *A Woman Killed with Kindness*, among others, all feature sexual jealousy. As for our authors in focus, besides *The Merchant* and *Volpone*, Shakespeare dramatized such

---

[1] See Lynn S. Meskill, pp. 16-20, for a comparison between "envy" and "jealousy" in the context of Shakespeare and Jonson.

jealousy in *The Merry Wives of Windsor*, *Much Ado About Nothing*, *Othello*, *Troilus and Cressida*, and *The Winter's Tale*;[①] Jonson did it in *Every Man in his Humour*, *The Magnetic Lady*, *The Devil Is an Ass* and *The Alchemist*.

Considering the frequency of the theme of sexual jealousy in English Renaissance literature and the absence of the stock character of a jealous man or woman, we may safely infer that Jonson had to use materials from his contemporary world, literary or otherwise. In close relation to characters, Jonson, as "the most intellectually self-conscious playwright of his time," attempted to "theorize 'humours' characterization" in *Every Man out of his Humour* in terms of humour's contemporary medical sense (Wiggins 74). As a result, Martin Wiggins notes, Jonson's character's humour was "not just a quirk," but "an obsession, a psychic imbalance comparable with Renaissance medicine's conception of mental illness" (74). Therefore, even if we do not say Jonson created the humour character, we can be sure that he greatly enriched it. In the case of Corvino, he created a pathologically jealous husband combining current medical knowledge and a contemporary literary theme, and because of this creation's entailment of realistic settings, events and characters, as Wiggins points out, this new realism "brought with it a vast array of kinds of experience hitherto excluded or treated only tangentially" in English comedy (78).

3. Corvino the fool and knave

The character of Corvino as an avaricious, flattering,

---

① Even Shylock has been accused of sexual jealousy for trying to shut his daughter Jessica up from suitors. See Stanley Wells, *Shakespeare, Sex*, p. 173.

surly and jealous husband is complicated by his response to Volpone's attempted rape of Celia, followed by a court accusation by Bonario who saves Celia. To save Volpone and himself, Mosca deceives Voltore the lawyer into believing that Bonario has abducted and forced Celia to accuse Volpone of raping her. Corvino, still hoping for Volpone's money, joins Voltore, Corbaccio and Lady Would-be, the other three major legacy hunters, to defend Volpone as a team of perjurers.

During their plotting for perjury, Corvino's worry shocks Mosca and the readers. Corvino asks Mosca if Voltore knows "the truth," and is assured by the parasite that a "formall tale" has been devised to salve his "reputation" (IV. iv. 6-8). Mosca thinks that Corvino is worried that Voltore knows the truth about his attempt to "prostitute [his wife] . . . freely, vn-asked, or vn-intreated" (III. vii. 75-76), and will therefore denigrate him. Surprisingly, Corvino's answer to Mosca's "tale" to salve his reputation proves that Mosca does not understand him: "I feare no one, but him; that, this his pleading / Should make him stand for a co-heire" (IV. iv. 9-10). What really worries Corvino is not the reputation of a cuckold, but the sharing of a dreamed legacy. This is to be proven again and again till the end of the play.

In the court, when asked to give testimony concerning his wife's alleged adultery, Corvino speaks about her in the foulest language:

> This woman (please your father-hoods) is a whore,
> Of most hot exercise, more then a partrich,
> Vpon record.

> (IV. v. 117-19)

Comparing his wife to a lustful bird ("partrich"),

Corvino echoes Voltore's false indictment of her unfaithfulness, but worse than Voltore, he calls his wife the most lustful of whoreson record. The familial association of a whore with an Elizabethan man was one of the ultimate ways of humiliating him. But here, even that does not bother Corvino. In fact, his charge, with strongest effects to mortify himself, is so repellently indecent that the court notary has to ask him to "preserue the honour of the court" (IV. v. 120).

Corvino now no longer seems afraid of becoming, or at least, being called a cuckold. Indeed, he is willing to project himself as a cuckold in public, as Mosca says to him:

> Mosca: [aside to Corvino] It was much better, that
>   you should professe
>   Your selfe a cuckold, thus, then that the other
>   Should have beene prou'd.
>   Corvino: Nay I consider'd that.
>
>   (IV. vi. 70-73)

In addition to his later readiness to be acknowledged a cuckold, Corvino openly declares in front of all people at the court that he hopes his "most impetuous, vnsatisfied" wife will go on to damnation (IV. v. 144-45, in his own words). Corvino's accusation is so hysterical that even one of the judges has become sympathetic with him: "His griefe hath made him frantique" (IV. v. 131). In reality, however, he has been turned into a foolishly contented cuckold, but he cannot realize that.

Celebrating the victory of wronging Bonario and Celia at court, Corvino joins the other legacy hunters in again asking Mosca for Volpone's legacy, each believing that only he or she is the exclusive heir (ess). However, each one, including

Corvino, is coldly and ruthlessly rejected and kicked out of Volpone's house. Corvino, especially, is humiliated by Mosca:

> Me thinkes (of all) you should haue beene th'
>   example.
> Why should you stay, here? with what thought? what
>   promise?
> Heare you, doe not you know, I know you an asse?
> And, that you would, most faine, haue beene a wittoll,
> If fortune would haue let you? that you are
> A declar'd cuckold, on good termes?
>
> (V. iii. 48-53)

Called "th' example" (of all greedy legacy hunters) and "an asse" by Mosca, Corvino is also told what he hated most to hear earlier: he is a "wittoll," a "declar'd cuckold." At the same time his reason to be a willing cuckold is exposed: greed for fortune.

With such humiliation and a complete loss of any hope, a person would find it natural and well-urged to seek revenge. However, Corvino's reaction is surprising. His perseverance to defame and defeat himself and his wife is exceptional. He warns Corbaccio, who has also lost all hopes outright: "We must maintaine / Our first tale good, for both our reputations (V. vi. 1-2). Obviously, Corvino remembers well that their charges against Celia are nothing but a "tale." However, Corvino's consciousness of his "tale" makes it all the more difficult to understand his intention to "mainteine" their "first tale good," that is, to hold on to their false accusations against Celia and Bonario. Theophrastus, as we remember, a source of Jonson's characterization, has described a stupid character who is "a slowness of mind in word and deed" like failing to understand a calculated account, attend a summon, or falling sound asleep during a play (75). Obviously, compared with Theophrastus's fool, Jonson's Corvino is much stupider. He does not fail to realize his declared cuckoldry or open humiliation or inheritance illusion; he chooses to bear the humiliation and exposed illusion and carry them through.

At first, Corvino charges Celia with unfaithfulness because he is still looking forward to inheriting Volpone's money. Now that Corvino's hope of inheritance is completely gone, and he has declared himself a cuckold at the court, there is literally no such thing as "reputation" for Corvino to keep, except that of innocence in the case. And this innocence is guaranteed by the nearly certain guilt verdict of Bonario and Celia. Perhaps the only explanation for Corvino's unconvertible insistence on his wife's guilt is his hope for a court decision that he is truthfully an innocent and suffering husband.

In any case, Corvino has chosen to persist in his wrong accusations, even when Voltore has confessed his own distraction in the second trial, intending plainly to subvert the previous court decision. When asked by one of the judges for testimony confirming Voltore's accusation against Mosca, Corvino swears that he will stand on his "first report" by his "state," "life," and "fame" (V. x. 43-44). Corvino willfully sticks to his perjury to the end regardless of the changes at the court, including the caprices of Mosca and Voltore. Eventually, when Volpone exposes himself and confesses to the court, Corvino has to accept a severe punishment:

1 Avocatore: Thou Coruino, shalt

>Be straight imbarqu'd from thine own house, and row'd
>
>Round about Venice, through the grand canale,
>
>Wearing a cap, with faire, long asses eares,
>
>In stead of hornes; and, so to mount (a paper
>
>Pin'd on thybrest) to the berlino—
>
>Corvino: Yes,
>
>And, haue mine eies beat out with stinking fish,
>
>Bruis'd fruit and rotten egges—'Tis well. I'am glad,
>
>I shall not see my shame, yet.
>
>1 Avocatore: And to expiate
>
>Thy wrongs done to thy wife, thou art to send her
>
>Home, to her father, with her dowrie trebled.
>
>(V. xii. 134-44)

Corvino is sentenced to row a gondola around Venice wearing a cap with fair, long ass's ears symbolizing horns or cuckoldry, plus a "berlino" or pillory, on which a piece of paper about his crime is pinned, telling the whole city about his "wittolhood." Also, he has to send his wife back to her father, with a fine of three times her dowry. Corvino envisions his upcoming miseries of rowing along the canal, with "stinking fish, bruis'd fruit and rotten egges" thrown at him.

From Corvino's offering of expensive gifts such as a rare pearl and a diamond, to his abusive chastisement of his wife, to his forcing his wife to sleep by Volpone, to the final events of distraught and headstrong false accusation of his wife, and to his eventual punishment, Corvino is shown to have two major humours; avarice and jealousy. His avarice, stronger than jealousy, is shown in his excessively passionate craving for Volpone's legacy at the cost of his own fortune, his wife and finally, his reputation. His jealousy of his wife almost results in her home imprisonment for the rest of her life. His pervasive fears of cuckoldry plus his tempting encouragement and violent urging of his wife to sleep by Volpone can be seen as extremely whimsical. His obdurate false accusation of his wife's infidelity at court absolutely erodes his dignity. All his misdeeds are caused by his avarice. Volpone's comment on Corvino in the face of Celia is a good summary of the merchant's sole ultimate concern for money:

> I, in Corvino, and such earth-fed mindes, [leaping
>   from his couch]
> That neuer tasted the true heau'n of loue.
> Assure thee, Celia, he that would sell thee,
> Onely for hope of gaine, and that vncertaine,
> He would haue sold his part of paradise
> For ready money, had he met a cope-man.
>
> (III. vii. 139-44)

Even Volpone is criticizing Corvino for lack of love for heavenly things. Indeed, Corvino only loves gains, or "ready money," for which he would sell anything and anyone, including his wife and even heaven ("his part of paradise"). However, in representing his avarice, Jonson brings in Corvino's fiery jealousy of his wife to contrast and highlight his desires for wealth, and then further complicates his character by letting him madly protect his reputation. Such are the passion, bad manners and, in other words, the corrupting power of a love only for earthly things rather than for God. And such is Corvino, precisely in the words of Volpone, 'a Chimera of wittal [wittol], foole and knaue" (V.

xii. 91). In terms of humours or stock characters, Corvino is at the same time the greedy legacy hunter, the flatterer, the surly man, the jealous husband, the willing cuckold, the perjurer, and the fool. In terms of sources, these characters come from Theophrastus's character sketches, contemporary character writers, and current theater productions. Dryden was right that humour was Jonson's "proper sphere," but he was wrong in saying that Jonson "delighted most to represent mechanic people" (XV: 353). As a character from his "full pen'd creature within fiue weeks" (*Volpone*, Prologue, ll. 13, 16), Jonson lets Corvino have different qualities, a combination of several types, allowing the character to develop according to his changing situation. Corvino is like a human being who can be sweet, fearful, angry, greedy, stupid and shameless.

ii. Bassanio

1. Bassanio the Prodigal Son

Different from the avaricious, flattering, mercenary and boring Corvino whose first appearance in the play is meant to bribe Volpone for a larger return of legacy, Bassanio impresses the reader as a merry-seeking noble man the moment he appears in the play: "Good signors both, when shall we laugh? Say, when? / You grow exceeding strange; must it be so?" (I. i. 66-67) Bassanio's blaming of his friends Salarino and Solanio for not having "laughed" together and "growing strange" is a greeting, but this greeting tells us about Bassanio's life of merry-making. Bassanio's question of "Say, when?" may mean that it is he, not Salarino or Solanio, who is eager for fun. By "must it be so?" whether Bassanio means "must you, Salario and Solanio, become exceeding strange" for not "laughing" with him, or as Horace Howard Furness notes, Shakespeare might mean it to be a stage-direction for their departure (note to I. i. 75). The phrase shows Bassanio's preoccupation with fun making with his friends. Harold Goddard assigns such a preoccupation to Bassanio's tedium, remarking that he, together with other characters, " give [s] the sense of attempting to fill every chink of time with distraction or amusement, often just words, to prevent their thinking" (84). When he sketches his characters of the vices, Joseph Hall describes the Unthrift in these words: "His senses are too much his guides and his purveyors; and appetite is his steward. He is an impotent servant to his lusts, and knows not to govern either his mind or his purse" (123-24). Seemingly, Hall was telling us about the character of Bassanio.

Indeed, Bassanio's first talk with his friend Antonio in private confirms such a description. Replying to Antonio's inquiry about the lady he has promised to tell about (I. i. 118-20), Bassanio says,

> 'Tis not unknown to you, Antonio,
> How much I have disabled mine estate
> By something showing a more swelling port
> Than my faint means would grant continuance.
> Nor do I now make moan to be abridged
> From such a noble rate, but my chief care
> Is to come fairly off from the great debts
> Wherein my time, something too prodigal,
> Hath left me gaged.

(I. i. 121-29)

Bassanio unequivocally confesses his unthrift. He has

been spending more than what he can afford, and has thus deteriorated his situation. He should cut down on his spending because of his "faint means." However, he does not because he wants to maintain his "noble rate." What he is concerned with most now is to get rid of his debts, although he knows clearly that his life is "something too prodigal." With these words, Bassanio precisely fits into Joseph Hall's character of the Unthrift:

> He ranges beyond his pale, and lives without compass.
> His expense is measured, not by ability, but will. His
> pleasures are immoderate, and not honest. A wanton eye, a
> liquorish tongue, a gamesome hand have impoverished him.
>
> (123)

A man who lives a life of willful free spending, seeking immoderate pleasures is impoverished. Such is Bassanio. He has not only squandered his own "means" (I. i. 124), but also "lost" "the much" which he "owes" Antonio (I. i. 146-47). And the result is he is not just "impoverished" (Hall 123), but in "great debts" (*The Merchant* I. i. 128).

Bassanio's self-aware prodigality is well known to Shylock. When Shylock tells his daughter Jessica about Bassanio's invitation to dinner, Shylock says he will go to feed upon "the prodigal Christian" (II. v. 15). Bassanio's employment of Lancelot Gobbo, Shylock's former servant, is also an act of prodigality. Shylock is somehow pleased to see Lancelot will serve Bassanio because he will "help to waste" Bassanio's "borrowed purse" (II. v. 49-50).

Bassanio's worst act of prodigality in the entire play is his giving away Portia's ring after the court scene, to Balthasar, the legal doctor, that is, Portia in disguise. While Balthasar does deserve a ring for having saved Antonio's life plus three thousand ducats at the least, and Bassanio can find it natural to thank Portia with an expensive gift, his giving away the ring means betrayal of his vow. Bassanio remembers well that "more depends on this [ring] than on the value" because when he receives the ring, he is made to "vow" that he "should neither sell, nor give, nor lose it" (IV. i. 430-39). [1] However, when Antonio asks Bassanio to weigh the doctor's merit and his friendship against Portia's "commandment" (IV. i. 446-47), Bassanio instantly asks Graziano to forward the ring to Portia. [2] Karen Newman remarks that "when the ring begins its metonymic [of Portia] travels from Bassanio to the young doctor, the ring picks up new meanings which contradict its status as a sign of male possession, fidelity, and values" (28). Therefore, when Bassanio breaks his word and fidelity by giving away the ring, he gives away his possession, too.

Bassanio's prodigality is, seen from another perspective, a result of his dominant humour. John W. Draper considers Bassanio's sanguine humour the reason for that generosity or prodigality: " Bassanio's sanguine nature, for example, explains . . . the liberality that depleted his former fortunes and the hopefulness with which he embarks on his career of borrowing and wooing"; it also explains the fact that " he is generous with Portia's ring " (*Humors* 28). However, as Aristotle points out in his *Nicomachean Ethics*, prodigal persons "exhaust their substance with giving" (1121^{a}17-18).

---

[1] See, Karen Newman, pp. 19-33, for a discussion of gift exchange in relation to giving and receiving gifts in *The Merchant of Venice*, including the ring episodes.

[2] See, Lawrence W. Hyman, pp. 109-116, for an analysis of the rivalry between Antonio and Portia for Bassanio's love.

Bassanio is prodigal rather than generous because he has not only exhausted his substance by extravagancy, but also in serious debt. As Bassanio says of himself when he tells Portia of his wealth, that "I freely told you all the wealth I had / Ran in my *veins* (III. ii. 252-53, italics mine). Bassanio means that all his wealth is his noble birth, his "noble blood. " This is consistent with his speech to Antonio in the beginning of the play. Before begging Antonio for another loan, Bassanio asks Antonio to " shoot another arrow that self way / Which you did shoot the first" so that he can find both this arrow and the first one back (I. i. 148-50). Lawrence Danson glosses Bassanio's request as " dubious analogy" (110), and Bassanio using such plausible language knows clearly about its falsity (Antonio blames him not to "spend but time / To wind about my love with circumstance" (I. i. 153-54)). Horace Howard Furness interprets Bassanio's uncontrolled expense as " obstinate in extravagance," or " wilful in his prodigality" (n. to I. i. 156).

Scholars and critics relate the character of Bassanio as an unthrift to the story of the Prodigal Son in the Gospel of Luke, which is also brought up by Graziano (II. vi. 14-19). Patrick J. Sullivan remarks that Bassanio is normally " decadent or prodigal in the manner of his biblical prototype" (31). Susan Mclean argues that " Bassanio is the most obvious parallel to the Prodigal Son. He wastes both his patrimony and the money that he had previously borrowed from Antonio " (49). Bassanio's experiences in the play is similar to the biblical story in that both Bassanio and the younger son from Luke (XV. 11-31) are wasteful when young, and then having gone through merry-making and poverty, are forgiven (Bassanio by

Antonio first and then Portia, and the younger son by his father). Comparing Bassanio with both Joseph Hall's sketches of the unthrift and his similarities with the biblical Prodigal Son, we will find it fitting to say there is clearly an aspect of the stock prodigal character in Bassanio. [1]

2. Bassanio the fortune-hunter

The prodigal and debt-entangled Bassanio is particularly conscious of money. When he comes to describe Portia to Antonio, the first expression Bassanio uses is "richly left" (I. i. 161). That is, Portia is an heiress of a large fortune. Money is the first point that comes into Bassanio's mind when he tries to tell his friend about the lady he is to woo. Perhaps because he feels embarrassed after this comment, Bassanio quickly adds "and she is fair" and "of wonderous virtues" (I. i. 162-63). [2] Then, failing to specify her fairness or virtues,

---

[1] Some scholars do not think the Prodigal Son is the source of Bassanio. See, for example, Barnet, p. 26; Mahood, Appendix, p. 199; and Wheater, p. 477.

[2] It was conventional to talk about money when it came to marriage in Elizabethan England. As Alison Wall argues that "arrangements about each side's contribution in land, money, or goods preceded marriage, even among poor people where the dowry could be simply a few household items," and for young people in the upper levels of Elizabethan society, their parents would negotiate widely "over the bride's dowry, the groom's land, and the jointure" (515). Another example about marriage and wealth can be found in *Much Ado about Nothing*, in which Benedick talks about his ideal wife. Benedick's standards, according to the note to the following quote from Arden edition (3 rd series) of the play, are a reflection of "conductbook recommendations for the choice of a spouse": "Rich, she shall be, that's certain. Wise, or I'll none. Virtuous, or I'll never cheapen her. Fair, or I'll never look on her. Mild, or come not near me. Noble, or not I for an angel. Of good discourse, an excellent musician, and her hair shall be of what colour it please God" (II. iii. 28-33). However, we need also remember that too much concern for money, to an Elizabethan, showed a perverted love for earthly things, something off the golden mean, especially considering the renewed or perhaps increased dominance of Aristotelian influence during this period of time. Although Lawrence Danson considers Bassanio's description of Portia "entirely appropriate," he is aware that Bassanio's intention of fortune hunting in courting of Portia is found in "most 'ironic' readings" of the play (43). John Russell Brown shares Danson's view on this point (*Merchant* xlvi-xlvii).

Bassanio again uses money: this Portia is "nothing undervalued" (I. i. 165) than the historical Portia, the daughter of Cato the younger and the wife of Brutus. He is aware that the "wide world" knows well of Portia's "worth" (I. i. 167). He continues to betray his monetary interest when he remembers that Portia's hair is like "a golden" fleece (I. i. 170). The reason for Bassanio's pecuniary mentality is clear: he wants to borrow money again from Antonio to compete with Portia's other suitors. He finds it likely that he will achieve "such thrift," and that he will surely "be fortunate," or, in other words, become rich as well (I. i. 175-76). M. M. Mahood remarks insightfully that "Bassanio's impecunious state at the beginning of the play leads the audience to suspect him of wooing Portia in an attempt to mend his fortunes" (4). When the ever generous Antonio confesses his shortage of money and is ready to seal a bond at a forfeiture of a pound of his flesh with a disreputable Jew, Bassanio attempts to stop Antonio, claiming that he will rather "dwell in my necessity" (I. iii. 154). This again betrays Bassanio's intention to marry Portia first and foremost for her money.

When he is to tell Portia about Antonio's depressing letter, Bassanio describes himself in monetary terms, too. He wants Portia to rate himself "at nothing" (III. ii. 255). That is, he wants her to rate his value of estate at nothing. He continues to confess to her his debts:

> When I told you
> My state was nothing, I should then have told you
> That I was worse than nothing.

> (III. ii. 257-59)

Clearly, Bassanio wants Portia to remember his impoverishment. Indeed, Bassanio is honest to admit that he is "worse than nothing" (III. ii. 259). We still remember that he was already in "great debt" before he borrows through Antonio the three thousand ducats (I. i. 128, 134). As is discussed earlier, Bassanio has thought of Portia as a wealth of riches for him to win.

Bassanio becomes unbearably impatient in the casket contest. He asks Portia twice to let him choose immediately, but the words he uses are: "But let me to my *fortune* and the caskets" (III. ii. 39, italics mine). It may appear that Bassanio is talking about trying his luck, but we know that this luck is firmly focused on real wealth. This is proven later when he has praised "fair Portia's counterfeit" (III. ii. 115), the proof that he has chosen the right casket. Bassanio takes out the scroll, on which he gives a happy comment: "Here's the scroll, / The continent and summary of my *fortune* (III. ii. 129-30, italics mine). Obviously, by "fortune" Bassanio now means more riches than luck. If he only meant luck, he would be seeming too unnatural and false in the context of his free talk associating marriage with money. Bassanio's happiness in winning Portia's riches is intensified by the words in the scroll:

> Since this fortune falls to you,
> Be content and seek no new.
> If you be well pleased with this,
> And hold your fortune for your bliss,
> Turn you where your lady is,
> And claim her with a loving kiss.

(III. ii. 133-38)

Within the space of fewer than one hundred lines, "fortune" is repeated three times; or exactly, between III. ii. 130 and III. ii. 136, Bassanio says the word three times. This intense repetition of the expression *fortune* cannot be pure coincidence, and Bassanio also knows it means more than luck. Bassanio's own following words firmly settle his intention of winning Portia as riches. As a winner, he tells Portia that he has come "by note," or as both Horace Howard Furness and M. M. Mahood agree (Notes to III. ii. 147 and III. ii. 140, respectively), [1] by money, and expects to receive a "prize" (III. ii. 140-41). Having chosen the right casket, Bassanio feels happy like a champion "giddy in spirit" (III. ii. 144), but he cannot claim the winning to be true until it is "confirmed, signed, ratified" by Portia (III. ii. 148). Obviously, as a sophisticated Venetian, Bassanio is clear how a transfer of fortune is done, and now, upon his success, he immediately brings Portia to the issue of confirmation and ratification. Certainly, Belmont means first money to Bassanio, not Portia his fair love.

Bassanio's comparison of himself to one contending in a "prize" (III. ii. 141) is also a sign that he expects to win Portia as something of monetary value. Both Jay L. Halio and M. M. Mahood argue that "prize" just means a contest or a match (notes to III. ii. 141). However, the *Oxford English Dictionary* defines it as "a reward, trophy or a symbol

---

[1] Jay L. Halio thinks "by note" means only "authorized by words in the scroll." He considers "confirmed, signed, ratified" by Portia refers to the kiss mentioned in line 138 (note to III. ii. 140). That is, Bassanio cannot kiss Portia as a symbol of claiming her without her confirmation, signature and ratification. This is good interpretation, but it also shows that Bassanio eagerly urges the transfer of fortune by those three formal expressions of business transactions.

of victory of superiority in any contest or competition"
("prize," def. 1a), citing another example from the same
play:

> Did I deserve no more than a fool's head?
> Is that my prize? Are my deserts no better?
>
> (II. ix. 58-59)

Here the Prince of Arragon does not or will not believe his
"prize" is just a "fool's head." In the same event of choosing
the caskets, Shakespeare could not have used the same word
"prize" to mean different things for different competitors.
Here, the *OED* compilers are right. It is true Bassanio
understands that making the right choice is like competing in
a contest, but he wants to win Portia as a reward. Because he
is fully aware how "richly left" Portia is (I. i. 161), he
clearly knows that the reward of Portia means a reward of a
huge fortune.

As a fortune hunter or competitor, the character Bassanio
does not match any stock types found in Theophrastus,
Joseph Hall or John Earle. But, as is generally agreed, the
most important source of *The Merchant of Venice* is the story
of *Il Pecorone* by Ser Giovanni, Florentino. Bassanio is
characterized based on the hero of the story, Giannetto. The
difference, according to Jay L. Halio, is Bassanio is a "noble
character" (15), and Gianetto is a stock character of the
Prodigal Son. In addition, Bassanio has to choose from the
three caskets for Portia herself and her fortune, and
Gianetto's motivation suggests an emphasis on
concupiscence, his strong sexual desire. In short, although
Bassanio's role as a fortune hunter is not so clearly a stock
character as his role as an unthrift, Shakespeare still draws

on a source which links Bassanio to the stock character of the Prodigal Son.

3. Bassanio the hypocrite

Although Bassanio is a prodigal as well as a fortune hunter, he does not appear to be a ludicrous and despicable person. Even though Bassanio himself confesses to be a "braggart" (III. ii. 257), he impresses Portia and Nerissa as "a scholar and a soldier" who is "the best deserving a fair lady" (I. ii. 110, 115-16). His good reputation in giving "rare new liveries" encourages Lancelot to leave Shylock to work for him (II. ii. 103-04). Harold C. Goddard has a good comment on Bassanio: "He fools the average reader . . . as completely as the dashing movie star does the matinee girl" (85). A more accurate description of Bassanio's truthfulness perhaps should be that he may appear sincere, but he is often hypocritical.

In a long-winded speech, Bassanio lectures on deceptive ornaments in various aspects of people's lives. In law, a tainted and corrupt plea " obscures the show of evil " if "seasoned with a gracious voice" (III. ii. 76-77); in religion, serious people with a biblical text "bless and approve" the worst evil and hide their "grossness" by a good show (III. ii. 79-80); beauty obtained from wearing make-up which is bought by weight, and therefore the one who wears the heaviest make-up is the "lightest" morally (III. ii. 91); etc. Bassanio claims, ornament is the "seeming truth" to "entrap the wisest" (III. ii. 100-01). Towards the end of his sermon, Bassanio declares, "Therefore thou gaudy gold, / Hard food for Midas, I will none of thee (III. ii. 101-02). Because gold is so showy and deceptive, Bassanio says he is not going to have anything to do with it, nor will he do with silver, the "pale and common drudge" between man and man (III. ii. 103). Instead, he will choose lead because its "paleness moves me more than eloquence" (III. ii. 106).

However, we do remember that, to quote Harold C. Goddard again, Bassanio, giving the speech about the deceptive appearances of gold and silver, is "clad in the rich raiment that Antonio's (Shylock's) gold has presumably bought" (86). We also remember that when Bassanio arrives at Portia's house to choose the casket, he is reported to have brought "sensible regreets" and "gifts of rich value" (II. ix. 88-90), that is, greetings of substantial gifts. It is certain he would not say at that moment such things "may the outward shows be least themselves" (III. ii. 73). His expensive shows of his gifts must not be anything like lead. Therefore, as Goddard argues, the real Bassanio is "the golden casket. He gained what many men desire: a wealthy wife" (86). He has everything to do with Portia's gold, instead of "none" (III. ii. 102). ①

By openly denouncing gold and silver, Bassanio succeeds in making the right choice and consequently winning Portia to whom he has sworn "a secret pilgrimage" (I. i. 120). Since Bassanio admires Portia so much, he should be sincere towards her. However, when Bassanio picks up Portia's portrait from the right casket, instead of affectionately

---

① John Dover Wilson considers Bassanio's sermonizing speech a "flaw in characterization. " Based on Bassanio's incongruity in making the speech, Wilson asks, "What has altered you [Bassanio] , that you, of all men, suddenly use this sanctimonious talk?" (xxvi). However, Bassanio's moralization here can be seen as an unsurprising speech by a hypocrite, rather than a flaw in dramatic art.

praising her beauty and grace, he teasingly chooses to use bawdy language in front of Portia and others:

> What demi-god
> Hath come so near creation? Move these eyes?
> Or whether riding on the balls of mine
> Seem they in motion? Here are severed lips
> Parted with sugar breath; so sweet a bar
> Should sunder such sweet friends. Here in her hairs
> The painter plays the spider, and hath woven
> A golden mesh t'entrap the hearts of men
> Faster than gnats in cobwebs.
>
> (III. ii. 115-23)

Bassanio's expressions, "riding on the balls of mine," "lips," and "hairs" sound vulgar. As Eric Partridge has shown, these expressions are often puns with sexual overtones (74, 77, 178, 150). Rex Gibson, in discussing the teaching of *The Merchant of Venice*, points out that Bassanio's description of Portia's portrait here is an example of a passage where "rhetorical excess becomes hyperbole" (127). He argues that "such elaborate and fanciful language" can be spoken "seriously, mockingly or in some other way" (127). Joseph Hall gives a sketch of the character of the hypocritical: he "hath always two faces; ofttimes two hearts: that can compose his forehead to sadness and gravity, while he bids his heart be wanton and careless within" (106-07). From Bassanio's speeches before and after he chooses the casket, we can see he perfectly fits such a sketch. On such an occasion, Bassanio's improper language can only show his light attitude towards Portia. ①

As Tony Tonner remarks, Bassanio, when reasoning with Antonio about his loan to woo Portia, compares Belmont to Medea's homeland "Colchos" (I. i. 171), and he himself to Jason, who succeeds in recovering the golden fleece with Medea's help but deserts Medea after marriage. Because Jason has deceived Medea, Bassanio's comparison can implicitly remind the audience that he will act hypocritically towards Portia. This point is proven when Bassanio quickly gives his sworn ring to Balthasar, the disguised Portia, becoming "unfaithful" to Portia "almost immediately after their marriage" (149). ②

Bassanio has also fooled his friend Antonio. In the very beginning of the play, he "urges his childhood proof" of shooting a second arrow in the same direction to find the lost first one (I. i. 143), but he has not told Antonio how many arrows he has shot, and he already "owes the most in money" to Antonio (I. i. 130). That is to say, he also owes debts to other friends. It is reasonable to infer that he has repeatedly told Antonio his arrow-shooting analogy to borrow money from the merchant friend. In his speech about deceptive good appearance when standing before the gold casket, Bassanio talks of cowards wearing the "beards of Hercules and frowning Mars" to hide their "false hearts" and "livers white as milk" (III. ii. 85-86). However, when

---

① Referring to Shakespeare's sonnets 127-52, ones mainly about the Dark Lady, Park Honan remarks that Shakespeare "might be obsessed with sexual experience since he has included bawdy puns even in poems on ideal love" (189).

② Again, as pointed out by Tony Tonner, Graciano reinforces Bassanio's comparison of himself to the deceptive Jason by claiming they are both Jasons when Bassanio selects the right casket: "We are the Jasons, we have won the fleece" (III. ii. 241) (149).

reading a letter about Antonio's "lost fleece" (III. ii. 241), Bassanio is so frightened that Portia says that some hurtful contents in the letter "must have stolen the colour" from his cheek (III. ii. 243). Bassanio becomes so cowardly pale that Portia immediately decides to intervene. And yet, at the court, when Shylock is to cut Antonio's flesh, Bassanio asks the merchant to have courage. Moreover, he brags that Shylock shall have his "flesh, blood, bones and all" before Antonio shall lose "one drop of blood" for him (IV. i. 112-13). However, when Shylock whets his knife, Bassanio has just one plain question, "Why dost thou whet thy knife so earnestly" (IV. i. 121), and is answered by Shylock that he is ready to cut the pound of flesh from Anonio. At this point, Bassanio does not know what to say for a long time and certainly takes no action at all. Much later, after Antonio makes his farewell speech, and when Shylock, pointing his knife at Antonio's chest, is ready to cut, Bassanio again says loud and empty words of "losing and sacrificing all [his life, wife and the world] / Here to this devil, to "deliver" Antonio (IV. i. 283-84), without the slightest action or proposing any real solution. Moreover, as R. W. Maslen points out, if Bassanio's use of "devil" is taken seriously, his speech would imply that " one man's physical survival can outweigh the salvation of two souls and even of the world itself, a notion hardly compatible with orthodox Christian doctrine" (111). It is cruel to see that Antonio is now almost losing his life for having borrowed those three thousand ducats for Bassanio. It may have been better for Bassanio to remain silent should he be unable to take any meaningful action.

4. Bassanio the honest husband

Despite his hypocrisy, Bassanio is an honest man. One of Joseph Hall's descriptions of an honest character is: "all his dealings are square and above the board: he is a faithful client of truth, no man's enemy" (93). Bassanio's accident with Portia's ring is a good example. When Portia formally declares Bassanio's money-seeking success and requires Bassanio to keep the ring she gives him, he swears solemnly to protect it with his life:

> . . . when this ring
> Parts from this finger, then parts life from hence:
> O then be bold to say Bassanio's dead!
>
> (III. ii. 183-85)

However, at the end of the court scene, in order to show his genuine gratitude to Portia/Balthasar, Bassanio entreats Portia to take "some remembrance" from him and Antonio "as a tribute" (IV. i. 417). They are willing to give her the three thousand ducats Antonio previously owes Shylock (IV. i. 408). When Portia declines the ducats and demands the ring on Bassanio's finger, Bassanio tells her honestly that the ring comes from his wife and he has vowed to keep it. Eventually, Bassanio yields at Portia's insistence on nothing else but the ring and Antonio's argument that the lawyer's "deservings" and his (Antonio's) love should be valued more than Portia's "commandment" (IV. i. 447).

Naturally, Bassanio comes back to Belmont ringless and faces Portia. Although he tells Portia that if he "could add a lie unto a fault," and he would deny giving the ring away (V. i. 186-88), Bassanio confesses and begs for forgiveness. The climax of the ring scene is Portia's forgiveness of Bassanio, who, like the Prodigal Son, is no longer money conscious, extravagant, hypocritical. Instead, Bassanio is shown to be sincere and honest.

Looking at Bassanio's complex character in summary, we find in him a combination of different characters: a prodigal or an unthrift son and friend, a money-minded fortune hunter, hypocrite and an honest husband who takes responsibility for his mistake. These characters have their sources in Theophrastus the classical character writer, stories from the Bible, contemporary theater and readings. Bassanio has inconsistencies, even contradictory qualities. He is so wasteful that he has absolutely " disabled " his "estate" (I. i. 123) and fallen into great debt. At the same time, he gives generously to his servants and has fostered a good reputation. He loves Portia, but he cannot keep the ring she gives him at their wedding. He has obvious strengths and frailties. In this sense, he seems like a real man living around us, but it should be noticed that his realism results from Bassanio being a hybrid of several types.

III. The facilitators

i. Mosca

1. Mosca the Elizabethan parasite

When writing about Jonson's Mosca as an Elizabethan dramatic parasite, E. P. Vandiver accurately remarks that he is perhaps " the most noteworthy so-called parasite in Elizabethan drama" who has the ability to " deceive people and make each one think he is his friend while he is plotting against all of them" (423). From the beginning to almost the end of the play, Mosca manages to not only deceive everyone who wants to have anything to do with Volpone but also make them believe that he is their friend. He also deceives Volpone himself.

As Volpone's parasite,[1] Mosca has qualities of his traditional Latin ancestor. As E. P. Vandiver notes, a parasite in Latin comedy is "conspicuous" for "his Gargantuan appetite, unctuous flattery, activities as pander, and intrigues" (411). Mosca does not seem to show a gigantic, or "Gargantuan" apetite, but tries to fill others' ears with oily flattery, seemingly to work with them like a pander and to devise intrigues for them and himself.

In the first scene of *Volpone*, when Volpone blasphemously praises the glory of gold, Mosca responds with similar impiety: "Riches are in fortune / A greater good, then wisedome is in nature" (I. i. 28-29). Then when Volpone brags about his uncommon ways of acquiring wealth, Mosca tells his master that he does not "deuoure / Soft prodigalls," nor use violence to rob wealth from "poore families." Mosca praises his master because his "sweet nature" abhors cruelty and violence, and because he loathes "the widdowes, or the orphans tears" should wash his pavements, and many other oily words (I. i. 30-66).

Mosca's oily responses to Volpone fit Joseph Hall's

---

[1] E. F. Watling considers the translation of "parasitus" in Latin comedy into English "parasite" "an unsatisfactory business." He remarks that the Roman parasite, "a kind of professional diner-out and jester, both as a social institution and as a stage type," is best translated as "table-companion," the "nearest literal equivalent to the original word and may perhaps stand as an approximation" (54).

description of a flatterer exactly:

> His speeches are full of wondering interjections, and all
> his titles are superlative; and both of them seldom ever but
> in presence [of the person being flattered]. His base mind
> is well matched with a mercenary tongue, which is a willing
> slave to another man's ear.
>
> (114)

Mosca's comparison of riches with wisdom are precisely "wondering interjections," and although he does not use a "superlative" here, he uses a comparative. His list of his master's ways of getting wealth matches perfectly a "mercenary" tongue, a tongue hired to suit words to his master's ears. Merely because of several lines of flattery like these, Mosca is well rewarded by his master, who calls him "my beloued" (I. i. 30), "good," "louing" (I. ii. 65, 122), "good rascall [, let me kisse thee]" (I. iv. 137), among other epithets.

Naturally, as a panderer, Mosca not only flatters his master. He will flatter all the legacy hunters desirous of Volpone's estate, deceiving them and assuring them that he is working only for them. When Voltore, the advocate, comes to visit the falsely sick Volpone, Mosca tells him that Volpone has decided on him as the heir and pretends to beg him for employment and care (I. iii. 27-37). Then in a long speech to convince Voltore of Volpone's favor, Mosca tells him that his "good chance" is Volpone's long-standing admiration for lawyers. Mosca says Volpone respects lawyers for their "course" [professional demeanor], their ability to "speak to every cause, and things mere contraries" [to defend any case and argue for exactly opposite causes] till they lose their voice, their "quick agility" to "turn and return, make knots, and undo them, give forked counsel" [ambiguous advice], their wisdom, their "perplexed tongue" [double speaking] and their ability to make money from defending either side of a case (I. iii. 51-66). Mosca's description of lawyers is sarcastic, but he is so careful and skillful in presenting it that it sounds complimentary to the exceedingly shrewd Voltore. Moreover, Mosca quickly turns his flattery to Voltore's hope to make plenty of money ("euery word your worship but lets fall is a *cecchine* [a gold coin]"), thus linking Voltore with Volpone on the basis of their mutual obsession with wealth (I. iii. 66). Mosca and Volpone easily succeed in tricking Voltore to give them his silver plate.

The second legacy hunter to try Mosca's ability is Corbaccio, "the old rauen" (I. iii. 81), and "a wretch, who is (indeed) more impotent" than Volpone can "faine to be" (I. iv. 3-4). Corbaccio brings two gifts: an "opiate" (I. iv. 13) and "a bag of bright *cecchines*" (I. iv. 69). Although Corbaccio claims that his opiate, that is, his poison in the form of a drug, is from his "owne Doctor" and he himself "stood by, while't was made" (I. iv. 15), his trick proves to be too simple for Mosca, who dismisses his idea by saying that Volpone does not trust any physician. To return the trick, Mosca tells Corbaccio that Voltore has visited with a silver plate, provoking Corbaccio to rival with the lawyer. Corbaccio offers his gold coins to Mosca to "quite weigh downe" Voltore's plate (I. iv. 70). Moreover, Mosca tricks Corbaccio into believing that if he makes Volpone his heir and disinherits his son, his generosity will move Volpone into pronouncing him as heir "out of conscience, and mere gratitude" (I. iv. 108). Mosca makes Corbaccio sincerely believe that he has not only done himself "a good," but also "multiplyed" the good for his son. Seeing that Corbaccio calls this plan "my inuention" and does not want to acknowledge his help, Mosca argues that "it hath beene all my studie, all my care [to work for him,]" and "You are he, / For whom I labour, here " (I. iv. 117-23). After these arguments, Corbaccio claims to Mosca that "I know thee honest" and "I doe not doubt, to be a father to thee" (I. iv. 125, 127). Mosca's pretended arguments thus send Corbaccio home excitedly to prepare his will to disinherit his son, offering his wealth to Volpone.

Mosca lures the merchant Corvino, a vulture, the raven, the third legacy hunter with two pieces of news: Volpone is almost dead and the freshly made will, although its content is still not clear, is most likely to reveal Corvino as the heir. Mosca says that he has helped to put Corvino down in all the places in the will. Therefore, Mosca makes Corvino believe that he is the only possible heir. With Mosca's help, Volpone successfully bilks Corvino out of his diamond and pearl, but the Fox is not satisfied because Mosca's mentioning of the merchant's beautiful wife has strongly aroused his lust.

Trying to pander to Volpone's seduction of Corvino's wife further illustrates Mosca's abilities as an evil adviser and an intriguer. Because Volpone determines to see Celia, Corvino's wife, Mosca devises a mountebank scene to satisfy his desire (II. ii.). As Alvin B. Kernan calls him a great theatrical " producer " (178), Mosca oversees Volpone's entire mountebank performance. Volpone's superior performance does enable him to catch sight of Celia, but also results in an attack from the jealous Corvino, who happens to see Celia's dropping of her handkerchief to buy from the moutebank/ Volpone his advertised medicine. Despite his wound from Corvino's attack, Volpone complains lustfully to Mosca about his burning desire. Therefore, Mosca promises to devise another plot to " bring success " to Volpone's " desires," invites Volpone to "applaud" his "art" (II. iv. 26, 38), and receives Volpone's praises as " my better Angell " (II. iv. 21).

Mosca's new plot works out fruitfully. As Mosca makes Corbaccio believe that Voltore is rivaling with him for Volpone's legacy, Mosca causes Corvino to believe that many people, especially one Doctor Lupo, is competing with him to cure Volpone, hoping for legacy. In spite of Corvino's jealousy and concern about becoming a cuckold, Mosca successfully leads Corvino to decide to offer Celia to bed with Volpone. Moreover, deeply trusting the parasite, Corvino wants Mosca to tell Volpone " with what zeale, / And willingnesse " he offers his wife; he also wants Mosca to swear to Volpone that he decides to offer his wife " on the first hearing [about the situation] " out of his " owne free motion "; when Mosca leaves, Corvino reminds him not to "forget to send [for their coming], now" (II. vi. 92-101). Mosca's flattery and plots are so effective that he not only wins Corvino's absolute trust as a friend, but also causes Corvino to voluntarily work against his own will but for Mosca's benefit at the same time.

An accident occurs again to prove Mosca's skills as an oily and deceptive parasite. Before he sends for Corvino and Celia, Mosca comes across Bonario. He decides to fool Bonario into believing that his father is going to disinherit him so that in a rage or dispute, the young man can kill or seriously wound his father. In the beginning, the upright but innocent Bonario despises and refuses to believe in Mosca. Mosca, however, is so cunning that he quickly changes Bonario's mind and wins his trust by pretended weeping and soft argument. In one of the most hypocritical speeches in the entire play, Mosca tells Bonario:

> Sir, it concernes you; and though I may seeme,
> At first, to make a maine offence, in manners,
> And in my gratitude, vnto my master,
> Yet, for the pure loue, which I beare all right,
> And hatred of the wrong, I must reueale it.
> This verie houre, your father is in purpose
> To disinherit you.

(III. ii. 38-44)

Different from his flattering talk with the legacy hunters, Mosca now tells Bonario something only a righteous man will do. He says that he knows his exposure of Corbaccio's plan of disinheritance is a major offence to his master's and his own benefit, but he chooses to reveal it because of his "pure loue" (for justice) and "hatred of the wrong." Then he goes on to tell Bonario of his only purpose in doing that—his "mere respect" for Bonario's "generall state / Of goodness, and true vertue" in which he "claims an interest" (III. ii. 47-50).

Hearing these words, Bonario declares that Mosca has lost "much of the late trust" he has in him. Bonario's disbelief is not a difficulty for Mosca. The changeful parasite swears that if he is not telling the truth, Bonario can draw his "iust sword / And score you vengeance, on my front, and face; / Marke me you villaine." He flatters the young man that "I doe suffer for you, sir. My heart / Weepes bloud, in anguish" (III. ii. 66-70). Mosca's attempt to divide Bonario from his father fits exactly the stock character of the dissembler sketched by Theophrastus:

> Every word, every action, of the Dissember is an artifice by which he labors to conceal some evil intention. A man of this sort approaches his enemy with professions of friendship; he flatters those against whom he is secretly plotting mischief; and he condoles with them in the day of their calamity: to one who has defamed him he proffers his forgiveness.
>
> (10)

Bonario is not able to see through Mosca's flattery any evil intention to plague his own family. Eventually, Mosca persuades Bonario to come with him to Volpone's house. Although Bonario's coming proves to be a mistake, Mosca's misjudgment turns out to be a critical incident to let him put on his biggest show of flattering and machination skills.

Mosca's masterwork as a superb schemer is achieved in the first courtroom scene in Act IV, Scenes v and vi, after a brief moment of despair and confusion. Because Corvino comes unsent for with Celia and Corbaccio arrives too late, Mosca has to adjust his plot. Celia, upon realization of her husband's intention, resolutely resists being prostituted. Mosca suggests Corvino bring Celia to Volpone's bed and leave the scene. Having Celia with him in the room alone, Volpone tries all ways to seduce Celia but fails. Just when he wants to use violence, the unguarded Bonario breaks in, wounds and threatens Volpone, saves and takes Celia away, and they immediately go to the local court to accuse Volpone of attempted rape. Both Volpone and Mosca are frustrated for a moment, but Mosca is clever enough to take advantage of Voltore's visit and call all the legacy hunters together to put on a victorious grand show. This arrangement of Mosca fits exactly Anne Barton's commentary:

> Mosca makes a terrible mistake in Act Three when he fails to entertain the possibility that Bonario may leave the gallery where he was told to walk and read, and so become a witness not only to Volpone's attempt to rape Celia, but to the fact that the invalidism of the Fox is all a cheat. Yet the miscalculation, as Jonson is at pains to show, is easily redeemed.

(*Dramatist* 115)

Volpone and Mosca's redemption occurs in the courtroom scenes. When Voltore, Corbaccio, Corvino all come together, Mosca tells each to lie and indict Bonario and Celia while continuing to make each believe that he himself is Volpone's only heir. At the same time, Mosca makes sure that these legacy hunters will lie as a team, despite their own private aims. Also, Mosca has to direct Volpone to act dead when he is called for interrogation. Besides, Mosca brings the gullible and confused Lady Would-be to stay ready to accuse Celia of being a deceptive prostitute. The most important person Mosca must make sure to lie consistently and effectively is Voltore the advocate; he must ensure Voltore puts his pleading skills to best use. As the production shows, Mosca proves to be both a superb director and " a Protean actor " (Bradbrook, *Living Monument* 96). All the actors and the actress perform perfectly according to Mosca's direction, and he himself also gives flawless acting. Consequently, the avocatori, or the magistrates, rule that Bonario and Celia be taken to custody and parted, and that Volpone "the old gentleman be return'd, with care." The magistrates at the same time say they are sorry because their "credulitie wrong'd him [Volpone]" (IV. vi. 54-57). As Alvin B. Kernan remarks, in these scenes, Mosca "takes a variety of widely differing capabilities and interests . . . and creates a smoothly working ensemble" (178). Or, as Robert Jones says, the trial scenes in Act Four are in fact "the parasite's own show" (110). In these scenes, Mosca is the successful leader of the deceivers.

Earlier, just after he succeeds in gulling Corvino into offering his wife to sleep by Volpone, Mosca becomes so satisfied with himself that he cannot help bragging, particularly about his "towne-arte," which he glorifies as divine, "a most precious thing, dropt from aboue, not bred 'mong'st clods and clot-poules, here on earth." He believes that his "arte" should be made a "science" that is worth academic study and gentlemen's pursuit. He sees the world as made up of only parasites, feeding on each other the way animals do, without any idea of civilization, progress or future common good. A panderer himself, Mosca looks down on people who merely flatter others in order to survive in town, and on those homeless wretches who are forced to make a living by pleasing the rich. He is contemptible of anyone who fawns and makes a fool of himself only for a good meal or a position in the court of a gentleman or the government. Unlike the gluttonous Falstaff, Mosca stresses the dignified side of a table-companion. His ideal parasite is a "fine, elegant rascall" who can "rise and stoope (almost together) like an arrow" and can "present to any humour, all occasion." Such is a born parasite, not taught (III. i. 5-30).

And now, after his brilliant victory at court, Mosca is even more satisfied with his direction of this performance than he was with his success in tricking Corvino and his wife. He tells Volpone that

> We must, here, be fixt;
> Here, we must rest; this is our master-peece:
> We cannot thinke, to goe beyond this.
>
> (V. ii. 12-14)

Despite being a braggart, Mosca thinks this is already the ultimate deception and entertainment they can succeed in; therefore, they should stop right there without going further.

Through these analyses of his complex character, we can see Mosca is simply no mere stock parasite of the Roman comedy. Although still a parasite in name, he is not a gormandizer. He is a panderer, a flatterer, a dissembler, a braggart, and a play director. So far, all his parts, or, all these types of characters, have been fused into Mosca to work a wonderful effect. To borrow a phrase from E. P. Vandiver, Jonson achieved a splendid "character amalgamation" in Mosca (421).

2. Mosca the Machiavellian villain

Although Mosca tells Volpone that they should stop at their masterpiece after the trial scenes in Act Four, Volpone, as Kernan observes, "is not content to let the deceptions rest here, and he insists on directing two more plays himself" (179). In both plays, Mosca is asked to play the

Machiavellian villain by declaring his master's death so that Volpone can come out from his bed and enjoy more pleasures of deceiving the legacy hunters. [1]

In the first performance, after Castrone and Nano go out in the streets to spread the news about Volpone's death, Mosca is arranged by Volpone to put on a gown and play the only heir with Volpone's will in his hand. While Volpone retreats behind a curtain to peep at what is going on in front of it, Mosca sits down to pretend to take inventory of Volpone's legacies. What follows is one of the most hilarious scenes in the entire play: Voltore, Corbaccio, Corvino, Lady Would-be come one by one, circling around Mosca, thinking him- or herself as the only heir (ess), asking about the will complacently. Mosca ignores them at first. Instead, he attentively and carefully takes stock of the "legacy": "turkie carpets, nine— . . . two sutes of bedding, tissew— . . . of cloth of gold, two more— . . . of seuerall vellets, eight— . . . Eight chests of linen" (V. iii. 1-11). Mosca's cool ignorance, the anxiety, doubt and suspicion of the three vulture-like legacy hunters and the foolish Lady Would-be collide into a noisy but non-violent discord that intensifies a comic irony to its culmination. Anne Barton commends that this scene is "the single most representative act of the play" (*Dramatist* 109). A villain as Mosca is playing, part of the dramatic fun comes from the technical terms of accounting in his speech. When discussing jargon as dramatic speech, Alexander H. Sackton remarks that Jonson's use of jargon as "a development of the

---

[1] Edward Partridge discusses the traditional associations of imagery among the fox, Volpone and a Machiavellian villain, see esp. pp. 84-85.

disguise convention" becomes "an integral part of the action, and produces or enhances dramatic irony. " Sackton says that "no other Elizabethan writer experimented so much as Jonson with such language, or produced with it such a variety of dramatic effects" (112). [1] In this scene in which Mosca enumerates the items of Volpone's legacy, the language is not as technical jargons as those in medicine or alchemy, but they are the terminologies of the book-keeper, and achieve the same dramatic effect.

Mosca helps Volpone enjoy a great deal of fun from ridiculing the legacy hunters, but the master is still not satisfied. Hoping to enjoy further pleasures, Volpone directs Mosca to take his "habit of Clarissimo [nobility]; / And walke the streets; be seene" so that they (Volpone will be dressed like a *Commandadore*, a court officer) can "torment 'hem [the legacy hunters] more " (V. iii. 105-06). Unfortunately for Volpone, his pleasures at deluding and ridiculing the legacy hunters are producing a deadly side-effect. When they are ready to go out, Mosca and Volpone have a highly menacing, even sinister dialogue:

> Mosca. But what am I?
> Volpone. 'Fore heau'n, a braue *Clarissimo*, thou becom'st it!
> Pitty, thou wert not borne one.
> Mosca. If I hold my made one, 'twill be well.
>
> (V. v. 2-5)

Mosca, probably having foreseen his next goal and

---

[1] See Alexander H. Sackton, pp. 72-112, for a detailed discussion of Jonson's use of jargon in medicine, alchemy and food as dramatic speech and rhetoric in Jonsonian plays; for jargon in *Volpone*, see pp. 75-77. I owe this reference to Dr. Zhu Ruiqing (朱瑞青).

possibility, pretends to ask Volpone what part he should play on the streets since Volpone earlier has already told him to walk on the streets in his clothes of a *Clarissimo*, a Venetian nobleman. Volpone, obviously failing to really understand his parasite's greedy intention, complacently tells Mosca that he feels pity for him for not being a borne *Clarissimo* while confirming that the parasite "becom'st it [is suited to the part]. " Similarly, Mosca's response "If I hold my made one, 'twill be well" means, in Mosca's context, not Volpone's, that it will be good for him if he can hold *on to* his made Clarissimo. Indeed, when Volpone goes out, Mosca sneers behind Volpone's back that he will "make him [Volpone] languish. " He immediately takes the keys to the house, sends Volpone's eunuch, dwarf and fool off into the city, and declares himself "possest [of Volpone's estate]" (V. v. 8- 12). [①] At this moment, Mosca is almost complete in both being turned (by Volpone) and turning (himself) into a Michiavellian villain.

Mosca's completion of this transformation comes in the middle of the last scene of the play when he appears in court to answer the charge of Voltore, who confesses his wrong- doing, accuses Mosca of fraud after being frustrated and humiliated and then recants his accusation thanks to Volpone's delusion at court. Therefore, when Mosca arrives at court unaccused by Voltore in the gown of a Venetian nobleman, he appears to be different from all the past roles he has been in: the flatterer, the intriguer, the evil adviser, the courtroom ensemble director and the cool inventory

---

① See Brian Parker, p. 15, for an excellent discussion of *Volpone*'s "ironic punning" of possession.

taker—in fact, he has been particularly cool since he played the inventory taker as Volpone's heir. Now he is even cooler, so that a judge orders him "a stoole," and another considers him "a proper man" and "a fit match" for his daughter (V. xii. 49-51). When Volpone tries to beg Mosca to collaborate again, Mosca on the one hand tries to openly dismiss the begging Volpone as a "busie knaue," and on the other, coldly negotiates for "halfe" of his master's wealth. Then, when Volpone agrees to share it, Mosca becomes greedier and tells Volpone that he cannot "afford it you so cheape" (V. xii. 55-70), and turns away from Volpone regardless of his entreatment. Mosca has turned a thorough Michiavellian villain. Perhaps Volpone now realizes that he has mistaken not to have taken his parasite's praise of gold seriously:

> It transformes
> The most deformed, and restores 'hem louely,
> As 't were the strange poeticall girdle . . . It is the thing
> Makes all the world her grace, her youth, her beauty.
> (V. ii. 100-02, 104-05)

Indeed, Mosca has also been an obsessive lover of gold, but is not noticed as such by Volpone. Therefore, when Mosca, to quote J. A. Bryant's wonderful comment, is "openly declaring his fatal admiration" for Volpone's gold, "Volpoone miscalculates in assuming that Mosca, who does not share his master's weakness for sex, also does not share the weakness of Voltore, Corvino, and Corbaccio for yellow gold" (*Compassionate Satirist* 88).

However, as Volpone miscalculates to let Mosca play his heir and a Clarissimo openly, Mosca mistakens his master for a tolerator of wrongs. Eventually, Volpone cannot bear seeing himself being whipped while Mosca becoming prosperous with his estate and decides to confess everything, bringing punishment to all, including himself. As J. A. Bryant says, "Mosca's miscalculation, however, is more serious; he fails to see that Volpone's pride in his cunning will not let him accept passively any serious challenge to that cunning" (*Compassionate Satirist* 88). Thus, in a fatal attack of avarice, like Vice in a morality play, Mosca, as Robert Withington says, "cozener, cheater, 'parasite-slave,' meets a villain's fate" (751). The cool nobleman in Mosca, who has bespoken "conscience and duty in the best manner of knavish hypocrisy" (Jones 111), is defeated by his own avarice.

Surveying the character, or rather, the characters of Mosca, we find that although he is categorized as an Elizabethan parasite and a Machiavellian villain, he is rather a mixture of many more character types because both an Elizabethan parasite and a Machiavellian villain can have a variety of subtypes. Herford and the Simpsons say that Jonson was "especially indebted to Sejanus for his conception of Mosca" (II. 60). As E. P. Vandiver says, in creating Sejanus, Jonson had broken "all bounds of the stock figure [of a parasite]" and "loomed up as an individual, a dramatic creation which one almost fears to call a parasite" (420). Presenting Mosca as the personification of flattery, deceit, craftiness, unscrupulousness, double-crossing, and as a pander, Jonson successfully transformed the stock figure of parasite into "an evil adviser, intriguer, and villain of serious plays," merging such stock figures as "the clever servant, pedant, pander, Vice, evil counsellor, and the Machiavellian villain" (Vandiver 426). Certainly, Mosca is even more composite than Corvino, the jealous husband, avaricious merchant, the fool and knave. He is not what Augustus William Schlegel branded as a personification of general ideas, nor William Hazlitt's stagnating and corrupting "leaden cistern" that cannot develop (*Lectures* 73-74). At least, their comments, if applied to Mosca and Corvino, would be quite beside the point. Mosca not only develops; in fact, he develops so cunningly that even his master who stays with him all the time fails to understand him.

ii. Antonio

1. Antonio the melancholic man

Unlike the avaricious, envious, foolish and knavish Corvino the merchant who attempts to bribe Volpone for legacy, Antonio in *The Merchant* is melancholic in the beginning of the play. He frankly tells his friends:

> In sooth I know not why I am so sad.
> It wearies me, you say it wearies you;
> But how I caught it, found it, or came by it,
> What stuff 'tis made of, whereof it is born,
> I am to learn.
> And such a want-wit sadness makes of me,
> That I have much ado to know myself.

> (I. i. 1-7)

Antonio confesses his sadness; he says it "wearies" him; moreover, he stresses that although he is going to explore the causes of his melancholy, he finds it difficult to know it himself. Sir Thomas Overbury's Character sketches were published over fifteen years after the composition of *The Merchant*, but it is worth quoting his Melancholy man here as a reference for the character of Antonio: "Hee carries a cloud in his face, never faire weather . . . His spirits, and the sunne are enemies; the sunne bright and warme, his humour blacke and cold; . . . foolish apparitions . . . suffer him not to breathe, according to the necessities of nature" (73-74). Such is almost a sketch of Antonio.

Salerio and Solanio, Antonio's friends, offer some reasonable causes for his melancholy. Salerio believes that Antonio is sad because he is concerned with his mercantile ships, his "venture" in many parts of the world, since there are many unpredictable dangers in the sea like violent winds and rocks. Antonio disapproves of his supposition, assuring them that his ventures are carefully made, and he has other sources to rely on besides trade. Then, the friends guess Antonio is sad because he is in love. Antonio disgustedly rejects this suggestion. Salerio and Solanio lastly suggest that Antonio is in a melancholic mood for no reason, but other friends come and their discussion about Antonio's sadness is interrupted (I. i. 8-56).

However, Graziano, the " unabashedly worldly chatterbox" (Anne Barton, Introduction to *The Merchant* 251), picks up the conversation and offers a third explanation that Antonio has "too much respect upon the world" (I. i. 74), that is, having too much concern over worldly things. However, Antonio, as Lawrence Danson remarks, rejects Graziano's "more comprehensive explanation as decisively as he has the previous ones" (24). Antonio says he holds the world as it is, nothing more than a stage where every man plays a part, and his part is a sad one (I. i. 77-79). Lawrence Danson says that Antonio's comparison of his own sadness to that of a sad actor in a stage play "appears to rule out any more guessing about his melancholy's motives" (24). In effect, Antonio's answer does stop his friends from further guesses, although Graziano continues to ask Antonio to put his melancholy aside. As the play goes on, Antonio's inexplicable sadness is either a *donnée* (Danson 24), a mood given to an actor (as Antonio says he is a player) or something forgotten by others. The only other mention in the play of Antonio's moods is by Antonio himself, who says he is turned "th' unhappy subject" by Bassanio and Portia's quarrels over the ring (V. i. 238).

Critics have endeavored to explore the causes of Antonio's unexplained sadness. John W. Draper claims that Antonio's "sad" humour seems to arise "not from his innate complexion, but from his momentary worries and the dangers that beset him" (27). Most scholars, however, hold that Antonio's sadness is long-standing. Among others, Lawrence Danson's view is particularly pertinent to our discussion. According to Danson, the *Croxton Play of the Sacrament*, "the only extant example of a complete English 'miracle play'" from the latter half of the fifteenth century, is both "an example of the conservative theoretical attitude towards 'merchants' in general" and "an analogue to *The Merchant of Venice* in particular" (27). In the *Croxton Play of the Sacrament*, the two merchants, Aristorius, a Christian, and Jonathas, a Jew, "alike in their fealty to Mammon," or determined followers of the god of wealth, have both sinned against Christ at first but are repentant in the end for their "sin of covetousness" (27-29). Danson remarks that Aristorius's penance to give up trade entirely and "the assumed irreconcilability of good deeds verses [*sic*. , a typo for *versus*] buying and selling are strikingly revelatory of an attitude [of the Elizabethans, esp. Shakespeare's audiences] towards the world's great ' merchants '" (29). Since historically, "Christian behavior could never be reconciled with a fully emergent capitalism," and "in England in the 1590s, the new order [of capitalism] had arrived, but not the respectability" (27), Danson concludes that Antonio is sad because Shakespeare " plays with his audience's expectations, giving them a merchant who is (apparently) so far from being guilty of a lack of charity" (29). [1]

2. Antonio the liberal friend

Contrary to Aristorius, his analogous covetous model in the *Croxton Play of the Sacrament*, Antonio in *The Merchant*, despite being a tradesman, appears to be gracefully generous, almost a liberal man in the Aristotelian sense. Aristotle says in his *Nichomachean Ethics* that " the liberal man is praised . . . especially in respect of giving [riches]" (1119^b 22-25); " the liberal man, like other virtuous men, will give [riches] for the sake of the noble, and rightly" (1120^a 24-25). Antonio is such a man to give for the sake of the noble. Murry J. Levith considers Antonio an opposition to Christopher

---

[1] Many critics argue about Antonio's sadness as a result of his homosexuality, which drives him to compete against Portia for Bassanio. For details of such discussions, see, for example, Barton, Introduction to *The Merchant*, pp. 252-53; Edelman, pp. 54-64; Hyman, pp. 109-16; Mahood, p. 51; Midgley, pp. 199-204; Benston argues against the homoerotic view, see pp. 367-85, esp. pp. 383-85; so does Danson, pp. 34-40. Another opinion attributes Antonio's melancholy to his feeling of alienation. See, for instance, Cynthia Lewis, " Antonio," pp. 19-31. Indeed, Bassanio's possible marriage to Portia means certain loss of his friendship with Antonio; this could cause Antonio to be sad, and he may not want to tell about this kind of sadness to Salerio, Solanio or Graziano.

Marlowe's Barabas, the Jew of Malta: "If Marlowe's merchant engenders all the clichés of Jewish and Machiavellian selfish greed, Shakespeare's embodies just the opposite" (*Italian Settings* 10).

The first man for Antonio to give to liberally is Bassanio. Although, as we have discussed earlier, Bassanio, Antonio's "most noble kinsman" (I. i. 57), is a prodigal, Antonio shows himself to be the loving father figure in the Prodigal Son story by giving Bassanio love and money. Because Bassanio confesses to Antonio that he has been living a more extravagant life than he can afford "showing a more swelling port / Than my faint means would grant continuance" (I. i. 124-25), Antonio's giving riches to Bassanio repeatedly may not be absolutely right. However, this is a kind of generosity and Aristotelian liberalism.

As a friend, Antonio has always been liberal to Bassanio in terms of wealth. Not bothered by the "great debts" Bassanio owes him, he tells Bassanio that "my purse, my person, my extremest means" are always open to his (Bassanio's) needs (I. i. 128, 138-39). When Bassanio wants to borrow yet another "good round sum" to woo Portia (I. iii. 102), Antonio, himself short of money or commodity at the moment, decides to use his credit "to the uttermost" to "furnish" Bassanio (I. i. 177-85). As a result, Antonio has to seal a bond with the money-lender Shylock, his enemy, on terms that if he forfeits, Shylcok can cut off a pound of his flesh in any part of his body that pleases Shylock. In other words, Antonio risks his life to lend three thousand ducats to Bassanio. Antonio's generosity to Bassanio is exactly like Joseph Hall's description of the character of a true friend:

"While he hath some, his friend hath all" (98).

Antonio's liberality to Bassanio can also mean that he does not expect return or paying back. Bassanio's repeated borrowing of large sums from Antonio is an example. Another good example is from Antonio's letter to Bassanio when he finds out that his hopes for mercy from Shylock are crossed:

> Sweet Bassanio, my ships have all miscarried, my creditors grow cruel, my estate is very low; my bond to the Jew is forfeit, and since in paying it, it is impossible I should live, all debts are cleared between you and I if I might but see you at my death. Notwithstanding, use your pleasure; if your love do not persuade you to come, let not my letter.
>
> (III. ii. 313-19)

Antonio's graciousness to Bassanio is apparent here. Although his life is endangered now because of his bond with Shylock for Bassanio, he does not blame Bassanio at all. He even declares that if he cannot live, the debts between them, no matter how much, are "cleared." Antonio's only hope is to see Bassanio once at his death if Bassanio feels willing and Portia allows him to come. Antonio is at complete ease, ready to let go all of his loans to Bassanio.

Antonio's generosity is not only for his friends. He tells his friends that Shylock hates him because he "oft delivered from his forfeitures / Many that have at times made moan" to him (III. ii. 22-23). He has not only helped many he might not know well, but also is ready to forgive Shylock, who almost takes his life. In the courtroom scene, when Shylock's malicious intent is frustrated, Antonio is asked to give mercy to Shylock. Antonio first begs the Duke and the court to "quit the fine for one half of his goods," that is, to remit the fine for half of Shylock's wealth, and promises to first have the other half given him "in use" or in trust and then transfer it to Lorenzo at Shylock's death (IV. i. 375-87). In this act, Antonio can be said to have shown his love for his neighbor. [1]

Another instance of Antonio's liberality is his suggestion of giving Balthasar / Portia a ring. When Portia in disguise will take nothing but the ring from Bassanio's finger since he insists giving "some remembrance" to Portia "as a tribute," Bassanio tries to dissuade Portia from taking it (IV. i. 419-40). Then Antonio tells Bassanio to "let him [Portia in disguise] have the ring" because he thinks that Balthasar's derservings are more important than Portia's commandment. Although the ring Bassanio gives Balthasar / Portia is Bassanio's, not Antonio's, and it does not stand for wealth alone, Antonio's suggestion in giving shows his liberality with wealth.

Antonio's generosity has won him many good friends. In addition to Bassanio, Salerio, Solanio and Graziano, the Duke of Venice can be counted as one. As the court leader, he articulately and explicitly shows his favor for Antonio, the defendant. He not only shows deep sympathy for Antonio, but also asks for mercy for Antonio from Shylock. He even asks Shylock to forgive some portion of the principal ("a moiety of the principal") Antonio owes the money-lender (IV. i. 25, 28), let alone the forfeiture. Moreover, the Duke says openly

---

[1]   Richard H. Weisberg considers Antonio's request here of the Duke / Court hypocritical: "Antonio merely reiterates the Duke's disposition of the half of Shylock's goods that are to go *to the state*! Antonio has no power over, nor any interest in, that half. Thus *he is in fact forgiving the 'fine' that only the state has a right to get.* So Antonio begins his speech by winning the hearts of his listeners through a gracious disposition of that which he does not own" (15).

to the court that "upon my power I may dismiss this court" (IV. i. 103). As the authority, the Duke's statement shows both his intended dismissal and at least his underestimation of Shylock's plea and his admiration of Antonio as a generous merchant.

Certainly, Antonio's liberality has also accumulated hatred, the worst of which is found in Shylock. For Shylock, Antonio's mistake is that he does not only lend money to his friends like Bassanio; worse yet, he "lends out money gratis, and brings down / The rate of usance here with us in Venice" (I. iii. 41-42). In monetary terms, Antonio's lending out money with no interest has "hindered" Shylock to earn "half a million" (III. i. 51). As a result, Shylock determines that if he forgives Antonio, "cursèd be my tribe" (I. iii. 48-49), and that he will "execute" the "villainy" Venetian Christians teach him in a "hard" way (III. i. 66-67). Consequently, Shylock is resolved to take "revenge" on Antonio (III. i. 50, 62, 64, 66, 87).

Despite the complexity of Antonio's character, he can still be regarded, at least in part, as the type Aristotle's "liberal man."

3. Antonio the "spiritual Jew"

One reason for Antonio to get into conflict of money-lending with Shylock is his belief in the ancient teachings against increasing money through interest. As mentioned earlier, Aristotle in his *Politics* argues that interest, "money born of money," is "the most contrary to nature" (1258^a 23). In his *Nicomachean Ethics*, Aristotle holds that "if a man makes gain [through interest], his action is ascribed to no form of wickedness but injustice" (1130^a 31-33).

Backgrounded by such influential classical and biblical exhortation, Antonio firmly believes that money-lending at interest as Shylock does is not right. He "rails" (I. iii. 46) at Shylock: "When did friendship take / A breed for barren metal of his friend" (I. iii. 131-32)? For Antonio, money-lending should be done without interest as a sign of friendship because money, a " barren metal ", cannot "breed. "

Antonio's belief in money-lending at no interest as an act of justice is in line with Elizabethan morality. Indeed, he does appear to have a sense of justice. When he knows that Shylock is filing a lawsuit against him, Antonio quickly points out, as Murray J. Levith observes, that "as a trading centre Venice had to be especially careful with its justice" (*Italian Settings* 26). Antonio tells Solanio that the denial of " the course of law" in Venice "will much impeach the justice of the state" because Venice's "trade and profit" "consisteth of all nations " (III. iii. 26-31). Because of this realization, Antonio confesses the bond and is ready to accept Shylock's legal revenge at the court even though he knows fully about its fatal consequence. "I am a tainted wether of the flock, / Meetest for death" (IV. i. 113-14) are the words he says to Bassanio when facing Shylock's knife.

On the other hand, however, Antonio does not seem to practice justice properly. Early in the play, Shylock complains that Antonio " hates our sacred nation" (I. iii. 46), that Antonio has "rated" him about his "monies" and "usances" in the Rialto, and that Antonio calls him a "misbeliever, cut-throat dog," spits upon his "Jewish gaberdine," voids rheum upon his beard, and foots him as " a stranger cur" over

Antonio's threshold (I. iii. 106-18). Antonio does not seem to feel bad at all for having said or done such things to Shylock; he responds to Shylock:

> I am as like to call thee so [a cut-throat dog] again,
> To spit on thee again, to spurn thee too.
>
> (I. iii. 128-29)

Apparently, Antonio admits the acts he is accused of by Shylock and has no intention to change his behavior at all, even at the moment when he is trying to borrow a large sum of money from Shylock. Perhaps, as Portia ironically tells Bassanio that she will become as "liberal" as he, Antonio's abusive words to and rough kicks at Shylock are another aspect of his liberality—his liberality of expression and action. We will not forget that when Portia accuses Bassanio of breaking his oath never to give away her ring, Antonio swears to Portia that "I dare be bound again, / My soul upon the forfeit, that your lord / Will never more break faith advisedly" (V. i. 251-53). Lawrence Danson keenly remarks that Antonio's " self-righteously unrepentant answer to Shylock at their first appearance together . . . is shocking to modern ears. No doubt it would have shocked some in Shakespeare's audience; others . . . might have applauded Antonio's openly expressed hatred" (31).

Commenting on Antonio, Murray J. Levith says that his name " recalls saints," and he is " the special Christian singled out by God for a higher calling—to denounce false religion and be a willing martyr for the values of the true faith" (*Italian Settings* 24-25). While there is a question whether Shylock's religion is " false " or not, Antonio is certainly not a willing martyr for the values of the " true " faith. At least, Antonio seems to have forgotten what the Gospel of Matthew teaches:

> Ye haue heard that it hathe bene said, Thou shalt loue thy neighbour, and hate thine enemie.
>
> But I say vnto you, Loue your enemies: blesse them that curse you: do good to them that hate you, and praye for them which hurt you, and persecute you.

(V. 43-44)

It is true Antonio loves his neighbor, but he hates shylock, and shylock, a lowly money-lender, is not a real enemy. Lawrence Danson sensitively points out: "The *malice* with which Antonio has, in the past and now, publicly reproved and humiliated Shylock, convicts him of being, in this instance, himself spiritually a 'Jew'" (32).

The Jews were a drastically stereotyped people in Shakespeare's time. In literature, as James Shapiro points out, "sermons, paintings, Chaucer's *Prioress's Tale*, Corpus Christi plays, and a host of other sources confirmed that Jews [until the sixteenth century] ... were the accursed descendants of those who had killed Christ and who continued in their devilish ways" (*Shakespeare and the Jews* 13). According to M. M. Mahood, the Jew was represented as "the greediness of worldly choosers, and bloody minds of usurers" (5). Marlowe's *Jew of Malta* had a strong theatrical influence upon the Elizabethans. In reality, the trial and execution of Ruy Lopez, the Queen's Jewish doctor, was fresh on Elizabethans' mind and a sign of bitter anti-Jewish feelings in England. The Jew, therefore, had become a stock character in early modern English literature, representing greed, cruelty and vengeance. Because of Antonio's usual hate and harshness toward Shylock, Lawrence Danson's comment on Antonio as a "spiritual Jew" seems justified.

Antonio's "spiritual Jewishness" is further attested by his response to Portia's direction in the form of a question: "What mercy can you render him, Antonio" (IV. i. 394)? To this direction, Antonio, besides his suggestion to "quit the fine for one half of his goods," demands that

> Two things provided more: that for this favour
> He presently become a Christian;
> The other, that he do record a gift,
> Here in the court, of all he dies possessed
> Unto his son Lorenzo and his daughter.
>
> (IV. i. 378, 383-87)

Antonio's demands, to borrow Richard H. Weisberg's interpretation, are:

1. Shylock must place half of his present wealth into a trust [run by Antonio], with Lorenzo and Jessica receiving the principal at Shylock's death;

2. Shylock must convert to Christianity;

3. Shylock must pledge to will all of his after-acquired wealth to Lorenzo and Jessica.

(16)

This means Antonio will reap a fairly good income till Shylock's death, and Shylock "must face the additional torment of being the enforced benefactor of a young couple he has every good reason to despise" (17). Moreover, Shylock, who will not "smell pork," "eat," "drink," "pray" with the Christians (I. iii. 31-35), will now have to do all of these. To quote Weisberg again: "It is here that Antonio, ostensibly the model of Christian courtesy . . . might be fully expected to outdo the Duke's generosity. Instead, Antonio proceeds to fail every test of moderation, mercy, and forgiveness that Portia has imposed upon him (14). If "Jewish" is taken to mean incorrectly hateful and unforgiving, Antonio in his treatment of Shylock is well worth the word.

From this discussion of the character of Antonio, we can see he is mainly made up of three types: the melancholy man, the liberal friend and the "spiritual Jew." His melancholy humour is not explainable; he is generous to his friend Bassanio and others from the beginning of the play to the end; he hates Shylock also from the beginning to the end. For Bassanio and other Christians, he is generous; but for Shylock, he is unforgiving. He is a complex character with strengths and weaknesses, but his characterization is clearly based on traditional character types. If we look at Antonio through the perspective of William Hazilitt and Charles Gildon, Antonio will be an individual with little development.

IV. The villains of passions

i. Volpone

1. Volpone the blasphemer

Volpone is a rich Venetian nobleman who openly eulogizes his wealth. In the opening lines, we hear Volpone enthusiastically greeting his gold:

> Good morning to the day; and, next, my gold:
> Open the shrine, that I may see my *saint*.
> Haile the worlds soul, and mine.

> (I. i. 1-3)

In this parody of a mass, Volpone passionately salutes and worships his gold as a "saint," calling it both the world's and his own "soul," and the closet where he stores it a "shrine." In these lines, Volpone is accurately what Joseph Hall describes as the character of the profane: "Perhaps himself be his own deity, and the world his heaven. . . At first, he sinned, and cared not; now he sinneth, and knoweth not" (110). At the same time, Volpone also fits exactly into Hall's character of the covetous since he so worships his gold: "A lifeless piece of earth is his master; yea, his god: which he shrines in his coffer, and to which he sacrifices his heart. Every face of his coin is a new image, which he adores with the highest veneration; yet takes upon him to be protector of that he worshippeth" (116). Indeed, as discussed in Chapter Two, the love of gold means an estrangement from the love of God, a natural consequence of profanity.

Volpone is enthralled by the power of gold. With a pun on *sol* (the solar mysticism of Italian Renaissance philosophers and an English term for the Italian coins known as *soldi*), soul and the sun, and an allusion to the alchemical belief in the Renaissance that gold is the son of the sun, Volpone continues his adoration:

> O, thou sonne of Sol,
> (But brighter then thy father) let me kisse,
> With adoration, thee, and euery relique
> Of sacred treasure, in this blessed roome.
> Well did wise Poets, by thy glorious name,
> Title that age, which they would haue the best;
> Thou being the best of things: and far transcending

All stile of ioy, in children, parents, friends,

Or any other waking dreame on earth.

Thy lookes, when they to Venus did ascribe,

They should haue giu'n her twentie thousand Cupids;

Such are thy beauties, and our loues!

(I. i. 10-21)

Volpone's calling gold the *son of Sol* parodies Christians'
worshiping of Christ as the son of God. He kisses the coins in
the way he would kiss the cross. He claims that it is right for
poets to title the best time in history the "golden age,"
venerating gold as the best of things.

Then Volpone specifically praises the limitless power of
gold:

Deare saint,

Riches, the dumb god, that giu'st all men tongues:

That canst doe naught, and yet mak'st men doe all
things;

The price of soules; euen hell, with thee to boot,

Is made worth heauen! Thou art vertue, fame,

Honour, and all things else. Who can get thee,

He shall be noble, valiant, honest, wise—

(I. i. 21-27)

Volpone knows that silence is golden. But he, at the
same time, poignantly shows that gold gives all men tongues.
Many people are affected by money, even consider it the goal
of their lives. That is why Volpone continues to say that
although gold itself can do nothing, it makes men do all
kinds of things. For many people, gold, or money in general,
is the measure to judge others, hence it is "the price of
soules." Because gold is so powerful and important, even hell

will become heaven if it has gold in it. To Volpone, gold, or wealth, is inclusive of all values and virtues, from honor, fame, and nobility, to wisdom. Commenting on these lines, Edward Partridge remarks that "Volpone's ethical system is almost point for point the reverse of Christian ethics" (94).

Critics have linked Volpone's blasphemous opening speech about gold to Marlowe's *Jew of Malta*. T. S. Eliot holds that it is "in the manner of Marlowe, more deliberate, more mature, but without Marlowe's inspiration" (154). James Shapiro says that "Volpone's opening speech also invokes a Marlovian restructuring of values and the playful undermining of theological and ethical claims" (*Rival Playwrights* 63). The common ground between T. S. Eliot and James Shapiro is Volpone's degenerative worshipping of gold as Barabas does. As Brian Parker remarks, "Gold is supposed not to have existed in the Golden Age, but Volpone puts it at the centre of his universe, praising it as brighter than the sun, the unmoved mover and creator of the world, lovelier than sexual beauty, and the ground for all human values" (25).

Volpone worships gold, but we soon learn that he glories more "in the cunning purchase" of his wealth, that is, he is more proud of earning his wealth than hoarding it because he does not work in any of the usual ways (I. i. 30-31). He does not invest in any industry, till any land or engage in any trade, not even in usury or money-lending. As he tells Mosca:

> I vse no trade, no venter;
> I wound no earth with plow-shares; fat no beasts
> To feede the shambles; haue no mills for yron,
> Oyle, corne, or men, to grinde 'hem into poulder;

I blow no subtill glasse; expose no ships
To threatnings of the furrow-faced sea;
I turne no moneys, in the publike banke;
Nor vsure priuate.

(I. i. 33-40)

Obviously Volpone is familiar with almost all industries: agriculture, animal husbandry, steelmaking, food processing, glassblowing, transportation, international trade, and banking. However, these are not his ways to acquire wealth. His is "no common way" (I. i. 33).

Because Volpone has "no wife, no parent, child, allie," not one in blood relations to inherit naturally his "substance," people around "obserue" him. Consequently Volpone draws "new clients, daily" to his house who bring him "presents," and send him "plate, coyne, iewels" with a hope to be made heir upon his death (I. i. 75-79). Taking advantage of the situation, Volpone plays with these people's covetous hopes to satisfy his own avarice.

Volpone's avarice is clearly shown in his conversation with Mosca. Before he sees Voltore, the first major legacy hunter in the play, Volpone tells Mosca that he is eager to receive Voltore's expensive gift: "Dispatch, dispatch: I long to have possession / Of my new present" (I. ii. 115-16). When Mosca returns from spying on Voltore's arrival and tells Volpone that the advocate brings a silver plate, Volpone asks: "Of what bignesse?" (I. i. 92) When Voltore comes in, Volpone pretends that he retains enough consciousness for simple communication. Voltore greets him at his bedside, and Volpone responds:

Volp. Bring him near, where is he?

> I long to feel his hand.
>
> *Mos.* The plate is here, sir.
>
> *Volt.* How fare you, sir?
>
> *Volp.* I thank you, Signior Voltore.
>
> Where is the plate? Mine eyes are bad.
>
> (I. iii. 14-17)

Although Volpone tells Mosca that he wishes to feel Voltore's hand, clearly he does not really mean to do it. It is the plate that he wants to feel and have. The repetition of the word " plate " is so obvious that Volpone's avarice is immediately apparent to the audience.

Volpone's seeming valuation and pursuit of money as the central and only important thing in life are also impressively displayed in a conversation between Mosca and Corvino, the merchant:

> *Corv.* Say,
>
> I have a diamond for him, too.
>
> *Mos.* Best show't, sir,
>
> Put it into his hand; 'tis only there
>
> He apprehends: he has his feeling yet.
>
> See, how he grasps it!
>
> *Corv.* 'Las, good gentleman!
>
> How pitiful the sight is!
>
> (I. v. 16-21)

Corvino genuinely trusts Volpone is dying and exclaims sympathetically at the sight of his weakening senses and movements. However, the audience or reader, knowing about this dramatic irony that Volpone and Mosca are merely putting on a vivid show, understands what Mosca and Corvino say more than Corvino does. Mosca tells Corvino that

Volpone's hand is the only organ left to him for understanding and feeling. While Corvino takes Mosca's words literally, the audience/reader understands that this is an accurate restatement of Volpone's grasping mentality: he understands the world not with his mind, but through his hand; he only values what he obtains materially from the world. Volpone's cooperation with Mosca in clenching the diamond put to his hand ("See how he graspes it") confirms Mosca's directions to Corvino. More importantly, the audience knows that " grasping " is certainly Volpone's conscious behaviour. Compared with Volpone's self-confession in the opening speech, this conversation is an example of emphasis on Volpone's money-grasping philosophy, but the difference is this one is made in front of someone outside of his household—someone whom he intends to fleece.

Another of Volpone covetous "clients" is Corbaccio (I. i. 76), who, according Mosca, is "a wretch, more impotent / Then this [Volpone] can faine to be" (I. iv. 3-4). Yet, even such an old wretch, Volpone does not let go. After deceiving Corbaccio's bag of "bright cecchines [gold coins]" (I. iv. 69), Volpone, with the direction of his parasite, even induces the old man to go home to make his will naming Volpone as his heir and disinherit his son. When the old man is sent home for the will, Volpone is so happy with his gains from Corbaccio that he claims that he "shall burst [in laughter]" (I. iv. 132). Clearly, Volpone is not just avaricious; as he himself claims, he enjoys more the tricking of other avaricious people. This shows that Volpone is more complex than a mere stock character of greed.

2. Volpone the voluptuary

Although he deceives in order to obtain money from "women, and men, of euery sexe, and age" (I. i. 77), including such a decrepit wretch as Corbaccio, Volpone should not be mistaken to be a miser. Volpone is also passionate for women and wine, or, as William Empson says, a "dashing lover" ("Volpone" 652). To be sure, Volpone is not interested in all women. He has a strong aversion to the ordinary but pretentious Lady Would-be, despite her "toy, a cap" of her "owne worke" (III. v. 15). Volpone's strong desire is for Celia, Corvino's beautiful wife.

Because Celia is under close watch by Corvino, Volpone manages to disguise himself as a mountebank working under Celia's window and see her. Although this sight is paid by a heavy price—the jealous Corvino injures him while beating him away, Volpone's desire for Celia continues to boil and burn. Volpone begs Mosca to "employ" freely his "gold, plate, and iewells" to help satisfy his "longings" (II. iv. 23-24). This shows that for Volpone, gold is but a means, not an end.

By Mosca's plot, Celia is finally tricked to and left alone by Volpone's bedside. Lecturing Celia against her husband's willingness to sell her "onely for hope of gaine, and that vncertaine," Volpone confesses his desires for her. However, his desires turn out to be more of an erotic game-play than a mere act of carnal satisfaction. He claims that he is willing to contend with the changeful Proteus or Acheloüs, the Greek river whose horned deity could change shapes, in order to win her love. Volpone introduces Celia to some "comedie," "entertainment" and "sports of loue" (III. vii. 160, 161,

166). He wants Celia to act out the games he imagines based on erotic old stories and classical poetry. When rejected by Celia, Volpone tries to assure her that he is her "worthy louer" (III. vii. 186). He shows and promises Celia all his wealth, including his pearls, diamonds, gold and other jewels. He tempts Celia with all kinds of rare food, such as "the heads of parrats, tongues of nightingales, / The braines of peacocks, and of estriches," even a phoenix if he could get (III. vii. 201-05). He also tries to lure Celia to other carnal enjoyments, like bathing in the "iuyce of iuly-flowres, / Spirit of roses and of violets, / The milke of vnicornes [a mythical animal, Gordon Campbell n. to III. vii. 215] and pathers breath / Gather'd in bagges, and mixt with cretan wines," and drinking "prepared gold, and amber." With his dwarf dancing, his eunuch singing and his fool making up a grotesque dance nearby, he and Celia should "in changed shapes" or Celia "in more moderne formes" act out the stories in Ovid's *Metamorphoses* (III. vii. 213-21).

Clearly, Volpone's enumeration of the overwhelmingly long list of sensual delights includes all aspects of a dissolute life, the life of "a voluptuary" (Dryden, XV: 343). We can therefore see that lust is among the least important of what he has for Celia at all. Indeed, of all the enjoyments Volpone counts for her, the central one is entertainment. At the very beginning of the play, Volpone has actually revealed such an attitude towards his life: "What should I doe, / But cocker vp my genius, and liue free / To all delights, my fortune calls me to" (I. i. 70-73)? Volpone's aim to "liue free / To all delights" that his fortune "calls "① him to is also seen previously when he says he wants to fill up every space of his time with either a trick of the legacy hunters or some sport. Volpone seems in one sense like Portia. Despite his wealth, Volpone is also "aweary of this great world" (*MV*, I. ii. 1-2). Therefore, Volpone always anxiously seeks out entertainments.

Like Bassanio's prodigal life, Volpone portrays one possible for himself and Celia to pursue. Again, Joseph Hall's character of the unthrift may partly apply here: " His pleasures are immoderate, and not honest" (123). Volpone also has "a wanton eye, a liquorish tongue" (123). But different from Bassanio, who accumulates piles of debt to keep his extravagance, Volpone gulls greedy visitors for wealth to spend. Brian Gibbons has an excellent comment on Volpone's voluptuousness: "Volpone's attempt to seduce Celia is an admirable parody of materialist rhapsodies . . . It is the main purpose of Jonson to show through satiric exaggeration the perverse and disgusting detachment of Volpone from natural and vital enjoyents" (128). Therefore, Volpone's obsession with money is not just a sign of avarice or prodigality. Rather, it is an act of corruption. M. C. Bradbrook points out, in *Volpone*, "Jonson had, as it were, shown a refracted and more distorted image of city corruption; the worship of gold, and the mutual trickery of Volpone and his dupes reach a more horrific scale" (*Living Monument* 96).

---

① This word "calls" is another signifier of Volpone's attitude of life. He does not think that his fortune allows him to enjoy pleasures of life; instead, his thoughts are that his fortune invites him to pleasures. This is an additional evidence that money can corrupt.

3. Volpone the Machiavellian villain

Tricking dupes for money and then using the money for sensuality is only part of Volpone's complex character. This is especially true when Volpone and Mosca have won the first hearing at the court. In other words, the character of Volpone is not just that of the covetous and the voluptuary. Volpone is a Machiavellian villain, too.

After Mosca superbly "picks up the shattered pieces of their plot" and "skillfully orchestrates the fools to transform Bonario and Celia from accusers into defendants" (Jones 112), Volpone asks Mosca to spread the (fake) news of his death in order to have a good laugh behind a curtain, looking at Mosca's torturing the fools one by one. Volpone does get a wonderful entertainment. However, Volpone makes a disastrous mistake in asking Mosca to wear his clothes (showing Mosca has become his heir and a nobleman). Quickly, Mosca takes advantage of his heir-and-nobleman charade to usurp Volpone's status and wealth. When Mosca in a Venetian nobleman's gown appears at court to testify to Volpone's reported death, he is on his way to succeed in getting Volpone physically out of his way.

Out of great frustration and terror, Volpone (in disguise) tells Mosca to say that he is still living. However, Mosca simply wants to dismiss him. "What busie knaue is this!" Mosca exclaims at court and tells the magistrates: "most reuerend fathers, / I sooner, had attended your graue pleasures, / But that my order, for the funerall / Of my deare patron did require me" (V. xii. 55-58). "I intend to bury" Volpone "like a gentleman" (V. xii. 59), Mosca continues. Then at Mosca's demand for a half of his wealth, Volpone hesitates. Volpone's hesitation perhaps convinces Mosca of his victory. When Volpone (still in disguise) insists that he lives, he is challenged by Mosca as "an insolence" (V. xii. 75). The magistrates lean to the side of Mosca and order Volpone to be whipped. Facing an imminent whipping, Mosca's betrayal and the parasite's prospect of marrying one of the magistrate's daughters, Volpone decides to bring all parties down. He loudly declares: "My ruines shall not come alone; your match/ I'le hinder sure; my substance shall not glew you , / Nor screw you; into a family" (V. xii. 86-8). Then, with the intention for a cruel counterattack, Volpone confesses to the court:

> I am Volpone, and this is my knaue;
> This, his owne knaue; this, auarices fool;
> This, a Chimera of wittall, foole, and knaue;
> And, reuerend fathers, since we all can hope
> Nought, but a sentence, let's not now despaire it.
>
> (V. xii. 89-93)

Expectedly, Volpone's confession concerning the villainy of himself, Mosca ("my knaue"), Voltore ("his owne knaue"), Corbaccio ("auarices fool"), and Corvino ("a Chimera of wittall, foole, and knaue") collapses all the tricksters and dupes. Although it does not result in death, it does cause heavy and justified punishment to all of them: Mosca is first "whipt," and then to "liue perpetuall prisoner" in Venetian gallies; Voltore, "banis'd from " advocates' fellowship and Venice; Corbaccio, to be "confined to the monasterie of San' Spirito" till death; Corvino, to be rowed around Venice wearing "faire, long asses eares" to announce his cuckoldry. He is also to send his wife to her father with her dowrie trebled; and Volpone is to "lie in prison, crampt with irons, / Till thou bee'st sicke, and lame indeed" with all his wealth "straight confiscate" to the hospital of "the Incurabili" (V. xii. 106-44). Thus, Volpone's final defeat, also his victory over Mosca, does not help him escape, but destroys himself as well as every participant in his fraud. [1]

On the whole, Volpone, as an idolatrous gold-worshipper, a voluptuary, and a Machiavellian villain, is a complex mixture of several character types: the avaricious, the covetous, the blasphemous, the lustful, the voluptuary, and the comic villain. Russ McDonald notes that in such "grand figures" as Volpone who "stand out from the rest of the dramatis personae and compel our attention by virtue of their elaborate speech, forceful personality, obsession, solipsism, intransigence, or prodigious imagination," Jonson "depicts trickery or foolishness on a heroic level" (100). Compared with Mosca who, although is cast as a parasite, is not a single-faceted humour or stock character, Volpone, as Carol A. Carr remarks, is even "less typical" than Mosca (155), despite their similarity of a rogue. Clearly, Volpone is not what William Hazilitt has described as one confined in a "leaden cistern" (*Lectures* 73). Instead, Volpone, in terms of complexity of character, can rival with Shakespeare's villains, such as Shylock.

---

[1] Ian Donaldson sees Volpone and Mosca as one of the many teams in Jonson's plays which feature competition and collaboration as "the central and conflicting impulses" ("Looking Sideways" 8). For Donaldson's full discussion of competition and collaboration in Jonson in a much broader sense, see Donaldson, "Looking Sideways," pp. 1-22.

ii. Shylock

1. Shylock the miserly usurer

Murray J. Levith observes that "Shylock shares with Volpone a gold-centered not God-centered Venice; both have sold their souls" (*Italian Settings* 17). Levith is certainly correct about Volpone and Shylock's attitude towards money and God. However, they have a big difference between their ways of making money. While Volpone handles "no vsure" or "moneys in the publike banke" (I. i. 39-40), Shylock is a usurer. [1] Shylock is acknowledged to have his prototype in Barabas of Marlowe's *Jew of Malta* (e. g. , Shapiro, *Rival Playwrights* 104-11), but he also fits into Joseph Hall's character sketch of the covetous: "He lets money, and sells time for a price; and will not be importuned, either to prevent or defer his day . . . He breeds of money to the third generation, neither hath it sooner any being than he sets it to beget more" (117). Shylock regards money as the prop of his life. This can be seen from his lament when all his money is confiscated at the conclusion of the trial scene:

> Nay, take my life and all, pardon not that:
> You take my house when you do take the prop
> That doth sustain my house; you take my life
> When you do take the means whereby I live.
>
> (IV. i. 370-73)

Naturally, as a usurer, Shylock is not happy about

---

[1] By present definition, usury means lending money at excessively or exorbitantly high rates. In Shakespeare's time, it was not necessarily so. As John W. Draper notes, although there were times that usurious rates of interest were regulated, usurers commonly used tricks to exact "outrageous" profits, and this aroused "general bitterness" against them ("Usury" 41-42).

interest rates being brought lower by such merchants as Antonio who lend out money gratis:

> I hate him [Antonio] for he is a Christian;
> But more, for that in low simplicity
> He lends out money gratis, and brings down
> The rate of usance here with us in Venice.

(I. iii. 34-37)

Although usury was permitted for Jews, Shylock does not like being called a usurer. He says angrily about Antonio, "he was wont to call me usurer, let him look to his bond" (3.1.37-38). Instead of *usury*, Shylock only uses the word *usance* for himself. He defends his practice of usury in an aside:

> He [Antonio] hates our sacred nation, and he rails
> Even there where merchants most do congregate
> On me, my bargains, and my well-won thrift
> Which he calls interest.

(I. iii. 40-43)

Therefore, to Shylock, usury is a venture, a risky investment, not only normal, but also decent and even holy because it is like the way Jacob used to thrive. Shylock quotes the story from Genesis 27 in which Jacob skillfully manages to acquire as many parti-colored sheep (i. e. wealth) as possible by letting his mother sheep look at partly stripped branches at the time of conception (*MV* I. iii. 63-82). Shylock proudly compares his profit from usury to Jacob's clever means to prosperity.

Shylock's words are the best exemplifiers of his avaricious attitude. Here are his first lines in *The Merchant of Venice*:

Shylock. Three thousand ducats, well.

Bassanio. Ay, sir, for three months.

Shylock. For three months, well.

(I. iii. 1-3)

The very first words Shylock is heard to say in the play are: "three thousand ducats," to be followed by "for three months," the time during which interest will be charged. This is a vivid characterization of a mind that is engrossed in money. [1] Moreover, as Simon Palfrey and Tiffany Stern have excellently pointed out, Shylock repeats Bassanio's phrases (e. g. "for three months") and "immediately turns them to his own use" by adding a word "well" ("for three months, well") as "indeed a kind of discursive 'interest', borrowing for the purposes of quickly hoarded increase" (195). This shows a miser is also at the same time a hoarder.

Indeed, Shylock's speeches before the trial scene in IV. i are all centered around money. Every other major character of *The Merchant of Venice*, although considering money to be important, cares first of all about his or her sadness or happiness. Antonio's first speech begins, " in sooth I know not why I am so sad" (I. i. 1). Bassanio begins his first speech with " good signors, when shall we laugh?" (I. i. 66). Portia, rather like Antonio, sighs about her melancholy, "by my troth, Nerissa, my little body is aweary of this great world" (I. ii. 1-2), but her concern is not about money, but about a human relationship. Only Shylock's opening speech deeply impresses the audience with his avarice, his obsession

---

[1] Shylock is even a miser with words. Besides repeating Bassanio's statements, he says only the word "well," not enough for Bassanio to form a clue to his intention.

with the specific amount of a large sum of money. His money-oriented mentality is evident.

When he has to go out, Shylock tells his daughter, Jessica, that he "did dream of money bags" (II. v. 18), exactly as Joseph Hall sketches in his character, "he fears to keep, and abhors to lose" (116). Money has become such an important part of his life that he thinks of it all the time during the day and dreams about it during his sleep. In addition, according to M. M. Mahood, in Shakespeare's England, dreaming was supposed to work by opposites; therefore, Shylock's dreaming of holding money bags means to him that he is going to *lose* money. Naturally, this frightens him (*MV*, n. to II. v. 18). As Joseph Hall describes, "in the avaricious man's short and unquiet sleeps, he dreams of thieves, and runs to the door, and names more men than he hath" (117).

For Shylock, money is not something that helps him and his daughter have a good and happy life. He inflicts his avarice on his daughter, too. As Tony Tanner points out, Shylock repeatedly warns Jessica to "look to my house . . . lock up my doors . . . shut doors after you" (II. v. 16, 29, 52) (148). ① He instructs her to avoid spending. When he hears of masques outside his house, he orders Jessica to turn a deaf ear to the music and merrymaking, because his philosophy of life is: "Fast bind, fast find: / A proverb never stale in thrifty mind" (II. v. 52-53). While ostensibly Shylock quotes this proverb to caution Jessica to lock up his house securely, the

---

① Tanner also hints that Shakespeare may have intended Shylock's name to signify his miserliness (Shy*lock*), in contrast with Antonio's open liberality or prodigality (148). Shakespeare's name Shylock only appears in *The Merchant*—it is not a borrowing from any other source.

expression is also a reflection of his avarice—to bind up his money bags fast to stop his money from leaking out, much like the maxim "a penny saved is a penny earned." Sylvan Barnet remarks that "Shylock, the mirthless isolate, is, of course, the embodiment of all that is antithetic to prodigality" (26). In sharp contrast with Bassanio, who borrows money to spend on romance, luxury and entertainment, Shylock shuns every kind of amusement as "shallow foppery" (II. v. 34). As Harold Bloom observes, "Shylock takes little pleasure in himself or anything else, despite his pride in his self identity" (*Invention* 183)

A critical example of Shylock's "fast-bind" philosophy is seen at the court when Portia in disguise as the young lawyer from Rome, Balthasar, asks Shylock to have a surgeon on hand to treat Antonio's wound:

> Portia.　Have by some surgeon, Shylock, on your charge,
> To stop his wounds, lest he do bleed to death.
> Shylock.　Is it so nominated in the bond?
> Portia.　It is not so expressed, but what of that?
> 'Twere good you do so much for charity.
> Shylock.　I cannot find it, 'tis not in the bond.
>
> 　　　　　　　　　　　　　　　　（IV. i. 253-58）

Balthasar / Portia has declared that Venetian law allows Shylock to cut a pound of Antonio's flesh, and Shylock is ready to act. Balthasar suggests Shylock pay for a surgeon to stop Antonio from bleeding to death when he cuts the flesh. This can be seen as Portia's final attempt to move Shylock to show mercy in the name of charity. This can also be seen as

Portia's giving Shylock a final test on his choice between mercy and money. This may even be seen as an obvious warning or a reminder to Shylock that he should be aware that the law only allows him to cut exactly a pound of flesh, not to shed a drop of blood. However, Shylock—avaricious as ever, too obsessed with his money and revenge—refuses to pay for a surgeon because hiring the doctor at his expense is "not in the bond" (IV. i. 258). As it will turn out soon, this choice Shylock makes is to almost totally ruin his life.

Another way Shylock avoids spending money is to calculate carefully. Before he leaves home to dine with Antonio and Bassanio and lends them the three thousand ducats, Shylock tells his daughter, Jessica:

> I am bid forth to supper, Jessica.
> There are my keys. But wherefore should I go?
> I am not bid for love, they flatter me;
> But yet I'll go in hate, to feed upon
> The prodigal Christian.

(II. v. 10-15)

Shylock for religious reasons does not like dining with Christians, but he decides to eat supper with the two, Antonio and Bassanio, here in II. v. in order to "feed upon" them. Shylock's miserliness is exactly like Celeste Turner Wright's summary of the usurer's character in the Renaissance, "starving himself and his guests at home or appeasing his 'dog-like appetite' at tables of others" (196). Or, in Joseph Hall's words, "He never eats good meal, but on his neighbor's trencher (116).

Shylock's miserly calculations concerning food consumption are also seen in his disparaging remarks concerning his former servant, Lancelot:

> The patch is kind enough, but a huge feeder,
> Snail-slow in profit, and he sleeps by day
> More than the wildcat.

(II. v. 44-46)

Lancelot has chosen to abandon Shylock, but his choice is just what Shylock wishes for. Being a "huge feeder", Lancelot, upon entering service for Bassanio, can help Shylock waste Bassanio's "borrowed purse" (II. vi. 45-50). Shylock also condemns Lancelot for slow service and excessive sleep. However, Lancelot claims that he has been starving and lost much weight. He tells his father about his starvation, "My master's a very Jew . . . I am famished in his service; you may tell every finger I have with my ribs" (II. ii. 85-88). Lancelot has starved so much in Shylock's house that his ribs are easy to feel through his shrunken chest. Again, in Joseph Hall's sketch, "when his guests are parted, talks how much every man devoured, and how many cups were emptied; and feeds his family with the mouldy remnants a month after (117).

Shylock's extreme harshness and stinginess in life eventually lead to Lancelot's leaving his service and, more importantly, Shylock's own daughter's forsaking him. Jessica can no longer tolerate her father. She tells Lancelot that "Our house is hell, and thou a merry devil / Didst rob it of some taste of tediousness" (II. iii. 2-3), that "though I am a daughter to his blood / I am not to his manners" (II. iii. 17-18), and that she "shall end this strife" (II. iii. 19). It is Jessica's elopement with Lorenzo, a Christian, taking with her a huge amount of money that gives Shylock his first, critical blow in the play, which can be seen from his reported lament for the loss of his daughter and his ducats:

> My daughter! O my ducats! O my daughter!
> Fled with a Christian! O my Christian ducats!
> Justice! The law! My ducats and my daughter!
> A sealed bag, two sealed bags of ducats,
> Of double ducats, stolen from me by my daughter!
>
> (II. viii. 15-19)

While the speech reported by Salanio may not be Shylock's exact words, it does reveal his equal valuation of his money and his daughter. In other words, Shylock, in his avarice, regards his daughter as just another part of his valuable possessions. His later speech with his friend Tubal may indicate that he actually values his money even more than his daughter:

> A diamond gone cost me two thousand ducats in Frankfurt! The curse never fell upon our nation till now; I never felt it till now. Two thousand ducats in that and other precious, precious jewels. I would my daughter were dead at my foot, and the jewels in her ear! Would she were hearsed at my foot, and the ducats in her coffin!
>
> (III. i. 79-85)

To Shylock, the loss of the precious, two-thousand-ducat diamond is regarded as a curse fallen on his nation.[1] He

---

[1] Katharine Eisaman Maus has a good point here: "Although Shylock identifies strongly with his "sacred nation" and apparently relies on fellow Jews like Tubal, the play gives little sense of Jewish community" (Introduction 390). Besides being mentioned by Shylock (I. iii. 49) and Jessica (III. ii. 284) once each, Tubal, Shylock's only Jewish fellow, appears in person in only one scene, in which he tells Shylock of news of Jessica's squandering of his money and Antonio's misfortunes. Tubal's single appearance is not enough to form in our mind Shylock's sense of belonging to such a thing as a Jewish community.

would rather his daughter died and the money was returned to him. If he had to choose between the money and precious jewels his daughter taking away and his daughter, he would choose the former. Blood is thicker than water, but Shylock's money is thicker than blood. Katharine Eisaman Maus makes an insightful remark on Shylock's materialistic and individualistic psychology:

> Shylock is an isolated figure, shunned by his daughter, abandoned by his servant. His calculating, loveless existence seems to result from the way he manages his property. Or perhaps isolation has made him cautious and selfish. Shylock has little motive to be generous with the Christians who despise him, and every reason to believe that he cannot depend on others to rescue him from misfortune.
>
> (390)

In fact, Shylock regards money as the benchmark of his value system, by which he judges the world. When Bassanio urges Shylock to decide whether he will lend money with Antonio as the guarantor, Shylock talks with Bassanio in this way:

> Shylock.　Antonio is a good man—
> Bassanio.　Have you heard any imputation to the contrary?
> Shylock.　Ho no, no, no, no: my meaning in saying he is a good man is to have you understand me that he is sufficient.
>
> (I. iii. 11-14)

Shylock laughs at Bassanio's anxiety and defensiveness, and then tells Bassanio that the word " good " in his vocabulary means "sufficient," that is, sufficient in terms of money. As Anne Barton remarks: although he shares the Christians' vocabulary, Shylock "tends to narrow its meaning." In the word *good*, "the moral implications which for Bassanio are primary do not count in Shylock's estimation of a man's worth" (Introduction to *MV*, 251).

Shylock's world is a money world, a stage where every man is judged in terms of money, a world where he and all the people in his family must try to spend as little as possible, regardless of necessity or charity, and a world in which Christians are prodigals whom he is glad to feed upon. His money is the prop whereby he lives. His money is so important to him that a raid on his money can be worse than the death of his only relation, his daughter, and as serious as a curse falling on his holy nation. As John W. Draper says of him, Shylock is "depicted as unprincipled in business and unfeeling in his home" ("usury" 37). In *The Merchant*, Shylock's money-centeredness has accumulated large amounts of wealth so that he could give his wife a diamond ring of two thousand ducats (III. i. 66-68), and he can lend large sums of money out, like the three-thousand-ducat loan to Bassanio through Antonio. However, at the critical moment in the trial scene, Shylock's obsessive avarice eventually results in the loss of all his money and almost costs his life.

2. Shylock the choleric old man

Understandably, all the humiliation Shylock receives and his daughter's elopement with a Christian, taking his money and ring, throw him into a desperate rage. He complains passionately to Salerio and Solanio that he wants to cut

Antonio's flesh because even if it will "feed nothing else," it can feed his "revenge" (III. i. 49-50). His reasons are:

> He hath disgraced me, and hindered me half a million, laughed at my losses, mocked at my gains, scorned my nation, thwarted my bargains, cooled my friends, heated mine enemies and what's his reason? I am a Jew. Hath not a Jew eyes? Hath not a Jew hands, organs, dimensions, senses, affections, passions? Fed with the same food, hurt with the same weapons, subject to the same diseases, healed by the same means, warmed and cooled by the same winter and summer as a Christian is? If you prick us, do we not bleed? If you tickle us, do we not laugh? If you poison us, do we not die? And if you wrong us, shall we not revenge? If we are like you in the rest, we will resemble you in that. If a Jew wrong a Christian, what is his humility? Revenge. If a Christian wrong a Jew, what should his sufferance be by Christian example? Why, revenge! The villainy you teach me I will execute, and it shall go hard but I will better the instruction.
>
> (III. i. 50-68)

In this detailed justification of revenge, Shylock first enumerates the wrongs Christians represented by Antonio have inflicted him: disgracing him, causing him a loss of "half a million," laughing at his losses, etc. ; then he gives the reasons of revenge: since a Jew is also a human being, exactly the same as a Christian, no better, no worse, the Christian and the Jew should treat each other the same way; now that the Christians have wronged the Jew so much, it is just for him to return the wrongs.

Jay L. Halio in his introduction to *The Merchant* has an excellent comment on Shylock's justification:

Out of context, without the framework of vengeance, the speech is an eloquent plea for Jews—and by extension, other minority groups—to be viewed as human beings also ... By endowing his villainous money-lender with 'organs, dimensions, senses, affections, passions,' Shakespeare identifies Shylock with the rest of humanity, but a humanity depraved of revenge. Utterly absent from Shylock's claims is any connection with purer or nobler human attributes.

(46)

Exactly, as we may start to sympathize with Shylock from his plea for the wrongs and humiliation he has suffered, we should, as Halio later reminds us, consider that neither Shylock's or Christian's religion " sanctions vengeance " (Introduction to *MV*, 46).

Later, Shylock continues to show his choler in his plea in the trial scene when he claims " the due and forfeit of my bond" (IV. i. 36). When the Duke tries to persuade Shylock to show Antonio mercy and forgiveness, the money-lender answers that

> You'll ask me why I rather choose to have
> A weight of carrion flesh than to receive
> Three thousand ducats. I'll not answer that—
> But say it is my humour.

(IV. i. 39-42)

Shylock's humour here is what he does not speak out but is understood by all at the court—the penalty of his bond. According to John W. Draper, as a Jew, " Shylock should be melancholy" (*Humours* 112). However, because of his " lodged hate " against Antonio (IV. i. 59), which is hardened by his double misfortune of Jessica's elopement and the loss of his jewels, Shylock's "natural melancholy" has turned to a violent inward choler, which is to "plague" and "torture" (III. i. 109) Antonio (Draper, *Humours* 112).

Shylock's changed humour to avenge himself upon Antonio, like Volpone's adoration of gold, causes him to become blasphemous. When he hears his friend Tubal says of Antonio's "argosy cast away coming from Tripolis," Shylock is thrilled and shouts "I thank God, I thank God" (III. i. 96). As is clear from the discussion above, Shylock, in addition to being a stock character of an avaricious man, is also shown by Shakespeare as governed by the humour of choler.

3. Shylock the Machiavellian villain

Shylock's anger leads him to reject all money offers from Bassanio and later, from Portia. His choler is taking total control of him. Unnegotiably insisting on the forfeit and penalty of his bond, he sees no possible danger to himself beneath the letter of the bond until Portia urges him to cut Antonio's pound of flesh[①] with "no jot of blood" (IV. i. 303).

That the hurt Shylock is ready to avenge may easily remind audiences of the name of dog Venetians impose on him. Shylock blames Antonio for having called him a "cut-throat dog," and footed him as "a strange cur" (I. iii. 108, 115), and later Shylock still bitterly accuses Antonio "Thou call'dst me dog before thou hadst a cause," and warns him to "beware my fangs" (III. iii. 6). Salerio has called Shylock

---

① James Shapiro discusses Shylock's possible intention of castrating Antonio based on the "consistent" use of *flesh* in the sixteenth century and in the Geneva Bible to mean penis (*Jews* 122), see Chapter 4 for more.

"A creature that did bear the shape of man" (III. ii. 273). Salanio tells Salarino of "the dog Jew" moaning in the streets about the loss of his daughter and ducats (II. viii. 14-15), and brands Shylock as "the most impenetrable cur / That ever kept with men" in front of Antonio (III. iii. 17-18). In the courtroom, facing the Duke, Graziano calls Shylock "damned, inexecrable dog" and "this currish Jew" (IV. i. 127, 289). As Paul Yachnin and Jessica Slights suggest, "Shakespeare seems to have conceived the character Shylock in large measure in terms of caninity", and Shakespeare's caninization of Shylock is of a piece with the anti-Semitism of early modern Christian culture. The association between dogs and Jews was widespread" (9-10). [1]

Anti-Semitism has been a major issue to interpreting Shylock, especially today. Rex Gibson points out that it would be "unusual" today to teach *The Merchant of Venice* or *Othello* "without serious attention to anti-Semitism or racism." According to Harold C. Gibson, "Our knowledge of the Holocaust, and the continuing anti-racist struggles give imperative urgency to features which in the past were often overlooked or ignored in school and college Shakespeare" (19). Jewish critics in particular find Shakespeare's depiction of Shylock repulsive. According to Harold C. Goddard, "Shakespeare is at pains to make plain the noble potentialities of Shylock," and "there is a repressed Shylock" (95). Talking about teaching *The Merchant of Venice* to modern students, Harold Bloom remarks that Shylock's

---

[1] Yachnin and Slights have further discussion of Shylock's "dogged style" of conversation and other traditions associated with the Jews, see pp. 9-12 for more. For Shylock's "stubborn" words, see also John Palmer, p. 69.

agreement to become a Christian is "more absurd than would be the conversion of Coriolanus to the popular party" (*Shylock* 2). Bloom says, "to recover the comic spendor of *The Merchant of Venice* now, you need to be either a scholar or an anti-Semite, or best of all an anti-Semitic scholar" (*Shylock* 3).

However, many critics advocate a broader approach to interpreting Shylock and Shakespeare. Jay L. Halio remarks that anti-Semitic slurs "do not appear to be important in Shakespeare's vocabulary or his thinking, with the outstanding exception of *The Merchant of Venice*" (*Merchant* 9). Halio stresses that "[Shakespeare's attitude to Shylock] is ambivalent, far more than Marlowe's attitude toward Barabas. But in neither author can we confidently proclaim an anti-Semitic bias that is more than abstract and traditional". However one looks at him, Shylock has a complex nature. As Halio says, Shylock's character transcends the type, shatters the conventional image with his appeal to our common humanity, and leaves us unsettled in our prejudices, disturbed in our emotions, and by no means sure of our convictions" (*Merchant* 13).

From the above examination, we can see that although Shakespeare has turned the Jewish money-lender into a round, complex dramatis persona that resembles a real person, Shylock is based on the typical stock character of Barabas, and embodies the features of Joseph Hall's character sketches. In addition to being a covetous usurer, a miser, a choleric old man, and a Michiavellian villain, Shylock is a devout Jew who will not eat, drink nor pray with the Christians; he has fond memories of the ring his wife gave him when he was a bachelor. Anne Barton in her introduction to *The Merchant* remarks that "by contrast with Barabas, Shylock is a closely observed human being, not a bogeyman to frighten children in the nursery" (251). Leo Kirschbaum confirms Barton's view: "in one way, Shylock *is* more real than the Christians in the drama, for he after all does derive from reality" (10). However, Shylock, after all, is not a real person. His complexity and realism come from the combination of numerous types of literary characterization.

Conclusion

When arguing about " the crisis in [Shakespeare] editing " in his new book, *Shakespeare Studies Today: Romanticism Lost* (2011), Edward Pechter, the editor of *Othello* in *The Norton Shakespeare Critical Edition*, patiently warns us: " If we are no longer sustained by the pleasure and value of what William Hazlitt claimed as the self-evident consequence of engaging with Shakespeare's plays, then I think the situation of Shakespeare studies may be irremediably desperate" (139-40). Certainly Pechter is right to say that Hazlitt was sustained by "pleasure and value" in engaging with Shakespeare's plays. As we have discussed, Hazlitt describes Shakespeare's plays as free-flowing "bubbles" and " sparkles " (*Lectures* 73). He argues that although François Rabelais (c. 1494 – 1553) and Miguel de Cervantes (1547 – 1616) "excelled" Shakespeare in one aspect of comic art, [1] Shakespeare's talents in comedy were " as wonderful as they were delightful " (55). Even Hazlitt's criticism of Shakespeare sounds complimentary: the fault of Shakespeare's comic Muse is " too good-natured and magnanimous" (64). However, Hazlitt is dismissive and

---

[1] Rabelais, "in the power of ludicrous description," and Cervantes, "in the invention and perfect keeping of comic character" (*Lectures* 56).

harsh concerning Jonson. *Epicoene*, the "perfect" Jonsonian comedy in Dryden's view (XV. 349), is, for Hazlitt, a story of "gratuitous assumption from the beginning to the end" and "the height of improbability"; and its author, "in sustaining the weight of his plot, seems like a balance-master who supports a number of people, piled one upon another, on his hands, his knees, his shoulders, but with a great effort on his own part, and with a painful effect to the beholders" (*Lectures* 80). Hazlitt thinks Kitely in *Every Man in his Humour* is "as dry as the remainder biscuit after a voyage," and *Volpone* is Jonson's "best play" but considers it "prolix and improbable." As for *The Alchemist*, he sees "one glorious scene" between Surly and Sir Epicure Mammon as "the finest example I know of dramatic sophistry" but complains that "compared with this, the rest of the play is a caput mortuum [an alchemy term: a dead head or worthless remains]" (ibid. 82-86). As for another of Jonson's great comedies, all Hazlitt has to say is summed up in twenty-three words: "*Bartholomew Fair* is chiefly remarkable for the exhibition of odd humours and tumbler's tricks, and is on that account amusing to read once" (ibid. 85). Hazlitt is convinced that, as discussed earlier, Jonson's plays "read like translations, want adaptation," and "produce little pleasure," and his characters are "like machines" (ibid. 72-73).

Why would Hazlitt find Shakespeare so pleasant but Jonson so unamiable? Ian Donaldson suggests that Hazlitt came to identify Jonson with William Gifford, editor of the partisan *Quarterly Review* (1809 – 1824) and Jonson's works, and whom Hazlitt hated. Hazlitt chose to "denigrate" Jonson as a sign of his "disparaging assessment" of the editor ("Cambridge Edition" 258). Tom Lockwood shares Donaldson's view on the enmity between Hazlitt and Gifford at the cost of Jonson: "through the process of working out his dislike for Jonson was Hazlitt able to formulate his distaste for Gifford" (122). Lockwood affirms that "Hazlitt thus takes Jonson, and with him his readers, into an explicitly politicized Romanticism" (113). [1] As D. H. Craig observes: " Of the English Romantics, Hazlitt elaborated the comparisons with Shakespeare most damningly " (34). Whatever the reason he disfavors Jonson, Hazlitt's "robust terms" (Donaldson, "Cambridge Edition" 258) helped to embed the antithesis between the comic art of Shakespeare and Jonson even more deeply.

In my introductory discussion, I have surveyed the development of some of the main contrasts between Shakespeare and Jonson since the seventeenth century. Popular tradition holds that Shakespeare's comedies are sweet, romantic, spontaneous, amiable, popular, and entertaining, while Jonson's are cold, based on humours theory, labored, satirical, pedantic, and moralizing; Shakespeare's comic characters are natural individuals, while Jonson's but caricatured types. These opposite appraisals are borne out if we read Shakespeare's and Jonson's works from a certain perspective.

Shakespeare's comedy may be sweet, romantic, and popular because Shakespeare himself frequently uses the

---

[1] According to Lockwood, Hazlitt thought that Gifford was a court "flatterer," a government "literary executioner" and a "Government Critic" (128-29). For a detailed discussion of the political aspect of Hazlitt's distaste of Jonson, see Lockwood, ch. 4, esp. pp. 122-30.

word sweet. Many of Shakespeare's comedies include love stories that feature dashing lovers and end in happy marriages. These romantic stories interest large groups of readers. Shakespeare's language is eloquent, beautiful, sometimes funny, sometimes thought-provoking, and sometimes both. Indeed, eloquence is what Shakespeare's early critics meant by sweet. While *sweet* is used to summarize Shakespeare's comedy, *gentle* is his early critics' epithet for his personality. Not only Jonson, but also Shakespeare's other contemporaries like John Heminge (c. 1556 – 1630) and Henry Condell (d. 1627) used *gentle* to refer to Shakespeare. According to Ian Donaldson, *gentle* was commonly used in the seventeenth century to mean "a river that was neither torpid nor in torrent, but which flowed steadily." One of the most common things said about Shakespeare in the seventeenth century was that his words flowed like "a river flowed with miraculous fluency" (*Magic House* 20). Donaldson believes that this point was Jonson's and his contemporary commentators' "primarily intending" when they used *gentle* to refer to Shakespeare (*Magic House* 20-21). We can now be certain that sweet and gentle used in reference to Shakespeare in the seventeenth century meant basically the same thing—praise of his free-flowing language.

In contrast to Shakespeare's sweet and gentle plays, Jonson created comedies that present humours-based characters. In *Every Man in his Humour* (1598), Jonson's first successful comedy, Thorello[1] (who became Kitely when Jonson revised the play for his 1616 First Folio), among other characters whose minds are fixated in various things, has an uncontrollable fear to being cuckolded. Also, *Every Man out of his Humour* (1599) features humours characters and is satiric, but *Poetaster* (1601) is only satirical, not humours-based. More important, however, is Jonson's contemporaries' response to his comedies. Charles Fitzgeoffrey (? 1575 – 1638), writing in a Latin poem, "Ad Beniaminum Ionsonium" ("To Ben Jonson") in 1601, praises Jonson's comedies effusively: "Moving to peals of laughter the Eternals, / And drawing smiles from Jupiter's grim visage. / Each pole of heaven thundering with applauses" (qtd. in translation in Craig, ll. 10-12). It should be noted that Fitzgeoffrey's praise was written before Jonson's more successful middle comedies, which means that Jonson's early humours and satiric comedies were already considered entertaining, laughter-provoking and popular, qualities that many later people would only associate with Shakespeare's comedies.

After detailed analyses of the didactic intentions and characterizations of *Volpone* and *The Merchant of Venice*, the most popular comedies of Jonson and Shakespeare, we are

---

[1] Critics have long observed the genetic relationship between Thorello and Othello. Anne Barton (*Names* 122), Ian Donaldson ("Looking Sideways" 22, n. 32) and E. A. J. Honigmann (*Othello* 334) all identify *Thorello*'s origin in *torello*: Italian, a young bull. They all suggest Shakespeare probably adapted *Othello* from *Thorello*—a minor example of the collaboration between Shakespeare and Jonson. Donaldson's article, "Looking Sideways: Jonson, Shakespeare and the Myth of Envy" gives an excellent insight into the friendly competition and collaboration between Jonson and Shakespeare, supported by a good many examples from their plays. In fact, competition and collaboration can be considered Jonson's characteristic relationship not only with fellow dramatists, poets, but also with his audiences and readers. See also, George E. Rowe, pp. 438-60.

able to critique the above-mentioned antithesis between the two dramatists. *Volpone*, because of its criticism of avarice, covetousness, extravagance, lust and pretentiousness, is satiric and didactic; it portrays two women and a kind of courtship, but is not considered a romantic comedy; however, it is not cold, either, but warmly funny, not labored, but spontaneous, not pedantic despite its medical jargon, but charming. The play is entertaining. It is, to borrow a phrase from Una Ellis-Fermor in her discussion of Jonson, Jonson's "most nearly perfect marriage of form and material" (101), or, in Jonson's own terms, the perfect marriage of profit and delight, and the very ideal of Horatian and Sidneyian art.

The characters of *Volpone*, at least the ones analyzed in this study—Corvino, Mosca and Volpone, contrary to William Hazlitt's notorious denigration as "machines" (*Lectures* 73), or such negative terms as "caricatures" used by Schlegel (II: 135) and Harold Bloom (*Ben Jonson* 9) and "general character" of Charles Gildon, are complex individuals. Corvino, the most likely to be typical among the three, is an avaricious merchant-flatterer, a jealous husband, a fool and a knave. He, however, rather than remaining the same throughout, changes and develops according to the situation. When he is sure of everything at home, Corvino brings expensive gifts to Volpone, flatters him and his parasite in hopes of becoming Volpone's heir. When he sees his wife drop her handkerchief before a stranger, he rushes to drive him away. When his hope for inheritance is challenged by a doctor who offers his daughter, Corvino makes the difficult decision to prostitute his wife to supplant the daughter in order to defuse this threat. When Volpone's attempted rape of his wife is interrupted by Bonario who, together with his wife, charges Volpone in court, Corvino angrily accuses his wife in the foulest language in order to make others believe that he is innocent and wronged. Finally, when all his hopes for inheritance are dashed and he himself has been repeatedly humiliated, Corvino persists in his false accusations against his wife and his perjury concerning Volpone.

Compared with Corvino, Mosca and Volpone are even more complex. These are real cheats (especially Volpone) that prey on greedy gulls and voluptuaries and readily spend what they have swindled. They are intriguers capable of ingenious tricks, blasphemers, and Machiavellian villains who are willing to bring death to other people in order to maintain their own interests. T. E. Eliot remarks: "Neither Volpone nor Mosca is a humour. No theory of humours could account for Jonson's best plays or the best characters in them" (79).

The Merchant of Venice, in comparison, is not the extreme opposite of *Volpone*. This is true despite the fact that *The Merchant of Venice* contains a typical Shakespearian romantic story that leads to two marriages after solving the riddle of the risky casket selection. The play has a sub-plot— the runaway and not-so-romantic marriage between Jessica and Lorenzo. Because the marriages, taking place in the Arcadian, paradise-like Belmont, include the normal Shakespearian beautiful lady, her maids, and handsome gentlemen, the play can well be considered a traditional Shakespearian comedy: sweet, romantic, and popular.

Yet the most important difference from the prevalent view of Shakespeare's comedies and the one which makes it similar to Jonson's didactic plays is *The Merchant of Venice*'s permeative moralizing. When Morocco, Arragon and Bassanio choose their caskets, they each make a speech moralizing on the proper match between the outside and the inside and especially the deceptiveness of outward show. Shylock's famous speech about revenge also moralizes on two issues: equal treatment of people of different races or religions and the right of revenge or justice. Certainly the most striking instance of Shakespeare's didacticism in *The Merchant* comes in Portia's discourse on mercy, also one of the best known teachings on the topic in Shakespeare, based on sources both inside and outside the Bible, calling on not merely Shylock, but every reader to consider justice tempered by mercy. As Lawrence Danson points out, "Seneca's *De Beneficiis*, the bestowing of benefits" on the general people means that "charity or love" is a "civic and humane obligation," but in the "specifically Christian context, it is more" (56). The Bible teaches Christians that they should "owe nothing to any man, but to loue one another: for he that loueth another, hathe fulfilled the Law" (Romans XIII: 8). In this verse, to quote Danson again, is contained "the essence of the Christian relation to his fellow man and to God" (56). In her speech, Portia means to teach the reader as well as Shylock that this "inflexible law" should be put into a "more proper relationship to individual men, to society as a whole, and to divinity" (Danson 63). Therefore, as Danson observes, because of the "centrality" of the relationship between mercy and justice in the Christian faith and because of the perennial popularity of mercy and justice as both a book and a dramatic subject in Shakespeare's England (67), the dramatist's Christian readers or audiences could not fail to appreciate the relevant moralizing of the play. By comparison, the didacticism in Portia's speech is much more direct, obvious and urged than in any speech in *Volpone*.

As for characterization, many believe *The Merchant* is one of Shakespeare's highest achievements. Antonio, Bassanio, Graziano and Lancelot Gobbo are alive in our mind's eye. Portia and Shylock have come down to the present day as two of Shakespeare's most memorable characters. Shylock, particularly, is one of the best-known characters in Shakespeare. John Gross says: "In the extent of his fame, Shylock belongs with Don Quixote, Tartuffe, Sherlock Holmes, Robinson Crusoe. He is a familiar figure to millions who have never read *The Merchant of Venice*, or even seen it acted" (209). Hermann Sinsheimer says that, in Shylock, Shakespeare created "the only post-Biblical Jewish figure" which "has impressed itself on the imagination of the world and become a universal symbol of Jewry" (9). Kenneth Gross informs us that Shylock's " complex afterlife " in performance, fiction, and criticism, and in the language of antisemitic cliché is "more extensive than that of any other character in Shakespeare's plays, save perhaps Hamlet, and even Hamlet cannot rival Shylock's chilling passage into the commonplace" (x). Certainly, Shylock has deeply frustrated some people. Harold Bloom complains that Shylock "contaminates" both the drama and the audience (*Shylock* 7). Clearly Bloom's antipathy of *The Merchant* comes not from Shakespeare's lack of ability as a dramatist, but from the towering reputation or infamy of the portrayal Shylock—a fact that precisely shows the dramatist's success in characterization. Whether we find Shylock worthy of sympathy or not, Shakespeare has given us a vigorous, individual and full-dimensional character. However, the vividness and fullness of Shylock, or even of Portia, does not imply that there is vigor and fullness of all other characters in *The Merchant.* Arragon is known to us only as an arrogant clown; Morocco is just a braggart; Graziano, despite his long-winded talk and noisy shouting, is but a typical hothead.

Therefore, if we compare characterizations in *Volpone* and *The Merchant of Venice*, we find both more and less lifelike characters in each play. Volpone, Mosca, Corvino, Shylock, Portia and Antonio are the more fully developed; Corbaccio, Lady Would-be, Celia, Graziano, Arragon, Morocco, Jessica appear to be more like "types." This is not surprising; Anne Barton says: "most dramatic characters" are "types" (*Dramatist* 107). Dramatic success is more a matter of the complexity of types than of avoiding traditional characterization altogether. In better developed characters, we find more complexity. Also, there is the matter of function. Northrop Fry's remarks about Shakespeare's characterization may apply to both Shakespeare and Jonson:

> All Shakespeare's characters owe their consistency to the appropriateness of the stock type which belongs to their dramatic function. That stock type is not the character, but it is as necessary to the character as a skeleton is to the actor who plays it.

(277)

Fry is definitely correct because each character in a play

has to play his or her own role. Naturally, it is up to the dramatists to decide what characters they are to feature for the certain effect or purposes they want to achieve. Discussing stock characters and humours characters, Martin Wiggins remarks that, compared to the "stock types" in romantic comedy inherited from Roman and Italian drama— "lovers and misers, clowns and braggarts, foolish fathers and cheeky pages," "humorous roles" can look "narrowly caricatured in their focus on a single dominant trait." However, they also "opened the genre to a tremendous range of human experience" (70). Therefore, each kind of character has its own merit. It is difficult to conclude generally that Shakespeare's characters are all like real people, while Jonson's are all caricatures or two-dimensional types.

The differences between Shakespeare's and Jonson's comedies and the characterizations therein are complex. We have seen that while some of their comedies are markedly different, like *Poetaster* and *Much Ado About Nothing*, some others may share more similarities. The tone of *Measure for Measure* is more satirical than some other Shakespeare's comedies, and *The Case Is Altered* is more romantic than many other Jonsonian comedies. In the case of Jonson, it is also important to remember that he was a long-time author of court masques, an entertainment Jonson had developed into a kind of literature that is an important part of his dramatic art. Stephen Orgel has remarked: "In a sense, Jonson produced the best masques because he had produced the best humorous comedies; the courtly form shows us the humorous theory applied to universals" (*Masque* 198).

In order to understand the conventional contrasts, or, rather, the myth of contrasts between Shakespeare and Jonson, it is necessary to explore the development of such a myth. Roughly, this development may be divided into four phases: seventeenth century, eighteenth century and Romantic Era, nineteenth century, and since the beginning of the twentieth century.

During the seventeenth century, Jonson was, overall, more popular with writers, literati, that is, those who left works for review. In Shakespeare's and Jonson's lifetimes, there were few comparisons of their reputations. Jonson achieved a fame beyond the world of stage in 1609 (Craig 7), Shakespeare spent his last years in Stratford; Shakespeare and Jonson did not begin to be compared until 1630s (Craig 8). Then, by the century's end, according to Gerald Eades Bentley, who compared the reputations of Shakespeare and Jonson based on twenty-two classes of allusions to the two authors, Jonson wins by far in twenty-one, such as reference by dramatists, allusions with the specific names of dramatists, and historical and critical writings about Shakespeare and Jonson. Only in one class, that is, allusions to specific characters, does Shakespeare clearly win. The top seven most popular characters are all Shakespeare's, Falstaff being by far the most popular (132-39). Another result of Bentley's research that may interest us is the most popular plays by Shakespeare and Jonson in the seventeenth century. They were: *Catiline*, *Volpone*, *The Alchemist*, *The Silent*

Woman, and *Sejanus*—all Jonson's.① Romantic comedies were particularly unpopular.② "Performances of Jonson's plays and masques were discussed by the literati nearly twice as often as Shakespeare's." As Bentley remarks, in the seventeenth century, Jonson, who could see that Shakespeare was "not for an age, but for all time," but whose own plays "best exemplified the accepted critical dogma of his time and who most vigorously preached the dogma," was "the man" for "lesser writers" (137-40).

Comparative criticism of Shakespeare and Jonson probably began with Milton, whose "L'Allegro" (1632) separated the dramatists by nature and art (ll. 131-34). These terms of nature and art were to be borrowed by Dryden and other critics in the seventeenth century to compare Shakespeare and Jonson, and Dryden "dominated" their criticism.

If the seventeen century was one of Jonson's "supremacy" (Craig 18), then the eighteenth might be seen as one for his decline. Gerald Eades Bentley has noticed that in the seventeenth century, although Jonson's reputation was much greater, Shakespeare's was "growing more rapidly than Jonson's" in the last two decades (138). Jonson continued to have advocates in the eighteenth century, among whom John Dennis and Peter Whalley were the best known. However,

---

① We should remember that this list of "popular plays" means popular with writers as reflected in their writings, which did not necessarily represent performances.

② According to Gerald Eades Bentley, two books about allusions to Shakespeare and Jonson, Edmund Chambers' *The Shakespeare Allusion Book*, and Jesse Franklin Bradley and Joseph Quincy Adams' *The Jonson Allusion Book*, are very careless and misleading. Bentley also lists inaccurate impressionistic statements by other critics on the reputation of Shakespeare in the seventeenth century. See pp. v-vii, 130-32, for details.

Jonson's reputation declined sharply, especially after the 1730s (Craig 20), and Shakespeare's continued to grow rapidly. One of the reasons was the spread of biographical writings. At the end of the seventeenth century, according to Ian Donaldson, popular anecdotes, which often present Shakespeare and Jonson in taverns, and anecdotes which turned upon "strikingly feeble pieces of wordplay," were distressingly showing the dramatists as "pedantic buffoons, trading laboured jokes" ("The Other Youth" 116). In the eighteenth century, when it was recognized that stories in the anecdotes could not be "reliably be verified," biographical narrative began to show itself, in which the focus was "no longer upon the witty quips of the two dramatists, but upon their inner character, their basic temperament and disposition" (*Magic House* 13-14). Then, when biographical narrative and literary interpretations of Shakespeare and Jonson became "intriguingly confused," Shakespeare was agreed to have a temperament and genius identical with those of Falstaff, not the Falstaff from a specific play, but one described by Corbyn Morris: "possessing Generosity, Chearfulness, Alacrity, Invention, Frolic and Fancy superior to all other Men; —The figure of his Person is the Picture of Jollity, Mirth, and Good-nature" (qtd. in Donaldson, *Magic House* 15). Jonson's personality, in this context, was "quite contrary to that of Shakespeare" (Donaldson, *Magic House* 15). In short, by the eighteenth century, the contrastive oppositions between Shakespeare and Jonson had all been postulated and solidified. As Ian Donaldson summarizes, Shakespeare was "generous, loving, open, quick, and amiable: not merely a national genius, but also as a thoroughly nice man;" and Jonson: haughty, morose, crabbed, pedantic, slow, grudging, sour, saturnine, envious, and splenetic (*Magic House* 17). In the Romantic age, despite reading and performance of Jonson's plays, praise of Shakespeare and criticism of Jonson reached a new height, as represented by Hazlitt.

In the nineteenth century, while Shakespeare had won a complete victory over his rival, the contrasts between Jonson and Shakespeare were even more solidly set. [1] Despite William Gifford's edition and Algernon Charles Swinburne's study to some how raise Jonson's reputation, those contrasts remained unchanged.

Since the beginning of the twentieth century, when Jonson continued to regain his reputation as a dramatist, the oppositions between him and Shakespeare began to change. T. S. Eliot, according to D. H. Craig, made the revival of appreciating Jonson possible (35). Complaining of Jonson's "most deadly kind of reputation that can be compelled upon the memory of a great poet," Eliot in 1919 argued that "Jonson has suffered in public opinion," that his plays are "worth reading," that "Shakespeare's characters are no more 'alive' than are the characters of Jonson," and that we can derive from Jonson "not only instruction . . . but enjoyment

---

[1] According to D. H. Craig, Jonson became for many Victorians a good lyric poet. Even Hazlitt called a Jonsonian poem "a perfect nest of spicery" (qtd. in Craig 34). With recognition of his poetry, Jonson was read as the "supreme in the lyric. " Shakespeare was considered the man in the drama. There were also some twists about Jonson's other works in the nineteenth century. Swinburne, as Craig observes, thought "a single leaf of his [Jonson's] prose work *Discoveries* was worth all the lyrics, tragedies, elegies, and epigrams put together," while an unsigned reviewer considered Jonson's additions to *The Spanish Tragedy* "the one effort of his dramatic imagination (supposing it to be his) which had the power of speaking to the great human heart" (qtd. in Craig 34-35).

(65-81). As we go further into the twentieth century and come closer to the twenty-first, studies on Jonson have flourished. As Katie J. Magaw, who has surveyed more than a hundred English-language monographs published between 1886 and 1998, calculates, on average, "more than one book a year devoted exclusively to analysis of Jonson or his writings has been published during the modern period, and in the last twenty years especially" (201). A year later in 1999, Clint Darby adds 25 books on Jonson only published since 1925 to Magaw's list of over a hundred (262-63). John Burdett and Jonathan Wright "deliberately restricted" themselves to list over three hundred books published between 1972 and 1996 in which Jonson is discussed but not as the sole concern (151). Despite the number of Jonson studies in the past century, change in the Shakespeare-Jonson antithesis does not seem to have followed suit. As we discussed in the Introduction, Jonson is still often perceived as Shakespeare's "Other" despite all the works of Harry Levin, Russ McDonald, David McPherson and others. It is high time we listened to James Shapiro:

> We need to be cautious about accepting dichotomies like "art" and "nature" (such as Jonson's claim that "Shakespeare wanted art"); neither the one nor the other is the province of Shakespeare or Jonson; rather they offer handy terms in the struggle for mimetic superiority.
>
> (*Rival Playwrights* 153)

And

> It would be a mistake to conclude by suggesting that our own critical age has been free of this kind of reductiveness. The portraits of Shakespeare and Jonson

have not changed all that much since the days of Dryden,
Johnson, and Wordsworth. We need to recognize the
constructedness of *both* "Jonson" *and* "Shakespeare," and
we also need to ask why we have chosen to accept
traditional versions of their development as dramatists . . .
If we are to break out of these constraining and constructed
ways of thinking about their respective careers and
dramatic output we also need to consider what purpose
these divisions serve us institutionally, especially in
relationship to the canon of authors that we teach, stage,
and anthologize.

(*Rival Playwrights* 167-68; emphases mine)

Certainly, we do not want to view the two greatest
English Renaissance dramatists in a reductive way. We need
to, as suggested by Shapiro, "break out" of those
"constraining and constructed ways of thinking," the simple
oppositions between Shakespearean and Jonsonian comedy
that have been largely invalidated in the present study. In
1960, Patrick Cruttwell in his *Shakespearean Moment and Its*
Place in the Poetry of the Seventeenth Century discussed the
spectacularly productive and creative period in which
Shakespeare was working. As Ian Donaldson remarks, this
period was "triggered no doubt by Shakespeare's own
prodigious example, but sustained by the converging energies
of other writers stimulated by him" ("Looking Sideways"
18). If my small study can in some way help the
understanding of this Shakespearian moment and Ben
Jonson's place in it, then its purpose will have been happily
achieved.

Works Cited

Abrams, M. H. , and Geoffrey Galt Harpham. *A Glossary of Literay Terms*. 9th ed. 2005. Boston: Wadsworth Cengage Learning, 2009.

Adelman, Janet. *Blood Relations: Christian and Jew in* The Merchant of Venice. Chicago: U of Chicago P, 2008.

Alexander, Gavin. *Writing after Sidney: The Literary Response to Sir Philip Sidney, 1586 – 1640* . Oxford: Oxford UP, 2006.

Alexander, Michael. *A History of English Literature*. London: McMillan, 2000.

Allen, Percy. *Shakespeare, Jonson, and Wilkins as Borrowers*. London: Cecil Palmer, 1928.

Aquinas, Thomas. *Treatise on Law*. Trans. Richard J. Regan. Indianapolis: Hackett Publishing, 2000.

Aristophanes. *Frogs*. Trans. Ian Johnston. Arlington: Richer Resources, 2008.

Aristotle. *The Nicomachean Ethics*. Trans. David Ross, revised with an introduction by Lesley Brown. Oxford: Oxford UP, 2009.

——. *The Poetics of Aristotle*. 2nd ed. Ed. & trans. S. H. Butcher. London: MacMillan, 1898.

——. *Politics*. Trans. H. Rackham. London: William Heinemann, 1959.

Ascoli, Albert Russell. *Dante and the Making of a Modern Author*. Cambridge: Cambridge UP, 2008.

Auden, W. H. "Brothers and Others." *The Dyer's Hand and Other*

Essays. New York: Random, 1962. 162-237.

Augustine. *De Doctrina Christiana.* Ed. & Trans. R. P. H. Green. Oxford: Clarendon, 1995.

Aziz, Jeffrey H. *Of Grace and Gross Bodies: Falstaff, Oldcastle, and the Fires of Reform.* Diss. U of Pittsburgh, 2007. Ann Arbor: UMI, 2007.

Baker, David Erskine. *Biographia Dramatica, or, a Companion to the Play-House.* 3 vols. New ed. London: Longman, 1812.

Baldwin, Edward Chauncey. "Ben Jonson's Indebtedness to Greek Character-Sketch." *Modern Language Notes* 16.7 (1901): 193-98.

Baldwin, T. W. *William Shakspere's Small Latine & Lesse Greeke.* Vol. I. Urbana: U of Illinois P, 1944.

Bamborough, J. B. "Ben Jonson." *British Writers.* Vol. 1. Ed. Ian Scott Kilvert et al. New York: Scribner, 1979. 335-51.

Banham, Martin, Roshni Mooneeram, and Jane Plastow. "Shakespeare and Africa." *The Cambridge Companion to Shakespeare on Stage.* Ed. Stanley Wells and Sarah Stanton. Cambridge: Cambridge UP, 2002. 284-99.

Barish, Jonas. *The Antitheatrical Prejudice.* Berkeley: U of California P, 1981.

——. *Ben Jonson and the Language of Prose Comedy.* Cambridge: Harvard UP, 1960.

——. "The Double Plot in 'Volpone.'" *Modern Philology* 51.2 (1953): 83-92.

Barnet, Sylvan. "Prodigality and Time in *The Merchant of Venice.*" *PMLA* 87.1 (1972): 26-30.

Barton, Anne. *Ben Jonson, Dramatist.* 1984. Cambridge: Cambridge UP, 1986.

——. *Essays Mainly Shakespearean.* 1994. Cambridge: Cambridge UP, 2006.

——. Introduction. *The Merchant of Venice.* By William

Shakespeare. *The Riverside Shakespeare*. Ed. G. Blakemore Evans. Boston: Houghton Mifflin Company, 1974. 250-53.

——. Introduction. *The Merry Wives of Windsor*. By William Shakespeare. *The Riverside Shakespeare*. Ed. G. Blakemore Evans. Boston: Houghton Mifflin Company, 1974. 286-89.

——. "Jonson, Ben." *The Spenser Encyclopaedia*. Ed. A. C. Hamilton, Donald Cheney et al. London: Routledge, 1990.

——. "The London Scene: City and Court." *The Cambridge Companion to Shakespeare*. Ed. Margreta de Grazia and Stanley Wells. Cambridge: Cambridge UP, 2001. 115-28.

——. *The Names of Comedy*. Oxford: Clarendon, 1990.

Barton, John, and John Muddiman. *The Oxford Bible Commentary*. Oxford UP, 2001.

Beattie, James. "Remarks on the Usefulness of Classical Learning." *Essays: On Poetry and Music, as They Affect the Mind*. 3rd ed. corrected. London: Printed for E. and C. Dilly, 1779. 453-515.

Beauregard, David N. "Sidney, Aristotle, and *The Merchant of Venice*: Shakespeare's Triadic Images of Liberality and Justice." *Shakespeare Studies* 20 (1988): 33-51.

Beckwith, Sarah. "Drama." *The Cambridge Companion to Medieval English literature, 1100 – 1500* . Ed. Larry Scanlon. Cambridge: Cambridge UP, 2009. 83-94.

Bednarz, James P. *Shakespeare and the Poets' War*. New York: Columbia UP, 2001.

Belsey, Catherine. *Shakespeare in Theory and Practice*. Edinburgh: Edinburgh UP, 2008.

Benston, Alice N. "Portia, the Law, and the Tripartite Structure of *The Merchant of Venice*." *Shakespeare Quarterly* 30.3 (1979): 367-85.

Bentley, Gerald Eades. *Shakespeare and Jonson: Their Reputations in the Seventeenth Century Compared*. 1945. Two

Vols. in One, Vol. I. 1965. Chicago: U of Chicago P, 1969.

Berg, Sara Van Den. "True Relation: The Life and Career of Ben Jonson." *The Cambridge Companion to Ben Jonson.* Ed. Richard Harp and Stanley Stewart. Cambridge: Cambridge UP, 2000. 1-14.

Berger, Harry, Jr. "Mercifixion in *The Merchant of Venice:* The Riches of Embarrassment." *Renaissance Drama* New Ser. 38 (2010): 3-45.

Berkowitz, Joel. *Shakespeare on the American Yiddish Stage.* Iowa City: U of Iowa P, 2002.

Bevington, David. *Shakespeare's Ideas: More Things in Heaven and Earth.* Wiley-Blackwell, 2008.

Bishop, David H. "Shylock's Humours." *The Shakespeare Association Bulletin* xxiii (1948): 174-80.

Bland, Mark. "Ben Jonson and the Legacies of the Past." *Huntington Library Quarterly* 67. 3 (2004): 371-400.

Bliss, Philip. Appendix: Chronological List of Books of Characters, from 1567 to 1700. *Microcosmography, or a Piece of the World Discovered in Essays and Characters.* By John Earle. 1628. A new ed. with notes and appendix by Philip Bliss. London: White & Cochrane, 1811. 246-314.

Bloom, Harold, ed. *Ben Jonson's Volpone, or the Fox.* Broomall: Chelsea, 1988. Bloom's Modern Critical Interpretations.

——. Introduction. *Ben Jonson.* Ed. Bloom. Broomall: Chelsea, 2002. 9-15. Bloom's Major Dramatist.

——. Introduction. *Shylock.* Ed. Bloom. New York: Chelsea, 1991.

——. Introduction. *William Shakespeare: Comedies.* Ed. Harold Bloom. New York: Bloom's Literary Criticism-Infobase, 2009. Bloom's Modern Critical Views.

——. *Shakespeare: The Invention of the Human.* New York: Riverhead, 1998.

——, ed. *The Merchant of Venice.* New York: Bloom's Literary

Criticism-Infobase, 2008. *Bloom's Shakespeare Through the Ages*.

——, ed. *Shylock*. New York: Chelsea, 1991. *Major Literary Characters*.

——, ed. *William Shakespeare's* The Merchant of Venice. New ed. New York: Bloom's Literary Criticism-Infobase, 2010.

Bloomfield, Morton W. *The Seven Deadly Sins*. Michigan State College P, 1952.

Boyce, Charles. *Shakespeare A to Z*. New York: Dell, 1990.

Bradbrook, M. C. *The Growth and Structure of Elizabethan Comedy*. London: Chatto & Windus, 1955.

——. *The Living Monument: Shakespeare and the Theatre of His Time*. 1976. Cambridge: Cambridge UP, 2010.

——. *Shakespeare and Elizabethan poetry: A Study of His Earlier Work in Relation to the Poetry of the Time*. New York: Oxford UP, 1952.

Bradley, Jesse Franklin, and Joseph Quincy Adams. *The Jonson Allusion-Book: A Collection of Allusions to Ben Jonson from 1597 to 1700*. New Haven: Yale UP, 1922.

Brennan, Michael G., and Noel J. Kinnamon. *A Sidney Chronology, 1554 – 1654*. Hampshire: Palgrave Macmillan, 2003.

Briggs, Julia. *This Stage-play World: Texts and Contexts, 1580 – 1625*. 2nd ed. 1983. Oxford: Oxford UP, 1997.

Bristol, Michael. "Confusing Shakespeare's Characters with Real People: Reflections on Reading in Four Questions." *Shakespeare and Character: Theory, History, Performance, and Theatrical Persons*. Ed. Paul Yachnin and Jessica Slights. Hampshire: Palgrave Macmillan, 2009. 21-40.

Brown, John Russell, ed. *The Merchant of Venice*. By William Shakespeare. London: Methuen, 1955. *The New Arden Shakespeare*.

——. "The Riddle Song in *The Merchant of Venice*." *Notes and*

Queries 204 (1959): 235.

Bruce, Susan, and Rebecca Steinberger. *The Renaissance Literature Handbook*. London: Continuum, 2009.

Bruster, Douglas. *Drama and the Market in the Age of Shakespeare*. Cambridge: Cambridge UP, 1992.

Bryant, J. A., Jr. *The Compassionate Satirist: Ben Jonson and His Imperfect World*. Athens: U of Georgia P, 1972.

——. "Review: Elizabethan Drama: 1956." *The Sewanee Review* 65. 1 (1957): 152-60.

Burckhardt, Sigurd. *Shakespearean Meanings*. Princeton: Princeton UP, 1968.

Burdett, John, and Jonathan Wright. "Ben Jonson in Recent General Scholarship, 1972-1996." *The Ben Jonson Journal* 4 (1997): 151-79.

Burnaby, William. "Letter V. Wherein Are Laid down General Rules to Judge of Tragedy and Comedy." *Letters of Wit, Politicks and Morality*. By Guido Bentivoglio et al. London: Printed for F. Hartley, 1701. 230-37.

Burnley, David. "Language." *A Companion to Chaucer*. Ed. Peter Brown. Oxford: Blackwell, 2002. 235-50.

Burrow, Colin. Introduction. *Horace, Of the Art of Poetry*. Ed. Colin Burrow. *The Cambridge Edition of the Works of Ben Jonson*. Print ed. Vol. 7. Gen. Ed. David Bevington, Martin Butler, and Ian Donaldson. Cambridge: Cambridge UP, 2012. 3-9.

Burt, Daniel S. *The Drama 100 : A Ranking of the Greatest Plays of All Time*. New York: Facts on File, 2008.

——. *The Literary 100 : A Ranking of the Most Influential Novelists, Playwrights, and Poets of All Time*. New York: Facts on File, 2009.

Bush-Bailey, Gilli. "Fitting the Bill: Acting Out the Season of 1813 / 14 at the Sans Pareil." *The Performing Century: Nineteenth-*

Century Theatre's History. Ed. Tracy C. Davis and Peter Holland. Palgrave Macmillan, 2007.

Busse, Beatrix. *Vocative Constructions in the Language of Shakespeare*. Amsterdam: John Benjamins, 2006.

Butler, Martin. "Chapter 19. Literature and the theatre to 1660." *The Cambridge History of Early Modern English Literature*. Ed. David Loewenstein and Janel Mueller. Cambridge: Cambridge UP, 2002. 565-602.

Cambridge University Press. Catalogue Introduction to *The Cambridge Edition of the Works of Ben Jonson* 7 *Volume Set*. 29 March, 2012. Web. http: //www. cambridge. org.

Campbell, Gordon. Introduction. *Ben Jonson: The Alchemist and Other Plays*. By Ben Jonson. Ed. Gordon Campbell. Oxford: Oxford UP, 1995, vii-xxi.

Campbell, Lily B. *Shakespeare's Tragic Heroes: Slaves of Passion*. Cambridge: Cambridge UP, 1930.

Campbell, Oscar James. *Shakespeare's Satire*. 1943. London: Oxford UP, 1945.

Cardozo, Jacob Lopes. *The Contemporary Jew in the Elizabethan Drama*. Philadelphia: B. Franklin, 1968.

Carlson, Marvin. *Theories of the Theatre*. Expanded ed. Ithaca: Cornell UP, 1993.

Carr, Carol A. "Volpone and Mosca: Two Styles of Roguery." *College Literature* 8. 2 (1981): 144-57.

Castle, Edward James. *Shakespeare, Bacon, Jonson and Greene: A Study*. London: Sampson Low, Marston, 1897.

Cave, Richard Allen. "Ben Jonson's *Every Man in his Humour*: A Case Study." *The Cambridge History of British Theatre, Vol. 1 : Origins to 1660*. Ed. Jane Milling and Peter Thomson. Cambridge: Cambridge UP, 2004. 282-97.

Chambers, Edmund. *The Shakespeare Allusion-Book: A Collection of Allusions to Shakespeare from 1591 to 1700*. 2 vols. Chatto &

Windus, 1932.

Chaucer, Geoffrey. "General Prologue." *The Canterbury Tales.* Ed. Paul G. Ruggiers. *A Variorum Ed. of the Works of Geoffrey Chaucer.* Vol. 1. Folkestone: U of Oklahoma P, 1979.

——. *The Riverside Chaucer.* 3 rd ed. Gen. Ed. Larry D. Benson. Boston: Houghton Mifflin, 1987.

Churchill, Charles. *The Poetical Works of Charles Churchill.* Ed. W. Tooke, F. R. S. London: William Pickering, 1844.

——. *The Rosciad,* 4 th ed. London: 1761.

Cicero, Marcus Tullius. *De Officiis.* Trans. Walter Miller. London: William Heinemann, 1928.

——. *Cicero's Three Books of Offices, or Moral Duties.* Trans. Cyrus R Edmonds. New York: Harper, 1868.

——. *De Oratore in Two Volumes.* Vol. I, Bks I & II. Trans. E. W. Sutton. Comp. H. Rackham. London: William Heinemann, 1967. The Loeb Classical Library.

Coghill, Nevill. "The Basis of Shakespearian Comedy." *The Collected Papers of Nevill Coghill: Shakespearian & Neduevakust.* Ed. Douglas Gray. Sussex: Harvester P, 1988. 256-88.

Coleridge, Samuel Taylor. *Omniana. The Literary Remains of Samuel Taylor Coleridge.* Vol. I. Ed. Henry Nelson Coleridge. London: William Pickering, 1836. 282-395.

——. *Specimens of the Table Talk of the Late Samuel Taylor Coleridge.* Vol. II, Ed. Henry Nelson Coleridge. London: John Murray, 1835.

Cook, Albert S. Introduction. *Sir Philip Sidney: The Defense of Poesy Otherwise Known as an Apology for Poetry.* By Sidney. Boston: Ginn, 1890.

Cook, Jeff. *Seven: The Deadly Sins and the Beatitudes.* Grand Rapids: Zondervan, 2008.

Craig, D. H. , ed. *Ben Jonson: The Critical Heritage.* London:

Routledge, 1990.

Cruttwell, Patrick. *The Shakespearean Moment and Its Place in the Poetry of the Seventeenth Century.* New York: Random House, 1960.

Cusack, Bridget. "Shakespeare and the tune of the time." *Shakespeare and Language.* Ed. Catherine M. S. Alexander. Cambridge: Cambridge UP, 2004. 101-21.

Danson, Lawrence. *The Harmonies of* The Merchant of Venice. New Haven: Yale UP, 1978.

Dante Alighieri. *The Divine Comedy of Dante Alighieri. Vol. I, Inferno.* Ed. & trans. Robert M. Durling. Oxford: Oxford UP, 1996.

——. *The Divine Comedy of Dante Alighieri. Vol. II, Purgatorio.* Ed. & trans. Robert M. Durling. Oxford: Oxford UP, 2003.

Darby, Clint. "Modern Books on Ben Jonson: A General Topical Index (First Supplement)." *The Ben Jonson Journal* 6 (1999): 261-75.

Demastes, William W. *Comedy Matters: From Shakespeare to Stoppard.* New York: Palgrave Macmillan, 2008.

Democritus, Junior (Robert Burton). *The Anatomy of Melancholy.* Oxford: Henry Cripps, 1638.

Desai, Rupin W. *Falstaff: A Study of His Role in Shakespeare's History Plays.* Delhi, India: Doaba House, 1975.

Dobson, Michael, and Stanley Wells, eds. *The Oxford Companion to Shakespeare.* Oxford: Oxford UP, 2001.

Donaldson, Ian. *Ben Jonson: A Life.* Oxford: Oxford UP, 2012.

——. Introductory. *Ben Jonson.* By Jonson. Ed. Donaldson. Oxford: Oxford UP, 1985. vii-xviii.

——. "The Cambridge Edition of the Works of Ben Jonson." *The Ben Jonson Journal* 5 (1998): 257-69.

——. "Jonson and the Other Youth." *Elizabethan Theater: Essays in Honor of S. Schoenaum.* Ed. R. B. Parker and S. P. Zitner.

Newark: U of Delaware P, 1996. 111-29.

——. *Jonson's Magic Houses: Essays in Interpretation.* Oxford: Clarendon, 1997.

——. "Looking Sideways: Jonson, Shakespeare, and the Myth of Envy." *The Ben Jonson Journal* 8 (2001): 1-22.

Dowson, Anthony B, and Gretchen E. Minton. Introduction. *Timon of Athens.* By William Shakespeare. Eds. Anthony B. Dawson and Gretchen E. Minton. Arden Shakespeare, 2008. 1-145.

Drabble, Margaret, ed. *The Oxford Companion to English Literature.* 6th ed. Oxford: Oxford UP, 2000.

Draper, John W. *The Humors and Shakespeare's Characters.* 1965. New York: AMS P, 1970.

——. "Usury in *The Merchant of Venice.*" *Modern Philology* 33.1 (1935): 37-47.

Dryden, John. *The Works of John Dryden, Now First Collected in Eighteen Volumes.* Vols. iv & xv. With notes & a life of the author by Walter Scott. London: William Miller, 1808.

DuBois, Arthur E. "Shakespeare and 19th-Century Drama." *ELH* 1 (1934): 163-96.

Dutton, A. Richard. Introduction. *Volpone* (1605) by Ben Jonson. Ed. Richard Dutton. *The Cambridge Edition of the Works of Ben Jonson.* Vol. 3. Gen. Ed. David Bevington, Martin Butler, and Ian Donaldson. Cambridge: Cambridge UP, 2012. 3-22.

——. "The Significance of Jonson's Revision of *Every Man in his Humour.*" *The Modern Language Review* 69.2 (1974): 241 – 49.

——. *Ben Jonson, Volpone and the Gunpowder Plot.* Cambridge: Cambridge UP, 2008.

Edelman, Charles. Introduction. *The Merchant of Venice.* Ed. Edelman. Cambridge: Cambridge UP, 2002. Shakespeare in Production.

——. "Recent Critical and Stage Interpretations." *The Merchant of Venice.* By William Shakespeare. Ed. M. M. Mahood.

Cambridge: Cambridge UP, 2003. 54-65. New Cambridge Shakespeare.

Edmonds, Cyrus R. Preface. *Cicero's Three Books of Offices, or Moral Duties*. By Cicero. Trans. Cyrus R Edmonds. New York: Harper, 1868.

Egan, Gabriel. *Shakespeare*. Edinburgh: Edinburgh UP, 2007. Edinburgh Critical Guides to Literature.

Eliot, T. S. *Essays on Elizabethan Drama*. 1932. New York: A Harvest Book, 1956.

Ellis-Formor, Una. *The Jacobean Drama: An Interpretation*. 1935. New York: Vintage Books, 1961.

Empson, William. *Seven Types of Ambiguity*. 2 nd ed. 1930. London: Chatto & Windus, 1949.

——. "Volpone. " *The Hudson Review* 21. 4 (1968-9) : 651-66.

Evans, Robert C. "Jonson's Critical Heritage." *The Cambridge Companion to Ben Jonson*. Ed. Richard Harp and Stanley Stewart. Cambridge: Cambridge UP, 2000. 188-201.

Everett, Barbara. "*Much Ado About Nothing*: The Unsociable Comedy. " *William Shakespeare*. Ed. Harold Bloom. Philadelphia: Chelsea, 2004. 167-80. Bloom's Modern Critical Views.

Fagan, Brian M. *The Seventy Great Inventions of the Ancient World*. London: Thames & Hudson, 2004.

Fairclough, H. Rushton. Introduction to *Ars Poetica*. *Horace: Satires, Epitsles and Ars Poetica*. By Horace. Trans. H. Rushton Fairclough. London: William Heinemann, 1942. The Loeb Classical Library.

Farley-Hills, David. *Shakespeare and the Rival Playwrights*, 1600-1606. London: Routledge, 1990.

Ferguson, Niall. *The Ascent of Money: A Financial History of the World*. New York: Penguin, 2008.

Ferrari, G. R. F. "Plato and Poetry. " *The Cambridge History of*

Literary Criticism. Vol. 1, Classical Criticism. Ed. George Kennedy. Cambridge: Cambridge UP, 1989. 92-148.

Finlay, Roger. *Population and Metropolis: The Demography of London1580 1650*. Cambridge: Cambridge UP, 1981.

Forgeng, Jeffrey L. *Daily life in Elizabethan England.* 2 nd ed. Saint Barbara: Greenwood, 2010.

Frye, Northrop. "Characterization in Shakespearian Comedy." *Shakespeare Quarterly* 4. 3 (1953): 271-77.

Furness, Horace Howard, ed. *The Merchant of Venice.* By William Shakespeare. Philadelphia: J. B. Lippincott, 1916. A New Variorum Edition of Shakespeare.

Galbraith, David. "Theories of Comedy." *The Cambridge Companion to Shakespearean Comedy.* Ed. Alexander Leggatt. Cambridge: Cambridge UP, 2004. 3-17.

The Geneva Bible. London: Robert Barker, 1615.

Gibbons, Brian. *Jacobean City Comedy: A Study of Satiric Plays by Jonson, Marston and Middlteton.* London: Rupert Hart-Davis, 1968.

Gibson, Rex. *Teaching Shakespeare.* Cambridge: Cambridge UP, 1998.

Gildon, Charles. *The Laws of Poetry Explain'd and Illustrated.* London: J. Morley, 1721.

Goddard, Harold C. *The Meaning of Shakespeare.* Vol. 1. Chicago: U of Chicago P, 1951.

Golden, Leon. "Reception of Horace's *Ars Poetica.*" *A Companion to Horace.* Ed. Gregson Davis. West Sussex: Wiley-Blackwell, 2010. 337-66.

Gosson, Stephen. *The School of Abuse.* London: Shakespeare Society, 1841.

Gras, Henk. "*Twelfth Night, Every Man out of his Humour,* and the Middle Temple Revels of 1597-98." *The Modern Language Review* 84. 3 (1989): 545-64.

Graham, Edward K. "Ben Jonson and the Character-Writers." *The Sewanee Review* 14. 3 (1906): 299-305.

Grebanier, Bernard D. N. *The Truth about Shylock*. New York: Random House, 1962.

Greenblatt, Stephen. General Introduction. *The Norton Shakespeare, Based on the Oxford Edition: Comedies*. By Shakespeare. Ed. Greenblatt, et al. New York: Norton, 1997. 1-76.

Gross, John. *Shylock: A Legend and Its legacy*. 1992. New York: Touchstone, 1994.

Gross, Kenneth. *Shylock Is Shakespeare*. Chicago: Chicago UP, 2006.

Guo, Hui (郭晖). *Ben Jonson's Encomia: Classical Tradition and Innovations* (《琼生颂诗研究》). Beijing: China Translation & Publishing Corporation, 2009.

Gurr, Andrew. "Prologue: Who Is Lovewit? What Is He?" *Ben Jonson and Theatre: Performance, Practice, and Theory*. Ed. Richard Cave, Elizabeth Schafer, and Brian Woolland. London: Routledge, 1999. 5-18.

Guthrie, Sir Tyrone. *A Life in the Theatre*. New York: McGraw, 1959.

Halio, Jay. L. , ed. *The Merchant of Venice*. By William Shakespeare. 1993. Oxford: Oxford UP, 1998.

——. *Understanding* The Merchant of Venice: *A Student Casebook to Issues, Sources, and Historical Documents*. Westport: Greenwood, 2000.

Hall, Joseph. *Characters of Virtues and Vices*. 1608. Oxford: Oxford UP, 1863. Vol. VI of *The Works of the Right Reverend Joseph Hall*. Rev. & corrected with additions by Philip Wynter. 10 vols. 1863.

Halliwell, James Orchard. *On the Character of Sir John Falstaff*. London: William Pickering, 1841.

Hannay, Margaret P. *Philip's Phoenix: Mary Sidney, Countess of Pembroke*. New York: Oxford UP, 1990.

Harris, M. A. "The Origin of the Seventeenth Century Idea of Humours." *Modern Language Notes* 10. 2 (1895): 44-46.

Hart, Jonathan. *Shakespeare and His Contemporaries*. Palgrave Macmillan, 2011.

Hawkins, Harriet. *Poetic Freedom and Poetic Truth*. Oxford: Clarendon, 1976.

Hazlitt, William Carew. *The English Drama and Stage under the Tudor and Stuart Princes, 1543 1664* . The Roxburghe Library, 1869.

Hazlitt, William. *Characters of Shakspeare's Plays*. New York: Wiley and Putnam, 1845.

——. *Lectures on the English Comic Writers*, delivered at the Surry Institution. London: Taylor and Hessy, 1819.

Hechinger, Fred M. "Why Shylock Should Not Be Censored." *New York Times* 31 March 1974, sec. AL: 23.

Herford, C. H. , Percy Simpson and Evelyn Simpson, eds. *Ben Jonson*. 11 vols. Oxford: Clarendon, 1925-52.

Herodes. *The Jealous Lady*. Ed. & trans. A. D. Knox. *Herodes, Cercidas and the Geeek Choliambic Poets*. Ed. & trans. A. D. Knox. London: William Heinemann, 1929. 124-35.

Hinchliffe, Arnold P. Volpone: *Text and Performance*. London: Macmillan, 1985.

Holderness, Graham. *Shakespeare and Venice*. Surrey: Ashgate, 2010. Anglo-Italian Renaissance studies.

Holdsworth, R (oger). V (ictor). Introduction. *Jonson:* Every Man in his Humour *and* The Alchemist: *A Casebook*. Ed. R. V. Holdsworth. London: Macmillan, 1978.

Honan, Park. *Christopher Marlowe: Poet & Spy.* Oxford: Oxford UP, 2005.

——. *Shakespeare: A Life*. Oxford: Oxford UP, 1998.

Honigmann, Ernst (A. J.) , ed. *Othello*. By William Shakespeare. London: Arden Shakespeare, 1997. The Arden Shakespeare 3 rd ser.

——. "Shakespeare's Life." *The Cambridge Companion to Shakespeare*. Ed. Margreta de Grazia and Stanley Wells. 2001. Cambridge: Cambridge UP, 2003. 1-12.

Horace. *Ars Poetica*. Trans. Ben Jonson. *Ben Jonson*. Vol. VIII. By Jonson. Ed. C. H. Herford, Percy and Evelyn Simpson. Oxford: Clarendon, 1947.

——. *Horace: Epistles II and Ars Poetica*. Trans. Ross S. Kilpatrick. Edmonton: U of Alberta P, 1990.

House, Humphry. *Aristotle's Poetics: A Course of Eight Lectures*. London: Rupert Hart-Davis, 1956.

Huang, Alexander C. Y. *Chinese Shakespeares: Two Centuries of Cultural Exchange*. New York: Columbia UP, 2009.

Huizinga, Johan. *The Waning of the Middle Ages*. Trans. Herfsttijd der Middeleeuwen. New York: St. Martin's P, 1924.

Hume, David. *An Enquiry Concerning the Principles of Morals. Moral Philosophy*. By Hume. Ed. with introduction by Geoffrey Sayre-McCord. Indianapolis: Hackett, 2006. 185-310.

——. *The History of Great Britain under the House of Stuart*. Vol. 1. London: A. Millar, 1759.

"Humour." *A Shakespeare Glossary*. By C. T. Onions. Enlarged and Revised Throughout by Robert D. Eagleson. Oxford: Clarendon, 1986.

"Humour." *Johnson's Dictionary Improved by Todd*. Boston: Benjamin Perkins, 1828.

"Humour." *The Oxford English Dictionary*. 2 nd ed. 1989.

Hunter, George K. "Elizabethan Theatrical Genres and Literary Theory." *The Cambridge History of Literary Criticism*. Vol. III, The Renaissance. Ed. Glyn P. Norton. Cambridge: Cambridge UP, 1999. 248-58.

Hyman, Lawrence W. "The Rival Lovers in *The Merchant of Venice.*" *Shakespeare Quarterly* 21. 2 (1970): 109-16.

Jackson, Gabriele Bernhard. "The Protesting Imagination." *Jonson:* Every Man in his Humor and The Alchemist: *A Casebook.* Ed. R. V. Holdsworth. London: Macmillan, 1978. 92-114.

Jardine, Mick. "Jonson as Shakespeare's Other." *Ben Jonson and Theatre: Performance, Practice, and Theory.* Ed. Richard Cave, Elizabeth Schafer, and Brian Woolland. London: Routledge, 1999. 105-16.

Javitch, Daniel. "The Assimilation of Aristotle's *Poetics* in Sixteenth-century Italy." *The Cambridge History of Literary Criticism.* Vol. III, The Renaissance. Ed. Glyn P. Norton. Cambridge: Cambridge UP, 1999. 53-65.

Johnson, Samuel. *Samuel Johnson: Selected Writings.* Ed. Peter Martin. Cambridge: Belknap-Harvard UP, 2009.

Johnston, Ian. Introduction. *Galen on Diseases and Symptoms.* By Galen. Trans. Johnston. Cambridge: Cambridge UP, 2006. 1-125.

Jones, Robert. *Engagement with Knavery: Point of View in Richard III, The Jew of Malta, Volpone, and The Revenger's Tragedy.* Durham: Duke UP, 1986.

Jonson, Ben. *Ben Jonson.* Ed. C. H. Herford, Percy and Evelyn Simpson. 11 vols. Oxford: Clarendon, 1925 – 1952.

——. *The Complete Plays of Ben Jonson.* Ed. G. A. Wilkes. 4 vols. Oxford: Clarendon, 1981.

——. "To the Memory of My Beloved, the Author Mr. William Shakespeare: And What He Hath Left Us." *Shakespeares Comedies, Histories, & Tragedies Being a Reproduction in Facsimile of the First Folio Edition 1623 from the Chatsworth Copy in the Possession of the Duke of Devonshire K. G. with Introduction and Census of Copies by Sidney Lee.* Oxford:

Clarendon, 1902.

Jowett, John. Introduction. *The Life of Timon of Athens*. By William Shakespeare & Thomas Middleton. Ed. Jowett. Oxford: Oxford UP, 2004. 1-154. The Oxford Shakespeare.

——. *Shakespeare and Text*. Oxford: Oxford UP, 2007.

Kantak, V. Y. "An Approach to Shakespearean Comedy." *Shakespeare Survey* 22 (1969): 7-14.

Kay, W. David. "The Shaping of Ben Jonson's Career: A Reexamination of Facts and Problems." *Modern Philology* 67 (1970): 224-237.

Keats, John. *Selected Letters of John Keats*. Rev. ed. Based on the texts of Hyder Edward Rollins. Ed. Grant F. Scott. Cambridge: Harvard UP, 2002.

Kendrick, Laura. "Medieval Satire." *A Companion to Satire: Ancient and Modern*. Ed. Ruben Quintero. Oxford: Blackwell, 2007. 52-69.

Kennedy, George A. "Hellenistic Literary and Philosophical Scholarship" (Sects. 1-7). *The Cambridge History of Literary Criticism*. Vol. 1, Classical Criticism. Ed. George A. Kennedy. Cambridge: Cambridge UP, 1989. 200-14.

Kernan, Alvin B. "From Introduction to *Volpone*." *Jonson: Volpone: A Casebook*. Ed. Jonas Barish. 1972. Hampshire: MacMillan Education, 1987. 173-88. Casebook Series. Gen. Ed. A. E. Dyson.

Khadawardi, Hesham. *Shylock and the Economics of Subversion in The Merchant of Venice*. Diss. U of Nebraska, 2005. Ann Arbor: UMI. 2005.

Kiernan, Pauline. *Shakespeare's Theory of Drama*. Cambridge: Cambridge UP, 1996.

King, Pamela. "34 Drama: Sacred and Secular." *A Companion to Medieval Poetry*. Ed. Corinne Saunders. Oxford: Blackwell, 2010. 626-46.

Kinney, Arthur F. *Shakespeare by Stages: An Historical Introduction*. Oxford: Blackwell, 2003.

Kirschbaum, Leo. *Character and Characterization in Shakespeare*. Detroit: Wayne State UP, 1962.

Knights, L (ionel) C (harles). *Drama and Society in the Age of Jonson*. New York: Norton, 1968.

Knutson, Roslyn Lander. *The Repertory of Shakespeare's Company 1594-1613* . Fayetteville: U of Arkansas P, 1991.

Kozuka, Takashi, and J. R. Mulryne. *Shakespeare, Marlowe, Jonson: New Directions in Biography*. Hampshire: Ashgate, 2006.

Krieger, Murray. "*Measure for Measure* and Elizabethan Comedy. " *PMLA* 66 (1951): 775-84.

Kuchar, Gary. "Rhetoric, Anxiety, and the Pleasures of Cuckoldry in the Drama of Ben Jonson and Thomas Middleton. " *Journal of Narrative Theory* 31. 1 (2001): 1-30.

Laird, Andrew. "The Value of Ancient Literary Criticism. " *Oxford Readings in Ancient Literary Criticism*. Ed. Andrew Laird. Oxford: Oxford UP, 2006. 1-36.

Landa, Myer Jack. *The Jew in Drama*. Jersey City: KTAV, 1969.

Langbaine, Gerard. *An Account of the English Dramatick Poets: Or, Some Observations and Remarks on the Lives and Writings*. Oxford: Prt. by L. L. for George West and Henry Clements, 1691.

Leitch, Vincent B. et al. *The Norton Anthology of Theory and Criticism*. New York: Norton, 2001.

Lelyveld, Toby Bookholtz. *Shylock on the Stage*. Cleveland: P of Western Reserve University, 1960.

Lennox, Charlotte. "On The Two Gentlemen of Verona. " *William Shakespeare: The Critical Heritage*. Vol. 4. Ed. Brian Vickers. London: Routledge, 1976.

Leonard, Nancy S. "Shakespeare and Jonson Again: The Comic

Forms." *Renaissance Drama* 10 (1979) : 45-69.

Levin, Harry. *Playbills and Killjoys: An Essay on the Theory and Practice of Comedy.* Oxford : Oxford UP, 1987.

——. "Two Magian Comedies : *The Alchemist* and *The Tempest.*" *Shakespeare Survey* 22 (1969) : 47-58.

Levith, Murray J. *Shakespeare in China.* London : Continuum, 2004.

——. *Shakespeare's Italian Settings and Plays.* New York : St. Martin's, 1989.

Lewis, Cynthia. "Antonio and Alienation in *The Merchant of Venice.*" *South Atlantic Review* 48. 4 (1983) : 19-31.

——. " 'You Were an Actor with Your Handkerchief' : Women, Windows, and Moral Agency." *Comparative Drama* 43. 4 (2009) : 473-96.

Lockwood, Tom. *Ben Jonson in the Romantic Age.* Oxford : Oxford UP, 2005.

Loewenstein, Joseph. *Ben Jonson and Possessive Authorship.* Cambridge : Cambridge UP, 2002.

Long, John H. *Shakespeare's Use of Music: A Study of the Music and Its Performance in the Original Production of Seven Comedies.* Gainesville : U of Florida P, 1955.

Loxley, James. *The Complete Critical Guide to Ben Jonson.* London : Routledge, 2002.

Lucas, D. W. Commentary. *Aristotle: Poetics.* By Aristotle. Introduction, commentary and appendixes by Lucas. Oxford : Clarendon, 1980.

Lynch, Stephen J. Preface. *The Jew of Malta with Related Texts.* By Christopher Marlowe. Ed. with introduction and notes by Lynch. Indianapolis : Hackett, 2009.

Magaw, Katie J. "Modern Books on Ben Jonson : A General Topical Index." *The Ben Jonson Journal* 5 (1998) : 201-47.

Mahood, M (olly) M (aureen), ed. *The Merchant of Venice.* By

William Shakespeare. 1987. Cambridge: Cambridge UP, 2003.

Mallinson, G. J. "Defining Comedy in the Seventeenth Century: Moral Sense and Theatrical Sensibility." *The Cambridge History of Literary Criticism*. Vol. 3, The Renaissance. Ed. Glyn P. Norton. Cambridge: Cambridge UP, 1999. 259-64.

Manley, Lawrence. "Chapter 13. Literature and London." *The Cambridge History to Early Modern English Literature*. Ed. David Loewenstein and Janel Mueller. Cambridge: Cambridge UP, 2002. 399-427.

Manlove, C. N. "The Double View in Volpone." *Studies in English Literature, 1500 – 1900* 19. 2 (1979): 239-252.

Marchitell, Howard. "Desire and Domination in *Volpone*." *Studies in English Literature, 1500 – 1900* 31. 2 (1991): 287-308.

Marlowe, Christopher. *Doctor Faustus. The Complete Works of Christopher Marlowe*. Vol. II. 2nd ed. Ed. Fredson Bowers. Cambridge: Cambridge UP, 1981.

——. *The Jew of Malta: With Related Texts*. Ed. with introduction and notes by Stephen J. Lynch. Indianapolis: Hackett, 2009.

Maslen, R (obert). W. *Shakespeare and Comedy*. 2005. London: Arden Shakespeare, 2006. The Arden Critical Companions.

Maus, Katharine Eisaman. *Ben Jonson and the Roman Frame of Mind*. Princeton: Princeton UP, 1984.

——. "Horns of Dilemma: Jealousy, Gender, and Spectatorship in English Renaissance." *ELH* 54. 3 (1987): 561-83.

——. "Idol and Gift in *Volpone*." *English Literary Renaissance* 35. 3 (2005): 429-53.

——. "Introduction to *The Merchant of Venice*." *The Norton Shakespeare: Comedies*. 2nd ed. Ed. Stephen Greenblatt, Walter Cohen, Jean E. Howard and Katharine Eisaman Maus. Norton, 1997. 1111-19.

McDonald, Russ. "Sceptical Visions: Shakespeare's Tragedies and Jonson's Comedies." *Shakespeare Survey* 34 (1981): 131-47.

——. *Shakespeare & Jonson, Jonson & Shakespeare.* Lincoln: U of Nebraska P, 1988.

McEvoy, Sean. *Ben Jonson: Renaissance Dramatist.* Edinburgh: Edinburgh UP, 2008.

Mclean, Susan. "Prodigal Sons and Daughters: Transgression and Forgiveness in *The Merchant of Venice.*" *Papers on Language & Literature* 32. 1 (1996): 45-62.

McPherson, David C. *Shakespeare, Jonson, and the Myth of Venice.* Newark: U of Delaware P; London: Associated UP, 1990.

Meskill, Lynn S. *Ben Jonson and Envy.* Cambridge: Cambridge UP, 2009.

Meyers, Carol. *Exodus.* Cambridge: Cambridge UP, 2005. New Cambridge Bible Commentary.

Midgley, Graham. "*The Merchant of Venice:* A Reconsideration." *Essays in Criticism* 10 (1960): 119-33. *Shakespeare:* The Merchant of Venice: *A Casebook.* Ed. John Wilders. Nashville: Aurora, 193-207. Casebook Series. Gen. Ed. A. E. Dyson.

Milling, Jane. "The Development of a Professional Theatre, 1540-1660." *The Cambridge History of British Theatre.* Vol 1. Origins to 1660. Ed. Jane Milling and Peter Thomson. Cambridge: Cambridge UP, 2004. 139-177.

Milton, John. *The Annotated Milton.* Ed. Burton Raffel. New York: Bantam, 2008.

——. *Paradise Lost.* Ed. Philip Pullman. Oxford: Oxford UP, 2005.

Morgann, Maurice. *An Essay on the Dramatic Character of Sir John Falstaff.* London: T. Davies, 1777.

Morris, Corbyn. *An Essay towards Fixing the True Standards of Wit, Humour, Raillery, Satire, and Ridicule.* New York: AMS, 1972.

Moss, Ann. "Horace in the Sixteenth Century: Commentators into Critics." *The Cambridge History of Literary Criticism.* Vol.

III. The Renaissance. Ed. Glyn P. Norton. Cambridge:
Cambridge UP, 1999. 66-76.

Moss, Joyce, and Lorraine Valestuk. "Volpone." *World Literature
and Its Times: Profiles of Notable Literary Works and the
Historical Events That Influenced Them*. Vol. 3. British and
Irish Literature and Its Times: Celtic Migrations to the Reform
Bill (beginnings—1830s). Detroit: Gale, 2001. 495-504.

Moul, Victoria. *Jonson, Horace and the Classical Tradition*.
Cambridge: Cambridge UP, 2010.

Mousley, Andy. *Re-Humanising Shakespeare: Literary Humanism,
Wisdom and Modernity*. Edinburgh: Edinburgh UP, 2007.

Muir, Kenneth. "Shakespeare's Open Secret." *Shakespeare Survey*
34 (1981): 1-9.

——. *Shakespeare's Sources*. Vol. i. London: Methuen, 1957.

——. *Shakespeare's Tragic Sequence*. London: Hutchinson, 1972.

Mullan, John. Introduction. *The Lives of Poets: A Selection*. By
Samuel Johnson. Ed. Roger Lonstale. Oxford: Oxford UP,
2009. vii-xxix.

Mullini, Roberta. "Streets, Squares and Courts: Venice as a Stage
in Shakespeare and Ben Jonson." *Shakespeare's Italy:
Functions of Italian Locations in Renaissance Drama*. Ed.
Michele Marrapodi, A. J. Hoenselaars, Marcello Cappuzzo and
L. Falzon Santucci. Manchester: Manchester UP, 1993. 158-70.

Murphy, Andrew. *Shakespeare in Print: A History and Chronology
of Shakespeare Publishing*. Cambridge: Cambridge UP, 2003.

Nash, Ralph. "The Comic 'Intent of *Volpone*.'" *Studies in
Philology* 44. 1 (1947): 26-40.

Newhauser, Richard. *The Early History of Greed*. Cambridge:
Cambridge UP, 2000.

Newman, Karen. "Portia's Ring: Unruly Women and Structures of
Exchange in *The Merchant of Venice*." *Shakespeare Quarterly*
38. 1 (1987): 19-33.

Nilsen, Don L. F. *Humor in British Literature, from the Middle Ages to the Restoration: A Reference Guide*. Westport: Greenwood, 1997.

Oldrieve, Susan. "Marginalized Voices in *The Merchant of Venice.*" *Cardozo Studies in Law and Literature* 5. 1. A Symposium Issue on *The Merchant of Venice* (1993): 87-105.

Orgel, Stephen. "Jonson and the Arts." *The Cambridge Companion to Ben Jonson*, Ed. Richard Harp and Stanley Stewart. Cambridge: Cambridge UP. 2000. 140-51.

——. *The Jonsonian Masque*. Cambridge: Harvard UP, 1965.

Ornstein, Robert. "Shakespearian and Jonsonian Comedy." *Shakespeare Survey* 22 (1969): 43-46.

Overbury, Sir Thomas. *The Miscellaneous Works in Prose and Verse of Sir Thomas Overbury*. Ed. with notes & a biographical account of the author by Edward F. Rillbault. London: John Russell Smith, 1856.

Pakaluk, Michael. *Aristotle's Nicomachean Ethics: An Introduction*. Cambridge UP, 2005.

Palfrey, Simon, and Tiffany Stern. *Shakespeare in Parts*. Oxford: Oxford UP, 2007.

Palmer, John. *Comic Characters of Shakespeare*. London: Macmillan, 1946.

Parker, Brian, ed. *Volpone, or the Fox*. Rev. Ed. 1983. Manchester: Manchester UP, 1999.

Partridge, Edward B. *The Broken Compass: A Study of the Major Comedies of Ben Jonson*. London: Chatto & Windus, 1958.

Partridge, Eric. *Shakespeare's Bawdy*. 3rd ed. 1947. London: Routledge, 1968.

Paster, Gail Kern. "The Humor of It: Bodies, Fluids, and Social Discipline in Shakespearean Comedy." *A Companion to Shakespeare's Works*. Vol. III, The Comedies. Ed. Richard Dutton and Jean E. Howard. Oxford: Blackwell, 2003. 47-66.

——. *Humoring the Body: Emotions and the Shakespearean Stage*. Chicago: U of Chicago P, 2004.

Pepys, Samuel. *Diary and Correspondence of Samuel Pepys*, F. R. S. 6th ed. 4 vols. Vol. III, as deciphered by the Rev. J. Smith, A. M. London: Henry G. Bohn, 1858.

——. *The Diary of Samuel Pepys*. Vol. IV. May 9, 1662-Dec. 31, 1662. Ed. Henry Wheatley, F. R. S. New York: George E. Croscup, 1893.

Perry, Marvin, and Frederick M. Schweitzer. *Antisemitism: Myth and Hate from Antiquity to the Present*. New York: Palgrave Macmillan, 2002.

Pechter, Edward. *Shakespeare Studies Today: Romanticism Lost*. New York: Palgrave Macmillan, 2011.

Phelps, Charles Edward. *Falstaff and Equity: An Interpretation*. Boston: Houghton, Mifflin, 1901.

"Philargyry." *The Oxford English Dictionary*. 2nd ed. 1989.

Philips, Edward. "The Life of Milton." *The Poetical Works of John Milton*. A New Ed. Complete in One Vol. Leipsic: Printed for Ernest Fleischer, 1834.

Plato. *The Laws of Plato*. Trans. Thomas Pangle. Chicago: U of Chicago P, 1988.

——. *The Republic*. Ed. G. R. F. Ferrari. Trans. Tom Griffith. Cambridge: Cambridge UP, 2000.

Potter, Lois. "Shakespeare in the Theatre, 1660 – 1900." *The Cambridge Companion to Shakespeare*. Ed. Margreta de Grazia, and Stanley Wells. Cambridge: Cambridge UP, 2001. 183-98.

Procter, Johanna, ed. *The Selected Plays of Ben Jonson*. Vol. I. Cambridge: Cambridge UP, 1989. Plays by Renaissance and Restoration Dramatists.

Prudentius. *Prudentius* I. 2 vols. Trans. H. J. Thomson. London: William Heinemann, 1949. The Loeb Classical Library.

Prudentius. *The Origin of Sin*. Trans. H. J. Thomson. London:
William Heinemann, 1949. The Loeb Classical Library.

Quennell, Peter, and Hamish Johnson. *Who's Who in
Shakespeare*. London: Routledge, 2002.

Quintilian. *Institutio Oratoria Books I-III*. Trans. H. E. Butler.
Cambridge: Harvard UP, 1996. The Loeb Classical Library.

Raffel, Burton. Introduction. *The Merchant of Venice*. By William
Shakespeare. New Haven: Yale UP, 2006. xvii-xxxi. The
Annotated Shakespeare.

Rathmell, J. C. A. "Jonson, Lord Lisle, and Penshurst." *ELR* 1
(1971): 250-60.

Redwine, James D. Jr. "Beyond Psychology: The Moral Basis of
Jonson's Theory of Humour Characterization." *ELH* 28.4
(1961): 316-334.

Reiss, Timothy J. "Renaissance Theatre and the Theory of
Tragedy." *The Cambridge History of Literary Criticism*. Vol.
III, The Renaissance. Ed. Glyn P. Norton. Cambridge:
Cambridge UP, 1999. 229-47.

Reynolds, Edward. *The Whole Works of the Right Rev. Edward
Reynolds, D. D.* Vol. 6. Ed. B. Riveley. London: Printed for
B. Holdsworth, 1826.

Riggs, David. *Ben Jonson: A Life*. Cambridge: Harvard UP, 1989.

Robinson, Matthew, and Daniel Murphy. *Greed Is Good:
Maximization and Elite Deviance in America*. Lanham: Rowman
& Littlefield, 2009.

Rogers, Samuel. "An ars naturâ sit perfectior." *Ben Jonson: The
Critical Heritage*. Ed. D. H. Craig. London: Routledge, 1990.

Roston, Murray. "*Volpone*: Comedy or Mordant Satire?" *The Ben
Jonson Journal* 10 (2003): 1-21.

Rowe, George E. Jr. "Ben Jonson's Quarrel with Audience and Its
Renaissance Context." *Studies in Philology* 81.4 (1984):
438-460.

Rowe, Nicholas. "Some Account of the Life, & c. of Mr. William Shakespear." *The Works of Shakespear.* Vol. 1. By Shakespeare. Ed. Rowe. London: Printed for Jacob Tonson, 1709. 6 vols.

Rowse, A (lfred) L (Leslie). *William Shakespeare: A Biography.* New York: Harper & Row, 1963.

Ruud, Jay. *Encyclopedia of Medieval Literature.* New York: Facts on File, 2006.

Russell, D. A. "Ars Poetica." *Oxford Readings in Ancient Literary Criticism.* Ed. Andrew Laird. Oxford: Oxford UP, 2006. 325-45.

Sacton, Alexander H. *Rhetoric as a Dramatic Language in Ben Jonson.* New York: Columbia UP, 1948.

Sackville, Charles. "Epilogue on the Revival of Ben Johnson's Play called, *Every Man in his Humour.*" *The Works of the Earls of Rochester, Roscomon and Dorset; the Dukes of Devonshire, Buckingham.* 2 vols. London: 1752.

Sale, Arthur, ed. *Volpone: or, The Fox.* By Ben Jonson. London: U Tutorial P, 1956.

Salingar, Leo. "The Idea of Venice in Shakespeare and Ben Jonson." *Shakespeare's Italy: Functions of Italian Locations in Renaissance Drama.* Ed. Michele Marrapodi, A. J. Hoenselaars, Marcello Cappuzzo and L. Falzon Santucci. Manchester: Manchester UP, 1993. 171-84.

——. "Shakespeare and the Ventriloquists." *Shakespeare Survey* 34 (1981): 51-59.

Sandys, John Edwin. *Shakespeare's England.* Vol. 1. Oxford: Clarendon, 1916.

Schelling, Felix E. "Ben Jonson and the Classical School." *PMLA* 13. 2 (1898): 221-49.

Schimmel, Solomon. *The Seven Deadly Sins.* New York: Oxford UP, 1997.

Schlegel, Augustus William. *A Course of Lectures on Dramatic Art and Literature*. 2 vols. 2nd ed. Trans. John Black. London: J. Templeman, 1840.

Seng, Peter J. "The Riddle Song in *The Merchant of Venice.*" *Notes and Queries* 203 (1958): 191-93.

——. *The Vocal Songs in the Plays of Shakespeare*. Cambridge: Harvard UP, 1967.

Shakespeare, William. *Much Ado About Nothing*. Ed. Claire McEachern. 3rd Series. London: Thomson Learning, 2006. The Arden Shakespeare. 3rd Series.

——. *Shakespeare's Sonnets*. 1997. Ed. Katherine Duncan-Jones. Arden Shakespeare, 1998. The Arden Shakespeare, 3rd se.

——. *The Oxford Shakespeare. The Complete Works*. Ed. Stanley Wells, Gary Taylor, John Jowett and William Montgomery. Oxford: Oxford UP, 2004.

—. *The Riverside Shakespeare*. Ed. G. Blakemore Evans. Boston: Houghton Mifflin, 1974.

——. *The Tempest*. Ed. Virginia Mason Vaughan, and Alden T. Vaughan. London: Thomson Learning, 1999. The Arden Shakespeare. 3rd Series.

Shapiro, James S. *Rival Playwrights: Marlowe, Jonson, Shakespeare*. New York: Columbia UP, 1991.

——. *Shakespeare and the Jews*. New York: Columbia UP, 1996.

——. *A Year in the Life of William Shakespeare: 1599*. New York: Harper Collins, 2005.

Sidney, Sir Philip. *The Defense of Poesy Otherwise Known as an Apology for Poetry*. Ed. Albert S. Cook. Boston: Ginn & Company, 1890.

Simkin, Stevie. *Marlowe: The Plays*. New York: Palgrave, 2001.

Simpson, Percy. Introduction. *Ben Jonson's* Every Man in his Humour. By Jonson. Ed. Percy Simpson. Oxford: Clarendon, 1921. ix-lxiv.

Sinsheimer, Hermann. *Shylock: The History of a Character*. 1947.

New York: The Citadel, 1964.

Smith, Adam. *An Inquiry into the Nature and Causes of the Wealth of Nations*. Vol. 1. Ed. A. Todd. Oxford: Clarendon, 1976.

Smith, Emma. *The Cambridge Introduction to Shakespeare*. Cambridge: Cambridge UP, 2007.

——. *The Making of Shakespeare's First Folio*. Oxford: Bodleian Library, 2016.

Smithson, Isaiah. "The Moral View of Aristotle's Poetics." *Journal of the History of Ideas* 44. 1 (1983): 3-17.

Spence, Joseph. *Anecdotes, Observations, and Characters, of Books and Men*. Notes and a life of the author by Samuel Weller Singer. London: W. H. Carpenter, 1820.

Spencer, Christopher. *The Genesis of Shakespeare's Merchant of Venice*. Lewiston: Edwin Mellen, 1988. Studies in British Literature 3.

Spencer, Hazelton. *Shakespeare Improved: The Restoration Versions in Quarto and on the Stage*. New York: F. Ungar, 1963.

Spenser, Edmund. *The Faerie Queene*. Book I. Ed. Carol V. Kaske. Indianapolis: Hackett, 2006.

Spivack, Bernard. "Falstaff and the Psychomachia." *Shakespeare Quarterly* 8. 4 (1957): 449-59.

Steggle, Matthew, ed. Volpone: *A Critical Guide*. London: Continuum, 2011. Continuum Renaissance Drama.

Steward, Stanley. "Jonson's Criticism." *The Cambridge Companion to Ben Jonson*. Ed. Richard Harp and Stanley Stewart. Cambridge: Cambridge UP, 2000. 175-87.

Stoll, Elmer Edgar. *Poets and Playwrights: Shakespeare, Jonson, Spenser, Milton*. Minneapolis, Minnesota: U of Minnesota P, 1958.

Stonex, Arthur Bivins. "The Usurer in Elizabethan Drama." *PMLA* 31. 2 (1916): 190-210.

Strabo. *The Geography of Strabo*. Vol. I. Trans. Horace Leonard

Jones. Ed. John Robert Sitlington Sterrett. London: William Heinemann, 1960. The Loeb Classical Library.

Suckling, Sir John. "A Session of the Poets." *The Works of Sir John Suckling: Containing His Poems, Letters and Plays.* London: Printed for Jacob Tonson, 1709.

Sullivan, Patrick J. "Strumpet Wind: "The National Theatre's *Merchant of Venice*." *Educational Theatre Journal* 26.1 (1974): 31-44.

Tanner, Tony. *Prefaces to Shakespeare.* Cambridge: Belknap P of Harvard UP, 2010.

Taylor, Michael. Introduction. *A Mad World, My Masters and Other Plays.* By Thomas Middleton. Ed. Taylor. Oxford: Oxford UP, 1995. vii-xix.

Theophrastus. *The Characters of Theophrastus.* Ed. & Trans. J. M. Edmonds. London: William Heinemann, 1929.

Thornley, G. C., and Gwyneth Roberts. *An Outline of English Literature.* New ed. 1984. Essex: Longman, 2003.

Thorton, Bonnell. "An Account of the Reviv'd Play, *The Silent Woman*." *The Spring-Garden Journal* 1 (1752): 12-15.

Tickle, Phyllis A. *Greed.* Oxford: Oxford UP, 2004.

Tillyard, E. M. W. *Shakespeare's Early Comedies.* London: Athlone, 1965.

Tosi, Laura. "Shakespeare, Jonson andVenice: Crossing Boundaries in the City." *Visions of Venice in Shakespeare.* Ed. Laura Tosi, and Shaul Bassi. Surrey: Ashgate, 2011. 143-65. Anglo-Italian Renaissance Studies.

Tyson, Brian F. "Ben Jonson's Black Comedy: A Connection between *Othello* and *Volpone*." *Shakespeare Quarterly* 29.1 (1978): 60-66.

Vandiver, E. P., Jr. "The Elizabethan Dramatic Parasite." *Studies in Philology* 32.3 (1935): 411-27.

Vickers, Brian. "The Emergence of Character Criticism, 1774-1800."

Shakespeare Survey 34 (1981): 11-21.

——, ed. *William Shakespeare: The Critical Heritage*, Vols. 1, 2, 3, 4, 6. London: Routledge, 1974 – 1981.

Voigts, Linda Ehrsam. "Bodies." *A Companion to Chaucer*. Ed. Peter Brown. Oxford: Blackwell, 2002. 40-57.

Wall, Alison. "For Love, Money, or Politics? A Clandestine Marriage and the Elizabethan Court of Arches." *The Historical Journal* 38. 3 (1995): 511-533.

Ward, John O. "Cicero and Quintilian." *The Cambridge History of Literary Criticism*. Vol. III, The Renaissance. Ed. Glyn P. Norton. Cambridge: Cambridge UP, 1999. 77-87.

Warley, Christopher. "Reforming the Reformers: Robert Crowley and Nicholas Udall." *The Oxford Handbook of Tudor Literature, 1485 – 1603*. Ed. Mike Pincombe and Cathy Shrank. Oxford: Oxford UP, 2009. 273-90.

Watkins, John. "The Allegorical Theatre: Moralities, Interludes and Protestant Drama." *The Cambridge History of Medieval English Literature*. Ed. David Wallace. Cambridge: Cambridge UP, 1999. 767-92.

Watling, E. F., trans. *Plautus: The Poet of Gold and Other Plays*. By Plautus. London: Penguin, 1965.

Watson, Robert, ed. *Ben Jonson's* Volpone (New Mermaids). London: A & Black, 2003.

Weber, Max. *The Protestant Ethic and the Spirit of Capitalism*. Trans. Talcott Parsons. 1930. London: Routledge, 2001.

Weisberg, Richard H. "Antonio's Legalistic Cruelty: Interdisciplinarity and *The Merchant of Venice*." *College Literature* 25. 1. Law, Literature, and Interdisciplinarity (1998): 12-20.

Wells, Stanley. Foreword. *Visions of Venice in Shakespeare*. Ed. Laura Tosi, and Shaul Bassi. Surrey: Ashgate, 2011. xv-xviii. Anglo-Italian Renaissance Studies.

——. *Shakespeare and Co.* New York: Pantheon, 2006.

——. *Shakespeare, Sex, and Love.* Oxford: Oxford UP, 2010.

Westbrook. Perry D. "Horace's Influence on Shakespeare's *Antony and Cleopatra.*" *PMLA* 62. 2 (1947): 392-98.

Wetherbee, Winthrop. *Chaucer: The Canterbury Tales-A Student Guide.* Cambridge: Cambridge UP, 2004.

Whalley, Peter. Preface. *The Works of Ben Jonson.* By Jonson. 7 vols. London: Printed for Midwinter et al. , 1756.

Wheater, Isabella. "Aristotelian *Wealth* and the Sea of Love: Shakespeare's Synthesis of Greek Philosophy and Roman Poetry in *The Merchant of Venice.*" *The Review of English Studies*, New Series 43. 172 (1992): 467-87.

Whitney, Charles. *Early Responses to Renaissance Drama.* Cambridge: Cambridge UP, 2006.

Wiggins, Martin. *Shakespeare and the Drama of His Time.* Oxford: Oxford UP, 2000.

Wikander, Matthew H. *Fangs of Malice: Hypocrisy, Sincerity, and Acting.* Iowa City: U of Iowa P, 2002.

Wilde, Oscar. *The Importance of Being Earnest.* Ed. Russell Jackson. New Mermaids. London: A & C Black, 2004.

Wilkes, Thomas. *A General View of the Stage.* London: J. Coote, 1759.

Wilson, John Dover. *The Forunes of Falstaff.* 1943. Cambridge: Cambridge UP, 2004.

——. Introduction. *The Merry Wives of Windsor.* By William Shakespeare. Ed. Wilson. 1921. Cambridge: Cambridge UP, 2009. vii-xxxix.

Withington, Robert. " 'Vice' and 'Parasite. ' A Note on the Evolution of the Elizabethan Villain." *PMLA* 49. 3 (1934): 743-51.

Wood, Michael. *Conquistadors.* Berkeley: U of California P, 2000.

Wordsworth, William. Preface (1800). *Lyrical Ballads.* By

Wordsworth and Samuel Taylor Coleridge. Ed. R. L. Brett and
    A. R. Jones. 1963. London: Routledge, 1991. 233-58.

Wright, Celeste Turner. "Some Conventions Regarding the Usurer
    in Elizabethan Literature." *Studies in Philology* 31.2 (1934):
    176-97.

Wright, Thomas. *The Passions of the Mind in General.* Ed.
    William Webster Newbold. New York: Garland, 1986.

Yachnin, Paul, and Jessica Slights, eds. *Shakespeare and
    Character: Theory, History, Performance, and Theatrical
    Persons.* Hampshire: Palgrave Macmillan, 2009. Palgrave
    Shakespeare Studies.

Yaffe, Martin D. *Shylock and the Jewish Question.* 1997.
    Baltimore: Johns Hopkins UP, 1999.

Yearling, Rebecca. "Jonson among the Romantics." *The
    Cambridge Quarterly.* 35.4 (2006): 404-07.

Young, Edward. *Conjectures on Original Composition.* London:
    Printed for A Millar, 1759.

Young, R. V. "Jonson and Learning." *The Cambridge Companion
    to Ben Jonson.* Ed. Richard Harp and Stanley Stewart.
    Cambridge: Cambridge UP, 2000. 43-57.

Zhang, Siyang, et al. *A Shakespeare Dictionary.* Beijing:
    Commercial, 2001. (张泗洋, 等. 莎士比亚大辞典 [M]. 北京: 商
    务印书馆, 2001.)

何其莘. 英国戏剧史 [M]. 2 版. 南京: 译林出版社, 2008.

——. 英国戏剧史 [M]. 南京: 译林出版社, 1999.

侯维瑞. 英国文学通史 [M]. 上海: 上海外语教育出版社, 2002.

姜春兰. "英语诗歌鉴赏"教学策略探讨——以本·琼生的《不像大树那
    样生长》为例 [J]. 黄冈师范学院学报, 2009 (4): 34 - 36.

李赋宁, 刘意青, 罗经国. 欧洲文学史: 第 1 卷 [M]. 北京: 商务印书
    馆, 1999.

龙跃. 《致西莉亚》的意境与韵律之美 [J]. 湖南工程学院学报, 2005
    (12): 62 - 64.

卢桂荣. 《狐狸》（*Volpone*）——本·琼生对喜剧创作新探索 ［J］. 继续教育研究, 2002（3）: 103 - 04, 106.

——. 《狐狸》（*Volpone*）的戏剧背景分析 ［J］. 牡丹江师范学院学报（哲学社会科学版）, 2002（6）: 27 - 29.

——. 《狐狸》的欺骗艺术分析 ［J］. 西安外国语学院学报, 2003（9）: 63 - 66.

——. 本·琼生——其人其作 ［J］. 哈尔滨学院学报, 2002（12）: 24 - 26.

王品品. 美酒·花环——介绍本·琼生的一首爱情诗 ［J］. 英语知识, 1997（5）: 10 - 11.

王永梅. 本·琼森宫廷假面剧与自我作者化研究 ［M］. 北京: 科学出版社, 2015.

王永梅, 刘立辉. 从舞台到页面: 本·琼生与英国戏剧经典生成 ［J］. 外国文学研究, 2012（5）: 49 - 56.

吴美群. 传承与超越——试论本·琼生《森林集》中的古典主义 ［J］. 外语学刊, 2016（2）: 142 - 46.

于永生. 戏剧背景与讽刺主题的完美统一——《狐狸》（*Volpone, or The Fox*）背景艺术分析 ［J］. 西安外国语学院学报, 2003（12）: 61 - 64.

郑有志. 英国文艺复兴时期喜剧的代表作家——琼生 ［J］. 外国语, 1993（3）: 46 - 49.